England All Over

Also by Joseph Gallivan

Oi, Ref!

England
All Over

JOSEPH GALLIVAN

SCEPTRE

First published in 2000 by Hodder and Stoughton
A division of Hodder Headline
A Sceptre book

Gallivan, Joseph, 1964–
   England all over
   I.Tour guides (Persons) – England – Fiction
   I.Title
   823.9'14[F]

ISBN 0 340 70862 X

Typeset by Palimpsest Book Production Limited,
Polmont, Stirlingshire
Printed and bound in Great Britain by
Clays Ltd, St Ives plc.

Hodder and Stoughton
A division of Hodder Headline
338 Euston Road
London NW1 3BH

for Spring Rain

Mentioned in D-d-d-d-d-dispatches:

Steve B, like a rock, and Sue, Simon Prosser, Neil Taylor my editor, Jon Wood and Sarah at Hodder, the usual hosts especially D-d-d-d-d-damian and Emma, George (that's a she), Boaz & Sarah, Teresa, Malcolm & Daire, Adam, Tim & Sadie, John, Chris & Auds, Dan, Henry & Lynda (thanx for the car), and all my English, a people who never stop giving . . . thanx also to David Noale and Stan McCarter of the Met's Thames Division (river cops), John Stocker kickass lawyer for advice, real Blue Badgers like Paul Basler, David Hughes, Dave Needham, Pamela McHutcheon and Katrine Prince, Agent Antony, Big Blue for the ThinkPad-i series, and last and most and always, for the Love that always goes one louder, Spring Rain Gunter.

JG, all over, 1999

Characters

And Their Ages

Clive Pointing	tour guide	(44)
Barry Bergman	Londoner tour guide	(36)
Alexander White	head of tour company, posh	(32)
Christina ex-Pointing	Clive's ex-wife (Tina)	(39)
Tess Pointing	their kid	(7)
Rose	female coach driver, from Meriden	(36)
Gordon Pointing	Clive's brother	(41)
Christine Bergman	Barry's wife (Chrissie)	(33)
Diana, Dawn & Shelley	Barry's kids	(2, 5, 8¾)
Donna	Christine's sister	(30)
Stuart	Barry's useless tout brother	(30)
Craig	Barry's street-seller brother	(32)
Trevor	Barry's inside brother	(34)
Ossie	Barry's nationalist brother	(38)
Ron	Barry's dad, taxi driver	(57)
Danny	Clive's Kiwi neighbour, bungee boy	(27)
Jo	Danny's Kiwi girlfriend	(27)
Ray	coach driver, old bastard	(64)
George	Clive's old Geog teacher colleague, Camberwell	(55)
Amanda	the schoolgirl he bonked now 18	(18)
Other nomarks:		
Dave	the dead guy, debtor	(35)
Derek Mountjoy	Clive's crappy solicitor	(44)
Marion Mound	Clive's crappy barrister	(55)

(Insert corny Shakespeare quote here)

PART 1

A - B

1

Barry and Clive

The way Clive saw it from his seat in the Shakespeare just outside Victoria it looked like a bit of a row. Thirty people stumbled from a coach which was illegally parked and had its hazards going. They spread across the pavement with shocked looks or scowls on their faces, as though they were emerging from a fart-filled lift. Several made a beeline for the nearest fast food. Six well-dressed women hurried into the pub, brushing past Clive on their way to the Ladies. After everyone was off the coach, a fair-haired, slightly podgy young man in a red parka emerged with a clipboard. One of the ladies, tall with silver hair, a belted raincoat and a silk scarf, moved into his path and began fiercely asking him questions. At first the man hung his head, then looked away, then wrote on his clipboard. As he went to the luggage compartment he said something to her over his shoulder. The lady followed, still talking, still castigating him. After thirty seconds he slammed the door shut and turned on her, talking very close to her face, his head bobbing. She shrank back in surprise, but when he paused, she started back at him again. Definitely telling him off.

She was now waving her umbrella at him, tapping him on the chest with the duck's head handle. The man came back at her again, explaining something with both hands, pointing at the coach driver with both hands, pointing at the engine with both hands, his broad shoulders rising and falling. Then he gently put an arm around her shoulder and turned her so she could see the name in gold and purple letters on the side of the coach: Britannia Tours.

Clive took a sip of his diet Pepsi and noticed the glass was dirty. Clinging to the other side were the remnants of a lower-lip print in pink lipstick.

'Eugh. How disgusting,' he muttered, and took out a white handkerchief to try to wipe it off. Stubborn specks remained, and the clear patch only made the rest of the glass look greasier. In his effort the glass slipped and he sloshed his handkerchief with Pepsi. 'Balls.'

When he looked up again the fair-haired young man still had his hand on the tourist lady, only this time it was placed on the back of hers as she stood, arms folded, listening to him. He leaned in and said something close into her ear. She smiled, after a slight hesitation, and looked around at her fellow travellers, who were watching the scene too. Then turning her back to them, she said something to him. All Clive could now see was the man writing on the corner of his pad, tearing it off the clipboard and giving it to her. She looked at it and they spent another thirty seconds nodding and bidding each other farewell, and the man laughed a lot and made her smile.

Then he hopped on the coach and shut the door. The brakes hissed, but it didn't move. Clive couldn't see in through the tinted windows. The tourists dispersed after a few minutes, some of them following the silver-haired woman and asking her questions, which she seemed to be shrugging off.

When they were all gone, the coach doors reopened, the man jumped off, took a quick look around, waved the driver on, and came straight into the Shakespeare. He looked around. Clive stood up and called to him: 'Er, Barry? Are you Barry from Britannia?'

The man in the red parka came over. They shook hands.

'Barry Bergman, Britannia. Who are you again?'

'Er, Clive. Clive Pointing. I'm interested in the tour guide position.'

'Yeah, yeah. You talked to Al on the phone didn't you?'

'Yes, er, you mean, Alexander White?'

'Yeah, yeah, *Alexander*,' he said in a put-on posh voice. He started to turn towards the bar. ''Scuse me, I'm dying for a pint. Me froat's like the Gaudi Desert. What you having?'

They both looked at Clive's glass.

'Er, nothing. Coke. Diet Pepsi, I mean.'

Barry didn't look too impressed but he took himself off to the bar. Clive waited, still a little nervous. Most of the six ladies from the coach were out of the toilets now, standing in a huddle, deciding whether or not to stay in the pub and have a drink. At the bar, Barry caught sight of them and hid his face. He came back swiftly with a lager and a diet Pepsi.

''Ere. Sit round this side and keep an eye on those old girls, will you?'

Clive did as he was told. The women had found a table of their own now and didn't seem to have spotted Barry. They were chattering away in some European language.

'What's that, Dutch?' asked Clive.

'Danish. Bleeding Danes. Don't miss a trick. All the Scanders, actually. Very hard to get anything past 'em.'

'Hard to please, eh?' said Clive, chipping in. He badly wanted this meeting to go well. He needed a job, desperately, and would say pretty much anything to get Barry on his side.

'No. That's the Germans. The Germans are hard to please. Impossible, in fact. I won't do 'em any more. I just won't.' Barry looked at him with a defiant glare, then took a big swig of his lager.

Clive was wrong-footed. He wasn't expecting a gravel-throated Londoner when he set off to meet the man from Britannia. He'd answered an ad in the paper and the Alex White he'd spoken to on the phone had been well spoken. Rather impressive, Clive had thought at the time. Mr White had invited him to have a preliminary meeting with 'one of our guides, Mr Bergman, as soon as possible. Just to begin the selection process. Start the ball rolling, as it were.'

'What was all that about then?' asked Clive. He was feeling bold. And he knew from experience, as a forty-four-year-old man would, that a bit of small talk showing curiosity, even chutzpah, was preferable to going right to the heart of the matter. The bit where he proved ineligible for the job.

'Ah, bleedinell. We 'ad a few problems with the air conditioning. It was stuck on "ON" all the way back. A bit cool that's all, nothing to get worked up about.'

'Oh. Where did you go?'

Barry breathed in, rubbed his hand down his thigh once, and looked around at the carpet before returning Clive's gaze. 'That was another problem. Windsor. Bleeding closed, innit? The Castle. How was I to know? It's never closed.'

'Extraordinary restoration, though. Just for one week . . .'

'I know that *now*,' he said testily. 'So I says let's carry on up to Oxford instead, Oxford's a doddle, but there was a massive pile-up on the turn-off from the M40. So then I tell 'em we'll have to do Blenheim Palace instead, or go home, and by now they're all moaning, and half of 'em want to come home and half of 'em want to stay cos they haven't done Blenheim before . . .'

'Had you?' asked Clive, then instantly regretted it.

'Course I *fackin'* have, what do you take me for?' Barry Bergman always pronounced 'fuck' with an 'a' in it like a hatchet. It was his heritage. He glared at him and took another swig.

'I meant this year. Since the flood?' said Clive nervously.

'Well ... no, as it happens, not since then.' He paused, then asked suspiciously, 'Why? What's so different?'

'Oh it's all changed. You go around in golf carts for a start, no one's allowed to walk. The Chapel, the Great Hall and the State Rooms are all closed until August. Really the only thing to see is the Kitchen Court and the gardens. And they're looking a bit bare.'

After a resentful pause, Barry said, 'I thought you'd never done this job before? I thought you was a teacher.'

'Erm, I ... sort of ...'

To Clive's relief, Barry cut him off.

'Yeah well, there's more to it than reading a book. A lot more,' he said, and drained his pint. 'I'll have the same again, and then I'll tell you what you have to do.'

'Um, right,' said Clive, and took their dead glasses to the bar. Was that it? He wondered if he'd got the job already. What did Barry mean by 'I'll tell you what you have to do?'

One of the Danish ladies was at the bar next to him. 'Eighteen pounds? Are you sure?' she was asking the bar girl. All the staff had on the corporate brewery uniform – black trousers, white shirt with logo, half-sized apron – but her attitude was distinctly old school. The bar girl shrugged, and slapped the change down in front of her, then went to a customer down at the other end of the bar.

Clive smiled apologetically, but the Dane just missed his smile as she scooped up her coins. When he got back, Barry was ready for him.

'Thing is, these Danes, they could be anyone. Could be OAPs, could be doctors, or professors, could be Euro Diplomats for all I know. They all dress smart and they don't stand for any monkey business. So they were pretty cheesed off when the coach broke down outside Banbury.' A smile came across Barry's face. He had been quite handsome once, and knew it, but now in his late thirties he was letting the years pile up on him, so that his square jaw and chin dimple were lost amid the fat of premature middle age. His forehead was lined, and his eyes were slightly occluded by lids that had drooped an eighth. Clive guessed he was not yet forty. But his eyes were about twenty-one. There was plenty of life in his light blue eyes.

'Nearly had a rebellion on me hands. We all stood around while Ray tried to fix it, but then it started raining.' Barry started to chuckle at the memory. 'I had all these old girls standing around in the lay-by complaining at me, asking if it was much farther, and could they get a taxi, I had to tell 'em, "Listen darlin' there's no taxis out here, you're in the countryside now, the English countryside. Maybe I can get you a ride on a tractor ..." Luckily we found a tea shop down the road, the girl behind the counter was quite fit an'all, and pretty soon they were all there eating scones and Devon cream and Twixes and having a great time. But Ray comes back with the coach after about an hour and we have to come straight back here. Their four hours were up. Well I've got the kids tonight. The wife's going out with her mates.'

Clive was alarmed. He was talking to a nut case. Even so, he felt a flicker of warmth for the mouthy Londoner. Here was someone who didn't appear to give a damn, and Clive wanted to know how he kept his job.

'I was watching you from here as the coach emptied out,' he said. 'What was going on with that passenger with the grey hair?'

Barry smirked, looked around the room, took a slurp of his drink, then leaned slightly closer to Clive. 'She was the leader. She was a schoolteacher. Wanted to have a go at me, you know, "We want our money back," all that. Well, they can't have their money back can they, it's a business, we make no promises, no guarantees, says so in the brochure ... Anyway, what she really wanted was what they all want. Single woman on holiday, good looking ... well preserved anyway. You know what I mean.'

'Er, no. I don't,' said Clive. His curiosity was mixed with dread for a second.

'*Company,*' he said leering and stressing the first syllable hard.

'Oh.' He paused. 'So what was that you wrote down and gave her?'

'Me number. Mobile. Know what I mean?' He finished his pint, slammed his glass down, belched politely, and smiled. 'What's yours?'

'Um, I haven't got one. Too expensive.'

'Nahhh, not yer phone number you prannet. What are you drinking? Same again?' And he laughed loudly at Clive, then swaggered up to the bar, casting a half glance in the direction of the Danes.

2

The Old Boy Network

Clive Pointing was desperate for a new job because his career as a Geography teacher had ended abruptly when he had sex with a pupil. She was fifteen. Fifteen and a quarter, to be precise. Actually, as he often pointed out, she looked a good sixteen. But although he hadn't even noticed her, some might say that technically he had first met her when she was eleven, when she started at his school. So the deck was stacked against him.

After this sorry incident his wife divorced him and gained full custody of their only child, a girl called Tess, the sweetest little seven-year-old imaginable: cool-limbed, brown-eyed and always singing. After a year of unemployment, protesting his spousal and child maintenance payments, and blowing most of his savings on lawyers in the process, Clive realised there wasn't going to be any more teaching for him. Not even private tutoring. Wherever he went the word would get out. Even the most negligent rich sod of a parent would be hawkish about leaving him alone with their kids. He was fucked.

Just as the personal finance crisis was mounting he saw an ad in a free newspaper:

TOUR GUIDES WANTED,
LONDON PANORAMICS AND COUNTRYWIDE GUIDING,
EXPERIENCE NECESSARY.

I could do that, he told himself. He'd done lots of Geography field trips, taking kids all over the place in the mini bus. North Wales. The South West. Milton Keynes. He knew how to keep them in line. His only wonder was what it paid. Going on about the importance of tourism in late capitalist society was one thing. Getting his hands dirty on the production side was another.

It was now a year and a half since he'd seen the ad in the paper. When he first enquired by telephone, Alexander White had sniffily told him he needed a Blue Badge certificate to become a guide. He had to do the Blue Badge Guide course, run by the London Tourist Board. It cost, as Clive told his lawyer one evening in the pub near his home in Streatham, 'a hell of a lot of money' and worse than that, it looked genuinely difficult. All that stuff he had to learn ... it seemed harder than his Geography degree at university.

Clive only lasted six months on the course. You had the option: cram the whole thing into half a year, or do it in two six-month bursts over two years. He was already paying his rent with cash advances from a credit card, so he couldn't even afford to do it all at once. And no one was going to lend him the money. The bank had gone off him after he had bounced a cheque for a children's entertainer for Tess's fifth-birthday party. The clown had threatened to chin him too.

That had been a bad week for Clive, and there had been many worse since.

So half way through the course, his money ran out. He had to move out of his temporary flat in Highbury and find something a lot cheaper. First he stayed in Camberwell with an old teacher friend called George. Then he ended up in a studio in Streatham. Getting a job became an urgent matter. He'd been told there was no chance of work without the coveted Blue Badge, but as the same ad was still running in the free newspaper he gave it a shot. The same person answered the phone. *Alexander*. Clive bit the bullet and lied, saying he was now qualified. So Mr White arranged for him to be interviewed by Barry. In a pub.

He saw Barry exchanging smiles and jokes with one of the Danes at the bar. The ladies were now on their second drinks. He came back to Clive's table with a big grin on his face, which slowly faded, then turned into a frown when he remembered why he was there.

'Right. You Blue Badge certified? Cos I'm not. That's all bollocks.'

'Er . . . yes,' said Clive, startled. 'I didn't bring my certificate though . . .'

Barry gave him a sceptical look, then laughed in his face. 'Yeah well, don't bother, keep your cestificate at home. What we're looking for is a bloke who can keep the punters happy. Give 'em a bit of chat when we're stuck in traffic on the A3. Make 'em smile. They're on 'oliday. They've paid to get away from it all, so what they want is *happy*. They want to see England but don't go overboard on the kings and queens. They're just as interested in Marks and Spencer's as in the British Museum. So we skip it.'

Clive was surprised. 'Oh, I see. No Blue Badge, no British Museum.' And no St Paul's or Tower of London. That was the rule. You couldn't take a tour round the big institutions without the badge. There was a whole layer of vergers, beadles, marshals, floating pensioners and jobsworths who checked this sort of thing.

'That's right.' Then he took his fresh pint in his hand and leaned back. Just before he put it to his lips he glanced at Clive and said quietly, 'But we can work around that.' Big slurp.

Clive was suddenly sunk into depression. The thought of continuing to look for a tour guide job made him miserable and scared. Forty-four years old, and scared. Everywhere he turned people said there was no chance without the Blue Badge, and definitely not without a strong second language. Fluency, not just an ancient O Level or a stint on the Berlitz tapes. The people on the course were always cursing the unqualified guides. Not just the foreigners – the influx of Russians, Germans and Japanese who at least restricted themselves to taking their own nationals around in hermetic splendour inside their luxury coaches. But the dodgy-looking English who stood in the streets around Victoria and Waterloo trying to poach unwitting customers with their unfeasibly low prices and confusing flyers. In the tea breaks at class, between Georgian England and the theoretical walk-through of Soho, they made spiteful jokes about how to recognise a ringer: he'd be wearing an anorak or a parka instead of a smart blazer and raincoat. And training shoes. And he'd be reading from a *book*. Oh how they laughed, and looked around at each other, calculating who amongst them could be one.

So here I am, thought Clive. He was trying to get on board with Britannia Tours and their shameless wide-boy guides. But that Alexander White sounded all right. They couldn't be that bad. If he got the job he could be getting paid within a fortnight.

'So tell us a joke.'

Clive was stunned. He didn't know any jokes. 'I ... I ... I ...'

'Come on, just tell us a joke. One joke. Everyone knows one joke.'

Clive's problem was he only knew one joke – the last one he had heard. They went right out of his head. He hated the joke press-gang. His mind went blank.

Barry was starting to get impatient.

'Erm, OK. But this isn't a family joke. I would never tell it on a coach.'

'That's all right, go on, tell it.'

'It's dirty.'

'Even better.'

'Um . . . OK. There's this chap on a TWA flight from London to New York, and he's sitting very comfortably in business class, when this rather attractive air hostess approaches him with the jug of coffee. So she says to him, "Can I interest you in some TWA Coffee sir?" And he looks her up and down and says, "No thanks. But I'd like some of your TWA Tea."'

Silence.

Barry seemed to be thinking about it. After five seconds a smile played across his lips and he snorted. Then he shifted his weight in his chair and started to laugh.

'Naaaar-har-har, naar-har-har! Naaaar-har-har, naar-har-har!' He threw back his head and Clive could see his big tongue. 'Assa good one that is. That's good! I like it. Takes a bit of finking but it's a good one. Na-har, har, har.'

'Yes, and it sort of has a tourism angle to it too,' said Clive, immensely relieved.

When Barry settled down again Clive felt he could go back to his interview counter-interrogation.

'So, how many people work for Britannia?'

'About ten,' said Barry with a defensive sniff. He had readjusted.

Ten? Only ten? he thought. 'And are you expanding?'

'Yeah well, it's been a rough start to the season you know, what with the rain, and the pound up and down like a whore's draws. We had a few people leave.'

They both paused for a moment, thinking. Clive's heart raced.

'So where you from?' Barry asked him.

'Er, all over really. We lived in a lot of different places.'

Barry didn't seem impressed.

'My father was with the Midland Bank, they kept moving us around.' He tried to get back to the subject of the business. He still knew hardly anything about Britannia. 'So what's the struc . . .'

Barry cut him off. 'Basically, there's five coaches, that means five full-time guides. Three relief. Then there's Maxine, the girl in the office, she does all the bookings and that, nice girl, black girl but does a good job, practically runs the place, and Alex. I don't know what he does. Sits round on his arse all day fiddling with his laptop computer. He likes to think he's the boss.'

He said the last word with withering disdain. Clive struggled to move on. He reached for his homework, opening a paper file. 'And you're part of Wonga Leisure?'

'Beats me,' said Barry, shifting on his stool. He looked bored. 'So anyway, we need someone who can start next week. You've gotta know your stuff though. London especially.' He drained his pint, signalling the end of the interview. Clive jumped to his feet and gathered up his papers. He'd barely made a dent in his Pepsi, his stomach was a knot of terror.

'Er, when will I be ... will you give me a call about meeting Alex?' He turned towards the pub door, expecting Barry to come with him, but he was surveying the room. The Shakespeare was Barry's West End local. Well, his SW1 local anyway. This was where he met friends, met clients, had a pint after work, had a pint before work, and sniffed about for totty. His brothers knew they could usually find him in there. His old dad was a taxi driver and drove past the place every few hours. And it was always full of birds. Foreign birds and English birds. Office people, train people, tourists, runaways ... Barry felt richly apprehensive in there, and richly satisfied. Really rich.

Clive was just apprehensive.

Barry was a biggish bloke, six foot, and wide too, with a strong handshake. Not strong in a sincere way, more in a *don't-fuck-with-me-or-I'll-frottle-you* way.

'Yeah OK, you've got it. Meet me at the office a week on Monday. Nineish. Alex'll want to meet you, but I'll tell him you're all right.'

Clive was shocked, then overjoyed. 'Oh thanks! Thank you. I'll ... I'll see you Monday then. Great. See you. Bye.'

Barry made no attempt to leave. 'I'm staying for one more. Still got some time to kill.' He rubbed his jowls, signalling for the other man to clear off, so Clive exited as fast as he could, before anything could go wrong. Glancing back through the window he saw the man in the red parka strolling over to the Danish ladies, already breaking into a Barry smile, and a Barry line of patter.

'Yesss!' said Clive quietly as he hurried along to Victoria Station. He was five foot ten, of medium build. His dark-brown hair had become a dry thatch that to his relief had stopped receding at a respectable widow's peak. He was too young for Brylcneem but too old for gel. It had turned grey at the temples and, if he should ever attempt a beard again as he had in his middle thirties, at the chops too. His forehead was high and wrinkled, and ended in sharp ledges about his eyes, giving him a brooding, serious look. There were other signs of ageing – his eyes had their fair share of wrinkles, his nose and ear hairs had to be tended. He was quite proud of his nose, which was dead straight until the tip, whence it curled downwards, showing no nostril from the front. However, he had a large space above his upper lip where a broad moustache would have fitted, but which he had banished, again due to greyness. His head was the best part of his body, whose topography was shifting to a paunch-and-love-handles scenario (with slight stoop) the longer he was unemployed. Clive had good strong thighs and big calves, from all his years of walking, and regretted that there were few opportunities for showing them off in metropolitan London. Now he walked purposefully for the first time in years.

'Yesss! I'm back in business!' And he allowed himself a silent 'Yahoo!'

It was a beautiful summer's evening – seven o'clock and the sun was still shining. The pavements were crowded with office workers with their jackets over their shoulders and their sleeves rolled up. Women bounced by in summer blouses and T-shirts, all bra seams and bare legs, confidence all over their faces. People waded between the traffic to get to the pubs and celebrate being in England when it's light and warm. Clive felt a surge of daring, as though he could go up to any woman and start talking to her, and when it came to finding out what he did for a living, he could say he was employed. He could say he was a tour guide, actually. That he knew a few people around town, and he knew how to get into things for free. Suddenly, he could put people at their ease, he would never be stuck for conversation, he'd be happy to lead. At the end of the week he'd have a wage and could pay his own way.

'Yesss!' He felt like veering into the rail bar in Victoria and standing himself a drink, with all the other blokes, and buying one for the barman too. Or barmaid. Then he felt the snap of the leash at his neck, and reminded himself he was off the booze, and that it was better not to tempt fate. It was better to stay out of those places. One Diet Pepsi session was hard enough. A second would be even more miserable. He'd probably end up on the beer again. He had to tell himself to stop and think of Tess. Think of little Tess.

He was off the booze because of his divorce. It was one more thing the judge had held against him when he lost custody of his daughter. He didn't even get unsupervised contact any more. His wife's lawyer had branded him a child molester, on account of the fifteen-year-old girl, and questioned his ability to keep his hands off his own daughter. But at the most recent hearing the genius in the double-breasted grey suit had had also made Clive out to be an alcoholic. Just because, like everyone else he knew, he liked to open a bottle of wine in the evening, after a long day at school, and watch TV, and behave like an adult. Everyone he knew did the same. His ex-wife did the same. Christina. The hypocrite. And if they were sharing it, she'd open the second bottle just as soon as he would, so they could both get their fair whack. Half a bottle of wine was nothing, especially over four hours. What was it, a couple of glasses? Pathetic.

So the court had him down as a bottle-a-night guy, and looked at like that, it sounded a lot. But what were the odds that both lawyers drank when they went home? And the judge. All the teachers did. Some of them even drank in *pubs*, Clive wanted to shout out. Beer. Tons of it. Every night after work. As soon as they were out of the catchment area of the school. His lawyer though, whom he'd picked because he did the conveyancing when Clive and Christina bought their house, had told him to keep his mouth shut. His barrister was bloody useless too, a fifty-five-year-old boiler from the Temple who specialised in family law and irritating the judge. He was told he couldn't accuse his ex-wife of being an alcoholic too, because it looked desperate. Had to think of the kid first. It was stupid. His solicitor was an ass. Clive fired him. Right after he paid him.

Though the need for a drink after nine months' abstinence was making his teeth hurt, he survived, and went to the train. His sunshine had clouded over though – here he was, celebrating his new job, and not a soul to do it with. It constantly amazed him that despite having met thousands of people in his lifetime, and selected scores of them as acquaintances, sometimes even friends, that he should end up, in middle age, with no one. Well, there were a few people, but none he could call at short notice on a Friday night and invite out for ... what? A lemonade? It was too depressing.

Clive was glad to get on the train and start the long haul back to Streatham. At least out there there was no chance of anything happening. No prospects, no disappointment. Except for a few stray yuppies, everyone in SW16 had given up on London.

3

Divorce

A few hours later, across the city to the north, Clive's ex-wife and daughter were just coming home from Brownies. Seven-year-old Tess hopped out of the people carrier and let herself in. She had her own key, hanging from a shoelace round her neck. Her mother, a thin forty-year-old with a sculpted blonde bob and an inky tan from Turkey, hauled in the Waitrose bags behind her. Tess ran into the lounge, sitting down in front of the television with the remote control. Top Of The Pops had just started. The first sight that greeted her was three girls who looked like aerobics instructors, wearing tight shorts and trainers shaking it around an ungainly, murmuring man in shades and a sparkly tuxedo. She ran back out to the kitchen to get a drink. Mother gave her some fizzy water, ignoring her pleas to hurry up as she retrieved a clean glass from the dishwasher.

'What do you say?' she asked wearily as the child ran back to the TV. 'Walk! Don't run with a glass!'

Tess said nothing. She didn't want to bother with her mother this time, she was too excited about the stars on Top Of The Pops, and too keen to see if they matched up with the discussions at Brownies.

'Ecstas-ee! I'm in ecstas-ee!
Ecstas-ee! I'm in ecstas-ee!' [sang the girls, then the bloke growled]:
'I'm a mover and a shaker,
Got an active money maker,
Keep it real don't be a faker,
Ecstasy come on ecstasy.'

After two more trips to the car, the fridge freezer and the cupboards were full. Christina sat down at the kitchen table and poured herself a glass of Merlot. She took a sip then leaned back and closed her eyes. She loved the dry, dark liquid on her tongue, and its room temperature innocence. *The fruit*, she thought. *Slightly oaky*. She let it trickle down her throat a little at a time. She felt her stomach warming, and then waited for the alcohol to kick in.

At last, a Friday evening to herself. No dinner parties, no drinks parties, no meat-rack singles bars, no blind dates with loose cannons ... *Thank God that's over*, she thought. Some of the men out there ... What useless, self-centred, talentless, tasteless, balding, cliché-ridden lecherous ... losers. That was the only word for them. Good riddance to dating, and never again.

Jeffrey was her date now, her steady boyfriend, and he was coming over on Saturday. *Jeffrey. Even his name sounds right. How could I have ever have married someone called Clive? I've never met a worthwhile Clive. What was I thinking? I know what I was thinking. Ack ...* She tried to stop herself but the thought came anyway: *'This sweet, sweet man, this kind teacher, this noble professional, untouched by ambition and greed, he's going to keep us on an even keel, he'll be my compass and my guide.' What a silly bugger I was ...*

She recalled how splendid Clive looked at their wedding, in the very same morning suit her father had worn at his wedding. He had no shaving cuts, his new haircut worked, and the dress rehearsals had paid off handsomely. He even looked quite handsome then, she thought, and then regretted her naïveté. She really hated herself for marrying a self-loathing nobody who ran off with the first piece of skirt that presented itself to him. *Teenage skirt! A little scrubber of a schoolgirl who couldn't keep her knickers on past fifteen. If that's really when they did it. Who knew how long it had been going on before he confessed?* She tried to stop herself from thinking again but the words and images kept coming. She recalled Clive's grovelling apologies, his tears, his desperate genuflection, his protestations at how things had been distorted, his promise never to be unfaithful again, his limp, silence-filled telephone calls that dragged on into the night, and she started getting angry. *Breathe in calm, breathe out anger. Breathe in calm, breathe out anger*, she told herself to quiet her racing heart. Her aromatherapist had told her to think lavender, and she tried, and failed. *Think of something nice. Think of ... Tessa's school marks. Top in spelling, top in maths. Our summer holiday coming up. Think of Jeffrey ... Mmmm, Jeffrey. Jeffrey and his passion for wine. His taste in music. His opera CDs, a whole case of them in the boot of his Rover. The way he does the right thing*

— always offers to go Dutch but ends up picking up the tab. He knows I'm struggling to pay the bills.

She opened her eyes and gazed around the kitchen. The French farmhouse look — the giant slabs of beech wood that made up the table and prep cart, the oak fascia on the fridge, the stone sink, the rough brown curtains, the rag-rolled walls . . . suddenly it all looked very tired and annoyed her. *This is so last century,* she thought. *I'm not a peasant. When is Clive going to make some money and contribute properly? The useless sod.* She was getting cross again. The cordless phone was right there on the table so she picked it up and speed-dialled Clive on number three.

She heard it ring five times. *Typical Clive. Hasn't got his act together. God I'd hate to see the state of his new flat.*

'Hullo?' said Clive. Nothing more. She sensed that she had interrupted something.

'It's me.' She paused, expecting him to acknowledge, but only heard him catching his breath. 'I hope I didn't catch you in the middle of something,' she purred, a malicious reference to the time she burst in on him having a handjob when they had been married only nine months. She was supposed to be out for another few hours but reappeared without warning. It was typical Tina.

'Uh, no. I just couldn't find the phone. Haven't unpacked properly yet. What's wrong. How's Tess? Is she all right?'

'Tess is fine. I just called to see how your interview went. You know, just wondering when the great Clive Pointing would be gainfully employed again.' Christina had a deep, flavourful voice that made even her sarcasm sound like it could be a come-on. Or at least, made her sound as if she was open to reconciliation. You had to get face-to-face with her to get the full power of her loathing. She was still an attractive woman, on paper and on the phone. As she sat there in her white Gap blouse, tailored to her thin waist, and her black 'cigarette pants', as she called them — Beatnik-short and tapered at the shins — it was easy to see how people could find her so attractive. On the phone she made her vowels rich and heavy, her consonants clear. She was husky, she was sex online. She also had an infectious giggle that cut across all this, the same sound she made at fifteen on the phone to friends. And though her blondeness came out of a bottle, her hair had kept most of its youthful bounce. One look at her and most people concluded that Clive had blown it. He was a plonker, he was an idiot, he was a twat to have got caught.

'The interview went well,' he said brightly. Then he realised he was celebrating with his ex-wife, and put the brakes on. 'I think.'

'You think? What does that mean? You were *there* weren't you?' She wasn't sounding as husky now.

'I had an interview with one of their top guides, and he said . . .'

'Where?'

'Er, in a pub . . .'

'Oh God Clive. Oh God. That's all we need.'

'Look I'm doing this for me, not you.'

'You're doing it for our daughter!'

'Whom I never see, because of you.'

'You're not fit to see her. Who's to say you wouldn't be as good a father as you were a husband? I.e., total crap?'

Clive knew the 'i.e.' was coming. She wrote letters all day at the estate agent's where she worked, and *i.e.*, *viz.*, and *to wit* were cornerstones of the house style. He knew she hated her job, that she was secretly ashamed of it, and he wanted to get her on it.

'Ergo,' he said, 'what's the point in me getting a job?'

'Listen Clive, you owe me nearly a year's child maintenance. You get yourself a proper bloody job and start coughing up.'

'Well, like I said,' said Clive, feeling calmer the angrier she got, 'the chap who interviewed me said it was in the bag. I start on Monday.'

'What about your course? Do they know you couldn't finish it?'

'Not couldn't, *wouldn't*. I didn't have time. Because of you nagging for money. Remember?' He stopped himself from adding the words 'you bitch'. 'They do know as a matter of fact. They said my being a teacher was a better qualification in the long run.' He liked that. Rubbing it in that he was a qualified professional. He knew it got to her that although they had both been to university (she was at Exeter, no less) he was the professional and had carried on using his education, kept his brain in gear. She, though, had lost her way somewhere, and after a series of false starts had drifted into estate agency.

Christina fumed. She still found it too distasteful to remind him of exactly why he wasn't a professional any more – because he did schoolgirls – so instead she said in a silky smooth voice, 'Clive, call me when you've pulled yourself together. Goodbye.' And hung up.

He heard the electric click and then the silence. He was sitting on the floor, next to one of his many cardboard boxes of possessions – mainly books — on which the phone had its temporary home. He leaned back against the wall and looked about the flat.

Through a combination of his own fault and his own bad fortune, Clive now found himself in middle age inhabiting a single room (with kitchenette — twin gas ring, a chopping board, and a sink to piss in) in a subdivided house in Streatham, one of the most depressingly crap parts of London. It was far from the overground train and even further from a Tube. There were buses — unpredictable, slow, expensive — but you had to take buses to get to them. Naturally, as part of the settlement, Tina had kept the car. His flat consisted of the two ground-floor rooms of a three-storey house knocked into one, with windows at both ends, one looking out on the street, the other on an overgrown garden with its own dysfunctional family of cats. At the end of the short garden behind a fence of barbed poles was an electricity substation which hummed day and night.

From where he sat, on the floor between the boxes, he could see the pipe again. It was suspended from the ceiling by brackets and ran the length of the room. Clive reckoned it was a hot-water pipe, as it creaked and pinged at different times. There was a big kink in it half-way as though a heavy object had pulled on it. The landlord, Mr Ahmet, had told him when he first came to see the place, that the previous tenant had moved out unexpectedly. It was only months later, when he was stopped in the hall by one of his fellow tenants that Clive found out the bloke had hanged himself. Danny, the Kiwi from upstairs who told him this, talked excitedly of how the word had spread through the house on a Sunday morning and everybody piled downstairs for a look. Even Danny's girlfriend Jo had come down in her dressing gown, but when she saw the figure hanging, its fat blue tongue sticking out of a shocked white face, its head cocked at an inquisitive angle, she ran straight back to their room.

Danny noticed that the dead guy — who was called David and was about his age, late twenties — had his feet touching the ground, folded backwards. He reckoned the pipe had given too much and the bloke had died of strangulation instead of a snapped neck. 'He could have been struggling for hours,' Danny told him, his pin-prick pupils boring into Clive and a trace of a nervous smirk on his face. 'Jo thinks I'm sick?' he said with an interrogative whine. 'But I think you *heff* to see everything? I'm a film student y'know?' he added, as if it explained everything. Clive mumbled his excuses and returned to his room, vowing to get the pipe straightened.

At least this David didn't leave a semen stain on the carpet, he thought gratefully. That's exactly the sort of thing I should have said to Danny.

He'd have loved that. Dave still got the odd phone call, usually from people wanting money. Each time Clive had to explain that Dave was gone. If they pressed, which they usually did, he told them about the suicide.

Clive was already depressed enough without thinking about the swinging man. There was nothing much to look forward to. Clive got a flicker of his own suicide, shuddered inside at the sadness of it, and forced himself to get up off the floor and make a cup of tea.

4

East

Way across London to the east, Barry Bergman was getting out of a taxi and walking up the path to his tower block. He went through his pockets as he walked: phone number on piece of paper – out. Elastic band – out. Office keys – in of course. Article ripped from *Financial Times* by Maxine – out. He screwed the rubbish together and tossed it into a flower bed, then let himself in. He took the lift up one floor and opened his front door. He and his wife Christine had lived in their council flat for over ten years. As the kids arrived they had shouting matches about moving, getting a place of their own, but each time something new came up – her old mum had moved in with them, costing them quite a bit in prescription charges and time to look after. They had another baby. The council made a balls-up and gave the flat they were expecting to some other family. At one point they thought they were moving to Docklands, but then they took a look around the place and decided it was too empty. The pub was a fifteen-minute walk away. Then they had another kid.

'Dad! Dadda!' piped the smallest one as he came through the door, and clamped on to his knees. 'All right Di, how's my little beauty today? Wossat you got there Dawn?' Diana was two, Dawn was five, Shelley was eight and three quarters.

'Daddy, Daddy, look what I drew . . . look what I did . . . look what I got . . . Shelley hit me . . . No I never . . . Yes she did . . .' They were off, and Barry resigned himself to an evening in. Bath time, a video, sorting them out for bed, then maybe, maybe if they were good, a few cans in front of the telly. His wife's sister Donna, who had been looking after them till Barry got home (nearly an hour late, as it happened) came up the hall putting on her coat.

'Thought you was never coming. Why's yer phone switched off?'

'Is it? Oh, I must have forgot. Fanks for looking after 'em Donna. So where you all going out tonight?'

'West End.'

Barry's wife Christine was over at his dad's, making his dinner. She was going straight out from there. 'Oh. Well make sure Christine doesn't have too many, in her state, you know it's bad for the baby.'

'She's well past that stage . . . anyway, I gotta go.' She smiled. 'Bye kids! Bye-bye my little sweethearts! Mwa!' She bent down and kissed each one of them. Barry struggled through the scrum of children to give Donna a chaste peck on the cheek, and squeezed her arm as an invitation to have sex should they ever find themselves alone with half an hour to spare. Donna, who was used to ignoring this, left Barry to deal with his overexcited spawn.

Once the girls' hair was dry and they were all in bed and just whispering instead of pinching each other and kicking with tiny feet, Barry leaned back on the sofa and popped the top on his second can of lager. He thought back on the afternoon. He still had the ticket money in his coat pocket from the abortive Windsor trip, a roll of twenties and tens. He thought back to the pub, and the Danish women. How they had soon given in and admitted they enjoyed the day, said they hadn't been to such an authentic English cafe before. 'What is it called again?' one of them said. 'An oily spoon?' And everyone was laughing and someone brought him another pint.

He couldn't get over the Danes. Or the Swedes. All that porn. He couldn't imagine them not thinking about sex all the time. Bending over for him and looking back with a becoming smile. It was just too perfect. The Norwegians too, and the Finns. Anyone with fur coats, blonde hair and a laid-back nature. Even in their forties and fifties, it was still there. *Scandinavian*. Just the word itself promised so much.

This was all reaffirmed when, a few minutes after leaving the pub, while he was checking the foreign exchange prices in Thomas Cook's window, he got a call on his mobile. It played Colonel Bogey in a tinny electronic tone. The caller was Annelise, the well-dressed Danish woman from the bus. The argumentative one. She wanted to know if he had any flyers. It was just the sort of pathetic excuse he liked, and it gave him a chuckle as he sped to her Paddington hotel in a taxi. He was in and out in an hour, on account of the kids. An hour which included twenty minutes of courtship/foreplay and five minutes of cleaning up/valedictions. The rest was the old horizontal Esperanto. He rinsed his knob in her sink, not very impressed with the towels. 'Only one hand towel for a double room?' he asked rhetorically. 'Sometimes I'm ashamed of the service in this country, I really am.'

He'd asked Donna to tape his favourite soap, *Eastenders*, but she'd cocked it up and got a load of rubbish instead. Flicking around between the channels he couldn't settle on anything, even satellite was boring for once. There was a square photo on top of the telly of Barry in his twenties with Christine. They looked shiny and happy, like they'd had a day on the beach, and they both had cocktails in front of them. Her bare arm was draped around his neck. There was another woman's arm round his neck, coming from the other side, but whoever it was had been cropped.

For over ten years, into his mid thirties, Barry had been a Club 18 to 30 guide. He saw them all. Groups of party-mad teenagers mixed in with blossoming young adults, geezers with fresh paunches and girls with caesarean scars, shipping 'em in and out of Gatwick and Luton like mutton to Europe. All sorts, but all basically the same. Van drivers and pipefitters, bouncers, barrow boys and bakery girls, production liners and fork-lift drivers, service-industry foot soldiers, clerks and temps and typists and 'Exec Asses', cuties who worked in jeans shops, the girls who served pies at the skating rink, the BT blokes who fixed your phone, trainee coppers, firemen, nurses – tons of nurses, lovely nurses out of uniform and wearing just bikinis – dole office people with their pallid skin and hangdog looks (they took a bit of extra cheering up but he could do it), the blokes who dug up the roads, already brown and hard and able to live on ten pints and four hours sleep a night (plus a nap on the beach), thieves and fences, e-peddlers, Aspirin launderers, barmen, people who worked in record shops, people who worked in exhaust-pipe centres, people who worked nights putting holes in washers, North Sea trawlermen (he had known it, six incomprehensible Yorkshire boys who drank until they fell down and had to be constantly rescued by hotel security), rastas even, aerobics teachers, dole-ites, dole-ites, thousands of dole-ites with their black-market money, non-specific slappers, blokes who sold cars and vans, blokes who sold insurance, boxers, lots of boxers for some reason, fake ID council workmen, baggage handlers, even a bus driver once, from Scunthorpe or Skegness or somewhere northern like that, on his own and horny as hell, all he wanted to know was where he could get off his face all the time and where could he get sex local even if he had to pay for it, mental, never stopped smiling for a week ... Polytechnic students, more and more students in fact, schoolgirls though they weren't supposed to, launderette girls, supermarket girls, product-demonstration girls who wanted to be models, Irish girls, the odd Asian and his mates, not very happy about that in the early days but attitudes seemed to change and they were accepted, Asian babes as they started to get a bit of money and attitude, waitresses, office managers, salesmen, trainee accountants, muggers, everyone. Everyone. Even the odd gaggle of public schoolboys looking for an easy ride.

Barry had been an alpha male among Club 18 to 30 reps. He shagged his way through half of England during his halcyon days, when he used to take two loads of punters a week to Greece. And Greece was the place for him. He'd done a lot of no-name tours pulled together in shop fronts in east London before he worked his way up to Club 18 to 30. He did a dodgy caravan site in the St Tropez for a year, cramming them in and dragging them out, though he thought the South of France was too posh and a bit too nudie in a German businessman sort of way. He knew all the service stations of the autoroutes and the names of all the cross-channel ferries, he knew what time the airports closed around Europe and how to avoid the more massive queues. Club 18 to 30 came after him because their reps had seen him around in various Mediterranean watering holes, always with a string of happy punters in tow. He did Ibiza for a while until it went trendy, then the Costas, which were OK, a bit common but the traffic was there. But Greece, Greece was the place. The Aegean Sea. Corfu, Kos, Dos, Tos, Rhodes, Faliraki, and even bits of Turkey, Bodrum and Marmaris. Names that had once seemed strange and now seemed like home.

Barry led them everywhere. From departure day, chasing stragglers out of the duty-free shop at Gatwick where they already had the tops off their litres of vodka and perfume and getting them on to the waiting plane which was already half full of moaning Mancs and Brummies ... to the last day when he signed off on hungover lads on crutches with moped road rash or sunburn and watched them wheeled away by their friends on luggage trolleys. Barry was the man.

He entertained them on the plane with stories of cheap ouzo, topless swimming parties and loud clubs, he sorted out the shy ones and made sure they got loaded or laid at least once by the middle of the week, and he threatened his lads with jail and the cricket bat when they got too out of order and clashed too violently with the locals.

But what Barry was best at was the extras. Charming unexpected tariffs out of the punters for the things they had seen in the brochure and naively assumed would be free: parasailing, windsurfing, dune buggies, snorkel gear, ping-pong, barbecues, wine tasting, donkey up the hill to the monastery . . . even a Frisbee was a fiver. Barry taxed with a smile and embezzled with a poker face, and everybody loved him.

Great days, those had been great days. The money, the birds, the laughs. Now, as Barry put it, things were tighter than a gnat's chuff and not half as much fun. Britannia didn't compare. The unpredictable tourists, the strong pound, the rain – England wasn't Greece. Barry didn't like that posh twat Alex, and didn't think the new bloke looked up to much either. He seemed pretty green. Still, it just meant more extras for him.

He sat there watching the car programme on telly, *Top Gear*, without really thinking. The mad northern bloke was going on about the new Rolls, looked like a Rolls but had a BMW motor. 'Facking stupid,' Barry muttered. The phone went. It was one of his many brothers, Stuart. Did he want to go down the pub? Of course he wanted to, but he was stuck minding the girls wasn't he? Stuart annoyed him. Stuart had never lifted a finger when it came to looking after their dad, after Mum died. Stuart just treated his dad the same, like he was still a kid coming to him for pocket money. That reminded him – pocket money for the girls tomorrow, Saturday. He peeled three fivers off the roll and put them under the clock on the mantelpiece. He said he'd see Stuart when he'd see him.

He decided that since the telly was crap he might as well go to bed. No point waiting up for Chrissie. It was better to get some sleep now, since the girls would be in bouncing on the bed in the morning, pulling at his face and shouting in his ear. In the bedroom Barry put his clothes over the back of the chair, giving them the once-over for silver hairs, then, in his navy-blue pants with the cut-away sides, he got into bed and fell instantly asleep.

Clive was sitting on the edge of his own sagging bed in his boxer shorts, feeling the flab around his waist. He sighed, lay down, and pulled the covers over him. He wondered if the room would ever get warm, even in summer.

The phone rang. He leaned over and found it amongst the boxes.

'Can I speak to Dave please?'

'Er, no, Dave's not . . . around any more.'

'Well can you give him a message then?'

'Er, no. I mean, it's not possible.'

'Tell him I want my money, *now*, the bastard.'

'He's dead.'
'What?'
'He killed himself.'
'Bollocks. When?'
'Just before I moved in. A few months back.'
'Humph. Did he leave any money?'
'I don't know.'
'Wanker.'
'I'm sorry.'
'Oh fuck off.'

As he lay back down again Clive could hear the street as though there was no front on the house. Cars straining past every few seconds, girls clacking by on high heels, shouting children out late looking for trouble. From the back he heard the dog barking a few doors down, and found it impossible not to follow its arrhythmic woofs. Every time the dog seemed to have got to the end of a sentence, he added another barking clause. When he finished a paragraph, Clive held his breath hoping it was the end of a chapter. And when he launched into a new, spirited sequence, Clive's pulse went up a few more revs. *Bloody dog, shut up!* he thought. His mind hummed, and he wished it would leave him in peace. About once an hour he looked at the digital clock and cursed himself. It must have been after two a.m. by the time he nodded off into a useless soufflé of sleep, only to wake, exhausted, with the dawn chorus.

5

Streatham Sucks

What does a lonely man do at the weekend? When Clive Pointing went shopping, walking the streets of Streatham with his plastic bags and hunched shoulders, it was as though he was accompanied by Elgar's mournful cellos. On Saturdays he fished amongst the discounted breads in Sainsbury's while post-coital couples stepped around him to get to the flavoured pita pockets. He bought his meat and cheese in vacuum-sealed polythene instead of taking a number and queuing with them – her hair so soft, his arms still pumped – for honey-glazed hams and reduced-fat Gouda. It was as though his fellow shoppers could hear the doleful scraping of horsehair on steel and kept their distance. He wandered into the electrical shop to look at the black boxes, the durables that were always changing, always two steps ahead of him. He had lost track of time, and lost track of television.

In addition to the stinging capital order effected by her shit-hot lawyer, Christina had kept the house, the car and almost all the contents when they had split up. This included the TV, and he had neither the energy nor the cash to get his own. Sure, he could have got a dusty and rain-spotted set for a tenner from the pile outside the second-hand store, the place where he got his bed with the stained mattress and where Mr Ahmet bought his gas cookers. But television no longer seemed to have any point.

He had lost track of music too. Tina ended up with all his records and CDs, and he no longer had his pupils' taste to keep him fresh. He had the scratchy little radio in the bedside clock, on which he mostly listened to Radio Three. Of the few stations he could get that weren't affected by the electrical interference from the substation, it was the only one he could bear. He admired the way they'd have three hours of incomprehensible opera followed by a talk by a philosopher. Not about one, but by one. Also incomprehensible, but authentic. Most of the media was alien to him. He was too thin-skinned to hear the soundtrack to his youth, his salad days, curated by Radio Two. (At the time he hadn't thought he would one day rely on old memories of pop culture for the bulk of his self esteem.) And he was too depressed for the nursing-home torpor of Radio Four. The interchangeable politicians and pundits were like crickets rubbing their dry legs together, all noise and no signal, and since he didn't have a life, the magazine programmes no longer spoke to him. Culinary tinkering. Consumer wrongs righted. Cyberyarbles. 'Me and My Stool'. The whole project passed him by.

Saturdays were extra depressing because that used to be the day he got Tess. The last time he had her, last year it was now, they went to the Zoo. London Zoo, Regent's Park – the whole horror and sadness of it. He even had to give up a day's studying for the course, the practical. Everyone else was going on a walking tour of Soho. He thought he might be able to join up with them at some point, bring Tess along; but then he remembered what it was like to be six, and abandoned the idea.

He and Tess tried to get into Madame Tussaud's Waxworks Museum, but after queuing for ninety minutes with fractious suburbanites and fidgeting French adolescents, the door was closed and they were told to wait another hour. Tess cried and wanted to walk on her own, so Clive kicked Plan B into action, and they walked through Regent's Park, picking their way around the boating lake and between the trees, hoping for an ice cream van. Inside the Zoo, with her second ice cream jammed in her hand (the first was upended on to the grass, as usual) Tess scampered ahead, excited by the threadbare lionesses and amazed at the scorched camels. Most of the animals stayed in the concrete bunkers, or dozed in the weak sun, pointing their scurvy arses the wrong way, sucking their offspring or chewing their mange. Clive had to hurry round after her. He was trying to read the placards so he could explain things, but there was nothing to satisfy her queries: 'Why does the baboon have a red bottom? Why does the giraffe have a broken pattern on it? Why don't the penguins use their slides?' He heard another dad, another ex-husband he presumed, telling his sons how great the penguin house was because it was famous, and that the architect was a chap called Rubik.

'It's Lubetkin, not Rubin,' Clive said helpfully. The man looked up. He looked like a reasonable man – fleece jacket, khaki trousers, designer glasses – and his boys were well turned out. All three of them looked at Clive, in his mackintosh and old hush puppies.

'Mind your own business,' said the man, looking him straight in the eye. His sons looked up at him and then back at Clive.

'Weirdo!' shouted one of them, and stuck out his tongue.

Clive reddened, looked at the floor a moment and said nothing. Then he set off at ninety degrees, calling loudly after Tess, trying to make it clear he was one of them, a father, a nuclear dad, divorced maybe but doing his best to keep it all together, to bring up happy, sensible kids, to keep the civilisation going. He was no weirdo.

Tess wanted to go home. She said the reptiles were creepy, she wouldn't look at them, and the birds weren't flying about in their saggy net. She thought it was all stupid, and said she wanted to see the pop stars at Madame Tussaud's. Clive's heart was so heavy with failure he could barely talk to her, aside from issuing basic instructions, like 'Pay the nice bus conductor' and 'Don't tell Mummy about the sweets.'

The problem with his daughter was, she didn't like him any more. Obviously it had been getting worse since he moved out of the house, but it had become critical in the preceding months: her instinct was to be ashamed of him. She sensed he was a loser, and they were both paying the price for it.

'Mummy's new boyfriend wants to take us on holiday.' He knew that was coming.

Looking back to his and Tess's last real day out together, Clive realised that at least back then he'd had the comfort of a drink or two after a day of misery. After dropping her back at her Mum's he'd taken the bus to Upper Street, just for old times' sake, and gone into the King's Head. It was some kind of theatre pub, but they had booze and that's what counted. Everyone in there was young, a whole new generation of people out getting pissed, flirting, blowing their money and talking about house prices. The big visual attraction for drunks crushed up at the bar was the old-school cash register with the shiny metal exterior. It had prices on little plates that ker-chinged up when the keys were pressed, like a manual typewriter. Everything in pounds, shillings and pence. Kerching! 6d. Six denarii. Sixpence. Students on dates and bearded types milled about waiting for a play to start – *Happy Days*, by Samuel Beckett. Some old girl up to her neck in sand from the looks of the poster. Clive heard a couple of pointy-faced men talking about it. They weren't much older than some of his pupils. His ex-pupils. He used to see the books they brought into his Geography class. Fat text books of History and French Grammar, and English stuff: *Women in Love*, and *Animal Farm*, and always *Waiting for Godot*. That was Beckett, he reflected. He'd never read it. He saw some of it on television once but Tina turned it over, she said it was boring. It was pretty boring too. Except it made him wonder where it could possibly go next. Why bother?

That night he left the pub alone and rolled home in a mini cab. Well, what was called home at the time – his friend George's futon in Camberwell. George was a Geography teacher he'd worked with for five years, back in his rich middle period. George was solid and tweedy and had taken Clive under his wing. Nothing was said when Clive turned up at school on the first day of his second term with brown leather elbow patches just like George's. And nothing had been said when Clive was successfully invited to apply for a better job, north of the river, earning more than his mentor. George shook his hand grimly as they departed on the last day of term outside the staff room. Kids were hurtling down the corridors full of the ecstasy of summer freedom, and George broke off to lecture the first two he caught.

They promised to keep in touch, and did, once Clive and Tina had moved to North London, bought a house and had a baby. They met up for a drink in a mock-modern pub in Docklands, which Clive chose because it was half way, but which George joked was slightly weighted against him, given the barrier effect of the river and whatnot.

They settled into the irregular exchange of Christmas cards, so when Clive called a few years later, his life in ruins, homeless and hated, George grudgingly said he could stay on his sofa for a week, until he found a place.

George was single. Loser single. That is he had never married, nor lived with anyone, nor was he a homosexual – in, out or unwitting. Now that Clive had worked at another school and even been head of his own department, he could see that teaching had sheltered George from taking any risks with his life. George had bumbled along, satisfied with making small dramas out of minibus mileage and curriculum changes, sowing the seeds of his wisdom in the increasingly flinty soil of young minds. Young minds who deserted him every year, but were replaced every year.

'One week' turned into two, and then into a month, and then into six months. They had a routine for sharing the bathroom and Clive made sure he folded his bed away and brought home the odd takeaway for two.

George was six foot three, wore a lot of brown, and cut himself shaving every day. Clive assumed he would be glad of a bit of company, but he was mistaken. George would come home from school and fold himself into his favourite chair like a praying mantis with the remote control and watch whatever cricket was on. He liked cricket, but he didn't particularly like talking about it while it was on, and Clive's comments were generally ignored. It was winter and England were having a shockingly good tour of the West Indies, drawing several games and even winning one, and George's facial expression remained one of bewilderment for several weeks. He had forgotten how to enjoy England. But slowly it came back to him. When they had worked together George used to watch the test matches during free periods in the staff room at school in Walworth. He would sit with his elbows on the chair arms, his fingers making a steeple before his face, occasionally pushing his gunk-encrusted glasses back up his nose. Now he sat in his chair at home like a gunslinger with his remote control, one leg across the other knee, ignoring Clive, mesmerised by the procession of crimson-capped West Indians trudging back to the pavilion.

Despite their routine, though, George found more to tut-tut about as the months passed. He never brought up the subject of Clive finding his own place, but eventually he started bringing home the free-ads paper and placing it carefully on the bed settee.

After much phoning and Tubing it out to the areas he could afford, Clive found a place at Mr Ahmet's in Streatham. Fate dumped him south of the river again.

When he moved out, George shook his hand solemnly in the hall and shut the door after him. As Clive walked past the front-room window he saw him settling back into his chair, remote in hand. England had just moved on to Guyana.

In the days before his new job started Clive was able to immerse himself in his books. He phoned Britannia Tours and Maxine confirmed that his first day out would be a panoramic of London – a quick shufty round the capital for the type of tourist with no time and less imagination. Nothing too taxing there, he fancied. He had his *London Encyclopaedia* out, his *Blue Guide to London*, and his dog-eared *A–Z* in which he had marked all his solo walks. He loved the fabulous beauty of the colour *A–Z*, its inclusivity. He could look at it for hours. Every road and *cul de sac* laid out, every pond, gasometer, runway, every scrubby patch of grass, every wharf, works, siding, footpath . . . He loved the made-up colour scheme (A-Roads in amber, B-Roads in gold), the speculative dates on the unfinished roads

– whoever at the Geographers' A–Z Map Company did it even put in the river's low-tide marks. He could imagine how shocked the American tourist might be at the knotty mess of London's roads, like an ancient organism, a thousand-year-old oak. He could see the trainee cab drivers on the Honda C90s doing the Knowledge, map and wish-list under polythene, probing side streets for difficult mews and long-lost lanes.

But sometimes it all just reminded him of Tina and her trade. One look at the map and all he could see was house prices. It depressed him. He could see how she would always be needed, since every home was different, and dependent on so many variables – age, size, transportation links, distance from (mythical) centre, crime stats, local council, aspect of sun, anecdotal potential . . . he could see where every single one had to be individually valued, and then that valuation be discussed in pubs and at dinner parties for years after. He thought of Tina, and what a mess he'd made of his life.

Place names swam in his mind as he lay in bed listening to the dog barking. Britannia had come along at the right time. Clive's own internal Knowledge guy putt-putted down a cobbled street, bouncing heavily on the suspension. Things were OK, they were turning a corner. He'd soon be back on his feet.

6

Panorama

Clive awoke with a start, his heart thumping. His bedside clock blinked 12.00.

'Balls!' he muttered. 'Buggeration!' The clock was plugged in. He could only assume the electricity had been interrupted in the night.

'I live by a ruddy power station and this has to happen to me?'

He didn't even bother turning on Radio 3, since he knew they were shy about vulgarities like time-checks. He could just make out what his watch said, through the fog under the glass (ever since his first shower in Mr Ahmet's badly ventilated bathroom it had supported its own tropical weather system): ten minutes to nine.

'Oh, not today of all days? Why now?' He was supposed to be at the Britannia office by nine to meet Alex. He pulled on his clothes, grabbed his files and rushed out the door and down to the bus stop. This was always the gamble – wait for a bus to the train, or walk it? He ended up waiting fifteen furious minutes for the bus before running across the Common to the train. Buses sailed past him as he ran, making him so angry that he didn't even allow himself to stop to grab a bite to eat or a newspaper.

When he got to the platform his heart sank as he saw three hundred people kicking their heels and grumbling.

'What's wrong?' he asked an old lady standing by the chocolate machine.

'Bleedin' delayed innit,' she said.

They stood in silence for another fifteen minutes, Clive shifting from foot to foot, until at last the train crept around the corner. He took his place in the queue and managed to get a spot up against the door with his bag pressed to his chest.

It was ten minutes past ten when he got there. He considered bluffing and apologising for being just ten minutes late, but chickened out when he reached the office. Maxine sat at one desk typing at a computer with yellow Walkman headphones on. At 90 degrees to her, where he could best monitor her through his door, and the street scene out of the window, sat Alex. His desk was three times bigger, but held just a laptop computer, some photos, and a coffee cup from the Upper Crust. On the walls were a few faded posters of stout, photogenic castles – Leeds in Kent, Warwick near Coventry – and a set of metal shelves holding boxes of brochures. A couple of older people sat around on chairs reading, a tall man with a moustache with a *Daily Mail*, a woman with a *Daily Express* and a moustache of her own.

Maxine smiled at him and shouted across to Alex, who was buried in his screen, 'The new bloke's here! Alex?'

'All right, no need to shout!' he boomed back. He stood up but neither smiled nor offered his hand.

'So you must be Clive Pointing. Hum.'

Alexander White was five foot eight but because he didn't stoop he actually looked taller than Clive. He had a complexion that matched his pink shirt, and a web of thinning hair like spun sugar that only drew attention to the emerging dome of his skull. Beneath his bulbous forehead and sandy eyebrows, sat his disturbingly close-together eyes. His nose was classed as noble (big) and his mouth was generous and fleshy. When he turned to one side his looks lost a couple more stars, as his chin was directly connected to his Adam's apple by a rampart of flesh. With his pink shirts he favoured conservative ties and navy-blue or grey suits (also slightly baggy), boxer shorts with humorous motifs such as bananas, flying pigs or rugby balls, or sometimes a pair of cream lace-and-satin women's panties from Knickerbox that he had shoplifted one Christmas, and always black socks with black shoes. Clive reckoned he was about forty.

'Er, yes,' said Clive.

'You've done this before, I take it?' he said. This was the posh, deep voice that Clive had heard on the phone. Suddenly it was the most impressive thing in the shabby room.

'Er, yes,' said Clive. 'Well, sort of.'

'Good. Barry—' he said the name as though it were in inverted commas '—said you were a good fellow but I thought I'd better take a look at you myself. Well, let's get you started then.'

He suddenly turned and looked out of the window. 'Doesn't look too busy today I'm afraid.' The office overlooked the bus concourse at Victoria Station where there was a permanent scrum of vehicles, with commuters and tourists threading their way between them. 'Must be the cloud cover. Should pick up later, though.'

Clive was handed a Wonga Leisure employee form to fill in his tax details. He was relieved to be getting back on the National Insurance and Income Tax rolls. Since having his dole cut off he had felt abandoned by the system, and missed its security. Paying tax was like protection money and Clive wanted his safety net back.

He looked again at the two people reading newspapers. Each of them caught his eye then quickly looked away when he raised his eyebrows in greeting.

Maxine handed him a Britannia Tours Contract that on one side asked all sorts of personal questions pertaining to previous employers and educational record, and on the back had the rules of Britannia (no smoking in view of the customers, no eating in view of the customers, no fraternising with the customers outside work hours ...).

Clive's pen was still hovering over the 'reason for leaving last job' section when the door opened with a kick and in walked Barry.

'Facking hell that coffee machine took my money again. When you gonna get it fixed?' he said glaring at Alex as he dumped his bag on a chair. He started taking off his red parka like a boy about to have a fight.

Alex waved his hand as if he was pointing out a twentieth-century extension to a Palladian building. 'I gather you and Barry have already met,' he said, then smiled for the first time, teeth that were large and yellow like a horse's.

Clive raised his eyebrows at Barry by way of saying 'Hello, remember me? We had a pint together? I'm still grateful you got me this job, I always will be,' but Barry took only the tiniest of glances then carried on talking to Alex.

'Facking quid I've lost in that machine now ...'

'It's nothing to do with Wonga,' said Alex with exaggerated patience. 'You'll have to fill in a form and give it to the Klix person.' He rolled his eyes, then changed the subject, raising his voice for all. 'Everybody, this is Clive, he's starting with us today. Basically he'll be doing panoramics to start off. With Barry.'

Barry sniffed.

'Great,' said Clive, trying not to assert himself too soon. He couldn't resist asking one question though.

'Er, Mr White, how can you *tell* it's not busy today? There seem to be plenty of tourists about? Is it something ...'

'It's just something you get to know with experience,' he said with a smile. 'Maxine, print me out the weservations for today please,' turning smartly away from her. Whenever he was feeling particularly stately, or powerful, or successful, Alex lisped slightly.

Maxine didn't even acknowledge him but a few seconds later a sheet of paper was exhaled from the laser printer in the corner.

'Hmmm,' Alex sat down to study it, saying nothing more.

Clive shrugged inwardly and went on with his form. After much agonising he decided go with 'Wanted a change of direction' in the dreaded box.

He wasn't sacked, and he didn't fancy a change of direction. He had resigned his teaching post, and looking back it was the last bit of good luck he'd had – the Government cracked down on teacher–pupil sex just a few months later. He shuddered to think it, but he could have been face down in Brixton Prison right now if history had moved at a different pace.

The school suspended him on full pay at first. Then when the headmaster had finally got his story and those of the girl and her parents, he told Clive he would have to resign. Nobody wanted to press charges. The girl's dad did, but he was eventually talked out of it by his wife, the headmaster and the girl. He also wanted to punch Clive's throat in. That was left optional. All parties tacitly understood that if he was seen in the Borough of Islington again it was open season on Clive.

When he finished the form he gave it to Maxine and made a steeple with his fingers, waiting for something to happen. Barry was reading his tabloid. Clive looked at some of the brochures, which were more like glossy flyers. Canterbury. Stratford-upon-Avon. Oxford. York. Hampton Court. Windsor. This all looked like easy stuff to him, right off the Blue Badge course.

Alex stood up and announced that it didn't look good for today. 'If it's going to get any better we're going to have to try harder,' he said.

Barry put down his paper. 'What, you mean the board?'

'Yes.'

'Er, what's the board?'

Alex disappeared into the toilet, a small cube in the corner, and came back with a yellow sandwich board with purple words painted on it:

Britannia Tours – tours of London daily, all the sights,
Royal Palaces, Tower, Abbey, West End, Harrods, only £19.95

'Oh no,' said Barry. The old pair shifted in their chairs and lowered their papers.

'So I'll need a volunteer to go out and get those people. Come on, I want bums on coach seats!'

Nobody said anything for ten seconds until Clive slowly put up his hand.

'Clive! That's the spirit! Good man. See what a trooper we have here? Thank you, Clive, thank you. What you do is walk around out there with the flyers and get people interested. Talk to them. *Engage* them. Sell them the idea of a panoramic! Tell them the times and all the details, but get them to come. Sell them a ticket if you can ...'

'Get the cash up front,' chipped in Barry, smiling.

'Remember, 90 per cent of selling a product isn't pushing it, it's chatting, being nice, being charming. Can you charm them, Clive? I think so! You'll get thirty quid cash for it, on account of missing out on the trips.'

Clive didn't know what to do. A great wave of shame came over him, then a wave of wretched embarrassment, followed by the third, big breaker of sadness. How could he be reduced to this? Sandwich-boarding? He considered telling Alex where to stick his board, but then he thought about the money. How he needed the money to pay his rent, his credit-card payments, for food even. He was able to rationalise it: he was starting out at the bottom of an industry and would have to shovel shit for a while. Besides, he could prove to his new boss what a worker he was.

'Er, I suppose so,' he said.

'Great! Maxine, sort him out would you please?'

Maxine fitted the board over his head and led him down the stairs into the street. She gave him a bundle of flyers, then ran back upstairs. By the time she got back everyone else was crowding round the window, pissing themselves laughing.

'There he is,' said Alex. 'Look at him! He's going up to that couple ... oh, no, they've dodged him,' and he laughed his deep throaty laugh. 'A-hock hock, hock, a-hock hock, hock!'

'Faaaackinell,' Barry shouted. 'What a plonker. Oh and he gets the brush off again. I think that was a commuter, mate, you don't wanna waste your time there. Ooh here's a couple of nice birds ... yes, yes, yes ... Oh no, he's blown it.' And Barry laughed too, 'Naaar-har-har, naar-har-har!'

The other two chuckled and Maxine tittered, but eventually they got bored and drifted back to their seats. Every so often Alex would get up and have a peek, and someone would shout 'Is he still there then?' and Alex would do the commentary and they'd all have another laugh. Alex said he'd give him another fifteen minutes, but he got a phone call and forgot about the time.

After half an hour Barry stood up, grabbed his stuff and said he was off. He knew he was doing the 11.30 a.m. London tour, he always did it. There was enough work for him. The other two were just killing time until their specialist tours started. The *Mail* man did Jack the Ripper tours, the woman focused on dead women authors and aristocrats. Each of them smirked and said a cheery 'Hi' to Clive as they passed him outside.

After an hour Clive phoned from a call box to ask Maxine if he could get a sandwich, and she laughed.

'You can come up now. It was just a little joke.'

'A joke?'

'Yeah, cos it's yer first day innit?'

'Oh,' said Clive. He took off his board and then went and got a sandwich and sat down on a ledge. He was so angry he didn't want to go back in case he blew his top, and so sad he couldn't face them. Different emotions welled up inside him like competing notes: he hated them for being so cruel, but he hated himself more – for falling for it, for not doing anything about it, and for not finding it funny. Most of all he hated himself for being a forty-four-year-old man with a sandwich board. Eating a sandwich. He wanted to sulk, but he hated himself for resorting to sulking. Wasn't he always telling Tess not to sulk? That it was a low form of behaviour – reactive, unproductive, unattractive?

Eventually Alex came outside for the payoff, but since it was just the two of them the joke was slightly lost, and Clive felt even more like telling him to stick his job, but then remembered the money and succumbed with a grim smile.

'He's a good sport,' said Alex to Maxine as they came up. There were a few more guides in the office now, back from their morning tours, seemingly killing time, reading papers and talking small amounts of shop. Alex had Clive put the sign away in the toilet and then suddenly switched to serious mode. He informed Clive in his deep voice that he'd be going out with Barry in the afternoon for two short tours of London, the first led by Barry, to show how it should be done, the second led by Clive.

Clive felt some relief at last. The pay packet had just come an inch closer.

After much waiting, during which Clive read all the papers and flyers and studied his boss's cranium until he was sick of the sight of it, Barry phoned in on his mobile and said he was on Buckingham Palace Road ready to go with the next lot. Clive jumped up, his heart racing. To work, at last! This was his chance.

The London panoramic followed a well-beaten path, wiggling through the West End and then along the river to the City and back. Britannia was competing against plenty of other guided tours of London – many conducted in a foreign language – as well as double-decker buses that played tapes as they went. Employing a human to actually talk to the punters was something of a gamble, but that was part of the Wonga Leisure corporate philosophy – 'Quality service, at any price.' That was the message Alex had tried to instil in the troops when he came back from the management seminar at Bournemouth. Having to compete with the cut-price buses, hustling for the dregs of the tourists, didn't make it easy.

They were almost all on board as Clive came panting round the corner. Barry was taking their tickets at the coach steps, 'All right darlin'? Lovely day innit? This is warm for May this is . . . Yes sir, you and your daughter step up here . . . oh she's your wife? Well I never . . . No, no French allowed . . . Naaar, just kidding sir, we *lav* the French really . . .' He ignored Clive. Britannia had new guides starting all the time and Clive was now just another face. The experienced ones worked in typical freelance fashion, making the rounds of the different sightseeing companies like a game of musical chairs. They lived all over the south of England and came from all sorts of professions. There were a lot of ex-teachers and ex-army who thought they knew a thing or two about the country, resting actors and people back from the colonies, but there were also people who couldn't settle in any profession and had just drifted in. It looked easy, after all. The newcomers, like Clive, fresh off the training course, had to work their way up slowly, and Barry had seen enough of them come and go to not take much notice.

'Good morning ladies and gentlemen, or should I say good afternoon?' said Barry, standing at the front with the microphone as the coach pulled out into traffic. 'Sit down,' snapped the driver, a grey-haired man with a beer gut and a severe mouth. 'You're in me fucking mirror.'

Barry silently moved to the steps, remaining standing, and carried on as though nothing had happened. He spoke quite formally, keeping his London accent under control with a hint of BBC pronunciation. 'Welcome to Britannia's London Panoramic Sightseeing tour on this beautiful May day, where you will be seeing all the sights our beautiful capital has to offer. We will shortly be passing Buckingham Palace, home of our Queen Elizabeth and her son Charles, who used to be married to Princess Diana. The British government, in its infinite wisdom, does not allow coaches to go down the Mall, so we will be approaching Trafalgar Square by the back way. There you will see Nelson's Column, which commemorates Nelson's victory over the French General Napoleon at Waterloo ...'

'Er, no it doesn't,' said Clive.

Barry glared at him. 'Shut it,' he muttered, then carried on. He had outlined the whole trip by the time they rounded Queen Victoria memorial in front of Buckingham Palace, where everyone strained to get a look at some royalty. Barry switched gear to a sing-sing tour-guide voice, slightly nasal and bureaucratic. 'As you can see the Royal Standard is flying today, which means that the Queen is in residence. When she is at one of her other palaces or castles, the flag is flown there instead.' Then he delved back into his BBC. 'Many of you will remember the outcry after the death of Princess Diana about the Queen's refusal to mourn her publicly, and the compromise that followed, whereby the Royal Standard was flown at half mast for a few days, an unprecedented occurrence.'

From the vocabulary, Clive could tell this was all straight from a book. Maybe even a pamphlet.

They set off down Birdcage Walk, made a circuit of Parliament Square (Mother of All Parliaments, Big Ben the bell not the clock, statue of Winston Churchill) and headed up Whitehall, where Barry was able to mention Churchill again and his Cabinet War Rooms. He hadn't actually been there but he was able to rhapsodise about the coloured telephones, the pins on the campaign maps and the bombs falling on three-foot-thick concrete ceiling. As they flashed past the end of Downing Street and the Horse Guards in their sentry boxes, the passengers sat bolt upright, hardly blinking as they took it all in. Some took photos or videoed but mainly they stared out at the sights and listened carefully to Barry.

Clive's nerves gradually eased as he noticed more mistakes and omissions. Barry mentioned the National Gallery but not what was in it. He said Prince Charles called the new extension 'a monstrous carbuncle on the face of an old friend' when that referred to a different design that was never built. And as they went round Piccadilly Circus he neglected to mention the statue of Eros. 'This is Piccadilly Circus,' he said grinning, his London accent creeping in as he smiled, 'where the neon lights shine.' He gestured up at the flashing signs. 'Here you can come for a McDonald's and a Coke, then maybe have a pint of Fosters and take some pictures with your Panasonic camera on TDK film and listen to your Sanyo Walkman.' Gradually the passengers caught on and laughed.

Barry paused, looking out of the front of the coach at the traffic snaking up Shaftsbury Avenue, and Clive saw a look of complete boredom on his face. He rallied though, and turned to tell the punters about London's world-class theatre reputation. '*Cats*, *Les Miserables*, *Phantom* . . . remember ladies and gents, next time you're in Hong Kong or New York, it all started here . . .'

They trundled east, looped the Tower of London and headed back, taking in the Strand, whose traffic caused the driver to swear a lot. After dipping south of the river along Lambeth Palace Road to see the Houses of Parliament from across the water, the coach sped up and headed for home. At this point Barry reached under the front seat and pulled out a beer glass, a dirty dimpled tankard. 'Ladies and gentlemen,' (London accent) 'the local government here in London, in its infinite wisdom, does not allow me to charge market rates for my services, forcing me to supplement my income in whatever way I can. Now if it wasn't for the fact that I love London so much, and I love showing our foreign friends around the place I would have retired long ago. As it is, I can't imagine doing anything else, so it is at this point that I ask you to show your appreciation in any way you feel appropriate. I'm sure you understand what I mean. Remember that this is just between you and me. Thank you for being such a great crowd.' With that he passed the glass to the Japanese man in the first row. He and his wife whispered embarrassedly and fumbled for change. Barry heard the clink of small coppers and silver, and watched the glass go across the aisle, where a Canadian backpacker put in a pound. 'Remember it can get very heavy with just coins, so banknotes and bills are always welcome,' he shouted, without using the microphone

Clive was slightly horrified, and failed to be impressed when the glass came back half-full.

When everyone had filed past Barry and said their goodbyes and thanked him, Clive spoke up for only the second time.

'Isn't that illegal?'

Barry was counting the money. He didn't answer until he had finished. 'Forty-one quid. Bollocks to illegal.' He stood up. 'Right. I'm gonna have a pint. You get the next lot on here and come and get me when they're ready. You coming Ray, you miserable git?' he said to the coach driver.

"'Orses,' grunted Ray.

'Bollocks to you then, I'll go on me own.'

Barry disappeared into the Shakespeare. Ray put on his hazards and shooed Clive off the coach, setting the door to 'Closed' behind them.

'Erm, will you be gone long? Don't I need to get them on?'

'I don't want those buggers on my coach messing it up with their McDonald's. You wait till I get back.' With that Ray pulled on his coat and headed off to the bookies.

Clive was left on the pavement looking around for his customers. Everyone seemed to know where they were going, lining up by the other coaches and talking to the ticket collectors. Clive saw no one holding the purple and yellow docket of Britannia Tours.

He waited a while, then saw an elderly couple who looked lost.

'Britannia Tours?' he asked.

'Victoria Coach station, where is?'

'Oh.' He gave them directions.

Two French girls in their twenties came along. He stepped out in front of them, saying 'Britannia Tours? Britannia Tours?'

'Ah, *non non*. Tower of London.'

'Yes, yes, I take you to Tower of London, see?' He showed them the itinerary.

'Inside Tower? See the jewels?'

'Er, no ...'

'Ah, non, thank you,' one of them said, smiling sweetly, and they walked away.

After half an hour Clive had gathered together six people with tickets, and ten more maybes whom he had to keep from wandering off. He promised them the doors would be open soon.

It started to spit and was really quite cold.

Ray the driver was ten minutes late. A German couple looked at their watches, shrugged and walked off annoyed. Just as he was getting worried Ray appeared around the corner.

'It's OK folks, we'll be off in a minute,' Clive said, trying to sound jolly.

The coach driver let them on. Clive was so relieved he was grinning like a fool. 'OK ladies and gents,' he kept saying, 'we'll have you out of here in no time. Buckingham Palace is just around the corner.' A few stragglers appeared from nowhere at the last moment.

When they were all on he dashed over to the Shakespeare. Barry was inside, on his third pint, laughing and chatting up the two French girls.

He seemed in a much better mood. 'Ready to go are we? What's the count?'

'Twenty.'

'Oh dear, oh deary me,' he laughed. 'Still, means we'll have room for these two. How about it girls, do you fancy a free tour of London? All the palaces, all the castles?'

They looked at each other, doing the calculation that tourists do with their time and their money – and in this case, their feelings about this bloke who kept looking at their breasts, how many drinks they'd had (one) and who'd paid for them (Barry).

'Ooh, yes, thank you,' they said. Barry held the pub door open and the three of them headed down the street ahead of Clive, the girls pretty in their faded jeans and tight sweaters, Barry leaning into them and making them laugh.

Ray was in a bad mood on account of the gee-gees and he cautioned Clive about getting in his fucking mirror. Barry hogged the front seat with a French girl squeezed in either side of him, so Clive had to lurk deep in the stairwell. He couldn't see the punters' faces. He had his cue cards out and he was nervous.

He'd only said a few words of welcome when Barry burst out laughing and whispered something to one of the girls. Clive tried to ignore them, but hearing his voice on the speakers he thought he sounded whiny and too earnest, so he quickly slipped into teacher mode, a delivery characterised by pedantry and a hint of weariness. He went into his speech about the formation of London, how it principally consisted of two cities, Westminster and London, which had merged over the centuries. They would be moving from Westminster, the administrative or political capital, to the City of London, known also as The City, the financial capital and site of the original Roman settlement, Londinium, and back again, 'taking in a panorama not just of landscape and architecture, but of 2,000 years of history too'.

Barry gave a loud yawn which turned into a rasping belch. 'Scuse me, ladies,' he said, and they looked at each other then giggled. Clive tried to ignore them. He tapped the microphone and asked Ray if he could turn it up.

'No,' growled Ray.

'Here you go,' said Barry, leaning forward and doing it for him. Clive felt a flicker of gratitude which vanished when Barry started doing his own running commentary on Buckingham Palace for the girls.

Clive was keen to point out that it was originally called Buckingham House and that John Nash, the star architect of the time, started converting it into a Palace for George the Fourth in 1825, but quickly overspent his budget. 'It wasn't until Queen Victoria's time that a monarch occupied the palace. The facade of the East Wing, which you can see here, in front of which the Changing of the Guard takes place, was not actually added until 1913.'

He thought that was an impressive fact.

'Tell 'em about Princess Di's funeral!' said Barry loudly. 'Queenie wiv her head bowed!'

Clive was stoic, ignoring him.

'Aw, bollocks,' said Barry, and told the girls about it himself.

Ray seemed to be in a hurry. They were soon passing the Abbey. 'The sumptuous stonework and carvings of the saints on the famous North Entrance to Westminster Abbey actually dates from Victorian times. The Victorians had a great love affair with all things medieval. And of course with chivalry. The statue of the man on the horse you can just see outside the Palace of Westminster, which we colloquially call the Houses of Parliament, depicts King Richard the First, who was killed in battle in 1199. The statue was put up in Victorian times, in 1860. King Richard was a dashing young man, more of a romantic cavalry leader than a king in fact. He was born in Oxford but spoke French and considered himself French, and thought of England as a useful way to make money for the crusades. He is supposed to have said "I would sell London itself if I could find a purchaser rich enough to buy it," although obviously it's not possible to verify that. He only spent four months of his ten-year reign actually *in* England, and was killed by an arrow besieging the castle of Chalus in 1199. As he was dying he chivalrously asked that the man who shot him be spared, but as soon as the castle was captured the captain of his guard had the archer flayed alive, and all his companions hanged.'

Throughout this speech Barry was muttering to the French girls.

It went on like this all the way round. The girls got a double dose of history, understanding very little except that one of these *types* was a bit of an alpha male, and the other wasn't.

Clive nobly plodded through his cards, telling the staring tourists about Nash (who did also Spencer House round the back of St James – despite the name 'Spencer', Barry didn't twig), Christopher Wren (St Paul's, and just about every white church with a spire east of Charing Cross Road) and Inigo Jones (Covent Garden piazza, and the Banqueting House, built for King Charles the First and outside which he was later beheaded – that made Barry laugh).

He got less reaction from the passengers. Not a chuckle nor a murmur of assent. The streaks of rain on the windows were making it hard to see – he thought maybe that was why. As they passed Lambeth Palace Barry got the pint glass out and ordered him to pass it around.

'No,' hissed Clive.

Barry grinned and got up anyway, and gave his ladies and gents speech about the infinite wisdom of the local government. He set the glass off (neither of the girls gave anything) and listened for the sound of coins.

By the time they lurched into place at Victoria, Clive looked tired and miserable. He bade the people goodbye on the street but most of them were more interested in getting their rain gear on. Barry presented him with the glass, grinning broadly.

'Two quid by my reckoning. Maybe less. What's wrong chief, you look knackered? Wait till you've done six of them in a day, then you'll know what knackered is. This ain't school any more you know. Oh yeah, make sure you do the seats.'

Then he got off and joined the two French girls who were waiting for him on the pavement, and headed back to the pub.

Clive asked Ray, who was getting his jacket, fags and paper together, what he meant.

'He means check under the seats to see if anyone's left anything.'

'Isn't that your job?'

'It is if you want it to be. If you want the keepings it's yours though. Finders keepers. Suits me.'

Slightly baffled, Clive left him to it.

He hurried through the rain and traffic to the Britannia office, but it had just closed. He phoned just in case but got Maxine's recorded message, talking about leaving messages for bookings or sending faxes after the beep. He left a long, hesitant message about not being sure what time to come in the next day.

Clive trudged off, thinking about Barry in the pub, and thinking what a shitty day it had been. He really wanted a drink. His teeth ached, like there was a wire stretched across the back of his mouth, pulled taut between his lower molars. He felt a particular kind of hunger he'd had since he stopped drinking, a hunger located right in the mouth. The world felt black and white and there didn't seem to be any point in doing anything if you couldn't have a pint. He went for a walk, unable to face the train and the thought of Streatham again so early. All around him he saw pubs, and peering in their windows he saw them filled with happy faces, office workers, tourists, the unemployed, professional drinkers, service-industry workers ... they were all in out of the rain. The cellos were starting up around him again. His mouth felt sad now, heavy with the echo of childish tears.

He ended up at Parliament Square and stood in the middle on the grass. Around him the city was whirling, lorries, bikes, despatch riders, taxis, cars, pedestrians. He stood looking up at the clock for a while, which he himself secretly thought of as Big Ben, and watched the minute hand creeping around, an inch every few seconds, and felt his life passing by, being wasted.

Standing there didn't help. There was no revelation, no epiphany. All the people he knew would be off doing their own thing right at this minute: Tess watching cartoons after school, Tina showing some Sloane Ranger of reduced circumstances around a studio flat, George listening to the one-day game on his earpiece, Danny the Kiwi upstairs ... doing what? He didn't even know that much about Danny. He hated himself. *How did I become Mr No Mates? Where did it all go wrong?*

7

Somebody's Daughter

It all started to go wrong when he had sex with a fifteen year old girl. That was the truth Clive tried to avoid, and in trying to avoid it he dwelt upon it daily. He always stressed that she was fifteen and a bit and fifteen was young, fifteen and a bit was well on the way. If you wanted to be fussy about it, she was fifteen and three months.

Mandy was by no means the most precocious girl in her year – there were plenty of others with seductive knowledge of themselves and in-yer-face breasts. There were fifteen-year-olds who could get into nightclubs and had boyfriends twice their age. But she wasn't a babyfaced naive either. She was fifteen, old enough for blokes to stare, young enough for them to go to prison.

To complicate things, she might not have believed she was attractive, but she knew she was attracted to Mr Pointing the Geography teacher, and she knew how to get his attention. Amanda wasn't thick. That was what confused Clive, and attracted him. She got B pluses and As in her essays on volcanoes and cocoa plantations and cloud systems and the distribution of services across a geographic plain. Her shopping centre project was exemplary – so neatly coloured in, each shop labelled according to what it sold and how much foot traffic it had. So descriptive, in the bald, unglamorous way a geographer prefers.

She had beautiful handwriting too, curvy, but clean and compact. That hadn't struck him until she sent him a personal note.

He hadn't noticed her, or taught her, when she was a flat-chested eleven-year-old who still cared about cute things like cats, and having the right coloured pencils. She didn't appear in one of his classes until the random reshuffle put her there in her fourth year. By then she had developed a heart-shaped face, a rosebud mouth and other curves. She used to sit in the middle of the second row in his classes, her blouse always clean and ironed, her skirt looking new, her dark hair combed straight and into a fringe. She had the soft, clear skin of the well-looked-after, never ruddy or scuffed like the kids with cereal stains on their uniforms and rings of snot round their nostrils. There were kids whose clothes smelt of mildew and damp, but Amanda always smelt of fabric softener and hair conditioner.

Although she would sit in the middle of the second row and ask the odd question, and always handed her homework in on time, that didn't make her remarkable, since at that age the kids were still pretty obedient. As they got older, though, they'd realise quickly that Geography was no use to them. The academic ones had no respect for such a soft science, they preferred Physics and Chemistry and computer work – subjects that stained your hands with chemicals, or later on money. Subjects with jobs attached to them. The arty ones had no use for Geography since it didn't relate to their budding egos. There was no poetry in it. There wasn't even a diary entry to be had from igneous rock formation or the development of the English canal system.

And that was the academically minded kids. The rest didn't really give a fuck about any subjects, apart from maybe making a bong in metalwork or an apple pie in home economics. It wasn't a bad school. A few kids went to university every year, and a few went to homes for young offenders. Clive just noticed her because she seemed to care about Geography. And as a teacher, he believed he should nurture that.

In September, he barely noticed her, but the mutual attraction built slowly over the school year. By the following July they were full of the heat of desire. By the following September Clive was suspended.

8

What's for Supper?

He had completely forgotten about his brother Gordon and their mother. When Clive let himself into his 'flat' after his first day as a tour guide the phone was already ringing.

He assumed it was another call for Dave and wearily answered, 'Clive Pointing, speaking.'

'Where the bloody hell *are* you? You were sposed to be round here an hour ago.' It was Gordon.

'Oh bugger. Was I? I completely forgot. I was at my new job today . . .'

'I've been pacing up and down for an hour waiting for you, what the hell are you doing home? She's going mad for you here, "Where's Clive, when's he coming, dear?" over and over . . . Get up here *now*. I'm going out tonight. It's all arranged.'

Gordon Pointing lived with his mum up in North London, Dollis Hill. She had Alzheimer's Disease. Gordon was her full-time carer, since he was unemployed, off work himself on a disability claim. She'd had full-blown Alzheimer's – as opposed to merely forgetting what she came into the room for, or leaving her purse in the fridge – for three years now and it was wearing on Gordon. Clive's younger brother was forty-one, he'd never been married and hadn't had a girlfriend now for more years than he cared to talk about. He'd slipped into a routine of watching telly, looking after Mum, and going to the pub when he could get cover. He read a bit too – he had a growing collection of books about the Nazis and the Second World War.

Clive was supposed to be his cover twice a week.

'Get in a cab now and get up here!'

'I can't afford cabs,' said Clive. 'Besides with the traffic it's quicker to get the Tube.'

'Is it bollocks! You can pay for a cab.'

'OK, OK, I'm coming ... let me just get my ...' He already had his coat on. 'OK, I'm setting off now. I'll call you if I get delayed.'

'Don't get delayed.'

'Bye.'

Clive took one look around the dim room then began the whole commute all over again, locking his door and making the long trudge back to the train.

Dollis Hill, like Streatham, was also a bastard to get to. It might have seemed accessible at first glance, given that it was the first piece of London inside the North Circular, near where the M1 starts at Brent Cross. But once you felt it on a human scale, as you did if you lived there and had to troop across the park to Dollis Hill Tube or worse, to Cricklewood railway station, you realised it was an inaccessible patch of old-school suburbia cut off by railway tracks and uncrossable roads. It was Edge City before Clive had even heard the term.

Three trains and a long hike later, Clive rang the doorbell of his brother's council flat. Gordon already had his padded grey jacket on one shoulder as he opened the door.

'Prat!' was all he said, and set off down the path, pulling it on and walking hurriedly.

Clive shut the door behind him and walked through Gordon's smelly hall into his smellier lounge. The cause of much of the smell was sitting there on the couch, staring at the TV.

'Hello Mum,' he said, bending down and kissing her. Her skin was soft and cool. It had lost all its elasticity and had a fine fuzz of hair over it. Despite the faint tang of urine coming from her, her face still smelt of her powder, as it had done since he was a boy.

'Do I *know* you?' she said in a strict, well-to-do voice.

'Yes Mother, it's Clive.'

'Oh!' she said, and looked embarrassed. She then looked as though she were going to ask him another serious question, but stopped and turned back to the TV.

'The lottery's going to be on in a moment. Won't that be splendid if we win? Daddy will be happy and we can all go to France. I've got my numbers.'

'No, Mother,' he said gently, 'I think that's later in the week. No lottery tonight.'

'Oh!' she said. Then after a moment, 'What are we having for supper?'

Clive got up and looked around, accidentally kicking her crossword where it lay on the floor, a mess of crossings out and improbable answers. He went into the tiny kitchen to see if they had eaten. A couple of dirty plates lay in the sink, covered in ketchup and chip shrapnel. There was a large piece of cod in batter sticking out of the pedal bin.

Clive spoke gently. He didn't mistake dementia for deafness, or vice versa.

'I think you've already eaten, Mum. Didn't Gordon feed you?'

'Oh!' She looked embarrassed again.

He sat down and looked about the room. His mother had taken over the front room as her bedroom so she didn't have to negotiate the stairs, but all her stuff was still in boxes, spilling over into the living room. Gordon hadn't been allowed to touch it because she thought he was trying to throw it away. Clive looked inside one of the open cartons at his feet. Books. All books. Old mould-spotted paperbacks from the forties, fifties, and sixties, mixed in with random hardbacks. A collected Auden. The Movement Poets anthology. A book about the Royal Shakespeare Theatre at Stratford. A biography of John Betjeman. Metaphysical Poets. *Lucky Jim*. A Doctor Johnson reader.

His mother had loved literature and would have been better educated were it not for the difficulty women had getting into university before the War, and for the fact that her husband the bank manager never quite approved of her being anything other than a housewife. Then, in her thirties, she had had her boys and that put an end to her hopes of being taken seriously. She still read to them though. Even in their teens she would read them poetry, until they found out nobody else's parents did and put a stop to it. When the boys left home she registered for the Open University and got her degree, rising early to study from the television. But by then it was too late to do anything with a degree. Her husband died and her will to better herself died with him. And so she had spent the last fifteen years reading romances and thrillers, if she read at all. More likely she was out walking in the countryside, or having tea with friends, or volunteering at the Sue Ryder shop in Milton Keynes, the last town their father had dragged them to.

As her brain started to go the boys had to sit down and decide what to do with her. Clive volunteered to take her, and installed her in the spare bedroom at the back of his house in Islington – much to Christina's selfish dismay, and Tess's childish delight. But after they broke up his mother had to be moved too, and as Gordon was now the one with more space, he took her. He went from twiddling his thumbs all day to having his hands full with dinner times, adult nappies and hassles with the Health Service.

'What are we having for supper tonight Gordon?'

'It's Clive, Mum. You've already eaten.'

'Oh!'

Clive did some tidying up in the kitchen, straightened some boxes (his mother's wary eye on him) and then stood around looking at Gordon's new books. *The Third Reich. Hitler: A Profile. Hammer of the Gods. War Crimes and Punishment. Carnival of the Animals: War Criminals in Rio. Hitler's Last Day's. And God Created Adolph and Eva.*

'Do you ever read any of these, Mum?'

'Ooh no. Hitler was a monster. I can still hear his voice now on the radio, nasty little man, full of hate. Always shouting. Did you know, the Poles had gun registration and the first thing he did when he marched in there was round up all the firearms? That's the sort of man he was. I can still remember it as if it was yesterday.'

'Where were you when he shot himself, Mum?' He always asked her this.

'Your father and I were at a dance and somebody ran in with a bit of paper saying "Hitler's done himself in!" And we all cheered and everyone was hugging each other, and then we went on dancing.'

'And did Churchill go on the radio?'

'Ooh yes, he was on the next day saying how great everything was. We never really liked Churchill much, your father and I, he was a bit of a bully boy in the Teens and Twenties, always trying to break up the strikes, but I suppose we got used to him in the War, we got used to hearing him on the radio. Those were dark times, Clive, very dark times, we didn't think we'd come through them. So it was comforting to hear his voice sometimes.'

'I've got a new job, Mother.'

'Have you dear? I always knew you would make a good teacher. Is it a good school?'

'Er, it's not a school, it's ... on a coach. I'm a tour guide.'

'Oh very nice, your father and I took some tours before we were married, we went up to the Lake District in the spring, I can still see the flowers, the snowdrops and the violets and the bluebells, and the daffs of course ... We took a walk up to Hill Top farm to see where Beatrix Potter did her writing, she was still alive then, and we were looking over the fence when she came out and she shouted "What are you two nosy beggars looking at?", Ooh, she had a sharp tongue, anyway your father and I just turned and ran, we were terrified. You used to love those books when you were little, you would beg to hear about Tom Kitten and Benjamin Bunny … I used to wonder how an old boot like her could have come up with Mrs Tittle Mouse …'

'Did you have a guide?'

'What?'

'On your trip.'

She looked puzzled, then afraid, then searched in her cardigan pockets.

'I've got my numbers here, put the lottery on, Gordon love.'

Clive sighed. She was getting worse. He tried to imagine how bad it could get. She already soiled herself from time to time, and she needed help getting in and out of the bath and washing. She made an almighty fuss, which he recognised from Tess, if she didn't get her favourite Boots apple soap and lavender talc.

Clive changed the TV channel for her. It was a comedian. He just caught a line: '… and so I said to her, that's not sperm, sperm tastes different …' and quickly changed channels. He had choices: Soaps, which were too dramatic, they might get her hooked or trigger something. News – too boring, too depressing. Nature – that was lucky, there was a programme on about ants. Plain old black ants that had no bite to them, like you'd find in any back garden. It showed what they were up to. It was soothing to see them busying away. Nice to know there were creatures worse off than himself.

Clive spun out the hours with his mother waiting for Gordon to come back from the pub. He tried to talk to her, but dealt with many of the same questions over again.

'What are we having for supper tonight?'

'You've already eaten, Mum.'

'Oh!'

All of a sudden she started reciting verse, her eyes blank like a blind person's:

> '"I wander through each chartered street,
> Near where the chartered Thames does flow,
> And mark in every face I meet
> Marks of weakness, marks of woe.

> '"In every cry of every man,
> In every infant's cry of fear,
> In every voice, in every ban,
> The mind-forged manacles I hear."'

'Stop Mum, stop!'
She carried on, not hearing him, and shaking her tiny fist.

> '"How the chimney-sweeper's cry
> Every blackening church appals;
> And the hapless soldier's sigh
> Runs in blood down palace walls."'

'Mother stop it. Let me get you a cup of tea. What tablets did Gordon give you?'

> '"But most through midnight streets I hear
> How the youthful harlot's curse
> Blasts the new-born infant's tear,
> And blights with plagues the marriage hearse."'

She went silent.

'Have you finished?' It rattled him, to think she had such a miserable poem bottled up inside her, but now she was back staring at the TV again. 'Are you sure you're OK, Mum?' He made some tea. He cooled hers in a saucer and helped her drink it.

After a while he felt hungry himself. He didn't think Gordon would begrudge him a can of beans or a sausage and some eggs but he found very little in the fridge, apart from some leathery cheddar and his mother's Complans.

She was wide awake. She talked sometimes, and sometimes gazed off into the television. He'd have to have a word with his brother about her 'sundowning'. She needed quiet times in the day, like a little kid, otherwise fatigue would make her very confused between six and nine in the evening. He put her to bed, amid much protesting that she wasn't tired and didn't know who he was.

At 11.30 p.m. he began to wonder about Gordon, worrying for a moment that he might have found himself a woman and be on their way to her flat. Or worse, bringing her home. At midnight he stood in the street and looked up and down for him. The last Tube would be going soon. At 12.25 a.m. he finally heard his key in the door, and the man walked in, unsteady on his feet. He waved Clive out of his armchair.

'Where've you been?' Clive asked annoyed.

'Lock in,' said Gordon.

'You could have rung.'

'Bollocks.'

'Don't bollocks me you little . . .'

'Bollocks.' He looked up defiantly. 'You're not one to talk.'

'I've got to get the last Tube.'

'Huh.' He crashed down into his chair. 'How's she been anyway?'

'All right. Thinks it's lottery day. Did you put her up to that? Waste of money.'

Gordon made no reply, he just stared drunkenly at the telly. When he realised he wanted to turn over he started fumbling for the remote control under him. He suddenly thought of something. He'd heard a great joke down the pub.

'Hey, listen to this. Bloke goes into a bank, right up to the cashier and says to her, really nasty, "Nice tits love, I want to open a *fucking* bank account." She goes "I beg your pardon, sir?" all shocked. And he goes "Listen, you dozy bitch, I said I want to open a *fucking* bank account." And she goes "I'm sorry, sir, but I can't help you if you're going to talk like that." So she leaves the window, walks over to the bank manager and whispers in his ear. The two of them come back and the manager asks, all formal, "What seems to be the problem here?" And the bloke says "There's no *bastard* problem. I just won five million quid on the lottery, and I want to open a fucking bank account." And the bank manager goes "I see sir. And this cunt's giving you a hard time, is she?" Heh-heh-heh, heh-heh-heh.' Gordon thought it was hilarious.

'That's not funny,' said Clive. 'It's . . . it's just sexist.'

'Oh, sexist my arse. You've just got no sense of humour.' Gordon looked pissed off.

'Look, who's going to put Mum to bed if you're this drunk?' asked Clive getting annoyed.

'You are, you twat. I do it every night don't I? Unlike you.'

'She almost wouldn't let me. She has her routine. You know I would if I could.'

'Yeah, sure.'

Clive wanted to argue but he didn't want to miss his Tube.

'I'm going,' he said. 'I've got work tomorrow.'

'Bully for you,' was the last thing his brother said.

Clive went in to see his mother. 'Bye-bye Mum, take care, see you in a few days, I love you ...'

'He was a bit of a bully boy that Churchill, they don't tell you that in school.'

Clive sighed and let himself out into the fresh air.

'What are we having for supper?' was the last thing he heard through the closed door.

He let one bus go past thinking he'd save money and still make the Tube on time, but when he got there all he heard was the rumble of the engines. He raced to the platform in time to see the tail lights, and to feel the flow of warm air being sucked after the train, dragging sweet wrappers and dust bunnies and human hairs deep into the system of tunnels.

He got the old 'Sorry mate ...' routine from a couple of London Underground workers and so headed off to look for a night bus. It was nearly 3 a.m. when he finally turned into his road in Streatham.

Danny's light was still on. The image of Danny going at it with his willowy girlfriend under a naked 100-watt bulb stayed with Clive as he lay in bed and tried to sleep.

9

Jump

It was well into Tuesday morning when Clive awoke. He could remember hearing the dawn chorus for a while, but after that was a blank. With one eye he could see that the clock was flashing 12.00 again, so he reached out and turned on the radio. He knew instantly from the programme that it was after 10 a.m., as the presenter was female. He felt guilty at being in bed while the rest of the country worked. It was like when he was a child and had a day off junior school. Every hour he would imagine what would be happening – sums, lunchtime, art, afternoon playtime, story. He was never sure whether he would rather be at home, reading comics and playing with his baby brother, or at school keeping up with the others, since he feared a conspiracy against him. Clive, according to his teachers, was a nervous child who took a long time to come out of his shell.

He dragged himself out of bed, feeling thick-headed. He might as well have been out on a bender the night before – he hadn't slept properly and felt like he had a four-star hangover. He put the kettle on and looked out over the garden, where the cats were prowling around the substation, fur standing up. He reminded himself that he had to call London Electricity and ask them about the outages. That was twice it had happened recently.

He was down to the dust in the tiny instant-coffee jar, so he sloshed it out with boiling water until it was too hot to hold. The milk was suspect, so he had it black. He sat down at the table and stared at the papers he had thrown down before leaving for his mum's: Britannia Tours.

'Buggeration!' Suddenly he remembered he had a job.

Maxine was nice to him on the phone, she said she got his message and didn't hold it against him that he wasn't there. 'It's just as well really, it's very slow today. We've had to turn others away. I doubt there'll be anything for you today.'

Clive was crestfallen. 'Oh. Can I call back later just to see? You might get something in?'

'Well, yeah, you can call back. But don't get your hopes up. I'll definitely call if we need you.'

'Er, is Barry working today? What did he ... I mean, what did he say ... about me. You know, did I do all right? I was OK wasn't I?'

'Oh Baz, he's OK, yeah, he said you were fine.'

'Is that what he said? He said "fine"?'

'Yeah. Or "OK". Something like that. Don't worry, love. Anyway it's not up to Barry. He's not the boss. Alexander's the boss.' She was looking across the office as she said this and could see Alex coming out of the toilet with his newspaper.

'Erm, OK. Bye ... Wait!' Clive was going to ask another question but she hung up.

He sat over his coffee in misery, thinking what an idiot he was, what a fool to lie in and what a loser to not be needed at Britannia. Although he was hungry he felt nauseous. The worries were building up – he'd already banked on getting a full week's work out of Wonga. He wasn't used to things being contingent on the health of the market. At school there was always a plentiful supply of kids to be taught. They were coming online at a furious rate. Little brothers of thugs he'd known, and boldfaced girls who looked just like their mums. Now there was this uncertainty to be faced every day. If the pound went up the bookings went down. If there was a plane crash or a terrorist bomb the Americans would vanish for the rest of the year.

He had his own personal money worries – shopping, rent, spousal maintenance, child maintenance, legal bills, new clothes needed for this job. His ex-wife had gone on a frenzy with the kitchen scissors when she found out about him and the girl, and his wardrobe had never recovered. Then he had his other worries – what if Tina found out what a consistent loser he was? Would the judge ever allow him full access to Tess again? What would the country be like when she was twenty-one and looking for a job? Would he ever find a non-alcoholic soft drink he liked?

'Come on Clive, buck yourself up,' he told himself, and decided to make a list of things he could do now until he got back into the guiding game.

He wrote on his pad:

1) Continue explorations. V&A Museum, St Paul's (inside), Oxford.
2) Library: *The Decline and Fall of the Roman Empire* (short version);
Samuel Pepys's Diary (ditto).
3) Tidy flat.
4) Shopping (food, etc.).
5) Activities for Mum: Zoo, bingo?
6) Call credit cards.
7) Bollock lawyer(s).
8) Sort out electricity.

He decided to do the last of these first, and spent a fruitless hour and a half on the phone trying to get some sense out of London Electricity. They swore up and down that his electricity hadn't been cut off and it must be a problem with the appliance. He said that was absurd, told them the make and model of the clock, and then played his trump card – he went outside and noted down the number of his substation from the plaque. The woman said that really wouldn't be any help but she took it down anyway. She promised they would look into it, and he should expect a call. When, she couldn't say.

By then it was lunchtime so he dressed and set off for the supermarket, where he ran the usual gauntlet of eyes prying into his trolley. He seemed to be the only one buying dried pasta instead of the squidgy fresh stuff, and instant coffee instead of whole organic beans. He wondered if it was maybe time to downgrade himself, as his Switch card was rejected and he had to pay by Visa. Maybe it was time to shop at Costcutters?

By the time he got home and had lunch the day was almost over. He felt a tiredness sweep over him, the payback for not having slept in the night, and lay down on his bed fully clothed. He was woken by the phone ringing. The clock had gone back to 12.00 again. From the light outside he had no idea whether it was that evening or the next morning, and missed the phone before it rang off.

He worked it out though by listening to the radio. The newsreader had a lethargy to his voice as though he had been reading the same old shit all day and was itching for a bombing or a constitutional crisis. It was six o'clock. Just too late to call Britannia, but not too late to start his entire day again, beginning with the instant coffee, and the eggs he'd missed first time around.

Clive decided to get an answering machine, because of the life he might be missing out on. He looked through the free ads paper and circled a few 0181 numbers which seemed near by, but calling them was like being a probation officer making house calls to the terminally mischievous. The first one was a man with a gruff voice who said it had gone and hung up. The second was a small child who went to get his mum, whom, after a long wait he then heard in the background, telling the child to hang up. The third was an old lady, a hoarse and breathless Londoner who kept telling him what a lovely machine it was and how it worked well and her son had got it for her. She really wanted to talk about her son, so Clive let her go on for a minute before steering her back round. Yes she wanted thirty pound for it, it was a nice machine, worked well most of the time, just needed a bit of fixing, she didn't use it much ... Clive bowed out.

Eventually he hit a respectable-sounding voice and felt relief (followed by guilt at being such a snob). The woman on the phone said yes, Forty pounds, she now had two of them, all-digital, come on over and see it, five minutes by car. No, she didn't know what bus it was. She sounded young. And good-looking.

The road only a couple of pages away on his A–Z. He never should have attempted it by public transport, but the sound of her voice lured him. He was a single man, he reminded himself. One never knew what might happen.

When he rolled up it was dark. A man answered the door. His gym-cut torso was crammed into a black T-shirt, and he looked at his visitor suspiciously. Clive said he had come about the machine. The man let his girlfriend deal with it. She was as attractive as she had sounded on the phone, friendly, borderline-perky, and not seeming to need the money. She explained to Clive that now they were living together they had two answering machines. To show it worked she plugged it in and called from her mobile, leaving a message.

As soon as he paid Clive noticed she stopped being friendly. She looked relieved and wanted him out of the house. The boyfriend shut the door after him rapidly.

At home he set it up and found there were still messages on it. Not just utilities people and telemarketing calls, but attractive-sounding girls making plans for the evening. Then there was a message on it from the untalkative boyfriend, date-stamped a fortnight ago. In his Cockney growl he was saying how much he was looking forward to coming over there that evening. '... I'm gonna rip your knickers off and give you a right seeing-to

... hur hur hur ...' Clive listened to it several times, loneliness building up around him. It seemed like something occurring on a different planet, so far had he drifted from the pleasures of life.

He got into bed and tried to sleep.

As though he were being mocked, Clive dreamed he was having sex with Amanda. His arrows of desire had straightforward flight paths. She was in her school uniform, and they were in her bedroom, a place he had never been. There were school books and pop posters and vestigial cuddly toys. She was fifteen, and they were fucking. She was a quick learner, he wasn't a bad teacher. Her parents must have been out, her little brother off bribed somewhere, playing on the rec. They had the end of the afternoon together. A summer afternoon, no school. Her alarm clock said 3.30 p.m. It was sunny outside. He wasn't remembering this, rather, he was making it up as he went, piecing it together from things that did happen and things that could have happened. Straight wish fulfilment, it felt nice, and there wasn't a person who could stop them, except for Clive.

He woke up with a start, feeling very ashamed. It was so long since he had had sex he had forgotten it had anything to do with him. He made himself some tea and sat at his little table. He worried that he was trapped in Streatham for ever, which set his heart racing, so he tried walking back and forth, but he was too self-conscious for that. He put on his black trousers over his boxer shorts and white vest and looked for something to eat. There was dry pasta, kidney beans, tinned kippers, salt. Remembering that Danny upstairs always stayed up late, he decided to borrow some food off him, just for company.

Danny's girlfriend opened the door, wearing what looked like underwear but which was on closer inspection her gym outfit. When Danny saw Clive a bright smile came over his face and he waved him in.

'Hey, come in! We're just watching some telly and smoking a bowl?' Danny was sitting on one end of the soft couch with a bag of grass and a small bong in his lap. Jo went back to lying at the other end, resting her bare feet up against him.

'Er, I just came to see if I could borrow some tinned tomatoes. Or paste,' said Clive, sounding as pathetic as he felt.

'Jo, do we have any tomato paste? We've got some pasta sauce I think? Go and have a look, love, see what we've got.'

Jo got up again and went into the kitchen. She shouted out, 'Is it just for one?' She sounded like a Kiwi too.

'Um, yes,' said Clive, feeling more like a loser than ever.

'Why don't you stay and have some dinner with us?' asked Danny, pronouncing it *dunner*. 'What are we having, Babe?'

'Lentil curry?'

'Lentil curry?' echoed Danny. 'It's nothing fancy, but it's food?'

Clive felt himself going into his 'Oh-no-I-couldn't-really,' routine which had served him well all his life, but Jo interrupted, 'No, no, stay a little, stay? Sit down.' She had big Brigitte Bardot eyes.

Clive surprised himself and stayed. He felt he had been thrown a lifeline, and made himself comfortable. They were drinking beers from the bottle, but Clive refused, which prompted Jo to bring him his own bottle of ginger ale and a glass of ice. They had a nice view from their flat, they could see over the substation to the patch of grass the kids played on. Even though the kids were little bastards, the green was a welcome sight. They had interesting stuff too – banks of videos and books, and lots of plants, and their bed was high and solid-looking, like an ancient marriage bed.

To his surprise, they asked him very few questions. Danny sucked in hugely on the bong and held his breath, his eyes glued to the screen. They were watching a home video of a guy rock climbing. It went on for ages. The climber was tanned and lean and wore yellow spandex tights. He took minutes to make each move. Clive looked around the room and noticed climbing holds screwed to the one wall.

'Who's the chap?' he asked.

Jo giggled.

'That's me,' said Danny, through a gargantuan exhalation. 'Want some?'

Clive wasn't much of a smoker. 'Sorry. It makes me thirsty. And a little paranoid,' he said.

'You have to learn to mellow out to enjoy it?' said Danny.

A huge cloud emanated from Jo's head, which was low down on the couch facing away from Clive. All he could see were her breasts, her hard belly with the navel ring, and her lean legs, wide open in front of Danny, who was still staring at himself on the screen.

'Where are you then?' asked Clive. 'Looks like the Peaks. Gardoms? Wimberry?'

'Gardoms. That's right,' said Danny, impressed.

A little while later Clive said, 'I used to climb a bit. But not like this. It was before all this high-tech gear. It was all leather boots and bobble hats. Don't you worry about falling?'

'Naw mate, there's a lot of elasticity in the rope. You just bounce.'

'What, like bungee jumping?'

'Yeah!' laughed Danny. 'Talking of which ... Jo, put that tape on for Clive, love?'

She got up and put a different video in. The title came up: *More Faces of Death*.

'Er, what's all this then?' asked Clive. He was worried he might be about to see his first snuff movie. He wasn't sure of his legal position.

'This is real life footage of deadly accidents?' said Danny with relish. 'Skateboarding, car crashes, planes going down, skiing, people falling off cable cars ...'

Clive watched amazed. The very first clip consisted of a young man bungee jumping off a tower in a desert. The first bounce went well, but when he reached the end of his tether the second time the ankle harness broke. The elastic went shooting wildly back up into the air, but the body carried on downward and hit the ground like a sack of potatoes.

'Ooh!' They all said at once. Danny grinned at Clive. 'Poor bugger eh?'

Since no one made a move to turn the tape off, Clive watched on. In a storm drain full of churning red water a small child was swept away like a leaf. A bi-plane looped the wrong-sized loop and crashed into a crowd of spectators at an air show, carving a path through them and scattering them like chopped liver. A parachutist dropped like a stone to the ground, his chutes twirling above him like a sycamore seed, and bounced slightly.

It went on, a death every minute. Jo served up the *dunner* and they kept watching. When that one was over, Danny told him where he could find *Even More Faces of Death* on the shelf and had him put that on.

After watching that, they were drained. Clive lay back, sighed, and asked a question he had been bottling up since he knocked on the door.

'What was Dave like?'

'Dave who killed himself?' asked Danny, then paused while he took a large hit from the bong.

At last he exhaled.

'He was quiet? Bit shy? Seemed all right to me?'

'So he didn't look ... shifty?' asked Clive. 'Only I still get a lot of phone calls for him, and it looks like he went out owing a lot of money.'

'*Reeeally?*' said Danny. He was fascinated. 'What do they say?'

Jo's face peeped over the arm of the couch now too. They both looked as eager as a person can who has a cubit of cannabis in their system.

Clive laughed, and tried to do the accent. 'Gimme moy farking manny, you cant!' He laughed again, and they joined in.

'Maybe he was a gangster?' said Jo, her eyes as wide as they could go.

'Sounds like he was deep in some heavy shit?' said Danny happily.

'I don't know,' said Clive. 'He could have just been an ordinary bloke, let his money get the better of him.'

'Shit,' said Danny. 'I couldn't imagine hanging myself over money, no matter how much?'

'No, I suppose not. There would have to be other things,' said Clive, and he grew despondent.

They all lapsed into silence. It was late. They watched a repeat of *Howzat!*, the hilarious cricketing quiz show, then the graveyard-shift news. Clive didn't want to leave, he was enjoying their company so much. Even their silence. Eventually though, Jo started getting ready for bed, brushing her teeth with the door open, so Clive got to his feet. He wished them good night, thanking them for supper, and headed back down the dark stairwell to his own darkened flat.

10

Cashless Society

'The trouble with Clive is, he's got no get up and go.'

Christina was talking to her psychotherapist.

'And I need someone with get up and go. I've got it, and I think I deserve someone else with it too. I mean you should see the state he's in. I rang him last week – he's supposed to have started this new job, as a ... I'm actually embarrassed to say it, really I am ... as a *tour* guide. On coaches. With *tourists*. Anyway, so I phone him and I say "How was it?" And he says "How was what?" And you know don't you, you just *know* from the start this is going to be hard, that he's hiding something, and God knows I know when he's hiding something I lived with him long enough. So after to-ing and fro-ing for a while it comes out that the job isn't even a proper job! When it's not busy he has to wait till they call him, you know, when the tourists aren't coming in for one reason or another, there's no guarantee of work, it's pathetic. So I asked him "Well how many days have you done?" He says "Er, just the one."

'"One?" I said. "One!" I was really ready to give him hell, I mean what kind of money is he going to be earning working one day a week? I've got bills to pay, I've got Tess's school fees and there's the car to be serviced, and I have to pay you ...'

'How does that make you feel?' asked the therapist.

'Um, well ...' Tina didn't like to be interrupted in mid-rant. 'I suppose ... I suppose ... if he doesn't pay me, how can I pay you?' She hoped that was the right answer.

There was silence for a minute, so she continued.

'I was never sure about Clive from the beginning. There was always something weak about him. I don't know why I married him. I suppose it was because he seemed honest, and had integrity, he cared about children and he seemed intelligent. Everybody else was marrying lawyers and people from the City and I thought "I've got my Clive, my teacher . . ." My father liked him. He seemed quite fond of Clive. They always had stuff to talk about, the environment and whatnot.'

She started crying at the thought of her late father, and at having given in to sympathetic feelings for Clive.

The therapist passed her a box of tissues. Christina snivelled and wiped for a couple of minutes.

'Daddy would be so upset if he could see me now. The worst thing is . . .'

'We have to end now, I'm sorry.'

She craned her neck and looked around. 'But I was just about to tell you something important!'

'I'm sorry, we're out of time,' said the therapist gently. 'We can talk about this next time.'

Tina reluctantly got up from the couch, sniffling and getting her bag together. She looked up at the therapist with sad, red eyes and left, forgetting to pay.

11

Test Material

After almost a week of being told he wasn't needed at Britannia Tours, during which he ploughed on with his books and took fruitless walks around Streatham, accompanied by the sound of cellos scraping out Elgar's Opus 85, Clive took matters into his own hands. He called Maxine one morning. As usual, she apologised, saying there wasn't anything for him, but she would call if anything came in. He was ready for her.

'Maxine, please tell me what's going on? I thought I was going to be working every day! This is no way for a ... for a man to live.'

'I'm sorry Clive, love, but you'll have to talk to Alex.'

'Well can you put him on then?'

Alex was standing by his desk with a cricket bat, practising his square cut. When he heard the name 'Clive' he began waving to her, mouthing 'No, no!'

'I'm afraid he's tied up at the moment.'

'Oh. Well tell him I'll be in town this afternoon anyway and I might drop in and see him.'

'OK, I'll tell him.'

Alexander White's problem was that he was utterly spineless. He was the most gutless manager in the whole of Wonga Leisure, perhaps even in the whole of English tourism. He hired people on the basis of whether they seemed like a good chap or not, without calculating whether their services were really needed, then refusing to fire them. In fact, going to great lengths to avoid them.

His working day consisted of having morning coffee at his desk while he read the front few pages of the newspaper. Next he would log on and read his e-mail, circulate anything humorous to his friends scattered about the landscape of corporate London, then polish his fantasy cricket portfolio. From there he would proceed to the toilet with the Sport section and drop a large log while reading about rugby and rowing, or cricket and athletics depending on the time of year. Sometimes motor racing, golf or tennis if there was a Brit involved. Next he would read the industry newsletters and his correspondence and make some calls. Then he would have lunch – either an industry lunch locally, or with a chum across town. After lunch he would play with his laptop a bit more, working on spreadsheets of customer bookings and the office accounts, and pretty soon Maxine would be bringing the tea and biscuits round and it would be time for a game of tip-and-run with whoever happened to be in the office. Maxine left at five on the dot, and Alex left at five fifteen.

It was a good enough job for now, the way he saw it. It had been quite a scoop at the time, landing a management position at the age of twenty-six. Previous to that he had been running a small English Language school in Earls Court, with no great success. After three years enrolment was down 27 per cent and not a single student had slept with him. Fortunately he was at one of the old Five Nations games at Twickenham when he ran into the father of an old school friend. Over a few beers in the bar he got the heads up on a Deputy Manager vacancy at Wonga Leisure. He jumped at the chance, coasted through the interview, celebrated the increase in salary by proposing to his girlfriend of one year, was promoted within three months when his boss left to go higher up the Wonga chain, got married, got divorced, got promoted again to Britannia, and here he was.

Clive walked in.

'Ah Clive! What's your bowling like?'

'Er, not . . .' He thought better of it. 'Well, I haven't bowled for a few years now.' This wasn't true. As part of his teacherly duties he had taken Games classes which included, 'B-team' cricket. There was no B-team, these were just the kids who were trying to get out of cross-country running. He would spend three hours on a lumpy field with a bunch of fatties, chatters and cat-torturers, showing them how to field a ball, kneeling down and using the body as a backup to a firmly cupped pair of hands, or how to bowl, over-arm and without a kink . . . pitch it up, pitch it up! His kids were so bad at cricket they made him look good. For the first few years he was amazed at their inability to learn, until he realised they didn't actually give a fuck about cricket and were refusing to learn.

'Bowl a few would you? I'm afraid I've worn Maxine out.' She didn't look up from her screen. 'Just a couple of overs.' He rolled the green tennis ball to him.

Clive put down his bag and grimly obliged. He had to find out what was going on with his job. He might as well prove he was a good sport first.

Alex scored eighteen off the first over, followed by ten off the next, followed by six straight fours.

'So Alex, about the work.'

'Oh, just one more over. Let's see if I can break my record of twenty-six in six balls. Come on.'

Clive had to duck as he smashed the first ball at him for a six. The next he bowled a little harder but it still went for a four. He tried to scare him by pitching the next one short but Alex hooked it for another six into the metal shelving. The batsman missed the fourth ball, calling vainly for a wide. He missed the fifth, slashing wildly outside the off stump, and cursed himself. Now he couldn't break the record. Clive bowled him an easy last ball which he lofted for another six, but Alex remained dissatisfied and muttered to himself.

Panting slightly, he put the bat down. They went into his office and Clive sat across the desk from him.

'Well,' he said in his deep voice, as though nothing had just passed between them. 'How do you like Wonga Leisure?'

'Erm, that's just it,' said Clive. 'I've hardly done a thing. I call Maxine every day and she tells me I'm on the list, but I'm sitting at home twiddling my thumbs. I thought when I got this job I'd be making a living wage ...'

Alex didn't like the phrase 'living wage'. It triggered echoes of militancy and labour unrest that he felt he was instinctively unsympathetic toward.

'The thing is, Clive,' he said, as sombrely as possible, '*basically* ... this arm of Wonga is very much dependent on a few fluctuating variables, such as exchange rates, weather, seasonal factors and suchlike ...'

Clive opened his mouth to say something ...

'The point is,' Alex said raising his voice and lowering his sandy eyebrows, 'we can't guarantee you work at this stage, because you are the newest person on our roster. When others are wecruited after you, you'll find you're given more and more to do. Now, if it makes you feel any better, even experienced people like *Barry* are not working at full capacity at the moment. It's been unseasonably quiet for the last week or so, but I'm sure things will pick up soon.'

'So Barry's not even working?'

'No. Not today. He did a half day. I expect . . .' He stuck out his arm, shook his cuff free of his watch and looked at it. 'I expect you'll find him in the Shakespeare right now. I wouldn't wonder. Might pop in there myself after work, in no uncertain terms.' He smiled at Clive, as if to say, 'There, doesn't that feel better?'

'So this is just a . . . blip?'

'Exactly. Stick around Clive. We want you to work here. We need people like you at Britannia. Your skill-set is uniquely suited to our twenty-first-century needs.' Clive felt a little better.

Alex suddenly said, 'You don't play regularly, do you?'

'What, cricket?' Clive shook his head.

'Hmm. We need a twelfth man next Sunday . . .'

'Er, no thanks. I really don't have the time,' said Clive. 'Got a little daughter. And an ex-wife, you know.'

'Yah, I know exactly. Divorced myself.'

'Oh really?' he said hopefully. A fellow sufferer. It warmed his heart.

'Two years we lasted.' He gestured at the photo on his desk, without turning it around for Clive to see. 'Felt like twenty-two.' And he laughed, 'A-hock hock, hock, a-hock hock, hock!'

Father Dear Father

Feeling slightly more optimistic, Clive headed down to the Shakespeare. Now he wanted Barry's take on the job market. He peered in through the window and saw him sitting alone at a table, drinking and studying the racing form. Clive went in and got himself a diet Pepsi at the bar then sidled up to him.

'Oh Barry, I thought I might find you here . . .'

'Awright,' said Barry, in a not particularly friendly way. It was a guttural gurgle with very minimal effort behind it. He carried on reading his paper.

'Um, listen Barry, I'm just . . . I'm a bit confused about the work situation here . . .'

Barry looked up, a little irritated. 'What of it?'

'I just think . . . I just thought I was going to be working every day, but all I've had was that Monday we did together and that's it. Alexander says it's just been a bit slow, but I was wondering . . . was it anything, was it something I said or did? Only I'm desperate to make some money right now . . .'

'Naaah mate. It's just been slow that's all. Look at me? I've been on three-a-day all week, and today all I had was one panoramic and a bunch of Spanish schoolchildren who wanted to go to the Tower of London.'

'I thought you couldn't do the Tower? You don't have your Blue Badge . . .'

'Yeah, so I took 'em to the London Dungeon, same thing really, they're not bothered, in fact it's more fun for the little bleeders . . . Listen Charles mate . . .' said Barry folding up his paper and looking him in the eye.

'Er, it's Clive.'

'Sorry, Clive. You see it's all about waiting, this game. It's a waiting game, is how I see it. There are slow periods, and then there are busy periods. And when it picks up it can be mental. You have to budget for the quiet times – that's the beauty of tourism. The people will come when they want to. You can lead a horse to water but you can't make it drink. Talking of which, I see you got yourself one ...'

'Oh, of course, hang on ...'

'Never mind, I'll get it, this time.'

Barry came back with a pint of lager for himself and a Diet Pepsi for Clive, and proceeded to tell him about the perks of the job. The main one, which took him quite a long time to explain with all the details, was the birds.

'Tourists mate, they're mad for it! *Begginfrit.* These birds come over here and they just want one thing: shagging. They want some prime English beef, that's all. Oh yeah I know, they want to see some castles too, but the main thing is, anything in trousers.' He lowered his voice. 'Anything from a bit of romance to a quickie in the coach khazi.'

Clive was feeling rather uncomfortable, and gripped his glass as he tried to meet Barry's gaze.

'Now you're a regular bloke right? What, forty-five, fifty?'

'Forty-four actually. Divorced.'

'There you go! There you go! Once you cotton on to how many women there are out there just dying to get to know their friendly English tour guide, you'll come to work with a smile on your face every day.'

'But I don't even get to come to work!' said Clive exasperated. 'I just talked to Alexander and he said ...'

'What did he say?' asked Barry, his brow furrowing.

'He said I was junior and I'd just have to wait.'

'Hmph,' Barry sniffed. 'Well he's a cunt. I'll have a word with him.'

'What about?'

'If I tell him you need more work he'll give it to you. I didn't know that was his attitude. Just like him to call someone "junior" ...'

'Well, he might not have actually ...'

'Nah, leave it to me, chief ... hang about, there's my old fellah!'

Clive looked out the window and saw a black cab, painted like newsprint to advertise the *Evening Standard*, dropping off a fare. Barry was already across the room. He went outside and banged on the roof of the taxi and had a word with the driver. They talked for a moment through the window and then the hazard lights went on. Barry came back in, looking serious and proud, followed by a man who looked like an older version of himself. The taxi driver had on Nikes, canary-yellow tracksuit legs, a white T-shirt that tucked in under his beer gut and showed off the remnants of once outstanding pectoral muscles and biceps, all topped off by that familiar Barry head – large features, a full mop of hair, and a sceptical scowl.

The older man looked like he was in his late fifties, although from behind he could have been any age, as his hair was dyed brown and his choice of sportswear was shared by many in the pub – tourists, builders, teenagers, senior citizens.

'Dad this is Clive, he's new. This is me dad. What you having, lager?'

Dad rubbed his chops while he made up his mind. 'Yeah. Lager.'

There was an uncomfortable few minutes before Barry came back with three more drinks, in which Clive tried to introduce himself but quickly gave up. Barry's dad wasn't interested.

'So Chrissie coming round tonight? I haven't talked to her yet today,' said Barry to his dad.

'Yeah, I hope so. She's an angel, your Christine, absolute gold mine. You treat her properly now, none of that monkey business,' he said gruffly.

'Shut up Dad, you're just scared of being left alone . . .' said Barry and laughed at him, 'Naaaar-har-har.'

'Oh, is your wife called Christina?' interjected Clive. 'So's mine. My ex.'

'No mate, Christine,' said Barry, then carried on with his conversation. Father and son talked about work, how quiet it was, how there were too few tourists and too many mini cabs, then they started using words such as 'Yankee' and 'Place' and Clive lost them till he realised they were talking about horse racing, then Barry's dad got a round in and told them about some old girl off the telly he'd had in the back of his cab and how he told her she'd been one of his first fares thirty years before and she remembered.

'So anyway, what's happening with that other TV bird then?' asked Barry.

'Fuck-all at the moment,' replied his father. He was referring to the young TV documentary maker who was hoping to make a film about a taxi driver. She was looking for someone colourful, someone traditional, someone like the people she was always hearing stories about but never seemed to meet. A 'gabby cabby', as she put it in her pitch. She'd narrowed her search down to three hopefuls, one being Ron, Barry's dad. Ron was dying to be chosen, but there was nothing much he could do to influence her. All he could do was sit and hope.

'I don't think she likes my skin,' he said glumly.

'So get a re-spray then,' chided Barry.

'What about the money? The *Standard* pays good money.'

'I suppose she wants all black? What about door panels for the time being?'

'All black. I'm pretty sure of it. You should have seen her face.'

'Silly cow.'

Then they talked about the EU and what a load of bollocks that was, Barry being slightly less vehement about it than his dad and Clive not being able to express his opinion succinctly enough for them in the time allotted, then they talked about football which left Clive out in the cold again, and then suddenly it was his round.

'Oh!' He said as they stared at him. 'Right. Same again?'

He went up to the bar terrified that he didn't have enough cash on him, but found that if he didn't have another Pepsi, which he didn't want anyway, he just had enough. He resigned himself to living off his cash advances on his Visa card until he got paid.

'There you go,' he said to the men. They both looked at him.

'Where's yours?' asked Barry.

'Er, I'm OK thanks,' he said, gesturing at his half a glass.

'So if you don't mind me asking,' said Barry, pausing for full menacing effect, 'do you *ever* drink?'

'Oh, well, sure, I love a drink ...' he said. They waited for the explanation. 'It's just that I'm still fighting for my contact rights, for my little girl, and one of the things my ex-wife said against me was that I drink too much, which is completely untrue, so as part of the probationary period I have to prove to the judge that I don't need it.'

'You poor bugger,' they both proclaimed at once.

'That's hard, that's really hard. So how old is your little girl then?'

'Seven,' said Clive gloomily. He got out a photo of her from his wallet and showed it round.

'Cor she's a pretty one. Here, have a look at these then.'

And Barry got his photos out, of three flaxen-haired angels. 'That's Shelley, she's eight, that's Dawn, she's five, and that little sweetheart is my youngest, Di, she's two, I think.'

'Yeah, two,' growled his dad.

All three men stared in pride and wonder at their photos.

'Apple of my eye.'

'I live for my grandkids. I *live* for 'em.'

'The only reason I get up in the morning.'

'And another on the way,' said Barry proudly. 'Scan next Friday, Dad.'

'Can they see his ticket at this age?'

'Yeah. Doctor says we'll know. Better be a boy this time. Same again Dad?'

Barry's dad looked at his watch, then out at his cab, still illegally parked, still with the hazards going.

'Bleedinell!' he exclaimed. There was a traffic warden standing by it, looking around for an owner.

'Naar har har,' laughed Barry as the yellow tracksuit legs rushed through the pub and into the street. He sang the chorus of 'Lovely Rita', the song about the traffic warden, wildly off-key. 'That's his theme tune, that is.'

They watched the show from their seats. Barry's dad was gesturing and pointing up and down the road, then they appeared to inspect his taxi licence, then they talked for a bit longer. The old man was joking, cajoling, trying to get her to laugh, and she hesitated several times to put pen to paper. Finally he got a little smile out of her. 'One,' he seemed to be miming, 'one more minute.' He touched her arm and she smiled coyly and started putting her book away, but gave him a bit more of a lecture, and Barry's dad bowed slightly and pretended to tug his forelock, and pressed his hands together in oriental supplication, and she smiled again and watched, in slight disbelief, as he strode back into the pub grinning.

Barry sang the song again. He was in very good spirits – loud, generous, forgiving, slightly deaf. He got up to see if he could find it on the juke box. It was evening now and the Shakespeare was filling up with its curious crowd. Clive looked around him at the crap on the walls. Bookshelves too high for anyone to reach, holding urns and old beer bottles, a miniature pram made of metal, a model of a chef riding a bike, wine bottles in a wooden box, a stooping duck. It was all stuff he used never to notice until he'd had a few drinks, but he would never remember if he was drunk. The floor was hardwood with large, industrial-strength rugs and the walls were dark green with framed pictures – a frontispiece from Shakespeare's *Comedies, Histories and Tragedies*, a drawing of someone in doublet and hose playing Cymbeline, some soldiers called the Newlancers, and an old etching of a pomegranate. It made no sense, but it made no sense to be looking at it anyway, when all around people were crowding in, slurping fresh pints, laughing and talking. It was still sunny outside and Clive was aching for a drink.

'So, Barry, do you think you can have a word with Alex about me working some more next week. Only I really have to make some money or find somewhere else ...'

'Oh no worries mate, I'll talk to him. This weekend. That Alex, he's a clueless prick. He does what I tell him to do. When I say "Jump", he says "How high?".'

''Strue,' said his dad, raising the thick Bergman eyebrows.

'Did he ask you what you had to *offer* Wonga Leisure?' said Barry in a poncey voice.

'Er, no, but I could have told him, I know London pretty well ...' They both stared at him. 'Well, obviously not as well as you two ...' The friendly wrinkles round their Bergman eyes returned. 'But I mean I know the country well, I used to be a Geography teacher ...'

'We had a crap Geography teacher at our school. Used to make him cry. Merciless, we were. Remember him, Dad?'

'I dunno, they were all the same to me, waste of time.'

'Remember the one we chased down the street?'

'Ah you kids, you were always causing trouble, I'm surprised you're not all inside like Trevor,' he said grimly.

'So how come you're not a teacher any more?'

Clive's face became stony. 'I'd rather not talk about it.'

'Ooooh!' said Barry, mockingly, 'He'd rather not talk about it.'

Barry's dad smirked into his pint.

'It must have been something well dodgy,' said Barry enjoying himself. 'Come on tell us, what did you do?'

'I said I don't want to talk about it,' said Clive firmly. There was a line beyond which he would not go, for anything. Barry got the message, shrugged his shoulders and looked around the room. The three of them said nothing for fifteen seconds.

Clive tried to steer things back to work.

'I mean, I bet I know more about equestrian statuary than Alex.'

Barry looked at him blankly.

'You know, statues with horses in them.'

'Oh. Yeah. I spose there are a lot of them about ...'

'A lot? There are tons in London alone!' said Clive getting excited.

'Hmm ... Well I can't think of any off-hand,' said Barry. 'What about you, Dad?'

'Buggered if I know.'

'Course you can. You just passed one!' said Clive. He was falling into teacher mode. 'Think! I bet you'll remember.'

'No, there's none round here,' said Barry decisively.

'Yes there are!'

'What, you wanna bet on it?'

'Well, no, not an actual bet ... I haven't got the money ...'

'No, no, come on, you say there's a statue of a horse round here, I say there isn't. Ten quid says there isn't one within a hundred yards of where I'm sitting.'

They both looked at Clive, waiting for him to take the bet, getting increasingly suspicious as he delayed.

'Well, no, you're going to lose, I'll win easily, it's not fair ...'

'Ten quid. Come on.' Barry was getting overexcited. He got the money out of his jeans and slapped it on the pub table. His dad immediately put it under the ashtray to keep it in place.

'I haven't got it,' said Clive.

'You can owe it me.'

'Um, OK then.' Clive shrugged. 'Done.'

Barry shook his hand roughly. 'So where's this facking horse statue then?'

'There,' said Clive, pointing out of the Shakespeare's window, past the taxi with the hazards going, to an enormous figure of a general on a horse.

Barry and his dad looked at it in amazement.

'Kinell.'

'Stone the 'ackin' crows.'

'Do I win then?' said Clive with a smile.

'Who's it of then?' asked Barry getting to his feet. Clive chased after him and they went outside for a closer look, crossing the road and standing dwarfed by the huge pedestal.

'It's General Foch.'

'Foch 1851–1929,' read Barry. 'He's not a Kraut is he? What's a Kraut doing up here? Is this new?'

'No.'

'I am conscious of having served England as I served my own country.' Barry read out loud. He looked puzzled as he stood, swaying, staring up at the metal man wearing a kepi, illuminated by the evening sun.

'He was a hotshot French soldier, commander of all the Allied troops in France. He was at the Battle of the Somme in the summer of 1916, and he saved the channel ports for the Allies by his generalship at Ypres. He also halted the German advance during the second battle of Marne in July of 1918. Basically, he helped us beat the Germans.'

Barry was well impressed, and stood with his mouth open, looking up.

'Generalissimo of the Allied Armies 1918. British Field Marshall 1919. Fuck.'

'Foch,' corrected Clive.

'No, *fack*, I never knew all that. Well I never.' He scratched his throat and headed back into the pub, stopping only to tell the traffic warden, who was back again, that his dad was coming right out.

'Here's yer ten quid,' he said handing it over.

'Oh, really, I can't take it.'

'Take it!' both men said at once, threateningly.

'OK, OK.'

'Your round. Same again please.'

Clive got the drinks in.

Barry got talking to some girl who brushed against him on his way back from the Gents, and his dad was only staying for a half so Clive realised it was time to make tracks.

'Er, Barry, you will talk to Alex this weekend won't you?' he said nervously, not wanting to interrupt.

'Yeah yeah no problem, consider it done.'

13

A River Runs Right Fucking Through It

While Barry spent the weekend with his wife and daughters, lending a hand with the shopping as the baby was due in September, and completely forgetting to call Alex, Clive passed it in the jobless, friendless purgatory of his Streatham home.

The highlight of Friday night was coming home and finding the new answering machine had four messages on it. One was from a debt recovery agency asking for dead Dave to get in touch. One was from a nameless, guttural frightener who also wanted his money back but didn't sound so accommodating. One was from Christina, ostensibly reminding him that she and Tess would be going on holiday in July. And one was from London Electricity, explaining that they had run some tests and there was no evidence the power had been cut off to his flat at any point. The voice suggested the fault must lie with the appliance itself. Clive took a look at his digital clock radio. It had no moving parts. For the moment, it was showing the right time. He wondered how the clock mechanism could possibly go wrong on its own, and if it had, how it could be fixed. He had always considered himself an 'If it ain't broke, don't fix it' kind of guy, as he unplugged it one last time. 'And if it is ...' He dropped it in the bin.

He spent the rest of Friday night in, trying to not think how fine life would be if he just had a simple, comforting vice, or at least the money for one. If he smoked he could lie back on his bed and smoke a cigarette in his vest and trousers. At least then he'd feel like a real prisoner. The world without alcohol was proving to be worse than black and white. It was dull like sepia, but without the warmth. Time was rigid and flat. He missed the old roller coaster of accelerated evenings, literally *spent* in the pub. Any pub. Instant taxi rides home where he relied on the driver to handle the geography. Analysis of the night before, like looking through a wallet of snaps taken on a forgotten disposable camera. Now there were just the slabs of the hours, all the same size, like a school timetable.

Saturday was another Saturday without Tess. He returned Tina's call, hoping to talk to his little girl but was told she didn't want to. It was true too. He could hear her refusing in the background and it broke his heart. Then he got an earful of questions about money. He asked her if she had been forwarding his mail lately, since he received very little of it, but she just scoffed and said it must be because he had alienated all his friends.

Clive wandered around the shops in Streatham in the afternoon. There was a modern-day match girl in the street croaking 'Four lighters a pound'. She also had toy pagers, cheap tamagotchis that committed *hari kiri*, and other bits of electronic flotsam. Clive bought a matchbox-sized radio with bud earphones for only £4.99, and was pleasantly surprised by the excellent sound quality – lush stereo that filled his head and almost took over his field of vision too as he walked the streets. It had a scan button, with which he searched for something bearable, but all he could find was breathless ads for mobile phones and presenters babbling about football.

In his sadness he gave George a call. He was just wondering how he was, and was going to ask if he wanted to meet for a drink – Clive was prepared to come over to his part of town.

'Oh, hullo Clive ... cricket's on.'

'Oh. How are England doing?'

'Rather well, actually, 404 for 6 declared.'

'Great. So, George, what are you doing tonight? Do you fancy ...'

'Oh I say he's gone! LBW! Nought for one!'

Clive had to listen to a description of the Australian opener's downfall and his trudge back to the pavilion at Edgbaston. Several times.

'I just thought ...'

'Ow-zayyyyy!' Shouted George. 'YESSSS! This is incredible! 0 for 2 – he's on a hat trick! You should see this, Clive ...'

Clive accepted defeat and excused himself, saying he was off to watch it. Instead he sat on his bed with the little radio trying to find the cricket commentary. When he finally did, he had missed all the excitement. Play was over. The Aussies were 12 for 2, bad light stopped play.

Saturday evening he read about the Fleet River, a dirty little stream

that dumps into the Thames near St Paul's. He learned that a poet called
Alexander Pope had written,

> 'Fleet ditch, with disemboguing streams
> Rolls the large tribute of dead dogs to Thames . . .'

He looked up this Pope and found he was a hunchback dwarf who was
banned from living in London because he was a Catholic. And that he used
to walk all the way into town from 'Twit'nam', had an unrequited thing for
some Lady or other in the time of Queen Anne, liked his drinking chocolate
and his coffee, and had frequent splitting headaches. And looked after his
old mum till she was about ninety.

He didn't know they pronounced Thames like 'themes'.

The Fleet River, he read, was mostly underground now, bricked over,
sometimes passing through a huge iron pipe. It rose above the bathing
ponds on Hampstead Heath. He thought it might make a good tour
some day. Maybe he could go it alone. Be like one of those Jack the
Ripper guides, leading keen-eyed Americans and Japanese around deserted
London on Sunday afternoons, looking for Dr Johnson's House, or places
where Sherlock Holmes prowled. Britannia wasn't everything.

On Sunday he was going to take the train into town and look around St
Paul's, to refresh his memory, but he had an attack of the blues and couldn't
raise himself from his bed. The Baroque splendour, the Whispering Gallery,
the soaring dome . . . they weren't enough to lure him. He tried listening to
his new radio but the sound was too clear, it went so deep inside his head
that he was afraid it might take him over. He worried about schizophrenia.
One minute you're listening to the Top Forty, the next minute the perky
DJ is telling you to top yourself.

He roused himself at 2 p.m. and began the long haul up to Dollis
Hill to see his mother. London was full of happy couples flexing their
lifestyles.

Mother was not well. She had been brought home by the police the
previous evening, discovered by good Samaritans wandering in nearby
Neasden. Clive only found out because he met the social worker on
her way down the path. She had just paid a follow-up visit and left a
few leaflets with Gordon.

Clive got on his high horse with his brother. What was he doing
letting her out of his sight? How long was it before he noticed she
was gone? Gordon let it slip that he had been playing video games

upstairs in his bedroom with the headphones on, which set Clive off on one.

'Look at you, you useless ... sod! What's got into you? You live like some ... like some laid-off navvy! All that school and college going to waste. What do you think Mum and Dad would think if they knew you were such a thicko? Video games? At your age? Why don't you get a ruddy job?' He was standing over him in the kitchen now, waving his arms about. Their mother was in the sitting room, sitting in front of the television. The crashes and shrieks of cartoons filled the air forcing Clive to shut the door. 'I can't believe you. You had a decent education and now you've sunk this low. You could have *been* someone!'

'Yeah, like you?' said Gordon. 'I hear Streatham's rather nice. You must invite me round next time you're having a dinner party.' He was openly contemptuous of Clive, a little brother unafraid.

Clive's biggest complaint against his brother was something he dared not say out loud: Gordon was a class traitor. They were raised in a firmly middle-class household, where it was the unspoken rule that you did not go down. One had a duty to maintain one's income, education, attitudes, contacts, lifestyle. But Gordon had been a rebel from the start. After his A-levels he had raised eyebrows by choosing to go to a polytechnic, then getting a degree in a default subject that didn't interest him – Economics. He had briefly worked for a packaging company in a clerical position that was supposed to lead upwards (eventually) to management, but after just three years of stapling, filing and kow-towing he quit. After a brief lay-off he moved from Milton Keynes nearer to London, to Barnet, using his experience to get a job with the council. He switched around within the council for a few years, his jobs taking him ever closer to London, until he landed his council flat in Dollis Hill. Then he moved to the private sector, taking a job in the office of a building contractor. In Clive's eyes he finally crossed the Rubicon one summer during the housing boom of the 1980s, when there was a shortage of unskilled labour and he started hod-carrying and wheelbarrow-pushing. The money was much better, he explained.

When the building work dried up one of the lads got him a job in a factory driving a forklift. He did that for a few years until he sustained a minor knee injury playing football in his lunch hour (it was a game of Germans; Gordon was in goal) and had himself relegated to sweeping up. The knee showed no sign of improving and after a year of complaining he was laid off with Incapacity Benefit. He threw himself into the system, learning everything there was to know about Benefits:

Statutory Sick Pay, Severe Disablement Allowance, Disability Living Allowance, Attendance Allowance, Invalid Care Allowance, Disability Working Allowance, Industrial Injuries Disablement Benefit, Housing Benefit, Council Tax Benefit, Income Support, Jobseeker's Allowance ... means tested or contributory, non taxable or taxable, he knew it all. He had earned his benefits, and now lived in a world where pennies were saved and hours were counted out in cigarettes.

Gordon had finally arrived in the underclass. The mean sixties pub (The Sailor's Fist) where he was recognised but not loved. The clapped-out car. The experimental glottal stops. The market stall tracksuit. He had it all. He now lived in a world of scratchcards, greyhound results and fenced goods, where the week's grocery shopping cost about the same as a round of Pimms.

He even told Clive he was thinking of getting a dog, knowing it would drive his big brother mad.

'You can't get a dog! What about Mum? Who's going to walk the thing? I can just see the three of you going to the pub together ...'

'Maybe I'll tie Mum up outside and bring the dog in for a pint,' he said with a grin.

Clive was so angry he went back in the other room with his mother.

'Hello, Clive,' she said. 'Your father and I have tickets for Kenwood tonight. I've made you and Gordon a tongue salad, and there's some pop in the pantry. Now be good boys and make sure you're in bed by ten o'clock.'

'Mother, Dad died over twenty years ago,' he said wearily. She looked at him, and became upset. She knew she had let him down and was embarrassed. Clive was always putting her straight and it made no difference. He was always having to explain to her that she was mad. Random memories rose to the surface of her mind, like criminal evidence in a canal.

'Let me read to you, Mum, what would you like to hear.' He looked in one of her boxes. 'Let's find you a nice poem. Here, what's this? Philip Larkin.' He flicked through it, looking for something short, something with the tang of her era – two-pin plugs and yellowed lampshades, overcooked food and chirpy bus conductors.

'Here we go. "The Mower".'

'"The mower stalled, twice; kneeling, I found
A hedgehog jammed up against the blades,
Killed. It had been in the long grass.

'"I had seen it before, and even fed it, once.
Now I had mauled its unobtrusive world
Unmendably. Burial was no help:

'"Next morning I got up and it did not.
The first day after a death, the new absence
Is always the same; we should be careful

'"Of each other, we should be kind
While there is still time."'

    She chimed in with the last line, 'We should be kind/While there is still time.'
    'Christ, that was depressing,' he said.
    Gordon came out of the kitchen putting on his denim jacket.
    'Where are you off to?' asked Clive.
    'Wheredyafink?' came the reply, and the doors slammed behind him.
    'I'll read you another,' said Clive gently to his mum.
    'What's for supper?' she asked with hopeful eyes.
    'Ooh, you've had your supper, Mum.' He choked up. For a moment he thought he was going to cry. He went over and put his arms around her neck, and whispered, 'I'm sorry mum, I'm sorry I'm such a mess.' She comforted him as if he were still a little boy, shushing him and stroking his hair.
    Clive couldn't speak for a minute, but in the end he recovered his composure and sat back in Gordon's armchair, and read her poems from an anthology. He didn't understand much of them, but his mother looked happy.
    It was 3 a.m. when he got back to Streatham.

14

Arise, Sir Clive

In the words of the Managing Director, fifty-five-year-old Sir Clive Tiddel, Wonga Leisure was in a spot of bother. Despite Sir Clive's predictions in the mid-1990s that the company was 'Well-placed to share in the unprecedented period of growth in English tourism that was fast approaching', Wonga was going nowhere fast. Its three holiday camps – in Southport, Whitby and Minehead – had been hit by a recession, caused mainly by an influx of members of the underclass. Their highly specialised social skills – particularly theft, vandalism and intimidation – had led to a decline in the numbers of respectable working families attending these traditional blue-collar sites. If there was one thing worse than crop-haired extended families driving around his camps burning rubber, throwing bottles, perpetrating rapes and robberies, selling drugs, intimidating staff, stealing the ping-pong bats and peeing in the swimming pool, it was the media finding out about it, Sir Clive had once confessed to some friends over dinner at his Soho drinking club the Black Box. The television documentary which he personally signed-off on had ended up being a total embarrassment for Wonga Leisure. And for Sir Clive personally, since it was made by the daughter of a very good friend. He had expected the series, slated to be called *Greencoats*, to paint a sensitive (and sympathetic) portrait of leisure expenditure in the Classless Society (a phrase made current by another of his friends). To his horror, what he saw trailed on the cover of every newspaper supplement and every TV news programme was a six-part sensationalist monstrosity called *Scum of the Earth*. The series made temporary heroes of the Shields family from Doncaster, thereafter known as the 'Hardest Family In Britain' as they perpetrated a week of drunkenness, disorder and Casualty trips on the campus of Wonga's flagship resort in Southport, 'Seatown'.

Sir Clive's frantic calls to the powers-that-be in the television industry, when leaked to the press, served only to fan the flames of debate, and the whole series became compulsive viewing for the nation, clearing the streets every Friday at 8 p.m. The programme's popularity was breathlessly documented by private utility providers: *SOE*, as it quickly became known, caused massive spikes in electricity usage (tea breaks) and cellular network usage (oral comparison of notes). It also made stars of such characters as Theresa, the forty-four-year-old Shields matriarch exceptional for her fighting prowess and her capacity for ale; Gary the Greencoat, the defiantly 'out' homosexual (to the tune of several beatings); and Wilf, the laconic caretaker with the twelve-inch goitre who was given to the overuse of the phrase 'Kiss my arse'.

Further bad news for Wonga came in the form of declining attendances at Hood World, its Nottinghamshire-based adventure theme park and resort. The push to attract middle and mid-to-upper income families with the opening of mountain bike trails, indoor snowboarding and a summer school for the under-twelves backfired badly. The normal Hood constituency – Midlanders tired of the poor showing of Britain's coastal resorts when compared with offerings in the Mediterranean and Florida – took one look at the bicycle-helmet and red-wine brigade on the adverts and spent their leisure euros elsewhere.

Other Wonga problems included decreased sales at its chain of 300 bingo halls due to competition from the National Lottery; a top-heavy management structure (a legacy of the pre-Tiddelian); a general slowness to market which led to Wonga's chain of money-losing tea shops in tertiary Royal markets (Tunbridge Wells, Brighton, Grantham); and a tendency to employ anyone with the appropriate accent so long as they didn't have a prison record.

Sir Clive had just spent six months touring his estate and espied a lot of dead wood.

Our Clive, on the other hand, having nothing to oversee except his own downfall, slept through most of Monday, only rising to a half slumber when he heard Maxine's voice on the answering machine telling him to come in for a meeting on Thursday. So deep was his sense of sadness and failure, he assumed he was being canned from a job he had never had, and rolled over.

He had to get up, however, to fit back in with the diurnal scheme. He was pottering unhappily about, when there was a knock at the door. He opened it a crack to see a strange man in a dark-blue suit, chewing gum. Clive wondered who he had pissed off now.

'Good evening, I'm from South London Financial. Are you the tenant here?'

'Ah,' said Clive. 'Yes I am, but the person you want no longer lives here.'

'I'm obliged to get your signature before I hand over these papers. Your credit card debts have been legally purchased and will now be payable to SLF on a weekly basis at an interest rate set by SLF,' he parroted.

'No you don't understand, the person . . .'

'Are you Mr Clive Pointing?'

'Er, yes.'

'Well it says here you've been a naughty boy,' said the man with a sudden grin. A curl of blue gum protruded from between his incisors. He was young enough to have been taught by Clive, but big enough to wring his neck. 'You owe twelve *farsand* pound.'

'Oh. I haven't had a Visa bill for months.'

'Ignorance of the law is no excuse,' said the man. 'Now if you'd kindly do the paperwork I'll be on my way.'

Clive showed him to the couch, where he sat on the edge as though not wanting to soil his suit. He quickly explained the procedure – Clive would pay 'SLF' (as he kept referring to it) a portion of his debt every month by cheque, in person. The APR was currently 29.4 per cent, but it could rise if he defaulted on the payment plan. He could send a cheque, come into the SLF office in Mitcham to pay, or he could have 'Collection', like this, which was slightly more expensive (APR 31.7 per cent).

Clive's heart was heavy with the feeling of people closing in on him. It was shameful to be so broke that he might end up being a punching bag for some crap gangster, and he was appalled that his net worth could plummet so rapidly. From head of his own nuclear family to stress-reliever for a psychopath in a few short years. Who knew, maybe Danny would catch it all on video? he daydreamed.

'Er, this isn't one of those companies . . .'

The young man cut him off. 'No sir, this is strickly financial. Though I can't vouch for what happens if we chose to sell the debt on.' He grinned. 'The worst we at SLF would do is seize your assets.' He looked about the room. 'Are you thinking of moving out . . . ?'

'Er, I'm still moving in actually.'

'And are we working at the moment?'

'Yes, I've just started tour guiding.'

'Oh, sweet — I've often thought I might be good at that myself. You must meet a lot of interesting people ...' he said, not really waiting for an answer.

'Er, yes.'

'Well, thank you for your time Mr Pointing, and good luck.'

'Yes, thanks. Bye.'

He showed him out and looked at the SLF calendar he had been given. The first payment was due in a week. June was almost here. He had his High Court custody hearing in August. He suspected it wouldn't be many more months before he was turned over to the loan sharks for their gruesome pleasure. South London had been a bad idea.

Clive sat down and considered the pros and cons of suicide again, dwelling on the pros.

15

On the Road

'You're on, Clive! Get your arse in here now!'

It was the next morning and Barry was on his mobile. 'Leaving in an hour. Two coaches of Yanks – Bath, Stone'enge and Windsor Castle.'

'All in one day?' asked Clive.

'Course all in one facking day! Gerrin here!'

He leapt out of bed, his heart banging. 'Yesss!' he shouted. 'This is it! Clive Pointing is back!' He raced around getting dressed and gathering his stuff together. There was no time for a bath, he estimated, but he didn't smell too bad. He got his loose-leaf binder together with all the relevant notes and ran down to the train station. He crouched on the platform muttering over his files. 'Yes yes yes, Queen Mary's doll's house, Sir Edwyn Lutyens 1924, American love all that doll stuff, Barbies and Alice in Wonderland . . . Aquae Sulis, Roman name for Bath, hot springs here since 860 BC, a Celtic hot spot . . . Hot spot, I like that . . . Stonehenge, built in three stages, from 3000 BC, PRE-DRUID! Also Silbury Hill, Old Sarum, Avebury and West Kennet Long Barrow . . .'

He ran into Barry on Terminus Place right outside Victoria.

'Where are they?' asked Clive looking around for the coaches.

'There's a problem. Sandwiches, you gotta do the sandwiches.'

'Eh?'

'Part of the deal was they'd get lunch on the coach, save us having to stop. Alex's fucking idea. Whacked the ticket price up to fifty though. That's why we can fit so much in in one day. But the prannet never ordered the sandwiches. You've gotta go and find two coaches worth of sarnies. That's a hundred. I've gotta go back and board them.'

'Er, OK. You'd better give me some money . . .'

'That's the problem,' said Barry, scratching his neck. It was against his principles to get involved in situations where there wasn't enough money. 'Have you got a credit card? We'll have to pay you back tonight from petty cash.'

'Er, well, I have but, there's a limit . . .'

There were no limits in Barry's world. He lent him his mobile to call Visa and MasterCard and jack up his credit limits, and strode off, turning only to remind him they needed drinks too.

Clive was surprised to hear the credit card people would co-operate. Both women were really nice and added 300 pounds each. Clive was on a mission, getting cash advances from the machine, then ducking into shops looking for fridges full of fast food. It was challenging. He ended up in Victoria Station and cleaned out the whole of the Upper Crust. Fifty sandwiches at three quid a piece. He then backtracked to the newsagents and kiosks and bought whatever the commuters hadn't picked over – sweating slices of Kraft cheese with raw onion on white rolls, boiled egg and cress in mayonnaise, ham slivers as pale and thin as pickled ginger. He had to buy a pack of bin bags to carry everything, then remembered the pop, and bought sixty Cokes. The rest he made up with miscellaneous dusty cans and jumbo plastic bottles of Tango, Irn Bru and Fanta.

Barry was waving him to hurry up as he came staggering round the corner, where two coaches were waiting, doors open, excited Americans milling on the pavement. Barry was shepherding them on, taking their tickets, in some cases taking cash. Ray was leaning against the wall reading his paper, having a smoke. He scowled at Clive when he said hello, then his attention was taken by a young woman walking past with a styrofoam cup of tea. She was smallish, wore a green zip-up anorak, jeans and trainers. Her fair hair was long and straight, her skin was clear, her features fine. She got on to one of the coaches by the driver's door and sat getting ready to go. Ray tossed his fag away and got on the other coach.

'You're with Ray today,' said Barry grinning and rubbing his hands together. 'I'm with the bird. So this is the deal – they're really up for the Stone Age stuff, so we'll blast on out to Stonehenge, then Bath, and do Windsor on the way back if there's time. Play it by ear. So keep 'em occupied. Keep 'em laughing.' Barry looked in one of the bin bags. 'Upper Crust? You *did* go to town, didn't you?' He grabbed the better bag and was off.

Clive was nervous. He spent the first twenty minutes introducing himself and talking about the day's itinerary. There was much craning of necks so he intercut with explanations of things they could see out of the window, such as the Ark office building at Hammersmith. He mentioned that the curved sides of the building acted like a sounding board, reflecting traffic noise from the elevated motorway on to the houses near by, so that now it was like living next to an airport and everyone had frayed nerves and their tellies permanently cranked up. He thought this irony might get a little smile of recognition from his people but they just continued gazing out of the window. He took a break once they got on the M3 and tried to talk to Ray.

'So, Ray, been in this game long?' he asked cheerfully.

'Five years.'

'Oh, that all? What did you do before?'

Ray sighed wearily. 'Prison warden.'

'Oh.'

'Before that I was in the merchant navy. Before that I was in a 'ome for boys. Satisfied?' He turned right round to look at Clive.

'Er, I suppose.' *Miserable bastard*, thought Clive.

No one asked Clive a question until they were well down the M3.

'What's all that yellow stuff?' asked an elderly lady. Most of Clive's coach were "seniors", a sea of white hair and pastel jackets.

'That's rape,' said Clive. 'Er, rape, a plant. When it's really in bloom the fields are bright yellow for miles. They take the seed and press it for oil, for cooking.'

'Like sunflower oil?' asked someone else.

'Yes. Although this particular plant was introduced with grants from the EU and has had a deleterious effect on the ecology of much our farmland.' He got on the microphone, so that his words wouldn't be wasted. 'One of the consequences of monoculture . . .'

'What's the EU? Is that the euro?' interrupted a raspy old man in a pale-blue fishing hat.

'Can we get change for euros? My fanny pack's full of them. Nobody will take them . . .' a woman shouted out.

'Can we stop and get a Diet?'

'Er, please, there are no stops now until Stonehenge. We should be there in . . .' he turned for Ray's input, who answered 'How should I bleeding know, depends on the traffic?', so he continued, '. . . in an hour or so.'

'I love that accent,' someone said to her deaf neighbour. 'So cute.'

'He's cute?'

The other coach overtook them. The female driver looked straight ahead with a serious face, but Barry was standing up with the microphone, yapping and smiling, and the punters looked like they were having a grand old time. Clive remembered his instructions.

'Now who's heard of Sarah Tisdall? Later today we'll be passing near . . . well, in the vicinity of, Cheltenham and GCHQ . . .' He went on to tell them about the young woman. It was a dreary tale that had nevertheless set Fleet Street – and consequently the staff rooms and modest dinner-party circuit of Clive's early married life – on fire. The passengers stared out of the window at the passing cows and clumps of trees.

He tried again. 'The inhabitants of Salisbury, which many of you know is not far from here, used to live in the Roman hill fort town of Old Sarum, until the twelfth century, when they moved because they couldn't stand the awful weather.' He grinned, hopefully. A few weak smiles passed across the faces of the deafer people, who assumed they had been told something amusing. 'So anyway, Salisbury. Erm, we're obviously not going there today but it does have a magnificent cathedral. The spire, which is 404 feet tall, is the tallest in England – was added as an afterthought around 1310. If we were just a little bit south of here you'd be able to see it. Erm . . .'

He went to sit down, but someone said, 'Excuse me, when are we having lunch?'

Clive had completely forgotten about the black bag stashed under his seat. Now seemed as good a time as any.

'Ah yes. With the compliments of Britannia . . .' and he went round with the sack letting people pull out whatever they could lay hands on.

As soon as they saw what they were getting they began grumbling.

'They call this a sandwich? Where's the beef?'

'Cheese, I don't eat cheese, I'm lactose intolerant. Hey Mister Clive, can I switch?'

'Is this kosher? I asked for kosher? Where's the label? Read this for me, Honey . . .'

'It says non-dairy vegetable shortening, sorghum, artificial flavourings . . .'

'What's this, Tango? Does it have caffeine in it? If I get caffeine I'll be up half the night peeing!'

'This food stinks. When are we getting a real lunch? Hey driver, pull over where we can eat!'

'. . . Artificial colourings E-134, E-198 . . .'

'Mine doesn't have a label. What do you think that dark stuff is, Hon? Does anyone wanna swap?'

'I had better rations when I was here in the war.'

Clive felt himself blushing as he handed out the last of the food. There was nothing he could do but sit quietly at the front.

'Where's mine?' asked Ray. There was only one left, so Clive handed it over, not wanting any more trouble.

16

Ray Was a Bastard Anyway

It had clouded over considerably when they pulled in at the coach park at Stonehenge. Barry was helping his old dears down form the coach and having a laugh with them. Clive tried to round his up but they ignored him, following their compatriots to the tunnel under the road to the stones.

Barry came over to Clive. 'Nice bunch really. Sandwiches went down well. We'll give it half an hour here and fuck off.'

'Half an hour?' exclaimed Clive. 'Is that all?' He had a lot of notes to get through.

'Yeah. It's boring as fuck this place, quick once round the rocks and everyone's ready to get back on the coach. Mark my words. Looks like rain too. I hate this fucking place.'

'I'd better lead then,' said Clive hurrying ahead.

The battered circle of whitish stones stood in a field behind a chainlink fence, remarkably close to the fork in the A303 which hemmed them in. Inside the fence about a hundred kagoul-clad tourists walked slowly round them, like monks. They stayed about thirty yards back from the actual stones, watched by guides and guards alike, and paused only to take photos of the constant shape-shifting. The air was quiet, except for the swish of the traffic.

Like a schoolteacher Clive stopped everyone in the corner to lecture them while they were itching to join the procession around the stones.

'Now this is our most ancient monument, and we don't know precisely when it was built. The theory is they were built in three stages. The first part was built around 3,000 BC, and this is the Outer Bank, the wide circle around the whole structure.' He pointed to a vague ditch that curved around the structure, and everybody looked, obediently. 'Just inside this was dug a ring of fifty-six pits which were later filled with an admixture of earth and human ash.' He paused for effect.

'The Heel Stone is over there by the road, and that casts a long shadow straight to the heart of the circle on Midsummer's Day, along what we call The Avenue. Which leads us to believe ... what? Anybody? OK, it leads us to believe that it had some astrological significance.'

'Now,' he said after a suitable pause. 'The next phase was the Bluestone Circle, the smaller piece of dolerite you can just see inside the larger ring. These stones were quarried in Perseli in South Wales and were never completed. It dates from around 2000 BC. By the way, they do not show any signs of having been deposited here by glaciation.'

Clive noticed people were starting to yawn, so he hurried up.

'The Sarsen Circle is the outer ring of large stones with the lintels placed across them, the ones we famously recognise as being "Stonehenge",' he said, making air quotes. Barry watched from the back, smirking. 'The Sarsen Circle, and the Sarsen Horseshoe inside the Sarsen Circle, date from 1500 BC. The stones are sandstone, hewn from the Marlborough Downs.' The first few drops of rain started ticking on people's rainwear.

He paused. Everybody waited a few seconds, then set off across the grass in an anxious herd.

'You never told 'em about the human sacrifices and the virgins,' said Barry coming up. 'What are you playing at?'

The Americans did their stint around the rocks, took their photos and waited to see what was next. Barry stepped up.

'Now no one really knows what went on here, but one thing we can be sure of, the Druids used this place for their rituals. And these pagan rituals included human sacrifice.' The crowd went 'Oooh!' and began chattering. 'Not true,' hissed Clive as subtly as he could. Barry raised his voice over them.

'Teenage virgin girls – and they had to be virgins – would be led by the white-cloaked Druids here on a full moon, and on Midsummer's Night, and tied there to what's known as the Slaughter Stone. This was originally a doorway to the circle, if you can use your imaginations for a moment.' Everyone stood stock still and stared. Stray tourists from other groups tried to eavesdrop, Barry taking them in with a glance. 'The teenage virgins, dressed only in thin white cotton gowns, would be prayed over by the tribal elders, who would ask the gods – the sun and the moon and whatever – for good crops this year, then they would ... Huh!' He made a sudden slashing motion with an imaginary knife at the throat of one of the old dears by his side. Everyone gasped and jumped and the little old lady went white, eventually joining in the laughter. 'Their throats would be slit, in a most gruesome fashion. Then, ladies and gentlemen ...' He tried to quieten them. 'There would be feasting and wine drinking, and dancing round the stones by moonlight, and naked revelry, and some people would wear antlers and goats' heads, and this would go on all night, the most massive pagan orgy of the calendar involving all the priests and priestesses and the prettiest young girls of the tribe, and the best warriors of course.'

The tourists were abuzz with excitement and had many questions, such as was it true it still went on today – Barry could only say it was rumoured to, in other parts, but the police had it pretty much under control these days, with the Criminal Whatsit Act. Someone else asked what happened to the naked virgins' bodies, and Barry speculated that they were probably eaten, or worse.

Tut-tutting in the background, Clive huffed and puffed, but no one was taking any notice of him.

Barry went on to explain how it was actually thought by some distinguished scientists that the stones, being so cumbersome and of a type of rock not found anywhere else in the country, may have actually been set up by an alien life form. 'If you look at aerial photographs, the patterns made by the stones are very similar to those where spaceships have landed in the California desert.'

'New Mexico desert,' someone corrected him.

'Thank you,' said Barry graciously. 'Of course we don't have your depth of history of contact with space aliens. Maybe they don't like the food here.'

And with that they all chuckled and began talking excitedly about Area 51, and a white-haired old guy who said he used to be in the Air Force started telling everyone about the time he was flying over Nevada and saw a series of bright lights moving in formation and when he told his commander he was transferred to ground crew for six months and told never to mention it to anyone again, on pain of court martial, and suddenly it was time to head back to the coach via the gift shop, with Barry conspicuously leading the way.

Clive killed some time by getting a cup of tea from the nasty little tea hatch, but eventually he had to face his crowd when he got back on the coach. Most people looked straight through him, still chatting about the virgin sacrifices, cannibalistic orgies and alien abductees' anal probes. He glanced over at the other driver – she was reading. He stared at her for several seconds, until she looked up, right at him, so he quickly looked away. Ray was nowhere to be seen. Eventually, with everyone waiting to go, Ray sauntered over from another coach where he had been talking with a fellow driver. Clive gave him a look but he took no notice.

The drizzle slowed them down a little – that and a three-car pile-up on the A350 – so it was well into the afternoon by the time they rolled into Bath and the punters were hungry again. Clive consulted with Barry and announced that there was a very nice pub down the lane where you could get a bite to eat but, when he led a good forty of them inside, the kitchen was closed. Clive's foggy watch had let him down, stopping over an hour ago.

Most of the people stayed however, Barry having recommended the scrumpy, and they ate crisps and kept out of the rain until it stopped. Clive wandered around until he caught up with the others and decided he would take them around the Roman bath. He explained to them that the actual bath came from a hot spring with a constant temperature of 46 degrees or 115 Fahrenheit, 'which is hotter than most hot tubs'. The Yanks liked that. He also said the Great Bath, which stood before them with its pea-green, lead-lined bottom and marble pillar stumps, was not discovered until the 1870s, and that the fancy changing cabins built around the side showed something of the changing fortunes of the Romans during their four-hundred-year occupancy of Britain. He went on a little too long about how a temple was built to worship Sulis Minerva, a mixture of the original Celtic water goddess Sulis and the Roman Goddess Minerva, when he should have just told them about the Celtic King Bladud rolling in the mud to fix his leprosy, because by the time he got on to the chemical properties of geothermal spring water he had lost most of them. He found them in the museum shop, but they avoided eye contact. He thought he heard someone say something about *him* needing a bath, but wasn't quite sure, and went off to have a surreptitious sniff at his pits.

So that was Bath, thought Clive. To hell with the marvellous Abbey, designed by God in a dream to the Bishop in 1499, with its stone angels climbing Jacob's Ladder to heaven. Never mind the Assembly Rooms, designed by Wood the Younger (younger than the bloke who designed the Circus, the round bit with the tree in the middle) in 1769 and host to many a glittering nob-filled ball. Clive wasn't too bothered, because the Jane Austen *Northanger Abbey* link didn't interest him much either. He took a stroll up Gay Street and along to the Royal Crescent, alone. The sun came out and made the honey-coloured stone look like gold, just the way it was meant to. He wondered who lived in such beautiful, such listed houses, looking for signs of life. A Volvo pulled up and a man got out, fishing for his keys, springing up the steps to his house with a pleasant look on his face. Clive had a sudden urge to call after him and ask him how he did it, how he'd swung it to have so perfect a place to live? The man probably would be greeted by a couple of kids in prospectus-quality school uniforms, and a bob-and-black-leggings wife who runs four miles a day. Clive hesitated, like he always did, fearful of invading another man's space, and the moment was shipped out to the scrapyard of history.

He looked at the curved and neatly railed lawn in front of the Royal Crescent – he liked towns that had boomed and still showed it. And planned towns that were all of a piece. Milton Keynes – now there was a place he was proud to have lived. A perpetual joke to outsiders, it had its advantages for residents, not least that you felt you were always within someone else's plan, within the mind of someone or something bigger than you. Bath was like being invited to someone's country home, everything was built to be beautiful, privately owned but publicly enjoyed, from a discreet distance. He noticed that Queen Victoria's crowd had got their oar in round the corner, building a huge park in 1830. He strolled back to the coach, running into Barry on the way, all the merrier for his three pints of cider.

'So, just time for Windsor Castle, eh?'

'It shuts at five thirty,' said Clive pessimistically.

'Does it? I always get that wrong. Oh well, better hurry up then. My lot are nearly ready. See you there.'

Clive waited by his coach until everyone was back, counting them in. Barry's driver roared out of the car park and they disappeared. He couldn't see how they'd be able to blast along the M4 and see anything of Windsor, and hoped no one would ask him about it.

Everyone seemed to be back except Ray the driver. Clive stood by the steps impatiently, then walked to the corner to search for him. Nothing. Back on board one lady said she had seen him disappear into the coach station, so Clive went looking for him. Nothing. No one had seen Ray.

He went back out again and stood helplessly in the coach park. 'This is ridiculous,' he muttered to himself. He wandered around some more, checking the food stands, asking at the information window if they'd seen a stocky, grey-haired man carrying a tabloid. Nothing. He decided to check the toilet. That was where his kids always ended up when they were missing. Boys smoking or dunking weaklings' heads, girls sobbing at some slight or wracked with cramps.

'Ray? Ray? Are you in here?' He checked the toilet stalls, one at a time, tapping on the door.

'Fuck off!' shouted someone within. Too young to be Ray.

The second-last one was locked. He bent down and saw feet, trousers round ankles. He hammered on the door. *This is it*, he thought. *I'm going in. Why do I always get the shitty jobs?* After a quick glance round he knelt down and looked, just as the other toilet flushed and a youth came out.

'You dirty queer, fuck off out of here!' shouted the lad, bristling and ready to stick the boot in.

Just at that moment Clive let out a yelp.

'Oh my God!'

The lad stopped.

'Oh my God!' was all Clive could say.

'What? What?'

Clive could see Ray's naked shins and thighs, his fallen tabloid, and part of his torso, leaning off to one side.

He stood up. 'He's collapsed. I think he's had a heart attack,' he said to the lad, unafraid. It was his teacherly instinct to be unafraid of anyone younger than him, especially in a crisis. He expected the kid to switch from wanting the beat the shit out of him, to wanting to help. And he did.

'What, what, who's dead?' The lad was excited. This was the real thing. This was security-camera stuff, like the compilation programme he watched every week, *Hidden Cameras of Outrage*.

'Give me a leg up,' ordered Clive, and the boy obliged.

Clive had a good view now of Ray's resting position. His body had fallen to one side and his head rested against the graffiti-covered wall. His eyes were open, his lips were blue lines, like a provincial Goth's. A fat tongue protruded from his mouth,

'Call an ambulance,' ordered Clive, jumping down.

The young man had his mobile out in seconds, and after he had relayed the details – he wasn't sure where they were, so Clive took over at that point – he asked whether they should kick the door down.

'No,' he said. He was a sensible man in an emergency.

'Is he dead?'

'Very possibly.'

'Jesus, fucking hell,' he said with a wide grin.

Pretty soon the word spread and the coach station Gents was bustling with paramedics and rubberneckers. They wheeled Ray to the ambulance and took him away. Clive had to face his people again, most of them straining to get a look and speculating loudly.

'Cardiac arrest? Jeez, so where's the defibrilator? What kind of outfit is this?'

'I hope I don't go here. Are we covered, Honey?'

'I've seen inside their hospitals, I'm tellinya, you don't wanna go here.'

Clive called the office, not knowing what to do. He couldn't drive a coach. Maxine said she'd get the AA to send another driver, they did things like that. She gave him Barry's mobile number so they could co-ordinate Windsor. Clive dialled and got though. He watched in horror as the pennies ticked down on the telephone screen, about one a second, and fumbled for some more change.

Barry didn't sound too bothered about what had happened to Ray. There was an edge of laughter to his voice when Clive to tried to arrange to meet up. Barry reckoned they were nearly there. He could hear happy old voices singing in the background,

> 'Goodbye, Piccadilly, Farewell Leicester Square,
> It's a long, long way to Tipperary,
> But my heart, lies there!'

'Er, OK then. See you there.'

The AA managed to get a driver to them within forty-five minutes, and after much moaning and placating, they set off down the M4. The driver was a stickler, however, and drove at a steady sixty-five miles an hour. Clive didn't attempt to point anything out on the way. He could have come up with something bilious about long-distance commuters, the M4 corridor and the stretching of the metropolis, but didn't think the Americans would be very impressed with the distances involved, reckoning a hundred miles was probably a trip to the outlet mall for most of them anyway.

They rolled up to Windsor Castle at twilight, just as Barry's coach was pulling out. Clive scrambled off and had a word with him.

'What shall I do?'

'Nothing you can do mate, it's all closed up.' Windsor was a sorry little town, dominated by the castle and Eton College, and haunted by the laziest sort of tourist and the keenest stalkerazzi chasing a shot of anything Royal. After dark it felt even more like a suburb of London, like a western Carshalton.

As he was about to leave he offered Clive some advice. 'You'd better offer them their Windsor Castle money back. These Yanks know where every penny goes and they're not afraid to ask for a refund.'

'Where am I going to get ... what, fifty tenners from? Is that what it cost?'

'Well, we paid wholesale of course — two quid a head — but they don't know that. You'll have to get it back from petty cash. Alex will deal with it.'

And with that he was off.

Clive flipped through his wallet counting his remaining change. He decided to come clean with them about the true cost of the non-entrance and hope they understood that business was business. To his surprise, there was some grumbling but a general acceptance that they would have been ripped off anyway, so he just had to go around making change and distributing two-pound coins like an almsgiver.

It was dark when they got off the coach at Victoria. Even the creakiest oldsters resisted Clive's offers of assistance down the stairs.

He was surprised when the driver asked him to sign his timesheet. 'What, are you not going to ask me to pay you too?' he asked bitterly. The driver gave him a dark look. 'Your driver died today and all you can think of is money? It's wankers like you that are ruining this country. Bleeding cowboy!'

Clive was dumbfounded. He was glad he had signed though. He knew he had absolutely no authority, and it felt good being reckless for once. For a second he thought of his own death. If someone came up and shoved his own death warrant in his face, he might just as easily have signed that. Whyever not?

17

Don't S-s-s-s-s-stand So C-c-c-c-c-close to Me

He entered the Shakespeare in search of Barry. He wanted his money back, but he also wanted to put an end to the day. To sign off.

There was Barry, holding court at a side table with his dad, and another young man with the Bergman face, who wore a blue baseball cap with the peak curved sharply. Clive came up behind Barry as he was telling a joke. The others were hanging on every word.

'Two paedophiles were walking down the road one day when they came across a pair of small lacy knickers on the ground. The first one picks them up, smells them and goes, "Ahhhh ... A seven-year-old girl." The other grabs them from him and also takes a smell and goes, "No, no ... Definitely an eight-year-old girl!"

'The two of them are smelling them in turns and arguing. "An eight-year-old!", "No, a seven-year-old!", "Definitely an eight-year-old!" ... and on like this, back and forth. So the local priest walks past and asks them what the commotion is all about. The first paedophile tells the priest, and asks him if he could mediate the argument, so the priest takes the knickers, has a good long sniff, and after pondering for a few moments he looks at the two men and says: "Definitely an eight-year-old girl. But not from my parish!"'

They chuckled and slurped their pints and called him a sick bastard and then laughed some more, and then he turned round.

'Clive. Yeah, he's back! He made it!' Barry was grinning widely. His dad even greeted him with the beginnings of a smile. The other guy looked away, down at his pint.

'You heard? Ray's brown bread!' said Barry excitedly.

'Pardon?' said Clive.

'Ray's dead. Snuffed it. Heart attack. Maxine told me on the mobile.'

'That's terrible,' said Clive, without much feeling. He prepared himself for those who knew Ray to wax eulogistic.

'He was a right cunt that bloke,' said Barry. 'A real moaning bastard. Right from day one he never had a good word for anyone, or anything. I'm glad to see the back of him.'

Barry's dad concurred. 'He was. He was a moaning cunt.'

In disbelief Clive looked to the third man for his contribution, but he just looked around the room.

'Oh, that's me *bravver* Stuart.'

'Pleased to meet you Stuart,' said Clive. He pulled up a chair.

Stuart nodded.

'So listen Barry, I have to get my money back. That's nearly four hundred pounds I'm down for the day.'

'Yeah, yeah, I know, you took a hit, that's not right, that's not right. First thing in the morning you get Alex to pay you back from petty cash.'

'Are you sure he'll have it?'

'Yeah yeah yeah, he's got loads of money in the office. Maxine takes care of it anyway. Ask her, if he's playing silly buggers. Coke is it?'

'Er, Pepsi. Diet.' Clive remembered his nightmare day. The relentless calls for Diet Coke.

He tried to make polite conversation. 'So Stuart, what do you do?'

'Tout,' said his father interrupting. Clive looked at him for more information. 'Tickets,' he added.

Clive decided to stay for just one Pepsi. He had very little to say, so low had he sunk. He just listened to the others talking.

Mainly it was Barry talking about football, kids, traffic and how funny he was (he edited out most of the birds), and the old man chipping in with corrections and historical perspective.

'S-s-s-s-s-same a—gain?' asked Stuart suddenly, getting up to go to the bar.

'Urrpp. Yeah,' said his dad.

'Lager,' said Barry.

'Er, Pepsi. Diet.' said Clive. He didn't want to seem ungrateful.

As soon as the stuttering brother was away, Barry and his dad both looked at Clive for a microsecond to gauge his reaction, but he showed none. He still had his teacherly gift of indifference in the face of inequality. He could have stood before a whole class full of stutterers and listened to them read aloud from Bradford & Kent and waited until every syllable had been dragged out of them. Clive Pointing didn't have much, but he had patience.

They were talking about drivers, and how much the AA replacement would have got paid if he was on overtime.

Suddenly Clive thought of a question. 'That driver you had – who was she?'

'Rose?' said Barry grinning. 'Why do you ask, you crafty bugger?'

'Er, no reason. It just seemed . . .'

'You liked the look of her, didn't you? Come on, out wiv it!'

'Not at all. It just seemed funny to see a young woman driving a coach . . . not that there's anything wrong with that, I mean, I'm all in favour of it . . .'

'Well, I'll save you any bother. She's called Rose, she's told me she lives with her boyfriend, and she's not interested. Personally I think she might be a bit of a lesbian, if you know what I mean – a real tuppence-licker, not just a dabbler. I think she's just waiting to get out.'

'You mean come out?'

'Yeah, yeah, whatever it's called.'

Clive was interested. 'Well how do you figure that, Barry?' he said with a thin-lipped smile. 'Did you ask her out and she said no?' He surprised himself with the harshness of his tone.

Barry leaned back and laughed. 'He's interested! He likes Rose!'

'I don't even know her,' said Clive trying to back out.

'Well, nor do any of us. She's new. She told me she used to be an AA Recovery Man, or Woman I spose, on the bikes. That's why I reckon she's a dyke. Chicks who fix bikes, gotta be. We just phoned the coach company and they sent her along. She'll be getting a bit more work now too, since old Ray kicked the bucket. Naaaar-har-har, naar-har-har!'

When he'd finished laughing, Barry looked him in the eye and said, 'So anyway Clive. You never did tell us why you stopped being a teacher.'

Clive's heart sank. There was no way he could stonewall again. There was something about persistence that overcame his untouchable superiority. Barry wasn't going to let him get away with it this time.

'Yeah, come on, don't keep us in suspenders,' said Ron. All three of them fixed their eyes on him.

'Oh, well, it was a misunderstanding . . .'

'It always is innit? What kind of misunderstanding?'

'All right, I'll tell you.' He took a deep breath. 'I had an affair with a pupil.'

Barry exploded with joy, high-fiving his brother and father. 'See! Told you! Didn't I tell you? How old was she? Was she sixteen?'

'Er, no,' muttered Clive.

Barry let out another cheer. 'Yes! She was under age, wasn't she? Oh yes. Come on then ... how old?'

'Was she fifteen?' asked the dad pushing his old face forward.

Clive blushed. Even his ageing skin was susceptible to a bit of colour. He said nothing.

'Yes!' shouted Barry. 'Told you, didn't I? Schoolgirl.'

It was Stu's turn to ask a question. 'Was she u————nder ...' The wait felt interminable. Finally he got it out. 'F-f-f-f-f-f-fourteen?'

'No she was not!' said Clive, outraged. 'She was fifteen and a bit' he yelped.

'Awww, bollocks, you win Dad,' said Barry, turning his nose up.

Dad was cheering. 'Yeah! Fifteen and a bit-of-all-right. That's a tenner son.'

Barry explained. 'Me old man said he reckoned she was between fifteen and a half and fourteen and a half. He was right.'

'Just out of curiosity,' sniffed Clive, 'what did *you* think?'

'Well, Me brother here Stuart went high – fifteen and a half to sixteen and a half. But that's only cos I'd already taken the low. I had you down in the thirteens.' He grinned. 'So anyway, what was she like? Was she well developed?'

'Some of these youngsters these days,' said Barry's dad. 'Strewth, I've picked 'em up from night clubs at four o'fucking clock in the morning and they're all dolled up, and we get talking and it turns out they're only fourteen, less sometimes. Push-up bras, lipstick, the lot of it.'

'So how come you never did any time? That's what I wanna know,' said Barry, wreathed in smiles. 'Cos I can tell you ain't seen the inside of a prison.'

'Er, well ... the school dealt with it. But you make it sound so sordid, it wasn't like that, it was ...'

'Beautiful!' And Barry exploded with laughter again. 'Naaaar-har-har, naar-har-har! Yeah, that's what they all say.'

'Ah, what do you bloody know?' snapped Clive getting up. 'She was a nice girl, and mature for her age, I made a mistake, it's over with. I wish people would just leave me in peace.'

'I wish you'd left me a piece,' said Barry and they all laughed again. Barry stood up too. 'Where are you going? Come on, sit down, sit down we're only having a laugh. Siddown!'

'S-s-s-s-sit down,' said Stuart, waving him back.

Clive didn't know what to do with himself. He didn't want to head back to Streatham. He didn't want to stay and be the whipping boy. He felt like mocking Stuart's stammer, just to restore the order of things, but a second later he realised that would be a bad idea. He'd learned his lesson, you don't take on families.

'Come on, stop feeling sorry for yourself,' said Barry. 'You only did what any bloke would do. Given the chance. Here's your tenner, Dad – it's your round an' all.' After a few more chuckles and cradle-snatcher jibes, the family settled back into a pattern of listening to Barry and arguing. It was dark outside now and the pub had peaked. The syncopated traffic rhythms of the Shakespeare meant it was dead again by ten o'clock. The juke box ran out of plays, so Barry went over, coming back smirking into his pint.

'This is it, this is it!' he nudged everyone as his song came on. Clive knew what it was in the first four bars. It was his era, and it was his theme song. It was The Police.

> 'Young teacher, the subject
> Of schoolgirl fantasy,
> She wants him so badly
> Knows what she wants to be,
> Inside her there's longing
> This girl's an open page,
> Book marking – she's so close now
> This girl is half his age.'

Then they all joined in the chorus, drunkenly caterwauling . . .

> 'Don't stand, don't stand so
> Don't stand so close to me
> Don't stand, don't stand so
> Don't stand so close to me . . .'

They were all on drinker's time, and Clive was in his sepia purgatory, with nowhere to look but down into his Pepsi. He tried to see the funny side, but it was fleeting. Pubs made no sense to him sober. Barry's batteries of laughter, his dad's snorts and wrinkly smiles, the stuttering brother's tentative persecution ...

'Pleeease, don't, s-s-s-s-s-s-s-tand, so, close, to, close-to-me!'

Clive politely waited till the song had ended before excusing himself. He had a skinful of Pepsi to piss up the wall. When he got back from the toilets he decided he'd had enough. He said his goodnights — his goodbyes, in fact, as he didn't think he'd be coming back. They were all suddenly nonchalant, barely acknowledging him, consumed with their drinking.

He stepped out into the night air. He still couldn't face the train so he took a walk down to the River Thames. Vauxhall Bridge Road was too depressing, too wide and straight and over-illuminated, so he wound his way through the side streets, past a playground, Grosvenor Estate, Westminster Hospital, until he came to Lambeth Bridge. He walked out along the short bridge, stopping to look at the water swishing by backwards. It was a flood tide, the natural flow reversed, running away from the sea. This was the best time to throw oneself into the jaws of death, to be turned head over heels by the opposing currents. The core of water at the bottom of the river would still be flowing out to sea while the vast flood of sea water was rushing upstream.

It didn't frighten him. And yet, Clive knew that this wasn't the time for killing himself. On the other hand, it certainly was a project he could come back to. He continued across the bridge to the south bank to find a Tube that might vaguely connect with his railway line.

18

Guided by Voices

Clive spent the next few days getting his things in order. As luck would have it, when he shuffled in from his disastrous daytrip to the historic south west of England at 1.30 a.m. he found a note on his door from the Metropolitan Police, telling him he had been burgled. Danny came down. He hadn't heard anything – he'd been in and out – but he called the cops on seeing that Clive's door had been kicked in.

They went inside together and saw that his boxes had been upturned, his drawers yanked out and his clothes pulled from their hangers. Danny was surprised that he took it so well.

'I didn't have anything valuable anyway,' said Clive, with a hollow laugh he'd never heard himself do before. 'My ex-wife got all that.'

'Ugh, look at this.' Danny pointed to the corner at a dark-brown stool, tapered at one end, bobbly at the other. 'That's a really British thing to do, isn't it? I've read about this in crime magazines, but only here?'

Without a word, Clive wiped it up with some pages torn from *ES* magazine, like he was a good citizen cleaning up after a dog.

Feeling sorry for Clive, the Kiwi offered to let him sleep upstairs on his couch till the door was fixed. He was concerned about gangsters. But to Clive the thought of being any nearer the bed on which they made their noisy love didn't appeal. He thanked Danny and said goodnight.

The next day he calculated that the only things of value he'd lost were his passport and his wedding ring, which had been by the sink. He didn't mind since he wasn't married and he wasn't going anywhere.

Days went by, and Clive slipped into paralysis. The coppers didn't even bother coming back about the burglary. He had a few calls for Dave but nothing from SLF or Britannia, for which he was grateful. He tried to get money out on his Visa and MasterCard but found they had been stopped. This gave him pause for thought. Killing himself was on the cards, but he had a flash of guilt — what if he didn't really deserve suicide?

What if his life wasn't bad enough to be ended by his own hand?

What about the schizophrenic, guided by voices to the parapet, who launches himself into the water? What about the person with real depression, clinical depression, not these feeble bourgeois blues? Depression where your body feels like lead every morning and it takes a heroic effort just to drag yourself to the shower? Depression where night time is dreaded because it ushers in long hours of insomnia and pain that make the soul itself ache. What about the person with a terminal disease who faces medieval torture at a cellular level? What about the abused and kicked around, those repeatedly abandoned by their families, for whom death really does seem like a logical end to an accidental existence? What about the grand criminal wracked by Judas-scale guilt? When it came to the circles of earthly hell that resulted in suicide, Clive wasn't even on the map. And yet, and yet, he could imagine all his minor pains and his view of an empty horizon adding up to something. Reason enough to take his leave of Earth. Maybe the bar had been lowered for that too.

He spent more days mooning about his flat, looking out of the window, thinking about his life, getting more and more depressed. How wrong it had all gone. The cellos followed him around, deep and insistent. At one point he had to go out and find something to eat, ending up at McDonald's eating cartoon food while sitting at plastic furniture, and he felt even sorrier for himself. The old Clive who had held his own at dinner parties against the neoconservatives and the champagne socialists, who had swept a woman off her feet and charmed her father, who had cracked the housing market at the first attempt with his instinct for profitable gentrification … he was reduced to this, breaking his last twenty so he could eat with Streatham's attention-deficient, sugar-high pre-schoolers and their hot-tempered parents.

In the afternoon he sat down and looked in his A–Z for a decent bridge to throw himself off. If he was going upstream on a flood tide he decided he'd like somewhere with a bit of scope for travel. Blackfriars looked like the best bet — that way he would probably die in some ancient spot, such as Charing Cross, or right outside the Palace of Westminster. If he did float for a few yards, at least the scenery would be nice — Cleopatra's Needle, the South Bank (whose architecture he had always stuck up for), the strands of lights along the Embankment. One bend was enough though – he hoped he wouldn't get as far as Lambeth Bridge. He also liked the look of Blackfriars (the road bridge of course, there was no way he was shuffling out on that rail bridge) because it pointed due north. Blackfriars Road had good *feng shui*, not that he really believed in that crap but Tina had a book on it, because it ran south to end at the six-pointed node of St George's Circus. He quite liked that chunk of London around Waterloo, the Cut, the Eurostar terminal – all the stuff that suffered from south-of-the-river stigma even though it was practically in the West End.

With that settled, he rang Tina and left a message saying he wanted to talk to her and to Tess, and that he'd be at his mother's in the evening.

He also rang Britannia and talked to Maxine. He asked her if she would send on his money, but make sure it was in a cheque payable to 'CASH' since he wasn't sure about his bank account, muttering something about it being frozen. He hoped the money would find its way to Tess if it wasn't used up in funeral expenses. He realised that ideally his body should never be found. That would really save some money.

Around 5 p.m. he set out on the topological tangle of the journey to his mother for the last time. He knew he was going to say goodbye to her, but knew that it was too little too late. Most of her mind had slipped away months ago, when he was still explaining to her how irrational her fears were. Every time he looked at himself he found new things to despise – here was the late-breaking news that he had learned nothing from having a child of his own.

When he got there, Gordon was keen to get down the pub. He had his arrows in his hand – the darts team had finally accepted him as a stand-in while one of the regulars was 'in the Scrubs' as Gordon put it, with the satisfaction of a novice namedropper.

'Er, Gordon, I ... I just want you to know, if anything happens to one of us, the other will ...'

He was out the door before Clive could finish.

'Oh! Have you come for the recycling?' said his mother looking up from the sofa.

She was wearing a flowery housecoat. The Pointings had always had a cleaning lady, wherever they lived. His mother wore skirts and lambswool polo necks with pearls around the house, not a housecoat. When she cooked or did her tidying, an apron. And when she gardened, wellingtons, gloves, and an old pair of his father's trousers that made her backside look big. He suspected the housecoat was Gordon's doing, but couldn't complain, considering the ignominy he had planned for himself.

'Hello mother, it's Clive,' he said quietly.

'Oh.' She looked sheepishly at him. 'You look just like your father.'

'Do I?' asked Clive, rather pleased.

'Yes, you have his eyes ...' She stared at him, then said brightly, 'He'll be home any minute, he must be working late.'

'No Mum ...' He stopped himself. He couldn't make her go through that again. 'Anyway, what are we having for supper?'

She smiled and went into great detail about a lovely piece of sole she had bought, and the lemon and butter sauce she had made, but on further questioning it turned out the year was 1970.

Clive let her ramble for a while, then did the crossword with her. Or rather, for her. Her synapses were sparking at random, but not in a useful way. As the evening wore on she launched into disconnected lines of poetry, which Clive encouraged, like someone blowing on a spark and producing tiny tongues of flame.

He rummaged in a box and found a fat anthology. He flicked through looking for something to read aloud to her. 'Wordsworth, Mum, do you like him?'

'Oh him. He's all right. A bit of a moaner though. And quite an old Tory at the end.'

Clive read silently for a minute. 'Listen to this then. It's called "To Milton". Is that the Milton, you know, wrote, er ...'

'Oh Clive. *Paradise Lost!* What do they teach you at that school? I'll have to have a word with your teacher.'

'Here, listen.' He read:

> '"Milton! thou should'st be living at this hour:
> England hath need of thee: she is a fen
> Of stagnant waters: altar, sword, and pen,
> Fireside, the heroic wealth of hall and bower,
> Have forfeited their ancient English dower
> Of inward happiness. We are selfish men.
> Oh! raise us up, return to us again;
> And give us manners, virtue, freedom, power.
> Thy soul was like a star, and dwelt apart:
> Thou hadst a voice whose sound was like the sea:

Pure as the naked heavens, majestic, free,
So didst thou travel on life's common way,
In cheerful godliness; and yet thy heart
The lowliest duties on herself did lay."'

'I like that,' he said. '"She is a fen of stagnant waters." That's how I feel.'

Tina rang. Clive couldn't speak long as his mother kept hissing at him to keep the phone line clear in case his father called. He persuaded her to put Tess on. He wanted to hear her babbling happily like she used to, but instead she was churlish. All she would say was Jeffrey had bought Off Peaks for all three of them. He'd seen Off Peaks in a shop in Streatham – they were cheap Chinese mountain bikes. She handed him back to her mother without saying goodbye, completing his broken heart.

His mother took the book off him and went off on another poem. She read the first few lines, but continued from memory, her small wrinkled mouth forming the words theatrically.

'"Fear no more the heat o' the sun
    Nor the furious winter's rages;
Thou thy worldly task hast done,
    Home art gone, and ta'en thy wages.
Golden lads and girls all must,
As chimney-sweepers, come to dust.

'"Fear no more the frown o' the great,
    Thou art past the tyrant's stroke;
Care no more to clothe, and eat;
    To thee the reed is as the oak:
The sceptre, learning, physic, must
All follow this, and come to dust.

'"Fear no more the lightning flash;
    Nor the all-dreaded thunder-stone;
Fear not slander, censure rash;
    Thou hast finished joy and moan:
All lovers young, all lovers must
Consign to thee, and come to dust.

'"No exorciser harm thee!
Nor no witchcraft charm thee!
Ghost unlaid forbear thee!
Nothing ill come near thee!
Quiet consummation have;
And renowned be thy grave."'

'Let's see that book, Mum . . . Shakespeare? Oh.'
Gordon came in at 11.
'You're early,' said Clive vacating the good chair.
'Fucking bollocks.'
'What happened?'
'Lost,' said Gordon, turning the TV up.
'Oh.' Clive didn't want to get into a discussion about darts, a subject
he knew nothing about. Especially this late in his life.
'Well, Mother, I'll be off now . . .' He paused. He was surprised how
little sadness he felt. She had already slipped away, and now it was just
his turn. His mother was watching telly. Clive put his arms around her
neck for a full ten seconds and kissed her, saying goodbye. As he left he
touched his brother lightly on the shoulder, who shrugged it off.
'Bye Gordon. Take care.'
'Hmph.'
He was lucky, the Tube was just pulling in as he got to the platform.
The silver train was almost empty heading into the West End, and it
had the end-of-day feeling to it. A Lucozade bottle rolled back and forth
across the grooved floor. A drunken young salaryman lolled and lurched
with the corners. Two trendy Asian girls talked animatedly, giggling and
mocking people on the platform. You could tell London was a media
capital – the carriage looked like a bomb had gone off in a newspaper bag.
There were bits of discarded journalism everywhere – giant flapping pages
of broadsheet, slippery advertising supplements, miniature TV guides and
going-out guides, blow-in cards from magazines, whole redesigned sections
balled up between seats, and fanned-out tabloids covered in footprints.
Someone got on and cleared a shred of *Evening Standard* off his seat, tossing
it across the car. It landed at Clive's feet and caught his eye: 'WONGA
LEISURE GOES BUST' read the headline. 'Hundreds face axe'.

Clive smiled, not bothering to read any more. That cleared up any
doubt there. It all made sense now. Everything was winding down. It was
time for him to shut up shop. This particular Pointing franchise was on

the outs. The brand name might continue, but it was time for Clive to close down.

He lay in bed listening to the radio one last time. He caught the end of a story, a bedtime story for all the nice people tucked-in across the country. It was read by an actress – it sounded like a Redgrave – with an *incredible* accent, upper class with injections of RADA, all magnified tenfold. She pronounced not just every syllable, but every consonant too. The voice mesmerised him. He felt like she had to be physically restrained from sounding the 'b' in 'climb' or the 'gh' in 'night'.

After that he listened to the Shipping Forecast, and heard the 'Sailing By' music pulling his heart strings one last time. Then he turned off his radio and slept.

The next day he took the train into town and jumped off Blackfriars Bridge into the river.

PART 2

Clive Live

The embarrassing thing is, I knew it was a mistake before I'd even hit the water. As soon as I stepped off the ledge and felt my balance go, I regretted jumping. I could have kicked myself, if I wasn't fifty foot up in the air flailing my arms and going 'Woooooaaaa!'

There's a lot of bollocks talked about jumping in the Thames, like it's this infernal place no one ever gets out of alive. To me the worst bit was the trip down. Thirty-two metres per second squared gives me the heebie-jeebies. People queue three deep for hours at Blackpool and Alton Towers for that feeling, paying good money too. And they're right. It scares the shit out of you. Metaphorically, of course. So with the water rushing up at me, and me thinking 'Hang on a minute, I've changed my mind about dying,' I only have about a quarter of a second to shut my mouth and take a deep breath, because who knows what's down there? There could have been great blocks of stone to smash myself on, coiled wire to snag my legs, old fishing nets, pipelines, sunken boats . . . I don't know. I should know because I'm . . . *was* a Geography teacher, but for a moment, I didn't. You know what fear does to your mind, you'd forget your mother's name if you were scared enough.

Luckily I went in straight and the soles of my shoes took the impact.

There's a lot of bollocks talked about jumping in the Thames, but one thing they're right about, it's dark as fuck down there. I landed like one of those aquatic birds you see on nature documentaries diving for fish, the way they come arrowing down and enter the water in a silver cloak of air, trailing bubbles after them, rapidly decelerating. That's another thing – the force of impact on the water isn't going to kill you. Maybe if you went off the Golden Gate Bridge, or the Humber – somewhere really high. But not poxy Blackfriars.

I reckon I was about twenty feet under water before my velocity reached zero – that's just like slamming on the brakes in a car, and who gets hurt in a car these days? Especially now everyone's got airbags, and side impact bars, and wings designed to crease. It's not a big deal. The big deal, like I said, is the darkness. I was thrashing about looking for the light and couldn't see a thing. It genuinely put the shits up me – I was tumbling around, not knowing which way was up, with about five seconds more air until my lungs rebelled and I had to gulp.

The good thing is – and not a lot of people know this – humanity divides fifty-fifty into sinkers and floaters. An expert told me – a river copper in fact. Try it next time you go to the swimming pool. Relax and see if you sink or float. I'm lucky, I turned out to be a floater. So as I was spinning around in the dark, not knowing which was up or down, I started drifting upwards.

Not before I'd felt the force of the water though. I was borne along by it, like on a moving pavement at the airport, swifter than the speed of walking. Now that was frightening. That was the bit I had hoped would kill me, so naturally, now that I'd changed my mind about dying I found it a bit worrying. I thought I was a gonner when I took a gulp and breathed in a load of water, that really hurt. That's like breathing in burning plastic fumes, the salty water getting down into your throat and windpipe, down further into the little branches of your lungs … it's really disgusting. But like I said, I was lucky – I am lucky – my natural buoyancy brought me back to the top. I'd never been so happy to see the pale light of London's sky above me as when I looked up and saw the surface of the water, five feet away.

And the sound down there – it's a soft roar, like distant traffic noise, which I can only guess is made by the stones being rolled along the river bed and the sound of boat engines. Sounds like those would carry well in the water and merge with each other. If you want to know what it sounds like, stick your head in a fish tank that has a pump. Or in the toilet cistern when it's filling up, if you can find one big enough. It's pretty creepy. Adds to the underworldy atmosphere.

One other thing I must point out – you also hear a lot of crap about the currents in the Thames. The water naturally speeds up under bridges to compensate for the displacement caused by the buttresses, and there are eddies too, just after the buttresses. So it *is* possible to get sucked in and whacked on the head or pulled under there. But that's about it. The stuff about everyone getting sucked under? Overrated. I used to tell my kids about the Mississippi, about what a fantastically complex body of water it is, how heavy with silt, how unstable, how wide, and how people would hear weird bangings on the bottom of their boats from the currents, which scared the shit out of them and made them think of dead men trying to rise, angry river spirits trying to capsize their craft ... well all that's true as far as I know (I only read about it in *National Geographic*, I didn't *go* there). But it's not true for the Thames. Old Father Thames, at least where I went in, is a pensioner sitting in his cardigan watching TV and grumbling about the price of things. He's not about to throw a fucking wobbler. In fact the biggest danger is being hit by river traffic. You could have some garbage barge or booze cruise plough right over your head without anyone knowing it, and if you didn't get your back broken by the bow you'd be chopped liver by the time the propellers finished with you. Just think of all those people dancing on the poop deck to the sounds of the Eighties while your last breath consists of salt water and your head is split open like a watermelon. Is that how you want to go?

I was fighting for the light. I had a stinging in my chest and more than a few worries. It seemed to be taking for ever, but I was fighting to get to the surface. You see, the terrible thing I realised just as I jumped – right at the moment I jumped, as soon as I lost my balance, was that this was a very silly idea. This was a terrible waste of life. I was right to doubt my eligibility for suicide – there were plenty more people in the queue ahead of me. There were probably millions of people worse off than me who struggled through the day with more dignity than I. I mean really, what fucking right did *I* have to be throwing my life away, apart from the obvious and pathetic right of ownership? It's embarrassing when I think about it. I can feel the heat of my cheek against the cool water right now as I think about it.

That's another thing about tossing yourself into the Thames. In winter, it's the hypothermia that kills you. (By winter I mean those six months in the south east when all streams run bitterly cold.) Three minutes is all it takes to chill you to a rag doll. I should have pointed that out before. So yes, it is a good place to kill yourself, but not the way you'd think.

This policeman, he told me some other stuff. For instance, the people who are *really* determined fill their pockets with stones, or tie bricks to their ankles. I thought he might be having a dig at me, calling me a lightweight or something. He also said a lot of people have a few drinks beforehand to get their courage up. I said that didn't really apply to me, since I didn't drink, but now that he mentioned it, a pint sounded like a great idea. He wasn't having a go at me at all really, I think he was just bored with his job and wanted to tell me some insider info, you know how people get. For instance, the ones who are dragged out pickled in brine and blended whisky are not to be confused with the knobheads who get pissed in riverfront pubs like the Founder's Arms in Southwark, or the Star and Garter in Putney, and then try and swim to the other bank to prove to their mates how hard they are. (Now that I mention this, I remember meeting a mad Aussie once who did this in Paris in the Seine, only he wrapped a large chain around his torso. Just to prove he was extra hard. He made it across too. But the next day he had a massive eye infection, some awful sewage bacteria had slipped under his lid and bred a busting colony. 'The French birds didn't like that,' he told me, laughing his Aussie head off.)

You know what else is bollocks? That thing about your whole life flashing before your eyes as you drown. I think I got pretty close and all I thought about was getting the fuck out. Actually I can remember *exactly* what I thought about:

What a prat I am.

This is scary – which way is up?

I wonder what Tess would think if she could see me now?

Does the Coriolis Force apply in this case?

The Coriolis Force is named after the nineteenth-century French physicist who formalised the concept of the Earth's deflecting force – the apparent deflection of moving air to the right in the northern hemisphere. It also applies to ocean currents, and I was just wondering if it applied to me and the water surrounding me as we bowled along. It's one of those bits of fluid dynamics you tell your pupils about and then you immediately say 'But of course you don't need to know this until you're at university,' and since not a single person I ever taught went on to do a Geography degree, it was pretty redundant.

I was lucky, I am lucky. I came bursting out of the water and into the light with a great gasp, a loud heaving that you'd have thought people on the river bank would have been able to hear. There were no boats coming – I'd checked before I jumped, because obviously I didn't want to tangle with the traffic. I'd have gone off a bridge over the MI otherwise. No, I wanted a watery death, a tragic death that would see my corpse picked up by the police and my story picked up by the papers.

That was a stupid idea. Such vanity.

For the first half minute back at the surface I could only just keep my head above water, and all I could see was the sky, the old grey lid on London, and God, was it beautiful. Never has the arse-end of a pile of cumulus looked so good to me. Once I got my breath I got my bearings – I saw the dome of St Paul's.

I have to admit to something really embarrassing at this point. Although I had intended to jump in on a flood tide to get the benefit of the subversive turbulence, all the better to kill myself, well . . . I ended up going the other way. I misread the tidal data in the paper. I know, I'm a teacher, I'm supposed to get these things right, but . . . But anyway, when I get to the Thames on this cloudy but warm June afternoon, a regular working weekday, the first thing I notice is the fucking water's flowing the wrong way. Or the right way I suppose – right out to sea. It's not even a high ebb tide – it looks as if it's on the way down already.

To use Barry's word, I felt like such a prannet. I didn't want to wait about for another eight hours, just to end it all, so I decided to go for it. And there I was, minutes later, bobbing like a buoy cut loose, heading for East London.

You've probably noticed, if only from the credits for *Eastenders*, that East London is very big, and that the river in particular goes into grand spasms of meandering after Wapping. It also gets very wide – especially around all those horrible places you don't want to go – Limehouse, Millwall, Blackwall, the wharves down at Woolwich . . . that copper in fact told me that the mud down there is pretty dangerous, like quicksand. They've found people in so deep that all they can see is the tops of their heads and they have to pull them out like newborns with giant forceps. All that stuff down there gives me the creeps, the scale of things is so monumental. I don't know if you've ever swum out to sea somewhere where it's clean, and seen the underside of a yacht at anchor. Well that's the creepy feeling I had – dwarfed by man-made things, which are in turn dwarfed by nature. I wanted to get out.

I was still coughing and spluttering and being borne along by the tide, but it didn't take a lot of brains to see I just had to head for the riverbank. I'm not saying the current isn't strong – but it's not impossible to go against the grain. That's another thing about suicides, they must be really up for it. If they float do they swim towards the bottom again? I mean, I just swam to the bank and got out. First though I had to let Southwark Bridge and Cannon Street rail bridge past. It was a bit frightening, the way things sped up under there. The water was all brown and choppy, and it was echoing off the concrete and steel. I was also worried about pitching up on the south bank, I just didn't fancy it. Southwark — what a place to end up. By swimming as hard as I could I made it between the river wall and the first support of London Bridge, and then skimmed along the wall looking for some steps or a ladder. It was like trying to hop a freight train. Or so I've read in *National Geographic*.

I could see the railing and the trees about fifteen feet above my head, and presumably there were pedestrians the other side of the wall going about their day. I wonder why no one just looked over and saw me? I guess my head was just a pink dot in a river of grey. Way over to the right was the battleship HMS Belfast hogging half the river, and ahead of that was Tower Bridge. I like Tower Bridge. Typical Victorian engineering — they used steam power to lift the drawbridges, then clad the whole structure in mock-Gothic brickwork. The metal walkway high up between the two towers was closed for most of the century due to its popularity with prostitutes and ... guess who? That's right. Suicides. I didn't fancy going under there either.

I was going to make a grab for one of these big wooden things sticking out of the water, they look like wigwams made of railway sleepers, with a concrete block on top. Who knows what it was, there's an awful lot of weird stuff out there when you start looking. But then I saw some steps leading right down into the water, so I started splashing over that way and suddenly kicked the floor and I was home free. I just sort of paddled the last bit and collapsed on the second step from the bottom in all my soaking tweeds and worsted wool. I remember spitting out a load of salty water and leaning forward on my knees like a Saturday-night drunk, then I rolled over on my back exhausted and looked up at the sky.

I was thinking 'Well here I am, back again. Clive Pointing, Mark II. This time it's going to be different.'

It must have been ten minutes before I heard the squish-squish of a pair of size eleven Doc Martens heading my way. Two blue serge legs and a tunic appeared above my head, and a face leaned over and casually said, 'Have we been playing silly buggers in the river then?'

That's it. No mouth to mouth (not that I wanted it anyway), no chopper to the hospital, not even an 'Are you all right?' Just a sarky City of London copper. I should have known.

He said he was going to arrest me for trespass but I talked him out of it. I told him I fell. My foot slipped.

He escorted me to the street where I leaned against the wall, dripping, while he got on the radio. After a bit of back and forth and much crackling, he let me go with a telling off. He said if he caught me down there again he'd 'throw me in the clink'. The clink! I nearly told him, the Clink's now a museum, and it's on the other side of the river, but I didn't want to push my luck. I wanted to ask him where he'd got the word 'clink' – was it passed around at Hendon, or did he get it off an old black and white film? But that was something I'd learned off Barry – don't wind up a copper when he's about to let you go. He says the time for that is when you're nicked and a bit of verbal can't make much difference.

So I set off walking west along Lower Thames Street, back the way I'd just come. It was a joy to see tourists all around – Gore-Tex jackets, chunky boots, khaki shorts with patch pockets, fleecy tops, sun hats, head scarves, greybeards, blondes, mousies, baldies, happy couples, stoic retirees, stout burghers, uncertain teenagers, soul-searching American women travelling solo . . . I could understand Barry's point of view now. I was walking with my back straight and the possibility of a smile on my face, and a BMW with tinted windows went by with a reggae tune thumping out from the passenger side, 'Head high, head held high . . .' That tipped me over into a smile, right as one of those women was walking past, she looked about forty, Mediterranean, she had deep, dark brown eyes and she smiled right back at me.

Everything seemed so different to me, so foreign. The stone of the river walls, the old buildings converted into offices, the drivers rushing by in their right-hand drive vehicles . . . I wanted to look in every window and ask, 'Who works here? Who lives here?' And stop every van driver, 'Where are you going, what are you carrying?' Doubtless they would have all told me to *fack orf* but I still felt like asking. Just being alive felt like a huge bonus.

I had nowhere to go so I just wandered round the City until I crossed into the Temple area and remembered my lawyer, my useless barrister Marion. It was afternoon by now and although I had mostly dried off – I was still a bit damp around the crotch and armpits, and had to carry my tweed jacket over my arm – I did look a bit rough. I saw myself in a shop window and I looked soiled, even though I didn't feel it. And there she was walking around the quadrangle talking to some other wigged poseur, a beanpole of a man, carrying files in their arms like a students.

'Hey Mrs Mound! Wait a minute!' She looked around and paused until she saw me coming then tried to hurry off. They were like two people afraid of being mugged, but I caught up with them.

'Mrs Mound, it's me, Clive Pointing. You're handling my case, remember?'

She started giving me the old 'I'm not at liberty to discuss it' line so I told her, I know the meter's not running but I think you should know I'm prepared to do whatever it takes to regain my right to see my daughter, including working two jobs, giving up alcohol, seeing a counsellor, whatever. And then she nearly took my breath away. She said, 'Well, you can start by having a bath,' and then she started walking away.

'That's it? That's all you have to say for yourself? Have a bath? You know what, missus? You're sacked. You're off the case.' That's what I said to her. She didn't even look round. I wasn't even sure she'd heard me. It's weird the way the law works.

I could see a security guard heading my way so I raised my arms and started backing off, and left by the other exit. It didn't bother me too much though. If that was the Establishment – Laurel and Hardy in wigs and a bloke who could probably earn more money looking for shoplifters in Top Shop – I wasn't impressed. I wasn't frightened either, for once.

I drifted north through some Yards and Lanes until I came to Lincoln's Inn Fields. Here's another legal industry stronghold, only this one's been taken over by dossers and bag ladies. The place where you would sit on sunny lunchtimes to have your chicken-breast sandwich and fat-free foaming latte is ruled by red-faced tramps who brawl over the dregs of sherry bottles or, on particularly fine days, take their shirts off and squeeze the spots on each other's backs. They've built little cabins on the grass from pallet planks and polythene sheeting, with adequate parking space for shopping trolleys stuffed with carrier bags. You can barely sit down for a minute without someone giving you a sob story as a prelude to asking for cash.

I sat down on a bench. Some bloke about fifty-five, already tanned, his stubble was turning white and his nose hair yellow, came over and started giving me the old story. He had a long black coat on like he was out of central casting for tramps, but he had a sense of propriety. He was trying not to get too close to me, as if he'd blow his chances if he violated my personal space. I just smiled at him and said, 'Look mate, I'm broke myself, if anyone needs any spare change . . .' He'd already turned away. The word must have shot around the tramp community because they left me alone, let me sit there and watch the world go by.

The funny thing is, about every hundredth person to pass me dropped a few coins at my feet or even forced them into my hand. Maybe they could read me – middle-class chap, down on his luck? Help him rejoin the job market, help him put his nuclear family back together again. I wasn't even trying and I was doing well. The light was fading when I started to feel peckish for the first time. With my six pounds thirty two chinking in my trouser pocket I took a walk up Kingsway and across to the Tottenham Court Road to the only fish and chip shop I knew – I'm surprised I knew any actually, Christina banned them. You should have heard the outburst when I took Tess for chips one time when she was little. She loved them so much she blabbed to her mother, despite my warnings, and the shinola really hit the fan. After that we were interrogated, separately, about what we ate after every outing we took together. Maybe Tina should have been a copper? Or a lawyer.

I lined up with the others – kids on their way to a concert, a cab driver, a skateboarder and a full-on fatty – leaning against the hot glass, staring in at the offerings. The Greek scooped me out a triple hopper of pale golden chips and threw on a huge curling cod. I don't remember what it cost, other than to say it seemed a lot more than it used to, but as soon as I tasted it I knew it was the best meal I had ever tasted. I bit the chips in half and watched their floury insides steaming, and the cod oozed hot fumes from under its bronze batter coat and warmed my lips. I stood in the street devouring them, transported back to Folkestone, to a time when I had just come back from France. I'd been on holiday with some university friends. It had all gone wrong and I was hitch-hiking back alone. Coming home was the best part of that holiday. I didn't mind being stuck on the south coast for a few hours, once I heard the first southern accents of the ferry workers. By the time I tasted the sticky inside of the batter and felt the vinegar fumes tickle my nostrils I was ready to kiss the tarmac.

It was dark now and the streets had changed completely. There were thousands of young people hurrying by on their way to pubs and restaurants, good-looking people dressed for summer, as though they were on a night out in one of Barry's resorts. I went into the first pub I saw, the Wheatsheaf just on Oxford Street, walked straight up to the bar and ordered a pint of bitter. Again it hit me – how lovely it tasted, and how lucky I was to live in this country. The bar was packed. I couldn't find a place to put my pint down, so after I'd drunk a long draught, I just stood there holding on to it.

When the alcohol hit my brain it all came back to me – the feeling of bonhomie (why isn't there an English word for that?), the optimism, my imagination soaring, the lovely way the music on the juke box spoke to me without language. If anyone was bothered at seeing a forty-four-year-old bloke standing alone in a crowded pub sinking a Speckled Hen, they didn't let on.

I felt so good I had another pint, and felt even better.

This pub had some crap on the walls too. It gave me an idea for a business: a prop service for kitting out pubs with stuff for people to look at when they're getting pissed. There was a row of books at basketball-player height. There was one my mother read to us when we were just teenagers: *As I Walked Out One Morning*. I couldn't see who it was by, but I do know how he felt. You just want to walk out of your little village in the summer warmth and see where life takes you – getting pissed, chatting to strangers, sleeping under hedgerows ... that's how I felt on this first night of true freedom.

If you're wondering where flaming June went, well that's what I'm telling you. This is how the summer began for me, Clive Pointing.

Feeling no compulsion to go back to Streatham, I wandered around until I found myself back at Lincoln's Inn Fields and sat down on my bench again, which was the only one that wasn't occupied by a snoring dosser. There was a different atmosphere in there now – sort of like a big scout camp, or night time in a boarding-school dorm. People were hunkered down in their bashes or under their blankets. There was the sound of muttered conversations in the dark, and I'm sure I heard the grunting of two tramps fucking. Maybe there are tramp babies born to tramp parents? Though I don't know how some of these fellows can get it up after a long day on the Special Brew and a diet of dustbin burgers. The human body is a miraculous thing. Apparently though, it's worse for their health when they come off the dustbin food. When they stop drinking McDonald's Cola dregs and eating panini stumps covered in people's saliva, sores and snot and teeming with fly eggs and whatever shakes out of a pigeon's armpit, when they start to detoxify, that's when they get ill. That's when everything hits them, when their defences are lax.

I had a pupil once who theorised that in cities in summertime, bees make honey from the leftover pop found in litter bins in the street. This pupil even claimed that you could identify different flavours of honey by region – Irn Bru in Scotland, Panda Cola in poor English neighbourhoods, and other variations in Coke and Pepsi. For a brief moment we proposed a joint survey with the biology department, mapping the bees' territory and classifying their output. But nothing ever came of it. That was my brush with originality. After that I went back to being a normal teacher.

The human body is a miraculous thing, and mine was getting sleepy. A warm front was working its way in, it was mild as day. I lay on my bench with nothing for a pillow and looked up at the clouds, which were lit from behind and then pierced by the lights of aeroplanes descending and heading for Gatwick and Heathrow.

No headache. No hangover. No beatings during the night. No robbery (I still had my wallet, albeit smeared with river silt). No bad dreams. No arrest for vagrancy (I'm not even sure if that's a crime, I'd have to ask a copper). No one pissed on me or tried to set me on fire. In fact when I woke up at half seven the next morning, I'd gained a sandwich. Someone had squeezed it into the crook of my arm. One time I would have thought this was because they didn't like to give tramps cash because they just go out and spend it on Special Brew. Now I reckon it might have been a way of giving me the whole value of a sandwich, since the bulk of the cost of a product these days seems to be distribution. Time is money, even for winos. I don't know. It was delicious anyway – cheese and ham on wholemeal bread, just like Tina used to buy, the expensive brown stuff.

I wasn't even that cold – there's a miracle for England in early June. And you know how it's darkest just before the dawn? Well it isn't. And another thing: 'Red sky at night?' – that's a load of shite. Red sky in the morning – this is your last warning. Don't listen to that crap.

When I told someone that instead of going back to my flat I'd slept out, in central London, they screwed up their face and said 'Eeeooough – why would anyone want to do that?' Like it was the biggest fucking outrage they'd heard all day (not counting daytime TV of course). I should have just asked – why's that so bad? If I were some multi-millionaire who liked to wander round his estate starkers you wouldn't be bothered, would you? If I were a businessman who checked into a hotel when he had a perfectly good home to go to, you wouldn't think that was weird, would you? But no, some things freak people out. Non-homeless people (what shall we call ourselves – homeful people?) sleeping out is one of them. Sleeping with girls under sixteen is another.

I could have been naked on the slab at the London Hospital mortuary and instead I was rolling off my bench, stretching and yawning and looking up at the birds. The park was emptying out. Tramps are pretty early risers – early to bed and all that. So I had all of London before me. All of my life in fact. I remembered something I'd been meaning to do but killing myself had interfered: check out the Fleet River, the best of London's eleven tributaries to the Thames. I love drainage systems, sometimes they're the only way to find your way around.

I walked down to Blackfriars and looked for signs of the outfall, but it must be underwater, probably one of those gated pipes that children are always getting stuck in so they can be on local television. No matter, I started walking along New Bridge Street, which quickly becomes Farringdon Street. That's always a good sign, when a road changes its name for no obvious reason. Wear and tear. Reassuring, like a dog-eared book. The street is a mass of boring offices, anonymous services like travel agents, sandwich shops, and raging traffic, but underneath you know the water's still flowing, only it's in a pipe buried 25 feet down. When the Fleet was a real river, back in the middle ages, it was deep and tidal and huge ships used to come up it, some past the Bridge of Fleet where Ludgate Circus is now, on up to what they called Oldebourne Bridge — or Holborn, from 'hollow brook' (whatever that means. Who knows what they were on about, these people with the tights and tunics?). In fact they've even found old anchors as far up as Camden Town.

If you counted all the scummy marshes on the west side, and the gravel slope leading up to where St Paul's is now, the whole Fleet River was 600 feet wide. It pretty much divided the West End from the City, people were always moaning about having to cross it. Not surprising since the dirty bastards used it as an open sewer. Just to add to the atmosphere there were loads of tanneries in the area too, churning out stinking gunk. But those medieval English, they moaned about the Strand being muddy too — if you had the cash it was better to go by boat — Eastward ho!, Westward ho! — all that. Course now you just get the District and Circle Lines, and a good thing too. Or a cab.

I walked on up to Holborn Viaduct, which is the one with all the painted Victorian metalwork. You can see where the banks would have been on either side. Christopher Wren had a plan after the Great Fire of London to turn it into a Venetian-style canal with lots of Bridges of Sighs — and that wasn't heritage industry idea then, that was state-of-the-art design. Course his entire plan to rebuild London never got past the 'artist's impression' stage. If it did we'd have a city with no gaps in it — no turd-strewn wastelands or closed-off parks. And who wants that?

They bricked it over in the end. They'd had enough.

I walked on up past Farringdon train station and Turnmill Street, now famous for its giant gay club, Turnmill's, but once home to a giant watermill. 'You spin me right round baby right round, like a record baby right round . . .' The DJ played that at our wedding. I didn't find out what it was about till years later. It always pays to look into the meaning of these things. Like Turnmill's. You have to think of the names like puzzle clues. Millers did a lot of grinding.

Onwards to Farringdon to where it changes its name to King's Cross Road. I love that area round there, it's so crap, so forgotten. There's people living round there in little houses like Coronation Street. I don't know how they do it, but there they are. I suppose you have to know someone, or be a real Londoner, because it's not money or wearing a blazer and cravat that gets you in. At number 61 there's a wall plaque with a head on it, where Bagnigge Wells was, which used to feed the Fleet, and off to the right, Wilmington Square has a dried-up fountain.

I went up past King's Cross Station, where I used to get the train up to Tina's father's place in the country on Fridays, getting Tess all dressed up and watching London recede from the window, she loved that. They both did. I found out that the name comes from King Edward the First who built a series of thirteen crosses on the route of his wife's funeral procession – that's all the way from Nottinghamshire to Westminster. Charing Cross was the last one. It was in Cheeringe, a hamlet outside Westminster. Well, you know where Charing Cross is. King's Cross was his penultimate cross. The were all jewelled and beautiful, and naturally they were soon looted and vandalised. The Victorians put up a copy of the last one, because they were like that, the Victorians. In love with love, and romance, and chivalry.

It's when you get up St Pancras Road that you get to the best bit – St Pancras Old Church, hidden away on the right with its own little church yard. It's hemmed in by road, rail and canal but it's been there since Roman times – there was once a temple to the god Mercury here, you know, the communications guy. The bloke on the phone company logo. So they say. Anyway the early Christians founded this church in the fourth century, way back before the Angles and the Saxons showed up. They used smashed up bits of the Roman temple in their walls like good recyclers. Of course most of the fourth-century stuff is gone. Here you're lucky to get a bit of medieval. You have to use your imagination. You can sense where the old pack-horse road followed the curve of the river bank. The church yard is still there – when the poet Shelley lived near by, this is where he met his missus, Mary Godwin, who was visiting her mother's grave. Very romantic eh? A good place to score. There's a wetland round the back by the Regent's Canal – one of those miserable local council places where London school kids are always being dragged when their teachers can't be arsed teaching. And I should know.

A lot of English people get fired up about this place. Anything Roman or before. Like William Blake, that chimney-sweep poet my mother knew. He got all excited about Albion. That's the England from before the Angles, the Saxons, and all those other yobs, before that lot came over, marauding and spoiling everything. The England of the Celts. Bangles and poems and naked virgins.

My feet felt hungry for road. I just wanted to walk and walk, loving every street sign, every billboard and graffiti tag. I kept going, walking up to Camden Town and beyond Kentish Town to Gospel Oak and the bottom end of Hampstead Heath. From the top of Parliament Hill, where the armchair Druids come once a year (I thought of Barry) I could see it all: the water of the Fleet in a row of ponds which were designed in the early seventeenth century as fresh-water reservoirs for London. They used to pipe it away in hollowed elm trunks.

People swim here, stark bollock naked and the female equivalent. Even in winter there are some old headcases willing to give it a go.

There's a road on the right, just like a country lane, Millfield Lane. I'm always surprised at the chunks of countryside that lurk in the midst of London. The actual source of the river, like most of them really, is an anticlimax. Somewhere in the grounds of Kenwood, the Palladian house, the rainwater creeps along the surface and hits the first pond.

That's when I thought about my mother for the first time. She'd be up there in north-west London being fed, watching *Tellytubbies*, fragments of poetry going through her head like a news ticker. I felt sad, but not sad enough to do anything about it. It sounds like an oxymoron but I felt numb. Scorched earth. Don't look back. I took this numbness as a sign that I should look after myself for the moment. Tess would be up to the north east in Islington, being chided and read to and loved by my ex-wife. People might be wondering where I am, but not much.

Self-pity can become huge. Huge and benign, like a goitre. There must be other people carrying around their own personal holocaust, or the apocalypse of themselves. Getting all their failures in a row. Spending a few hours a day nursing their weakness and their woe.

I noticed, standing at the top of the heath, where the orchestra plays in summer, that my cellos had stopped. I took that for a good sign too.

I spent two more days freely walking about, eating at chip shops, drinking from water fountains and sleeping outdoors. I stayed a night in Hyde Park, and when I woke up I saw several others had had the same idea – not dossers like me but respectable back-packer types. As I walked by one blond youth he stirred, looked at me in sleepy-eyed terror and tried to sit upright in his glow-worm bag. I just laughed and asked him why he was there. He stammered that he'd missed his plane and couldn't afford a hotel. There were others like him creeping out in the dawn light, some to the Kensington side like me, some to Bayswater Road. Maybe they were afraid of getting a hit by a Daktari dart from the park rangers or whatever they call them, but I don't think those boys and girls gave a fuck – it would take a bomb to shift them from their cosy vans during the breakfast show. Smoking and drinking tea and waiting for the outside to warm up.

I knew I had to go back south of the river at some point and I was starting to feel like a real tramp – stubbly, ready to engage with strangers and smelling like a giant gusset. I wandered over Vauxhall Bridge and stopped at a greasy-spoon cafe for breakfast. I had a bacon sarnie and a pot of tea. The girl serving me was of the old school – she must have been about twenty but she acted like it was still 1947 – fag in her mouth, bustling, thinking out loud, shouting orders to the cook. Again I was struck by how much pleasure I got from the food – the bread was cold and white, the bacon was rubbery and tasted of salt and smoke, the tea was like hot caramel. The thought that I had just tried to throw all this away made me feel very stupid. For a while there I'd been a bit put out that nobody gave a flying fuck about me jumping in the river. Now I changed my mind. I realised it was a good thing that no one knew. It was like winning the pools – tick the box for NO PUBLICITY if you fear you can't handle the consequences. Other people are weird. People have issues – as they say on daytime TV – about you killing yourself, and about you surviving.

I walked past the Oval. There was a test match on. The stadium had the same bustle that you get around Wimbledon or a football ground – people hurrying in, men in duster coats directing traffic, souvenir geezers hawking their cheap crap. There was a ripple of applause, then another as I got closer. Strange how slow the rhythm of the game was from the outside, with nothing to wait for but the sound. I thought of George, probably watching at home right now. Saturday morning, sitting in his giant Y-fronts, talking through a mouthful of Frosties, 'Oh I say! He's gone!'

Just as I was rounding the corner I distinctly heard the *tock* of the ball, followed by a gasp and a roar from the crowd. The next thing I knew a dark shape skittered off the pavement in front of me, hit the fibreglass panel of someone's Mazda and ricocheted wildly past my face. It came off a wall and bounced past me again, coming to rest under a Mercedes. There were a couple of kids running around and screaming trying to follow it but I got there first, knelt down and plucked it from behind a wheel.

I pocketed the ball and carried on walking. A few people looked at me but there was nothing they could say, it was finders keepers. They must have been really pissed off when they realised that I was just passing by, that I wasn't part of the game. But I just thought 'Fuck it, it's about time I had a bit of luck.'

I enjoyed myself with that young girl Amanda. The sex. I know I've spent a lot of time defending myself and saying it was a mistake, but that doesn't take away from the fact that I really enjoyed it at the time. Yes, I felt a bit guilty afterwards – during, sometimes – but nothing can really erase the pleasure I felt at getting my hands on her body. It's a memory.

I thought I'd better point that out in case anyone got the wrong idea.

I mean, ultimately it was stupid because I lost my family over it, and my job, and my home – and she felt bad about that too. But walking down the ugly streets of Lambeth and Brixton to Streatham, I was happy to be alive, and happy to have nothing other than my memories and the clothes on my back. And they would have to go soon.

To come back to the subject of her age again, let me put it this way: She was almost a girl, but she was almost a woman too. Normally I'm a glass-is-half-empty kind of bloke. But she was definitely half full.

There was a second note from the police on my door saying I'd been burgled. It didn't say 'You've been burgled again, please do something about this. See me!' It just said, you've been burgled. I like that about the police. Plodding. This time my boxes had been totally emptied out on the floor, my notes trashed and anything worth selling – most of my books, my cutlery and crockery – carted off. It was like a squat. It must have been a semi-professional, someone who knows how to get rid of low-margin items. At least the burglar didn't leave a curling clinker this time.

I sat down on the floor. The bent pipe started getting on my nerves so I pulled up the chair and tried to straighten it, pushing hard upwards on the cold metal. The paint flaked and I got dust on my hands but it bent quite easily.

Danny the Kiwi must have heard me coming in because he came downstairs. He rushed up behind me and grabbed my legs.

'What are you doing man? Don't do it man! Things aren't that bad ...?'

'What ... Danny what the fuck are you doing? Get off me!' I shouted.

'Don't kill yourself, you've got lots to live for?'

'I'm not, I'm straightening the pipe!'

He looked up at me suspiciously, still hanging on to my legs.

'Let go,' I said, and started laughing. 'I'm getting down. It's done.'

Danny was a bit ashamed, but managed to laugh it off. 'It's bad karma?' was all he could say.

We stood around in the flat looking at the mess.

'Where've you been, man? I thought something had happened to you? You had more visitors? Man, you look really rough. You need a wash.'

I told him I'd just lost it for a few days, I'd been bumming round the city, but now I had a plan and was glad to be back home so I could put it into action.

'Tour guiding, Danny. When Wonga Leisure folded our business went down the pan with it. But what do you think of this? Tours of the *real* England. Places that aren't on all the tourist maps. Come on, as a Kiwi, doesn't that appeal to you?'

'Like where?'

'Well, like anywhere. The Fleet River. Power stations. Shopping malls. The other prehistoric sites not just Stonehenge. Have you ever heard of the Devils Arrows in Yorkshire? The Merry Maidens and the Pipers in Cornwall? The Hurlers? Long Megg? Men-an-Tol?'

'No.'

'Anyway. Housing estates. Old markets. Race tracks. The sewers. Slaughterhouses. Ruined seaside towns. Places of overpopulation.'

'You could go to Glastonbury? Me and Jo are going in a few weeks, for the festival. I've always thought ...'

I was at least glad he was thinking. It seemed to me there must be a world of interesting sites out there that are not yet in the grip of the dead hand of history. The Kiwi perspective could be useful.

Danny offered to help me clean up, but I said no thanks. I saw his cinema eyes scoping the room for another jobby. I did accept his offer of some jeans and a T-shirt though. There was a skip outside, I just wanted to scoop everything up and drop it in. I saved a few things: one of Tess's drawings of me, looking like a snowman, and some ring binders that not even the thief wanted. The rest got binned, and good riddance to it.

I got out of my old clothes and lay in the deep, hot water with the sun pouring in through the pimply glass, thinking about England and all it could do for me. First of all it could hand over its treasures. Its green fields and country pubs, its tolerance and good humour, its smouldering liberalism and lower-case conservatism, its sense of history and its provincial naiveté. Yes.

All these things were mine to sell to the foreigners. Or rather, I'd be selling information about them to foreigners, but that's about as close as ownership comes these days. It was the same as teaching really. The only difference with teaching was the state was paying you to prepare the workforce for the future. I don't know if I ever achieved anything there. How many of the kids I taught that are now swiping groceries over the old scanner or clicking with the old mouse ever remembered anything about glaciation, pebble beaches, distribution of service centres or bites taken out of the population pyramid?

I should add here that I was born before the last bulge in the pyramid myself. You know how live births peaked in the UK in the mid Sixties, just after the contraceptive pill became available? Well, that was just after me and Gordon, my little brother. My father was a bank manager, with the Midland Bank. I assumed he was a pioneer in the field of the indispensable executive, in that his talents were so valuable that the bank would move him around every few years to manage a new branch. I'm not sure about that now. I think they just took advantage of his loyalty. Nowadays everyone is more mobile – everyone's biding their time, waiting to move on somewhere new where they won't be known, where people won't know how crap they are, where they'll be given the benefit of the doubt. I suppose that's how my last school saw me at the end. The quiet Geography teacher with a taste for young girls. Even though she was actually fifteen. And a bit.

We moved wherever my father was posted – Derby, Plymouth, Norwich . . . modest towns. For a couple of years there we had to live in Alnwick, which is right up in Northumbria. England doesn't end at Newcastle you know, although really there's bugger all up there, unless you like castles and rambling in the rain. Alnwick doesn't even rate a mention on the weather map. The Romans considered the nearby Cheviot Hills *ad fines* or 'the end of the road'. Which is why they built Hadrian's Wall around Newcastle, to keep the nutters out.

So we lived in Wolverhampton and in Southampton, we lived in Bury and we lived in Brighton. Actually I think someone had it in for Dad and moved him as far as possible each time, so that we'd never have the benefit of a community. Gordon and I would make friends at school, just start learning the local lingo, then it was off again to the next place. There were letters exchanged with old friends from defunct cheese and wine circuits at the other end of the country, and sometimes telephone calls (at the right time of day), but I don't recall much visiting. Our family was just us four, and our baggage was our culture – my dad's toy railways, or *model* railways as he called them, and my mother's books. That was about it.

Father was what you would call a bit of a stiff. But what choice did he have? You weren't supposed to express yourself in those days. Wearing a bowler hat was about the limit of it, and even then you had to know the time and the place. You couldn't get away with that up north, or after about 1975. He wore a suit, he carried a furled umbrella, he was niggardly with loans ... basically he did what he was supposed to do, to keep people in line, to make sure their money didn't get the better of them, whether it was savings or loans. I don't know what he'd say now if he saw all the teenagers with credit cards and charge cards and petrol cards ... maybe he'd just say 'Fuck 'em, I'll have some of that!' Maybe he would have changed with the times too?

We had a nice middle-class upbringing then – music lessons, charades, ITV was banned, Party Political Broadcasts were watched closely, service at the Church of the Holy Hypocrite every Christmas, holidays once a year ... I always loved holidays, even though my parents barely behaved any differently. We had two choices: either go to a boarding house at the seaside, somewhere nice like Torquay or Robin Hood's Bay (Mother loved the old book shop Cuvvins). Or, we'd go CHA. With the boarding houses it was an art to avoid the rabble – we didn't want to end up amongst a load of beer-swilling, child-cuffing blue-collar types (Dad always checked the calendar for the industrial holidays and the wakes). We wanted nice places with rambles, tea rooms and local history museums, antique book shops and provincial theatres. My dad had a thing for model villages – preferably with model railways. And don't talk to me about fucking Thomas the Tank and his 'live appearances', I don't mean that sort of crap. What the hell is that anyway? Ten quid to see a plastic mask stuck on the front of a choo-choo? I took Tess once, what a load of bollocks. It's just literature reborn as a smiley face. She loved it of course.

CHA was less risky. This is the Countrywide Holiday Association, where you stay in rooms in a big converted house, usually an old rectory or something. The main thing is walking – there are different grade walks every day, you have about ten minutes after breakfast to get ready and grab your packed lunch as you get on the coach. Then you walk all day and come home weak with hunger but happy. We used to love that. In the evenings there were suitably middle-class activities – Scrabble, chess, ping pong, folk dancing ... and if I'm not mistaken, there was no bar! Yes, now that I think about it, there was no bar. No fruit machines, none of that. All the other families were nice people, and their kids were nice too. I remember Gordon getting into a fight with one kid over a cricket bat or something, and me having to join in and help him win. But generally there was no dark side. Just wholesome fun.

There was no dark side to my family either, I should stress this right now. You know what it's like nowadays – as soon as someone starts mentioning their father they're usually trying to talk about destiny, and blame their failures on him. Same with their mothers. Or they wax nostalgic for the good times and their emotional growth. But this doesn't apply to us. My father was a bit of a stiff, not as affectionate as we are nowadays, with our hugs and our pastel baby slings, but still a loving man. I don't choke up when I think about him. And I don't think he would have wanted me to. And anyway, what he lacked our mother made up for. I just don't want you to think that inheritance is destiny, because no one can untangle which things we choose to inherit and which things are hard-wired into us.

I have hopes for Tess. And fears. The principal hope being that she doesn't watch too much daytime television, Jerry Springer and all that. I don't want her blaming me and her mother for every little bump in the path of life. I'm seriously thinking of suggesting to Christina that she sets the TV chip so she can't watch any of that rubbish.

Around the time she was born the fashion in our circle – such as it was – was to give your child a really old-sounding name, I suppose for its heritage associations: Edna or Ethel, Archibald or Wilf. At the same time, a few streets away, the proles were giving their kids speculative names like Phoenix or Diamond, names that suggested something eternal or even futuristic. I lobbied for the latter, I wanted something that sounded modern and seemed to break with the immediate past. She wanted something old and flowery. We locked horns and ended up with a compromise, Tess, which neither of us was overjoyed with. Don't get me wrong – we loved the baby, from the beginning, with all our hearts. Just that I always thought she could have been given an even better start in life with a better name.

Clive eh? *Clive*. So what do you think of Clive? I asked my dad once. He said it was a very sensible name, very respectable.

Fair rolls off the tongue, doesn't it? Clive. Who's a fucking Clive anyway? Clive Dunn, the old *Granddad* actor? Clive Lloyd, the great West Indian cricketer? I didn't have much to go on. I am Clive, hear me roar. Doesn't work does it?

That is our storied past, the Pointings. As for my grandparents, I never met them. What with two World Wars, rickets, filterless fags and rationing, they never made it very far into the century. As for the lot before that, there were old photos and vague suggestions of some sort of industrial proletariat recently displaced from the countryside. Inhabitants of Thomas Hardy Land, all hobnailed boots and no underwear, staring grimly at the camera.

So I hatched my plan to sell England, the bits of it that were still lying around, to the foreign tourists. One good thing about London is we get the cream of the crop – the educated, the affluent, the bohemian, the year-off brigade, the retirees, all with a stack of sterling burning holes in their bum bags. I've seen them, especially these older people who are determined to soak up the entire British Museum and fight their way round every room of the Tate. They want to see every plaster cast, every bronze bangle, every splash painting and every shrunken head, to find out where they came from, or to see what we've been up to in this island for the last two thousand years.

That's another thing – History. I know about space but no one ever really taught me about time. I mean, why is our history only two thousand years old? Have we that much to thank the Romans for? What were the Beaker people up to? They were the ones around before the Celts and no one knows much more about them. Apart from that they were buried with their clay beakers. Pretty sad, I know. Where's their national holiday? Beaker Day Disco. Free drink with beaker purchase! It's not going to happen, is it?

The Romans, in case you didn't know, because I didn't really know until I read about for the Blue Badge course, came for a reccy in 55 BC but didn't bother taking us seriously until AD 43. A bit like the British in the nineteenth century. We'd just mark out a bit of African or Pacific shoreline on the map, send in the gun boats, pound them from offshore till they were ready to submit and hey presto – another colony. I don't know what the Romans wanted with us. A bit of slavery and some necklaces I think. Still, look what it led to. Bath, the first London Bridge, and all those straight roads. The roads before then were all over the place – sheep and cattle trails like the Ridgeway from Avebury to Ivinghoe. I suspect the Romans never really gave a fuck, we were just a big war game to them. Look how they pulled out in the 400s. They even buried their treasure, a lot of them just to spite the Brits. The wankers. If my reading of history is correct, it was shortly after that we became a nation of Barries.

Maybe he'll be buried with his pint glass?

I decided I needed to talk to Barry. I needed someone with a way with people. I needed to talk to Alex too, despite the fact that he was a rather dim Sloane. At least he knew about the business side of things. Finding new people would take for ever, and now it was June, High Season. Lovely days when you could rely on not wearing a jacket, when you could be sure the major sights were open. If I was going to start a business guiding people around my version of England, I was already locked in with these two.

Streatham I'd written off as a bad place, somewhere that was beneath me, until I needed some new clothes. The next day Danny lent me thirty quid and I took a stroll down the high street and found my level at a cheap and cheerful seconds shop. Two pair of trousers, Bruno Sacchi, five pounds. Everything had sad names like that – Giorgiou Amandi and Talvin Cline. The stuff was piled up in big bins to be rummaged through by crumpled people who looked like refugees. Six pairs of socks for two pounds. Five T-shirts (seams slightly twisty) – four pounds. Five white vests – £2.99. Boxers – the same. Thin as handkerchiefs, yes, but boxers all the same. I got some no-name trainers too, and a grey padded jacket, the kind the very poor wear to their night cleaning jobs. It was quite hard to find one without a logo on it, or a cartoon character, but I managed it. 'I'll wear them now, if you don't mind,' I said to the girl behind the till. She shrugged. I got my wallet out, and decided to save the cash and chance my credit cards. They were stuck together with silver silt but I gave them a shine and they came up nicely. The Visa went through first time (such bounty! Such generosity to the less well-off) and I walked out into the street in my new gear. I'd made it. I was now an invisible person, a crowd man clad in the nameless gear of the poor, the immigrant, the loser, the nevereventried-er. I was right off the fashion map. I kept telling myself, 'So this is how low you can go!' and it didn't feel so bad. I was warm and comfortable, and looked quite well maintained. It's not until the grey padded coat gets shiny with grease and the shoes start to flap that being poor becomes a liability, and I had no intention of going that way.

I also stopped in at the Sue Ryder shop and got quite a result – a black

wool suit for only four pounds (I beat the woman down) and a decent
white shirt by Lanvin for fifty pence. Someone must have died, someone
with class. I was so pleased I went and sat in the pub and, following the
prescription painted on the outside sign in gold lettering, ordered myself
one of their 'chilled strong lagers'. There was a random demographic sample
in the pub, which seemed quite full for a weekday afternoon. So I wasn't
the only one who thought it an excellent idea to have a few pints in the
day instead of working. There were two blokes at the bar in jeans, black
T-shirts and gold chains, rabbiting away in the *Sarf Landan* manner about
things they had seen (on TV) and done (unto others). One of them had a
little logo on his T-shirt reading *D&G*. He was explaining how he'd got it
in Milan that morning. And now here he was in a boozer in London, and
wasn't that what it was all about? Europe. The shrinking globe. I wondered
how my Bruno Sacchi's would go down, if I just walked up and showed him
my label (it was on the outside, below the belt loop) but I knew better than
to ask for trouble. I was just enjoying listening to them. A country that
was fanatical about designer clobber, and here I was kitting myself out for
thirty quid. A nation of Barries and Sue Ryder women. The strong, chilled
lager was a blessing and set my thoughts free.

Britain isn't top nation any more.

I know – old news can have quite an impact, can't it? It shows you the
depth of your denial. But Britain hasn't been top nation since early in the
twentieth century. The good thing is, that news has finally trickled down
from the businessmen, who have been humiliated all over the world for
the last fifty years, to people like Barry, who have been abroad a bit, and
seen English sport in tatters, and even, hopefully, to Alex, who can't be
sure of the complicity of the people he lords it over any more. (When Alex
says jump, people like Barry say 'fuck off posh twat'.) We're all fucked, but
we're all on the same page, and that's a good thing. It seemed to me there
in the pub that my country had great potential for becoming top nation
in tourism again, by giving people what they want. All we had to do was
open it up to them – like the Americans. Over there famous people are
barely cold in the casket before their house is turned into a museum with
free parking, disabled access toilets and a gift shop. We could do that. And
we've got a lot more to sell. We've got layers of stories on stories. The fields
are chocka with old bones and the slippery clay of dead men, the churches
and country homes are a mass of add-ons and re-thinks. Everywhere you
go there's the sign of a battle or an uprising, a place someone got burned
or gibbeted, a devil's hollow or a holy spring. We've got all those old

generals and Royals, yes, but we've also got a stack of old writers to flog. Looking at my mum's books I realised that. Something must be done with them, all those Wordsworths and wotchamacallits. All we have to do is take this stuff out of the hands of the official guides and show them how we would do it.

I went looking for Barry. The Britannia number was disconnected, and the office was locked up. The bar staff at the Shakespeare didn't have a clue who I was talking about when I enquired – they must be trained to not notice people any more. So I took a stab in the dark. I remembered him telling me about his London, how it consisted of boozers where he could pick up foreign girls. It was all laid out like an Alsatian's invisible circuit, there to be routinely sniffed and checked.

I went to the Zetland Arms in South Kensington, which he said was neck deep in ripe Foreign Language students. I could see what he meant – these girls weren't just sweet and fresh, they were organic too. They had been brought up in the best-possible European manner, to care about culture, the environment, their health, their sanity, and the sanity of the world. I could tell all this just by looking at them, and by eavesdropping on the common language. I just stayed for a couple of drinks, as no one seemed to know who he was. Me and a girl from Barcelona had an animated discussion in the name of Barry – 'Big bloke, fat face, *tawks like "a"*,' but she didn't get it. She and her friends seemed to like talking to me though – I guess even a wrinkled wreck like yours truly has a chance around there since I've got something they all want – English.

I walked all the way up to W2, the posh white triangle above the top right end of Hyde Park, and looked in at the Duke of Kendal on Connaught Street. This was the sort of random pub you would never hear about, used by the local mix of mews-dwelling divorced businessmen, independently wealthy loafers, Arabs sneaking a drink, vestigial old folk who had seen the area gentrify around them, and sitting at the bar the odd mysterious woman with nothing to do. The barman was defensive and everyone strained to hear what I was saying. Yes, he did know Barry, but wanted to know why I wanted to know. Soon as I said it was personal the trail went cold. I didn't mind so much, as I'd had another pint and was feeling happy.

His next place was the Sawyer's Arms up by Praed Street, near Paddington. It's where all the cheap hotels are that cater for international travellers stunned by how expensive Britain is. Very Barry. I bought the girl behind the bar a drink. She knew who he was, he'd been in there just the day before, but there was no pattern to his comings and goings. It was evening now and the place was filling up with young Americans, cock-a-hoop at being able to drink legally under twenty-one. They sat around at tables, leaning back in their chairs and taking it all in – the weird TV, the strange currency, experimenting with crisps and stale cigarettes from the machine. Every time someone came in they all looked to the door. More and more of them arrived. I got talking to one lad who was six foot ten and wore a nylon basketball vest over a T-shirt with some kind of high-school insignia on it. He'd had two pints of Woodpecker and would alternately rabbit like a speed freak then stare off at the majesty of it all – the sunshine, the hanging flower baskets, the pulsating lights of the fruit machine. He told me they were all staying round the corner in some college dorm that was let out for the summer. They were over in London on an 'intern program' – basically their parents had paid a shit-load of cash to send them over here to work for free in whatever profession would have them – law firms, media, caterers, internet companies. They worked a few afternoons a week, and went on cultural trips arranged by the group leader – a dodgy Englishman with a waxed moustache. One of the kids said he described himself as a magazine publisher but no one knew of what. Culture consisted of *Cats* (block bookings – when they told me what they paid per head I nearly blushed), outings to Windsor, Oxford, Madame Tussaud's, Paris . . . all the usual suspects. Maybe it was the cider but they all seemed very happy.

I was listening avidly to a couple of girls who were interning in the 'London fashion industry' – fetching coffee and cutting up magazines – when a nearby cell phone suddenly triggered a memory. I had Barry's number somewhere. I looked in my wallet and there it was on a shred of paper torn from a Britannia flyer. 0976 238973.

'Here, you can use my phone, my dad's paying for it anyway,' said one of the girls. She was about twenty, big boned, and big breasted too and stuck them out in a friendly, open way that the locals never seemed to do. She had dry brown hair and a strange nose, long and straight – it might have been altered – with coiffed eyebrows that almost met in the middle. There was a weird beauty to her, maybe a trace of Slav or Russian. I was staring at her when I got right through to Barry. He was in his local.

'Barry it's Clive, Clive Pointing from Britannia. I've a proposition for you.'

'Clive? *Fackinell* what do you want?' He said it with a smidgen of curiosity.

'Where are you anyway?' I said. 'I want to talk business with you.'

It went quiet. I could hear pub noises in the background, music and the pumping of puggies paying out.

'What did you have in mind?'

'Listen I can't talk now, let's meet up ...'

He wanted to know what it was, so I told him about the idea of forming our own tour company with Alex and he told me to fuck off.

The girl giggled as I re-dialled. Her name was Amy and she went to the bar and came back with a half of lager for both of us.

'Barry, listen ... I'll come and meet you. Just say where. Let me buy you a drink ...'

He gave me the name of some place out in the East End – his version of the East End, out Stratford way – and said make it tomorrow, although he didn't want anything to do with any fallout from Wonga. He perked up when I told him what pub I was in.

'Oh yeah? What's it like in there tonight?'

I told him it was rammed and he sounded well pleased, like an emperor hearing good things about an outpost of progress.

The American girl was from Durham, North Carolina, which I had only ever thought of as a state with an impressive drift coast and a lot of monster-truck driving rednecks, but she had almost no accent and soon disabused me of that notion. She said it was a progressive state, and when she told me about her college with all the labs and computers and whatnot, I had to agree. So I gave her a bit of blather about County Durham and the cathedral, which she said she wanted to see and I said don't bother, it's too far away, and then I went on about Salisbury because they had a Salisbury out there too, and the next thing I knew she was inviting me back to her dorm room.

Well I never! As George would say. Clive Pointing – he's back!

You don't know what it's like, after so long, having a woman. I wanted to devour every cubic inch of her. I got a taste of the madness that afflicts Englishmen in the summer, when the light is good and the women seem to have abandoned caution. We walked along the street chatting amiably but we were both old enough to know what was going on. She liked my talk of West Kennet Long Barrow. She loved that – the idea of the 'prehistorics' as she called them, building a big mound to bury their dead in, a smooth green hill. Pretty soon she was expressing an interest in the Cerne Abbas giant, a mad cartoon caveman with a club and a hard-on drawn in chalk on a hillside in Dorset. That was it.

Her little room was painted a dirty green. There were blu-tak marks and pinholes where the previous occupant's posters had been. There was a narrow, studenty bed, a sink, and some white bookshelves, on which Amy had placed her *England: The Rough Guide* and a single soft toy, a horned ram. She waved it at me and said 'Go Tar Heels!' and I pretended I knew what she was talking about. I could barely take my eyes off her chest. She got a bottle of white wine out of the wardrobe. Didn't apologise for it being warm. I drank from her coffee mug, she drank from her toothbrush glass. We talked about London, I exaggerated the charms of Streatham, and suddenly we were snogging on the bed, leaning against the green wall, our heads beneath the shelving.

I mean really, is it my fault that women are getting younger every year, while I stay the same? I'm forty-four. Four years ago I was exactly the same as I am now. But four years ago she was just sixteen. She didn't even have a passport. It's a trick of parallax that makes me seem like a dirty old man.

The sight of her purple bra, a little worn from over-washing, took my breath away when she stopped to remove her sweater. And she smiled.

I felt fantastic as I rattled home on the Tube to Streatham. I walked all the way home from Balham, borne along by my happiness.

Barry wanted to know all the details of me shagging this American bird. I wasn't going to mention it because I didn't want to seem like I was poaching on his territory, but I couldn't stop myself. And in the event he was generous. We met the next night at the Swan in Stratford.

'So straight up, this geezer's got them in his fridge, I swear . . . Fucking hell, look who's here!'

They all stopped and looked at me while I pulled up a chair. The empty glasses were piling up in front of his dad, stuttering Stuart the tout, and another of his brothers, Craig. They were having it big, for a weeknight anyway, and Barry was talking at the top of his voice.

But I was determined to get my point across. I asked Barry what he had been doing since Wonga went under.

'Bit of this, bit of that.'

'B-b-b-bit of the o——ther,' Stuart chipped in.

And Barry goes 'Oi, you watch it! Anyway Clive's the expert on the other . . .' And they all laughed, including Craig, who had been briefed.

It turned out Barry had been helping his brothers in the interim. Doing a bit of 'ticket brokering' with Stuart, and helping Craig with what he called his direct marketing. Craig sells perfume outside Harrods, and Barry was the lookout. They'd given the usual lookout – a black kid called Errol – the fortnight off. The point of being the lookout was not to spot the police and give the signal to clear up and scram. That was unnecessary since the police were in on it too. The point was to provide a bit of authenticity for the tourists and rich tarts who liked to think they were streetwise and so were always on the lookout for the lookout. When they saw an eagle-eyed black kid leaning on the railings at the corner, they knew this was the real thing. Stolen goods. Black market. *Offabackovalorry* darlin', yuck yuck yuck. Anything to please, really. Anyway, Barry was being 'it' for a while, though he didn't like it. The money wasn't very good, and worse, he hated sharing it with the 'filth', as he called them. 'Fucking pigs. Don't talk to me about pigs.'

That's not to say he was willing to come and work with me. Until I bought a round of drinks.

'Oh, so you boozing as well as bonking again?' he said loudly as I came back holding six pints of Pentagram. (Special offer – buy five pints, get the sixth free.) 'What about your lawyer then?'

'Fucking lawyers. Don't talk to me about lawyers.'

I soaked up the abuse until they ran out of it, and then I started explaining to Barry how we should go into business together. With his knowledge of the tourist trade and my historical knowledge we could pick up a few of the old Britannia customers, and gradually expand. We'd work the same coach and learn off each other until we had enough customers to run two coaches. Then we'd expand, hire more people, it'd be brilliant.

He looked interested, especially when I laid it on thick about his gift with people, his Cockney charm, his long experience with tourists, his unique knowledge of London ... I kept quiet about the fact that we'd make more money doing day trips outside the capital.

Then I mentioned Alex and he said no.

'I'm not working with that cunt,' he said. 'What's he gonna do?'

'Well, we have to have someone to take the bookings.'

'What about Stu? He does nothing all day.'

I looked at Barry pleadingly. Luckily Stu spoke up.

'I'm too b-b-b-busy this time of year. I can't sit on the f-f-f-f-facking phone all day for you lot.'

'I think Alex has the experience,' I said. 'I haven't asked him yet anyway. Do you know where he lives?'

Barry tossed his head derisively. 'Out west some fucking place. Richmond.'

'Have you got his number?'

'No I 'kin' haven't. Try Directories.'

'I just have to find out how much a coach costs now ...'

'Four and a quarter for a fifty-three seater for eleven hours max, after that you need a new driver,' said Barry immediately.

I was surprised he knew, but I was a bit pissed by now so it was straight on to the next thing.

'Four seventy-five if you want *vijoes* and a toilet. But that's a forty-eight seater. Peak period, summer.'

'So ... what about drivers? What firm was that girl with we had that time, when Ray died?'

'Rose? Naaaar-har-har, naar-har-har! He's still interested in her. Silver Lining. What, you want to try your luck?'

I mumbled my excuses while he smiled at me over the rim of his glass. When I asked about Maxine it was a different story. He said he didn't know what happened to her when Wonga went bust, she must have gone back to Brixton. 'Anyway, she was tight,' he said. It was beginning to dawn on me that Barry probably tried it on with every single woman who crossed his path.

After another couple of pints I made him promise he'd at least think about it seriously.

'What was you saying about P-p-p-p-p-p-p-princess Diana's p-p-p-panties?' said Stu.

This must have been where I came in, because Barry realised he hadn't finished his story. He included me in his audience.

'Straight up, I talked to this geezer who knows a geezer in New York who swears blind, on his mother's grave, that he's got Princess Di's death knickers! He's got 'em in a plastic bag, you know, one of those little ones with the thingy ...'

'Ziploc?' I said trying to help.

'Yeah ... he's got 'em in his freezer. White and lacy he says they are.'

'The Royal death panties? Phwoar, they must pong a bit by now,' said Craig.

Barry cuffed him round the back of the head. 'Shut up you, show some fucking *rispeck!*'

Barry's dad belched. 'Urrrrrp. They must be worth a few bob.'

'Apparently they were spirited out of the hospital by a wotchamacallit, a ...'

'Nurse?' I said.

'An orderly,' he said frowning at me. 'And flown to Switzerland. Then the bags were switched and a dummy pair were sent to Berlin and the real ones ended up in Bermuda. Now they're in fucking New York somewhere.'

'In this geezer's f-f-f-f-reezer?' said Stu in awe.

'Yep.' Barry leaned back, all satisfied.

A Royal expert. Just what I needed. Personally, I've never been a fan of the Royals, they're just a quango on skis, but I can see where they keep the plebs quiet. I stuck it out to the end. I was in on every round of drinks. I didn't piss either, because they didn't, except for the old man. I remember Barry telling my TWA joke, without acknowledging it. He did it much better too. It sounded good in Cockneyspeak.

At chucking-out time they all piled into the taxi, which had a new paint job. It was now completely pink, with the word 'Digit' down the side in discreet letters, that was all. Barry saw me looking at it.

'New sponsor innit? Dad did it to impress the TV bird but personally I think it's a big mistake.'

I asked him what 'Digit' was but they drove off. I think it must be some new mobile-phone thing. Who can keep up with this stuff?

The buses and trains from Stratford to Streatham take hours, but I was happy. I hadn't been this pissed for years – I could barely see to get my key in the door, but somehow I made it, and had a good long lie in the next day.

The next few days were spent getting information from the library on starting a business, sending off for forms, and trying to track down Alex. I called a few A. Whites listed in Directories until I got a machine message that sounded like his voice, deep and posh. But he never called back.

At first I didn't mind, because I was enjoying walking through Hyde Park and up to Amy's in the evenings. But to use her expression, I soon got *antsy*. She wanted to go out and do stuff but I wanted to be getting on with my work. I had to get this business sorted out. She offered to help, but I sort of said 'No, you're American, you wouldn't be able to.' That's when she hit the roof, and I had to put in several kilo-joules of boyfriendery to placate her.

The need to get hold of Alex became so urgent I just got on the train to Richmond and went looking for him. Page 88 on the *A–Z* is not somewhere I've been before but it's a really nice place. Another one of those villages London is supposed to be made up of. Walking around the quaint streets and smelling the cut grass from the Old Deer Park, I could see how you could have a cosy life of restaurants and rowing and not really need to go into London much. When we did urban morphology the first thing I'd teach the kids is that the average industrial city in Britain has all the nicest bits in the south west, and all the real shit out on the east-north-east. The prevailing winds from the south west mean that your factory chimneys need to be downwind of the people that matter. It was funny seeing how long it took to locate themselves on the big map of London. Right in the thick of it, Hackney and Tower Hamlets are.

The people in Richmond looked almost Californian with their sunlamp tans and designer doggies, I was quite enjoying myself. I stopped to get some cash out and got talking to a fellow who told me where the best pubs were.

The Grace was snug. Even the puggie pumped quietly. The barman didn't know who Alex was – I suppose my description of a balding rugger bugger didn't give him much to go on, so he suggested I try the Trader's Arms. I got the feeling he didn't like me – strange face, cheap clothes – and he took ages to get me my half. These chaps are trained to police their clientele.

Just up the road I ran into Alexander White himself, in all his cricket gear. I surprised him – he looked very worried. The first thing he said was 'This isn't about your money is it? Because I haven't got it.'

I was surprised too – I hadn't even thought about the lost money. Details like that seemed distant and hazy.

'It's no big deal,' I said, but then thought better of it. 'Well, actually . . . I do have a proposition for you.' I steered him into the Trader's and we sat on stools at the bar. He kept his foot on his cricket bag. I came right out with it, how we should go into business, how he would be a great manager, how we could treat the six hundred as my share of the capital. He looked relieved, and even perked up at the word 'capital'.

'You know I had a similar idea myself, but it's really hard to find good people . . .'

I let him go on like this for a bit, starting to see why Barry couldn't stand him. He was an arrogant wanker and no mistake.

At one point I asked him what he'd been up to since the fall of Wonga and he made a batting motion and clicked his teeth like he was sweeping someone for four. 'Lots of this,' he said with a big grin.

It always amazes me how some people manage without work. What was he living off? Mummy and Daddy? Savings? Was he naturally thrifty? And then at the other end of town you have Barry downing gallons of premium lager every night and buying the family Bergman designer trainers and watches ... And then there's me, stony broke and chased by creditors. Don't the middle classes ever get a break? I mean, we run things, we run this country and yet we're the first to get squeezed by taxes and burglaries and insurance and broker's fees and fucking garage mechanics who rip us off and suit-wearing snobs who jet around the world in business class and fall asleep in the best seats at the opera ... It just pisses me off.

I looked him in the eye at the end and said, 'Next time I ring, get back to me, OK?' He just nodded, looking nervous again. You have to hate a bloke like that. Spineless, that's what I call him.

I set a date. We'd meet in the Shakespeare Monday lunchtime and plan our business. I declined his offer of a lift to the station – it was only a few hundred yards away. Twat. As Barry would say.

Monday, after much prompting by telephone, the two of them turned up. Late. An arrogant fifty minutes, and an insulting one and a half hours late. I myself was spot on time, so I had a couple of drinks.

'We can clean up if we get started right away,' I said. 'The season's only just begun, there's a good three months left. All we need is a coach, Barry and I guiding, and someone in the office and we're set.'

'What about the legal aspects?' asked Alex. 'You can't just start a company like that.'

'Well, I've looked into it ...'

'Bollocks to legal,' said Barry. 'I'm not registering for *naffink*. Besides it'll take months. No one registers.'

'Well what about your dad's cab?' I asked.

'Well, that's different innit? He's got the Knowledge. That's a real skill. This tour guiding ... it's bollocks really. Anyone could do it.'

Alex and I exchanged looks. We secretly wanted him to be right. I suggested we take a vote on it. Press ahead, or wait for official status. Barry's hand shot up. I decided that since successive governments were keen to simplify the process of starting a new business, I would vote to press on. Alex's hand crept up slowly.

'Unanimous.' I had a list of points on a beer mat. 'Now, capital. Alex reminded me that I'm still owed money by Wonga. I estimate our start-up costs at a thousand pounds, covering coach hire, literature and per diem expenses (personal meal allowance, etc.). How much capital can you two bring to the table, and what happened to Britannia's assets?'

Barry rubbed his neck and said he only had about three hundred quid at the most. Alex plucked at his chins and, trying to best him, said he had a grand. You could tell he loved the idea of being Chief Executive Officer of the company. Fuck Managing Director.

'I really need to go into the Britannia office and collect my stuff,' he said. 'I left my second-best bat there for starters. But they just locked us out the day we were let go.'

'That's no problem.' Barry looked stealthily round the room. The ancient Bergman housebreaking gene was kicking into action.

'What about the computer?'

'Oh I took that,' said Alex. He had a dead serious look on his face, as though he was owed it.

I was surprised to hear that, but then, I'm always hearing about white-collar crime, this was just my first actual taste of it. Barry got a round in. I was beginning to feel much better, we were flying through our agenda. Which coach company to use: Silver Lining, the one that Rose girl worked for. What colour flyers to use: I went for green with silver lettering, Barry wanted purple and yellow like Britannia's, Alex wanted red, white and blue. I talked them round.

'So this is it – high impact, in-your-face tours of the sites . . . we need a name.'

'What about Cool Britannia Tours?' said Alex. 'We could go for the trendy market.'

I groaned.

'Fuck off,' said Barry.

'What about Anglia?' I suggested.

They shook their heads. Bad associations – cheap television and double glazing.

'What about Club Britain 18 to 30?' said Barry.

Alex looked aghast, I groaned. 'It's not about Britain anyway, it's just England. We're not doing Edinburgh and Cardiff and all that.'

Alex got on his high horse. 'Excuse me but what's wrong with Scotland? You can't just cut it off. I went to university in Scotland and it's a fine place . . .'

Barry leaned back and scoffed, 'Yeah, I bet you're one of them cunts who wears a kilt to weddings, aren't you? I say bollocks to the Jocks.'

I agreed. 'There's only five million of them anyway. They get far too much attention for their numbers.'

'Same with the Taffs. How many of them are there?' asked Barry.

'Three million,' I said.

'Yeah, there's fifty million of us,' said Barry, taking a swig. 'Bollocks to 'em.'

'Besides, we shouldn't go too far afield because of the driver limits, it has to be places you can reach in a day ... think of England, think of something that sums us up ... What about Mercia Tours?'

'What the fuck is that?'

'The Saxon Kingdom. You know, like Essex, Wessex, Sussex ...'

'What about just Sex? Sex Tours With Barry? Naaaar-har-har, naar-har-har ...'

'Oh be serious,' said Alex. 'What about White's? Why not?'

'Fuck off,' we both said.

We tossed around a few more names. Barry didn't like Albion Tours because he thought it had something to do with football. Camelot was the lottery. Alex made a big deal about Shakespeare – Sceptred Isle Tours – but Barry said it sounded like septic. Later I found it came from one of the Britannia brochures anyway. 'What about A to Beeline?' I suggested? Nothing. 'Or A-to-Z?' said Barry, so I had to explain to him all over again that we had to not sound too London.

We tried Little England, Forever England, Made In England, Lions, Tygers, Horses For Courses ... In the end I said we should go back to Albion, and though Barry grumbled I got it through on a two-to-one vote.

So we got a round of shorts in and toasted Albion with room temperature Gin. The other two seemed suddenly very keen to see the old office so we all went up there. They just nodded to the security guard, who was watching his portable TV in the lobby. Britannia was just one door in a corridor on the first floor, and Barry took the fact that it was locked as a personal challenge. He made everyone stand back while he kicked at the doorknob. As we were all a bit pissed it took us a minute before we realised it wasn't going to spring open like on *The Sweeney*, and Alex wandered off. He came back with the key.

'Black chappy downstairs just gave it to me. I said we'd come for our stuff.'

Inside Barry made a beeline for Maxine's desk where he found the petty cash box with a few hundred pounds in it, and Alex appeared out of his old office with a small fireproof filing cabinet and his bat. Of course Barry made him open it. It had about a thousand pounds in it, and the Britannia cheque book.

'This is the alternative petty cash,' he said, and shrugged drunkenly. Barry was impressed and praised him for being a crafty bugger. Normally I would have been terrified to get involved – white-collar crime will out and all that – but as the company had ripped me off I decided it was OK to pay myself back. Barry voted with me, two to one, that I be subbed a few hundred quid living expenses for the time being. For a moment there he felt like my best mate and I wanted to tell him so, but I kept quiet.

The rest of the night is a bit of a blur. Someone suggested we celebrate in the West End, so we cabbed it up to Soho and had a Thai meal sitting outside. There were thousands of people around, all brushing past us and making remarks but that didn't bother the other two, they seemed well versed in the new etiquette of eating out.

When some prostitutes waved to us from a window Barry revealed that after the fall of Wonga he had tried to go it alone and do a Jack the Ripper tour of Whitechapel and the East End. He was most annoyed because he ploughed through a whole book on the subject, then when he was taking his first dozen punters round he ran into the author, who was doing his own tour, the the chap I'd seen reading the *Daily Mail* in the Britannia office. Barry was standing about in Hanbury Street making stuff up about the second victim, Annie Chapman, a tatty whore who was strangled and disembowelled in a passageway. The guide, Donald, embarrassed him in a loud voice, calling him a cowboy in front of his punters, so he retreated quickly with them. But what really put him off was the book itself. The more he read the sicker he felt. He didn't realise that a Ripper *rips*. Vaginas. Jack the Ripper, Yorkshire Ripper – same thing. He was indignant that no one had ever told him. Kill a woman and then spend a few minutes cutting her in half from the crotch up. There was also a photo in the book of one who had been killed on her bed with her legs wide open. It looked like her face had been eaten off, and the caption said her breasts and kidneys were on the bedside table. He reckoned anyone who wanted to go on a tour like that was a fucking freak, and was glad to have nothing more to do with it. He also said he was amazed that people were so violent in those days, the 1880s, 'before vijoes'.

It was then that I knew I had him. He didn't have the stomach to go it alone. He needed me.

I asked them if they thought we needed a motto, but Alex started saying how pleased he was with the re-branding of Britain and how he thought the country itself needed a new motto.

'What is it at the moment then?' asked Barry.

'Er ... I ... It's something in Latin, I can't remember exactly.'

I had to help them out, saying 'Dieu Et Mon Droit' was French and had been the Royal motto since Henry V, meaning 'God and my Right'.

'So what's that one, honey swot wotchamacallit you see everywhere?' Barry asked.

'You mean "Honi Soit Qui Mal Y Pense"? That's French too. The motto of the Order of the Knights of the Garter.'

They both looked blank, the ignorant prats. Because of all the beer I said, 'Don't you two know anything?' They were both silent so I explained. 'Edward the Third was this very chivalrous King, very into the old myth of the Round Table, and he decided to form a band of knights, and their symbol became the garter. He was dancing at a ball at Windsor castle with Joan, Countess of Salisbury, when her garter fell off her leg. When Edward stooped and picked it up all his mates started taking the piss so he said to them, dead serious, in French — because they all spoke French then — "Bollocks to you if you think there's anything wrong with that!" That's a rough translation. And you wonder why everyone in Europe thinks Englishmen are such a kinky lot.'

Barry was open mouthed with admiration and surprise, Alex sniffed and hid his face in his pint.

'The other one you might be thinking of is the Prince of Wales's motto, "Ich Dien", which is German for "I Serve". That was adopted by Edward the Third's son the Black Prince — no Barry, he was white — who defeated the King of Bohemia in 1340 and decided he'd help himself to his three-feathers crest and maxim.'

'Fuck.' You could see his mind working. 'I wonder what my crest would be?'

'Probably three pints of lager and a packet of crisps,' said Alex, and snorted at his own wit. 'And your motto could be "I swear."'

'Bollocks to you, you poof. Yours would be a glass of Pimm's, and cricket stumps with no bails ... and your motto would be "Please Don't Hit Me!" Naar har-har-har ...'

'Actually, pleb, my family already *has* a crest and motto. It's been in the family for centuries. It's a hunter with a crossbow on one side, and a scholar on the other with a book, supporting a shield with ...'

'Oh shut it, you cunt.'

'Come on lads let's not argue.'

'So what do *you* think the motto should be?' said Alex sniffily.

'For Albion Tours? What about "England — The Way It Is"?'

'What about "The Way It Ought To Be"?' said Alex.

'What about "The Way It Was"?' said Barry.

That made me laugh. '"My Country Right or Wrong"?' I said. 'Anyway, I know what the country's slogan should be ...'

'What?' asked Alex. 'Something majestic I think. Like "England – Number One".'

'That's as bad as Top Nation,' I said.

'That's it! "Top Nation" is even better,' said Alex. 'Actually it sounds familiar ...'

'How about "England – The Dog's Bollocks"?' said Barry. He made a sign with his hands. '"England – The Bollocks"?'

'How about just "England – Bollocks"?' I said.

'Nah, you're just taking the piss now. Fuck off.'

'The Bollocks of Europe. Europe's Bollocks.'

'Shut up.'

I was enjoying myself so much he forced me to tell the whole story of me and Amanda again, including how old she was and what she looked like, how well developed and what she was like in the sack, which made Alex look at me with what seemed like more respect, it must have been the dark-horse effect. And then I had to tell all about 'the American bird'.

A car went by blasting that reggae song, 'Heads High', the one I'd heard just after dragging myself out of the Thames. I was starting to see the funny side of things, since they both admired what I'd done, especially the way I'd ditched the American ('Best thing for it, clean break, don't let it drag on too long, last thing you want is some nutty Yank boiling your bunny,') when my heart was struck cold: my ex-wife was walking down the street towards us.

She'd already spotted me, so there was no way out. She was with a man – he wasn't handsome but he looked like he had money. Especially compared to me with my cheap shirt and my grey padded jacket slung over the back of my chair. Jeffrey.

'So this is what we get up to on a Monday night is it?' said Christina. The chap she was with made no attempt to hang back, as I would have done. The lads went very quiet.

'We're celebrating,' I said a bit too loudly. 'The birth of our new company. Albion Tours. We're legit and we're ready to go,' and raised my glass. Tina came up to me and snarled,

'You've got a daughter whose school fees are in arrears and who asked me the other day "Why does Daddy only give me a pound a week for pocket money?" Well now I know.' Then she started prodding me in the chest. 'You're an arsehole Clive. You hear me?' Poke. 'You're a fucking' poke 'arsehole!' poke.

I lost it. I brushed her arm away and stood up to say something but I was a bit unsteady on my feet. The bloke lunged forward, all chivalrous, so I started having a go at him, and then Barry stood up and started separating us and shouting 'Come on, leave it out you two,' and Alex joined in, and he was shouting 'Be cool! Be cool OK? Be cool!' and that made things worse. I just wanted to get my word in with this bloke Tina was with, to tell him what he could do with his cheap Chinese mountain bikes and to keep away from my daughter, but with all the shouting no one could hear me. The maitre d' rushed out, a big burly sumo of a fucker he was, and about a hundred people in the street turned round to see what was going on, I could see a few hopeful lads watching to see if they could get involved, but Tina pulled Jeffrey away, and Barry pulled me away, and then I found myself raising my hands and saying 'It's OK it's OK it's OK it's OK, that wanker, that fucking wanker,' (not words I'd used in public before, especially that loud) as they backed off, and after a lot more standing around and mutual soothing, we all sat down again.

Barry said never mind her, and Alex said his ex- could be a real bitch too sometimes. I didn't say anything. I did mind. Mainly I was thinking, 'If she's a bitch, what does that make me?'

Just when I thought something good was about to start – my own business, freedom, responsibility – along comes a reminder of sourness and suffering. What is it with the past that it always comes back and haunts you? How do you get the freedom to move on? My brush with death wasn't quite enough.

Soho still crawling with people at one in the morning is a sight to behold. The three of us chatted on the kerb for a few minutes, all a bit pissed, Alex with his cricket bat over his shoulder, Barry with the file in his arms and his eyes following the girls passing by. Alex announced that he was off to get his Jeep from the multi-storey. Barry was going to see some mates who were doing security at a club around the corner. I staggered off to Trafalgar Square in search of a night bus. Then I remembered my new cash and stuck my arm out for a taxi.

I love maps. Like a lot of kids I spent hours staring at maps, globes and atlases. It's a good way of losing yourself. You feel the strangeness of foreign countries, and the potential for escape. Wide-mouthed rivers

like the Amazon, square states like Wyoming. Most people grow out of
it, and end up with few in their lives – the local train route perhaps,
or the cartoon of a holiday town – but I just kept going and going. I
had a two-yard collection of Ordnance Surveys at my school, pin-sharp
detail down to the crappiest wind pump. I had rubberised relief maps
hanging on the walls which the kids would poke and trace. I had giant
charts showing the hidden beauty of the country – the candy-coloured
swirls of geology that centred on the south west like water going down
a drain, rainfall contours that showed how depressing it was to live in
Wales, land-ownership maps showing how the government, the church
and the monarchy had everything sewn up despite being incompetent,
unpopular and unnecessary. I had the ever-changing Counties and Unitary
Authorities of England, the Nine Regions of England, the National Parks
and the Areas of Outstanding Natural Beauty. I sent off for lush print-outs
of satellite images showing every channel of a river delta and every cat's eye
in a city. I was the first person I knew to install a GPS navigation unit in
his car, at great expense.

Every time there was a map exhibition I was there. I love *old* maps.
The extravagant cartouches – that's what the titles of maps are called –
are almost as big as the engravings themselves. I remember this one, a
World Map drawn in the time of Charles the Second. Along the top it
said 'A MAPP OF ALL THE WORLD, In two Hemispheres in which are exactly
Described all the parts of the Earth and Sea'. The landforms looked like
they'd been drawn by a seven-year-old – but what did they know in those
days? The top of Canada, they just left it blank hoping someone would
fill it in later. There used to be maps with Britain on her *back*, maps with
big coats of arms showing who owned what . . . you've probably seen that
laughable medieval *mappa mundi* in Hereford Cathedral that's so bad it looks
like a sheep's fleece, but there were some good efforts. Like a bloke called
Christopher Saxton who created a massive 21-sheet map of England in
1583 with a scale of eight miles to the inch. They were doing their best.

I should have gone into cartography. Computers. Joined up with the
Ordinance Survey or the European Space programme. Anything like that.
Something that didn't involve humans. Instead of fucking teaching. I was
such an idiot. I lost everything when Tina divorced me, I should just make
that clear. I lost the material crap, yes, and I lost my heart. It may not have
been the love of the century, but a few years after the wedding when the
romance cooled, we did get more and more familiar with each other, more
and more intertwined. It was a kind of love. Good enough for most people.

Yes, she had some annoying habits, and she used to tell me I had some. But I never really thought what I did with Amanda would end my marriage.

End my job, maybe. That made my heart beat faster – the thought of being castigated by the entire staff room and drummed out of school. A lot of them were walking dead anyway. Limited horizons. I had a colleague who wouldn't join the union because the meetings were after school and he'd miss *Countdown*, his favourite quiz. What the fuck can you expect from people like that?

Amanda was delicious. Her neck was like poured cream. I came within inches of it when I leaned over to help her with a problem. She didn't know how to plot a logarithmic scale, in fact she didn't even know what one was. I don't know what the maths teachers were up to – probably teaching them about Base 2, useless crap like that. But she wanted to learn. If you plot the rank sizes of cities against population, then made the axes logarithmic, the curve would become a straight line. She found that interesting. A place like England has a primary set-up – London is by far the largest city, nine million, then there's a big jump down to Birmingham, 1 million, then Manchester, Leeds, Sheffield, on like that, until you have a big group of towns of 100,000. She was a Londoner so she could have just accepted being in the top city. But she was curious to straighten things out, and to know what was beyond the M25. As a Geography teacher, you cling to anything like that.

I must confess, I've conflated two things here. She had the problem with the graph in the class before we had ever touched. But she told me she liked straightening things out much later, when we were in bed together. It was after we'd made love for the fourth time. See, that's the real crime – not the old in-out, but the lying around together afterwards. That's what gets people's goat. That's probably what her father thinks about when he wants to punch my throat in. It's not on – a middle-aged bloke with all his wrinkles, greying hair, and superior knowledge, lying around with a newly minted woman. Using her parents' bed was a big mistake, in retrospect. We should have gone somewhere neutral for an afternoon, like a field. Of course it's complicated by the fact that she really liked the lying around and talking. Where else could she talk to an adult with equal rights? Wasn't it better for her sentimental education to be with a real man, rather than in the back of some pustulant teen's Nova? Some scrawny lad who would have his way with her, only to get the heebie-jeebies and not phone her for a week?

I spend most of my time defending myself. I wonder if I'll be pleading my case for the rest of my life, or if I'll get to put all this behind me? I'll be like that Ancient Mariner, buttonholing people. It's too complex a case, and most people just want the simple version. And it's made harder by the fact that Amanda's getting older all the time, but I just stay the same.

To my surprise, the Tina encounter in the street didn't depress me for long. It made me more determined to succeed. I got hungrier for work, and less aware of the world around me. I barely ate, and when I did it was just to live. I noticed that the really poor pretty much live off chips with curry sauce poured over them – that counts as a meal. I suppose when you live on fifty quid a week it makes sense. The fact that I had no possessions felt good – I had less irrelevant crap to worry about. Less baggage slowing me down. Life became urgent. Barry was right – it was bollocks to wait for the government to let us start a business. Do it today!

I ran off a couple of thousand flyers at Kinko's saying Albion was taking tours to Stonehenge, forty quid round trip. That was undercutting, but there you go.

One good thing about this industry – the customers *were* born yesterday so it's easy to take advantage of them. What do they know? They just drift towards the centre of whatever town they've arrived in, looking for photo opportunities. On the first day we got thirty-three people. Barry and I stood outside Victoria giving out the flyers while Alex worked from home trying to get a deal with the coach company, and call in a few favours with the different ticket offices around the country – Windsor, Blenheim, Leeds Castle, Castle Howard, Chatsworth House, Ann Hathaway's cottage ...

It didn't go very well. He used some other coach company, Gray's, who sent us the wrong vehicle and a twat of a driver called Colin who didn't know his way out of the West End. Barry got on the wrong side of him by calling him a 'fick norverner' (he was from Leicester) and on the wrong side of me by chatting to some birds all the way down and not lifting a finger. I did all of the talking at Stonehenge this time, and when we rolled back into London he got the damned pint glass out. He only raised about ten quid, and blamed me.

But since we'd paid for the flyers we decided to stick to Stonehenge for the first week. The next day we only had twenty people, and most of them were from Taiwan so we couldn't get any banter going with them. They seemed a miserable bunch, and so were we. I told the driver I didn't want to see him again – he got us lost coming back.

The next day no coach showed up and we had to give everyone their money back (or at least the refundable portion that Alex and Barry put in the small print). I summoned Alex into the Shakespeare and asked him what was going on, why was the coach company so crap and couldn't he sort them out? In return he wanted to know why our sales were so low (nineteen that day; after refunds we netted the price of a few rounds).

'It's not our fault it's the flow, the flow was down today,' I said.

'I had a copper following me round half the morning, I couldn't do a thing,' said Barry. 'What about you anyway? What have you been doing? Where'd you find that crappy coach company?'

Alex said Gray were cheap and they were owned by his brother's godfather, so Barry told him to tell his brother's godfather he was a twat. I agreed.

'Right,' said Alex. 'We'll go with Silver Lining. But it'll eat into our profits, mark my words.'

'Since we've made fuck-all this week that won't hurt us,' said Barry, then he turned on me. 'And if *you* don't pull your finger out you'll be on the sandwich board again.'

'Balls to you,' I said. He looked at me funny, but he didn't do anything. Good job too.

We agreed to give it another shot but none of us was in a good mood. Things cheered up a bit when Barry's dad turned up. He was chipper – he'd had a call from the girl making the documentary about London cabbies and she wanted to interview him again. 'And it turns out one of the other blokes is a fucking Asian, so really it's down to two of us. Things are looking very handsome,' he said rubbing his hands.

I suddenly felt like shutting him up. 'Twenty quid says you don't make it,' I said.

His jaw dropped. He looked at Barry, and Barry said, 'You're on. Twenty quid each.'

'Count me in,' said Alex.

I don't like people who don't like Asians. And now it might cost me sixty quid. Oh well.

When you hit the bottom, you bounce. Some bounce higher than others. Some bounce right back. Me, I landed heavily. Then lay there for a long while. Finally I stirred. Picked myself up. And began the long climb, back to my station in life.

I don't think it would have happened without Rose. She came along in the middle of June and turned everything upside down.

PART 3

O Rose

1

New Albion

Rose was just like he remembered her — fair skinned, unsmiling. When the fifty-three-seater pulled up Clive rushed out to tell her where to park it. They had a new spot around the corner where the police weren't likely to bother them. Barry was still flying around the entrance to the tourist information centre. Or rather, he had been. Now he was talking to Hiroko and Akemi, two Japanese girls, pocket sized and giggly. He could see himself going through both of them with barely a pause for breath.

Albion was in a shocking state. Alex, AKA the Chief Executive Officer, spent most of the day at home in his boxer shorts, drinking tea, eating toast and downloading junk from the internet. With his free hand he worked the cell phone, trying to drum up business amongst his industry contacts. He was disappointed to discover how many people did not think he was the most skilful negotiator since Pitt the Elder. His landlady had been on to him about the back rent, a ghastly inconvenience that after three months was becoming a crisis. He was thinking of giving his godfather a call to see if there were any jobs going.

Barry spent his days and evenings in a fog of lager and cigar smoke. Now that he had a good excuse to sniff around the West End again the supply of women had resumed, but enjoyable though that was, he knew he still had to make a living. He was a partner in a business that had to be a success. To hear the other two talk about it, establishing the brand, growing the company and getting into the black were the most important things in life. The idea that being a businessman was the only way to be a man had hopped across from the other two like rape across a hedgerow. The traditional values — fucking and fighting and drinking and making a few nicker on the side – didn't seem to count for much compared to business plans and spreadsheets and corporate identity. Taking the piss out of Alex had become increasingly ineffective, and even Clive seemed to know what he was doing. For Barry that was the trouble with the upper classes, they had so many invisible advantages. Their expensive schools, their contacts in the City, their dickie bows, and their weird ideas about what he was capable of. When it got too much for him he lost himself in foreign fanny, beer and fantasies of getting out. His dream was that his dad would make it big with this taxi documentary, with lots of cut-aways to Barry, who would end up being his dad's manager for the spin-offs – the clothing line, getting in free to clubs, opening supermarkets ... Maybe even a docusoap of his own?

'Clive Pointing, Albion Tours,' Clive said holding out his hand to the driver. She looked smaller than he remembered. In the driver's seat, her back looked short and her thighs spread out in her faded jeans. She was more normal.

'I'm Rose.'

'My, er ... Barry'll be along in a minute.'

'Oh, is *he* coming?'

'Yes. I don't know if your boss told you ...'

'My boss? What boss?'

'... But we started our own company, a spin-off from Britannia.'

'Oh yeah, I heard about them,' she said, and broke into a wide smile which showed off her straight white teeth. 'That lot were a joke.'

'I'll just go and ... you know ...' Clive smiled nervously and ducked back off the coach. The first punters were gathering on the pavement, bothered and bewildered, muttering to anyone that passed 'Is this Albion? Is this bus going to Stonehenge?'

'Yes ladies and gents, have your tickets ready!' He made his voice as stentorian as he could, as though addressing assembly at school. Just as the first dozen scrambled on Barry arrived with more. Rose saw in her wing mirror that as he helped one of the Japs up the steps he patted her bottom. She rolled her eyes, then ignored him.

Clive was feeling edgy, worried that Rose might think they were a bunch of losers. As they sped along the M3 he hoped she was listening to his commentary. Passing Winchester he mentioned the school, how it was the oldest public school in the country, founded in 1382 by William Wykeham.

'Has the government been involved with education that long?' shouted out a middle-aged American. She was all ready for a debate about the nanny state and by extension, the Englishman's taste for corporal punishment.

'Aha, no madam, "public" in this sense merely means that in 1382 it was rare for a school to be open to the general public, that is, anyone who could afford it. What you call a public school we call a state school.'

He noticed Rose didn't bat an eyelid but Barry was listening, with a little scowl.

'Winchester itself was once the capital of Wessex and the *de facto* capital of England until the Norman conquest. You'd be surprised how the balance of power has shifted around the country. Before the Romans arrived, for instance, London was actually a rather pathetic little village. The Celtic tribal chiefs preferred to live in what we today call Kent and Essex. Nowadays, Essex is synonymous with nouveau riche vulgarity and brainless materialism, Beverly Hills with a fiftieth of the money and less sunshine, if you will. And there were times when other cities were important: Bristol, for instance, was once the third-biggest city in the country, now it's just another theme-parked dockland with nothing new to sell and a load of ugly flats full of bored kids. Oh, the University is quite posh.' He knew this because Tina used to go on about their rowing rivalry with Exeter, and he had seen Alex nod approvingly when the place came up in conversation.

'Now is anyone interested in King Arthur and the Knights of the Round Table?'

Most of the hands went up, and the Japanese girls conferred excitedly.

'William the Conqueror built one of his first castles at Winchester. The only surviving part of the design is the Great Hall, which itself is a replacement from 1235. But it's here that you'll find the famous Round Table. It looks like a giant dart board with a picture of a king where the twenty would be. Just so you don't waste your time, it's a fake, made in the thirteenth century. King Arthur was supposedly this King of Britain who resisted the Anglo Saxons when they invaded in the sixth Century. Well when I say "resisted", he got his arse kicked enough times and ended up in the south-west corner of the country. But stories about him didn't really get going until the mid 1100s. The English love a loser – Boadicea, Harold, any revolting peasants who get cut down by men on horses with swords. Wat Tyler, for instance. He was this fellow called Walter, a roofer from Essex, who on the 14th of June, 1381, led a load of blokes from Kent and Essex into London, ransacking Lambeth Palace, killing the Archbishop of Canterbury and the Lord Treasurer, shredding the King's mum's sheets in the Tower. They even sprung the famous preacher from prison, John Ball, and shouted "Death to all lawyers! John Ball hath rungeth your bell!" Anyway, the King was some spotty fourteen-year-old, Richard the Second, whose granddad had gone prematurely senile and whose dad, the Black Prince, never made it to the throne. He went to Smithfield, where the meat market was, Jack the Ripper and all that, and which they're now handing over to the art yuppies and café-bar crowd, where Wat got into a bit of a barney with the lord mayor, a fishmonger called William Walworth, who knocked him off his horse. Wat got stabbed, like a lot of other men after him, and died. Of course when they went after the King he did the ballsy thing and rode towards them saying "Sirs will you kill your King?" and they ended up dispersing. That's the thing about the English. We're good at raising a mob, but we're also very good at dispersing.'

He glanced at Barry, who was frowning at him. He decided to talk about land use.

'One thing I always love about summer in this country is how soon the hay comes in. Over there you'll see a machine that forms haycocks.' Bouncing up a country lane perpendicular to the motorway was a red combine harvester. 'In a few weeks you can come back here and there'll be rows and rows of hay stacks, round like two-metre wheels of cheese, sometimes wrapped in black plastic to help turn them into silage. And you'll know the harvest's in and the little bit of wheat this country still produces has gone to market. The process may be mechanised, from harrowing the soil to turning the loaves out of the bread tins, but there are still ways in which we are connected to the seasons. Our farmers still have to know their weather and their soil. Some people still work the land instead of watching telly. It's not quite all over for us yet.'

Rose glanced at him in the mirror. The passengers stared out of the window, searching for the world he was describing.

Just before Stonehenge they were stopped at a police check point. It was a couple of days before the Summer Solstice and the people were on the move. Clive grabbed the mike. 'Ladies and gentlemen, they take the Solstice very seriously around here. As you can see, there are a lot of scruffy people around. These are the hippies, the hippie punks, the squatters, the tunnel dwellers, the tree-occupiers, the New Agers, the New Age ravers, the white-collar druids, the travellers, the travellers who live with their mums nine months of the year, witches, warlocks, and school kids having a laugh ... these people are trying, between them, to forget the world of cashpoints and microwave ovens by staging a pagan spectacle, a celebration of the sun coming up. That sound you can hear is the police helicopters patrolling the exclusion zone, which is put up every year. Some say it's standard procedure crowd control, some say it's to protect the stones, some say it's part of a Masonic conspiracy to control the sacred sites at the peak of their power. Personally I think it's just a media spectacle contrived to kick off what we call the silly season, the time when journalists are given free rein to say what they want, a sort of three-month Anglo Saxon media *mardi gras*. Roll up your sleeves and let your hair down. But I'll leave it up to you to decide.'

The police waved them through and soon everyone was walking around the monument, trying to keep their disappointment in check by making observations about the stones' size and their greyness. The sky was almost clear and there was a strong breeze blowing across Salisbury Plain. Rose stood listening, a slight flush in her face from the cool air. Barry asked them all to imagine the virgins, *etcetera*, *etcetera*, but he seemed a little subdued. As soon as he'd done his spiel he disappeared for a cigarette.

'I've heard some rubbish in my life but that takes the biscuit,' she said when Clive came over and stood next to her.

'What do you mean?' He said, looking her straight in the eye. He liked having the chance to talk to Rose, about anything.

'Him. Who d'you think I meant?' She had a smile that could change meaning depending on how long she held it for, or what she did with her eyes or her voice. Right now Clive could feel she wanted to poke fun at him, and his back stiffened slightly.

'Yeah well, Barry's very . . . he's very popular. Especially with the ladies. I mean women.'

She gave a little laugh and shrugged, but didn't walk away.

Clive was content just to stand next to her, pretending to care about the stones.

'Do you like all this?' he asked.

'Not this time of year. All the tourists. I've been here with me mates for the winter solstice though, that's a laugh.'

Me mates. The words went through him like a sword. It was the first indication of any sort of outside life. *Me mates* was more working class than he had hoped. When he'd seen her reading that book he assumed she was *one of us*. And the fact that she had friends meant she would be harder to win over — a lonely person would be better disposed to him . . .

Clive scolded himself for letting his imagination get the better of him. But he wanted to go on talking to her. He tried mild mockery.

'Oh – a coach driver who tries to avoid the tourists eh?'

'I wasn't a coach driver then,' she said coolly.

'That's right. You were a motorcycle despatch rider.' He tried to say it without seeming superior.

'Did that Barry tell you that? God, he can't get anything right,' she sighed. 'I was an RAC Recovery person, on the bikes.'

'Why did you pack it in?'

'Too much carnage. I saw one too many families get pulped in their tin boxes.' She gazed out at the stones. Clive imagined she was replaying some horrible scene in her head and thought he could take advantage of her vulnerability. He was still thinking of the right question when she asked him, 'What about you?'

What about Clive? The question struck fear and joy in his heart. Joy because she might just care, fear because of the answer – that he had slept with a pupil.

'I was a Geography teacher for eighteen years, but I decided to get out of it. Fancied a change, you know.'

'Yeah, I know,' she said with that sly smile again. 'I often fancy a change myself. But people think it's weird. Most people here think change is bad. Which is not surprising, since they're used to waiting for it to happen. It's like my dad. He's run an estate for forty years, but he's never thought about what he'd do if it all went belly up.'

'Yes! I know exactly what you mean.' He smiled at her. She was six inches shorter than him so he could see down into the parting of her hair. He got a good look at her eyes for the first time. He'd assumed they were blue, but they were the sort of greeny-grey that changed with the colour of her surroundings. Out here in the sun on the grassy plain they were very grey.

'This company, Albion,' she said. 'It's a load of crap isn't it?'

'Eh? Why do you say that? We're only just getting going ...'

'I can just tell, you don't know what you're doing, because you don't know much about this country.'

'Well, no one's asking you,' said Clive, immensely pissed off. 'When I need a coach driver's advice I'll get back to you.' As he stomped off she shrugged and went back to staring at the stones.

2

Information Nation

Barry was in no mood to chat on the way back. Not even Akemi and Hiroko, the Japanese girls, interested him. He took an empty seat behind them and re-read his tabloid. When Hiroko put her face in the gap and tried to be cute he sent her packing. This whole thing of not knowing any history was getting him down. For the first time in his life he felt inadequate. He equated educated with posh, and normally with posh people he could stare them down, or out-drink them, or out-spend them, or shag their women, but this was different. He felt he had been lured into brainy territory to be humiliated.

He also didn't like the bird, the driver, the lesbian. She was trouble.

He got his mobile out and called a few people. First his dad, who was having a cup of tea in the taxi shelter in Knightsbridge. Ron hadn't heard any more from the telly girl but he was quietly confident.

'Who's that lad you used to know who works in telly? I'd like a word with him.'

'Who's that then?' asked Barry.

'You know, breakfast telly, docklands, fat fucker . . .'

'Oh, Fat Paul? He never worked in telly. He delivered the break-fasts, that was all. Van driver. He knows fuck-all, you don't wanna talk to him.'

'Giss his number, son, I need to cover all me bases.'

Barry looked him up on the screen of his phone. 'I'm telling you he knows fuck-all. He's still driving that old van,' he said with a derisive sniff.

He called Alex to see what the fuck he was up to, the lazy posh twat.

He handed the phone over to Clive with a glare. 'It's *Alexander*, he wants to say something to you.'

Clive took it sitting in the front seat, from where he had been silently fretting about Rose for an hour.

'You what? Pack it in already? You can't leave us in the lurch. Bloody hell we've only just started ... I don't care what your father says ... Well you'll just have to move somewhere cheaper. You're in this for keeps now ... What are the bookings like? Nothing? *Nothing?* Oh Lord, what are you doing all day? Look, look, we're heading back now. Get your arse in gear and meet us in the pub at five. Yes, *five*. The Shakespeare. Yes. And bring your damn computer.'

Rose waited a few minutes before she spoke.

'Trouble at mill?'

Clive mumbled. He didn't need this.

'Where is the mill anyway? Your office.'

'Alex works from home. Richmond.'

'What system do you use?'

'Pardon?'

'What computer?'

'Oh. Yes, he has a computer. A laptop. Don't ask me about systems though. I don't have anything to do with all that.'

She said nothing more until they were churning their way through Belgravia. Rose was a good driver. She had wiggled through strange back roads to get them on the M4, and seemed to have an instinct for where to go. In the country they'd whistle down country lanes, the long grass touching both sides of the coach, cows' faces so close you could see their taste buds, only to cut under an aqueduct and swing on to the motorway. Now she threaded through the Duke of Westminster's creamy neighbourhood until boom! there was Victoria again, seen from an angle he never knew existed.

'So when do you pay me?' she asked.

'Ah yes,' he said guiltily. 'Well, Alex is in the pub with his cheque book ...'

'OK. I'll come in.'

Barry sized up the whip-round money in his pint glass, ignoring the passengers as they departed.

'This'll just about cover the flyers and a round each. Bollocks!' He banged the glass down on the dashboard.

'Eh, easy! Take it easy!' said Clive.

'Watch me frigging dash!' said Rose.

'I'm fucking sick of all this. Where's that Alex plonker ...' Barry stormed off.

Ten minutes later Barry was in a slightly better mood. He'd bought himself a lager, put some songs on the juke box, and watched a couple of blokes playing the new trivia machine. They didn't know *anything*.

He went over to Clive and Rose who were sitting at a table with their own drinks. Clive had a pint, she had a Pepsi.

'I thought you'd be a Guinness girl.'

'Why?'

'Never mind. Or bitter.'

'You're bitter,' she said with an innocent smile.

'Come on now, let's not ... ah here he is.'

Alex walked in, wearing a cricket jumper and jeans. He sat down with a grim expression.

'This is Rose, the driver. She needs paying.'

'Er ... I'm afraid ...'

'Just get your cheque book out.'

'That's just it. I used the last one half an hour ago to get petrol.'

Rose stayed calm, but the other two rolled their eyes and protested.

'Plonker.'

'Al-ex!'

'Tell you what,' said Rose. 'Show me your computer and I'll let you off until Monday.'

They were all puzzled.

'Go on then,' Clive urged him.

He handed it over with a rueful look.

Rose began clicking through the directory structure. They watched her for a minute, until she looked up and said, 'This file called "Book 1". Is this your database?'

They all gathered round the screen. 'Book 1' was a spreadsheet Alex kept the bookings on. He explained that 'Book 2' was his contact list. Rose glanced at him, carried on, then looked up smiling.

'These figures in the cells, what do you do with them? Some of the totals are wrong.'

'I, I add them up ...' he said feebly.

'How?'

'Er, with a calculator.' Clive groaned. Barry looked for clues in the others' faces and quickly figured it out.

'The whole point of a spreadsheet is that it does all that for you. You give cells values and it adds the whole column up or whatever. How long have you been doing this?'

'Er, since Maxine ... Maxine used to take care of the number crunching ...'

All three of them groaned. 'You daft fucker,' said Barry, surprised, elated and ready to stick the boot in.

'Well it's not my fault, I'm supposed to be management not clerical,' he whined.

'What do you think management does?' said Clive. 'For Christ's sake.'

'Yep, your contact list is just the same, just a load of names and phone numbers in a spreadsheet. Nothing linked. How do you do form letters?'

'Form letters?'

They groaned again, Barry loudest of all. 'No wonder we're pissing our money away! Fucking hell.' He looked round at the bar, to trigger the next round, but the others were watching Rose.

She addressed them all. 'Where do you advertise?'

Clive and Barry hadn't even thought of advertising beyond flyers. Flyers were cheap and you could see who was getting them. They stared at Alex, who admitted they didn't, they couldn't afford to. Except for a small box in the free ads paper. Rose groaned.

'It's advertising, don't you get it? You don't pay unless it works. No one does. Show me your flyers then.'

Alex had a new one ready. It said 'It's Grand up North' and included a vague itinerary, some ambitious pricing, and bad clip-art of York Minster with a coach going past it.

'Oh dear. You lot haven't got a chance, have you,' she said. Barry marched off to the bar, shaking his head. Alex blushed. Clive looked at her hopefully.

'Can you help us?'

Rose put a falling strand of hair behind her ear and started tapping away at the keyboard. First she changed everything about the flyer — the colour, the font, the destination, the price, the file name ... she even found better clip-art deep on his hard drive. 'I'm going to do one for the Midlands too, just to compare.' She called it the 'Heart of England Tour'.

Then she went through his spreadsheets, inserting rows and columns, setting values, copying data. She rationalised the Albion address book and imported everything into a more powerful database programme.

'There now. Every time you phone, fax or e-mail someone it'll find them and make a journal entry, so you'll know who you've spoken to.'

'That would be good. It does get confusing remembering who you've said what to.'

Barry came back from the bar with pints for everyone.

'Who said I wanted ale?' she asked him coldly.

'Go on, drink it. It'll put hairs on yer chest.'

'I never said I don't drink. I'm driving.'

'Ahhhh,' he mocked.

'I could drink you under the table any day,' she said.

'Woo-hoo!' Barry rocked back in his chair delightedly. 'Don't kid yourself darlin', you might be a bit different, but don't think it makes you a man. Naaaar-har-har, naar-har-har ...'

'Oh what are you talking about? Anyway ...' She shrugged and went on with what she was doing.

'Where did you learn all this?' asked Clive. He was melting with admiration, especially at her ability to stand up to the other two. He felt she had leadership qualities, like himself. Perhaps she wasn't from some grotty estate after all.

'Just a hobby. I don't suppose you have a website do you?'

'That's all bollocks innit, the internet. I read in the paper where it's just for perverts and Greeks.'

'Not yet,' said Alex. His voice had gone back to being deep and boomy, as though the recent humiliations had been forgotten. 'But I'm in the process of setting one up.'

'I can do it right now if you want. Who's your ISP?'

They all looked blank. Barry tugged at his chin flab. She was getting to be a bit of a smartarse with her three-letter acronyms.

She tapped away for a few minutes, asking Alex questions. Barry and Clive found themselves cut out so they went over to the trivia machine. Barry wasn't very generous with selecting the categories. He picked sport whenever he could.

'Who was the first goalkeeper to captain his side to an FA Cup final victory?

'A) Gordon Banks, Leicester City

'B) Peter Schmeichel, Manchester Utd

'C) Dave Beasant, Wimbledon ...'

He read it out for Clive's benefit, but his hand had already flashed to the C button.

Clive didn't have a clue.

'What did Cassius Clay first change his name to?

'A) Cassius X

'B) Mohammed Ali

'C) Cassius Ali ...'

He tapped A with barely a motion. Correct.

'Which Kentucky city calls itself the Horse Centre of America?

'A) Frankfort

'B) Lexington

'C) Bowling Green ...'

'Frankfort!' shouted Clive. Barry slapped B.

'What are you on about? It's Lexington, innit? What's Frankfort anyway?'

'Oh I think it's the state capital ... um ...'

'Shut up if you don't know the answer.'

Rose was still fiddling with the computer when they got back. Barry bought everyone a drink with his twenty quid winnings.

'It's a real mess this,' she said. 'Anyway, I've done you a basic website, you'll have to fill in the details later. Where do you go anyway?'

'Er ...'

'All over,' said Clive. 'Canterbury, Brighton, Bath, Henge, Corfe Castle, Cotswolds, Stratford, Warwick Castle, York, Manchester ...'

'What's in Manchester?' asked Rose.

'Coronation Street,' said Barry. 'Birds love it.'

'Right on up as far as we want,' said Alex. 'Basically it's all in the embryonic stage. Actually we're looking for permanent drivers ...'

Rose just laughed. 'Right, let's connect. Give me your cellphone.'

Barry handed it over reluctantly, but she took one look and tossed it back. 'Wrong type. What about you, blue eyes?'

Alex's she approved of, then rummaged in the laptop bag for a cable and adapter. She plugged in, dialled up and was away.

'Credit card number?' she said.

They all looked at each other.

'Maxed out I'm afraid,' lied Alex.

'Cash man,' said Barry, pointing to himself. 'Cash only. Do everyfink with cash.'

Clive painfully reached for his wallet. He knew that if it was cancelled now it would be very embarrassing.

She put the numbers in and it was accepted. It took about five minutes to load the site, then she showed it to them, live online. They were like kids being shown a magic trick.

'You don't seem to be very organised,' she said, snapping the computer shut and sliding it back to Alex. 'I mean, where's your office again?' She didn't wait for an answer. 'You should be taking advantage of this technology. Get yourself a virtual office. Do everything through your website. Forward your phones. Advertise. Send out fax and e-mail bulletins, get your website mentioned in guide books, all that stuff. It's all practically free, and no one need know you're just a bunch of ... three people. You should go for it. I know how tourists make decisions. They start as though they are going to shop around, then they get really sick of it and go for either the cheapest, or the name they like best. And you're certainly cheap.'

'Albion's not a bad name,' said Clive.

'No you're right, it is good. Foreigners get it. Though if you're going for the lowest common denominator I don't see why you didn't just call yourselves "England". Seriously though, this is the sort of company I'd be up for investing in, if you knew what you were doing. A small tour company that's quick to respond to the market and has low overheads ...'

Clive snorted. 'Low overheads, low profits to match.'

'That's his fault,' said Barry digging his elbow in the posh boy's direction.

'Just shut it, bloody yob,' said Alex, his eyes flashing. He wasn't going to be humiliated on both flanks.

'Steady on ...'

'Calm down, calm down!' said Barry in a strangulated accent, waving his hands. Rose was the only one who smiled.

At that moment Barry's dad and his tout brother Stu turned up. Barry proudly showed them the Albion website, and both agreed that it was f-f-f-f-f-facking amazing. Stu said he had five hundred tickets he was trying to shift for the Glastonbury Festival. 'It's one hundred and ten quid a head at the gate.'

Everyone shrugged and said they weren't interested, but Rose piped up. 'What did you pay for them?'

Stu looked at his brother to see if she was safe. 'T-t-t-t-two q-q-q-q-quid each, wholesale. Selling f-f-f-f-face value.'

'What did you say?'

Barry glared at her, as if to say 'no one makes my brother repeat himself'.

She got the message, and continued hurriedly, 'Two quid, that's good. And it lasts three days? Well, you know what we should do?'

This 'we' was new, and it warmed Clive's heart.

'Why don't you sell Barry fifty at say, a fiver a piece, and we'll run a coach there. Bring some tourists in for the day. Charge them the usual plus the coach, plus a mark-up.'

Stuart was shaking his head but Barry thought it was a good idea. They went over to the corner to hammer out the deal, then announced that twelve quid was a fair price, and they'd charge the punters one hundred and fifty quid for the package.

Barry had hit upon the idea of taking the armbands back off the punters at the end of each night and reselling them the next day. Over three days each ticket could bring in £450.

Rose looked very happy. And she still hadn't touched her pint. 'Well I'm off. I'll do you an advert tonight and send it out, all formats.' she said to Alex. 'See you in a few days.'

They all turned to watch her go.

'So that's the lezzy?' asked Barry's dad.

'Don't think m-m-m-m-much of her arse.'

'She's not a lesbian,' said Clive. 'She's a very nice girl. Or woman, I should say.'

3

Barnas-s-s-s-s-s-selling

Albion Tours took three days off in anticipation of the Glastonbury cash bonanza.

Alex White spent the time looking at flats. His landlady had recently caught him red handed stealing from the laundry room, and while she would have been flattered into forgiveness had the wares in question been her own cavernous M&S knicks, because they were another tenant's she reluctantly drew the line. He had a week to get out.

He searched for a flat using the internet, and through its disregard for geography found himself looking outside his ideal catchment area, the theoretical centre of which was the Pitcher and Piano, a Sloaney pub in Fulham. The West End seemed like a good idea, or so the estate agent said. She said a lot of young executives were moving back into the city centre and leading the sophisticated urban existence enjoyed by continental Europeans. He could have his latte and his laptop in the bar café and not miss a trick.

'Fan-fucking-tastic!' he said at one point. He could feel a bond with her already. This was exactly what he wanted. He ended up accepting a dim studio just west of Portland Place, and spent a day throwing out Wonga ring binders, takeaway menus and mouldy sports gear, before loading up his Jeep and starting a new life in W1. Parking, he told his father, was a bit of a nightmare, but then you *were* at the centre of it all.

Barry spent a few days helping his wife look after the kids. Summer holidays were always a pain in the arse. The girls were all right, they could play outside the flats till it got dark at ten. It was just that there

was so much sport on TV he ended up arguing with Christine a lot –
'Stenders versus Wimbledon, Coronation Street versus the cricket highlights
… and that was just early in the evening. Later Barry himself would
be torn between watching his comedies like Canned, or The Surreal Student
Factory, or The Blokes Who Drink Beer, and Formula I racing. Still, he had
his little son to look forward to. One day they'd be able to outvote the
others democratically.

They were already talking baby names. Phil (after Phil Collins) led the
pack, although Chrissie kept saying that since he'd named the last one,
this one should be her choice, and she was thinking something exotic,
something Hollywood-ish, like Ocean or Leaf or River. Luckily Barry
had a good memory for certain bits of history and he pointed out that
River was the name of that kid who choked on his own puke outside
that night club, it was inallapapers. He tried to imagine managing his son's
international football career – the merchandising arm, the Bowie Bonds,
the night club grand opening, the film premières, the standing in the frost
in his sheepskin challenging the sanity of various managers – and cringed
to think the little thumb-sucking foetus with the visible tadger and the
apparent ambidexterity would be saddled with a name like River.

There was still the question of money for the boy, the question of a
legacy. Barry was confident that he could give him the best moral education
available – he would know right from wrong and when to do either, he
would love women, hate the Old Bill and treat everyone else with rispeck –
but he was still worried about him growing up poor. Tower blocks were
all right in the 1960s and 1970s when he was growing up, but nowadays
nobody who was anybody ever came from a tower block. He needed to
make some money, and he was worried that joining up with those two
ponces might be a mistake. Even middle-class people could be useless
fuckers, but it was hard to know at the beginning. Certainly Alex was
a waste of space. And Clive seemed just as interested in getting in that
girl's knickers as making Albion great.

The Swan wasn't a cure-all either. There were only so many conversations
he could have with his brothers down the pub. Lately his other brother Oz
had been in there a lot. He was the white-collar black sheep of the family.
He had left The Bulldog, the patriotic publication where he had worked his
way up from ad sales to Associate Editor, due to ideological differences,
and had helped set up a splinter publication, Pit Bull. The concept was a
forward-looking patriotism and the establishment of a new English identity.
This meant lots of articles about greyhound racing and pub singalongs, and

while Barry thought his brother's heart was in the right place, he didn't like being quoted in every single issue.

There were only so many taxing conversations he could have down the pub, and only so many nappies he could change at home. By the time Glastonbury came around he was dying to get back to work.

Clive Pointing gave himself three days off. His only chore was to fetch the tickets off Stu the tout. Unfortunately he had to go to Wembley Stadium for them. He felt a whisper of guilt to be passing so near to his mother's house without stopping. He imagined her sitting on the edge of the couch in her housecoat watching *Mastermind* or *Blue Peter*, or Gordon towelling her after a bath and putting her to bed. Then his selfish streak cut in and reminded him that he had been dead to them for the last few weeks without being missed. And that she had been dead to him too, for a lot longer.

At Wembley he joined the crowds hurrying to the new stadium. It didn't look like a sporting event to him, the people were too middle aged and too middle class. They seemed like a nice bunch. Couples. Parents. It was only when he was nearly there that he noticed all the Elton John tat for sale from the vendors. 'Sir Elton John', he read on a nylon flag, and wondered how this could have passed him by. He and the piano player were practically the same age. When he was growing up he loved 'Rocket Man' and 'Crocodile Rock' and 'B-b-b-benny And The Jets,' and 'A Song For Guy' (which he informed his mother wasn't about a gorilla, it was about a dead post room boy). What was it he said once in the paper? 'You can call me a fat, talentless poof, but you mustn't tell *lies* about me.' Then he played Princess Diana's funeral and now he was a knight. Pitying himself, Clive wondered that such a normal little bloke, such a Reg if ever there was one, should still be around, twenty-five years after his sell-by date, not just making music and loads of wonga, but being called Sir by everyone too. How Clive had misjudged everything. He wondered if everyone else had as bad a sense of history-in-the-making as he. His Elton records, which might have been worth something, were long gone. His CDs too.

There were clumps of men, a few black, mostly white, all wearing jeans, hanging around touting. 'Barnasellin, barnasellin,' they muttered. 'Tickets mate tickets?'

'No thank you,' he said.

Many of them had crushed Cockney faces like Barry, fidgety eyes and stiff necks. He watched as one of them approached two girls.

'How mach you got, girls?'

'*Firty* each,' said the talker. She nervously showed the cash. They were nice looking, but that didn't spare them the treatment. The fellow flashed them some tickets, took their money and turned on his heels so they had to hurry to keep up. He got into a conversation with two other touts. Meanwhile the girls got more nervous, about losing their money, about the police, and about missing the start. They had to have seats together. The lad kept them waiting by calling over yet another person, who eventually sold them a pair for ninety quid and told them they were great seats.

Clive had never bought from a tout before, but now he realised the value of them. They bought low, and sold high or not at all. They cleared a profit an hour before the gates even opened. Everything after that was gravy, and they preferred to go home with a pocket full of unused tickets than let the punters know they were weak and would drop their prices. They didn't stick around for the entertainment.

He found Stu on his own, his baseball cap pulled low on his face. 'Barnas-s-s-s-s-sellin,' he was saying. 'All tickets, all p-p-p-p-p-prices.' He didn't look busy. He seemed quite pleased to see Clive, and pulled a brick of Glastonburies out of his denim jacket pocket.

'Thanks,' said Clive, and turned to go home. A big roar went up, the honky-tonk piano began, and Elton kicked in with his piss-take falsetto version of 'Goodbye English Rose'.

'S-s-s-s-safe!' said Stu.

Clive enjoyed his few days off wallowing in anonymity. The cellos had definitely stopped, the stress and sadness had gone from his mouth, and he even looked forward to morning. The phone was disconnected, he wasn't getting any mail, and no one had knocked on his door for a while. He pulled up the carpet to find a decent hardwood floor, and threw out the rest of his possessions — paperwork and old text books, it all had to go. He kept one chair's worth of clothes, one shelf of library books, the cricket ball, and enough kitchen gear to make tea and sandwiches. The weather became warm so he climbed out of the window and sunbathed on the patch of grass in his underpants while reading the *Anglo-Saxon Chronicle*.

This was a cock-eyed history of the country that went from before the Romans up to AD 1154. Just to make things more complicated, they didn't start writing it until the ninth century, so the further back it went, the sketchier it got. Once they'd caught up with themselves they wrote it at the end of every year, just a few lines at a time. Added to that, they used to copy the whole thing out by hand every now and then, to distribute to different monasteries, inevitably making more mistakes. Sometimes someone would insert a poem, or revise something, or a big chunk would go up in flames. If the authors had a motto it would be 'Getting It Wrong, All The Time'. It reminded him of school, the staff room trying to put together a letter or a petition. How it would be passed around and photocopied and tinkered with until there were four different versions and no one could agree on anything.

Never had Clive seen such a sad old document.

'671. There was the great death of birds.'

That was it for 671.

Poor old King Alfred spent years trying to get the thickos to read and write, while fighting off the Vikings, and his men got their arses kicked many a time.

'900. Alfred, son of Aethelwulf, passed away, six nights before All Saints' Day. He was king over all the English, except for that part that was under Danish rule; and he held that kingdom for one and a half years less than thirty.'

It was one long tale of invasions, priest deaths, comets and cattle-slayings. And not much about anyone being born, since this was history on the fly and you never knew who might grow up to be famous.

'1087. One thousand and eighty-seven years after our Saviour Christ's nativity, in the twenty-first year that William reigned and ruled over England, as God granted him, fell a very heavy and very pestilential year in this land. Such disease came among men that full night every other man was in the worst way, that is, with fever, and that so severely that many men died in this evil. After, through the severe bad weather, as we told before, came very great famine all over England, so that many hundreds of people died a wretched death through hunger. Alas, how miserable and how pitiful a time was that, when wretched men lay fevered full near to death, and after came sharp hunger and undid them withal.'

A bit later someone wrote, with weary optimism, 'Their troubles passed on; so can mine.'

Clive put his book on his lap and sighed, staring at the blue sky, listening to the hum of the transformers and the hiss of traffic. It was hard to believe this was the same country. Alfred sounded all right though.

He spotted Danny and his girlfriend looking at him from their window and waved them down. 'You'd better climb through my window. The door's nailed shut.'

They came with eight cans of lager, a radio and a giant Toblerone, and passed a happy afternoon talking about the state of things. Danny wanted to know if the gangsters were back.

'Danny, if they are then they're only white-collar gangsters. And frankly I'm not worried. I've spent my whole life worrying about consequences. Over here we spend so long looking over our shoulders that we never get a good look at the future. Well *I* say bollocks to that. Some chinless knobhead brings down a two-hundred-year-old merchant bank and instead of being shamed he's a celebrity. Why should I worry about a couple of credit cards?'

The youngsters sat at his feet and lapped it up. The FM station played oldies. A dance record came on, proud of its artificial drums and plastic noise, delighted with itself. A girl's voice spoke some lines, amateurly: 'O, to be in England in the summertime, with my love ...' Clive heard them through the gauzy pleasure of the alcohol and knew for certain the words applied to him. Danny started going on about all the breakthrough indie films that had been backed with plastic and Clive egged him on to do the same.

'Exactly! What's the worst that can happen? Your film bombs, you declare bankruptcy, and you start again. By the way, do you two fancy Glastonbury this weekend? We're doing a sweet deal on a day trip ...'

4

Triumph

The first sign they were getting near Glastonbury was the scruffs walking purposefully down country lanes carrying plastic containers full of pale-brown liquid.

'Wossat then? Piss? Do they drink their own, these Crusties?' said Barry loudly. He and Clive were standing at the front of the coach staring out at the scene before them. Rose had them on a B-Road to avoid congestion, squeezing around post-boxes and brushing the weeds growing from ancient churches.

'Scrumpy,' she said.

Barry raised his eyebrows, but Clive ignored him.

'Three quid a gallon.'

'What, you've been here before?' asked Clive.

'Couple of times.' She paused, then volunteered just enough information to make Clive's ears burn. 'Old boyfriend was in a band.'

'Oh yeah?' said Barry. 'Anyone I've heard of?'

'Probably not.' She paused again while she changed gear. 'They were shite anyway.'

Clive was happy to hear it. Though her language worried him. He didn't want to compete with some leather-trousered stud who choppered in from his rock-star hotel and spent all his time in shades. Attitude was beyond him.

Everyone was in a good mood. Thanks to Rose's advertising they'd sold out their batch of tickets. The motley crew that assembled – Scandinavian hipsters, suburban school kids, middle-aged tourists, even a few Yanks – suggested she'd hit a commercial sweet spot. Danny and his girlfriend were along too, and they boosted morale by passing round a hypermarket-size bottle of vodka and playing their boom-box. By the time they got to Somerset people were hopping off the coach to piss and hopping back on with cider. Rose wasn't bothered. The first time Clive asked her to stop, she just shrugged.

'The customer is always right,' was all she said, and gave a giggle he hadn't come across before.

'This whole region is known as the Isle of Avalon,' said Clive, taking the mike, 'partly because King Arthur is supposed to have come here on a barge when he was mortally wounded, accompanied by weeping fairies, to be buried alongside his Queen Guinevere. Two bodies were found in Glastonbury in 1191, which were transferred to the local abbey's choir in 1278. In Celtic folklore Avalon was the meeting place of the dead, and Gwynn the god of the underworld was supposed to live here. That was good enough for people like William of Malmesbury and Thomas Malory to make a story out of. The tower, or Tor, you just saw on the top of the hill is at an elevation of 512 feet. Which must mean the water round here was pretty deep once.'

The passengers murmured, confused.

'The other big myth of the area — and this will probably make you laugh — is that Jesus Christ was here. Supposedly Joseph of Arimathea, one of the Virgin Mary's relatives, owned a lead mine in the Mendip Hills near by, and he brought his kinsman Jesus here during the Saviour's slack period. Hence William Blake's lines in the poem we refer to as "Jerusalem": "And did those feet in ancient time/Walk upon England's mountains green?" It was just the preface to his long poem called "Milton", although if he'd known it would end up being belted out by public schoolmasters and fifty thousand rugger buggers at Twickenham I don't think he would have bothered.' Clive didn't bother to explain the public school/private school thing again, he had too much to say.

'Another legend is that Joseph was imprisoned for twelve years after the death of Jesus, and was kept alive by drinking from the Holy Grail — the cup that was used to collect blood from the spear hole in Christ's side. Some other jokers say it was the chalice used at the Last Supper. The grail and the spear were later taken to Glastonbury by Joseph, where he founded the abbey and commenced the conversion of Britain. Of course this is all bollocks because there was no Glastonbury Abbey till the fourth century. But what do you expect from people in those days?

They'd believe anything.' Clive was enjoying himself again, saying whatever came into his mind.

They arrived at the farm where the festival took place, to be greeted by a breathtaking view. The hills were a sea of vehicles, glass glinting silver under the sun. A valley spread out before them, flooded with coloured tents and moving bodies. The stage, a metal pyramid, looked tiny in the scale of things, and other tents and marquees ran up the side of the hills into the fields. There was a large metal fence around everything like it was Belfast.

Rose asked for the microphone. The men were unsure of whether to give it to her – she was only being paid to drive, and besides, she wasn't one of them – but Clive handed it over.

'We'll meet back here at eleven after the last band and have you back in London by two at the latest. If you don't already know, Glastonbury is a great modern tradition, easily the best of all the rock festivals. All profits go to the charities Greenpeace, Oxfam and WaterAid, and all mess is cleared up by volunteers. Be careful of the hot sunshine, watch your belongings. And don't buy drugs from anyone with a Liverpool accent, they're probably fake.'

'Oh and hang on to your armbands. We need them back for s'curity purposes,' shouted Barry.

Everyone piled off the coach and Barry helped them through security. He knew how to handle people with walkie-talkies and coloured tennis shirts.

It was really hot. Rose put her hair up, then took off her sweatshirt and tied it around her waist. It was the first time Clive had got a good look at her. She had a lean, smooth neck, and her breasts pointed downwards. Barry took one glance and downgraded her to a backup bang.

'So,' said Clive, rotating his green wristband.

'Bar,' said Barry, hurrying off.

'I really have to eat,' said Rose.

Clive tagged along with her. He was amazed at the crowd – so many young people. He heard a lot of London accents and Bristol accents among the vendors whether they were selling chips or trips, but most of the kids had a neutral, home-counties sound, a south-east accent rubbed smooth by television, education and relocation. There were Welsh voices too, and Scousers, West Midlanders, generic northerners, but mostly it was a southern sound. His heart stopped for a moment when he thought he saw Amanda – a girl in a silver vest and shorts, soft brown hair, graceful arms, dancing with two boys — but when she turned the face was different.

They threaded their way through to a food stand. Rose went for a baked tofu and broccoli-sprout wrap, so Clive had the same.

'I've never had this before,' he said.

She laughed at his innocence, and he was surprised how easy-going she was. She didn't fit into the annoy-or-impress matrix that seemed to have governed most of his relations with women.

Rose bought him a beer and they sat down on the grass to watch a band. The programme described them as 'folk rock', and Clive listened for some trace of connection with the past. 'This one's called "From Lollards to Dullards",' barked the lead singer, a long-haired man in army trousers, but Clive couldn't make out the lyrics.

'See that drummer? He used to be in my boyfriend's band. He's dead kinky.' She laughed and lay back on the grass, chewing a stalk and looking at the sky.

Clive wanted to ask in what way, but was worried about opening a hypermarket-sized can of worms.

'I love the countryside here. We're so lucky to have pale-blue sky and grassy fields,' she said. 'Everywhere else seems so coarse, so overdone. You know, abroad.' He looked at the logo on her black T-shirt. It said Triumph.

'Have you travelled much?'

'I've been around Europe and Asia. And a bit of South America, the jungle.' She sat up on her elbow. 'You know that feeling when you come back from abroad, and everything looks so gentle and muted, the grey sky and concrete, small houses and hills? Well I get that feeling all the time now. It's like I'm permanently coming home. I can't really stand to be abroad for too long. Fortnight, max.'

'That's nice,' said Clive, enjoying being taken into her confidence. 'It must be nice to feel at home everywhere. Where are you from originally?'

'Meriden.'

'Centre of England?'

'Yep,' she said proudly.

'When we were growing up we lived in Coventry for a bit. That's a bit of a hole,' said Clive.

'It's one of those places nobody likes but nobody's been either. I haven't got time for that nonsense.'

'Not enough tourism for them. What have they got – Rover, the Cathedral . . .'

'Philip Larkin, the poet,' she said.

'Oh, you've heard of him?'

'Course. Haven't read all his poems though. We had to do him at school. The teacher tried to get him to come and do a talk but he told her to get lost.'

Clive made a mental note to get hold of the hedgehog poem again.

'By all accounts he was a bit of a cu . . . I mean, a wanker.'

She laughed and lay back on her elbow.

'And Lady Godiva,' he said.

'Now if you're looking for tourist crap, that's Class A.' She explained how the story of Leofric's wife riding naked through Cov town centre as a dare to make him repeal taxes didn't come into circulation until the late 1100s, one hundred and fifty years after they lived, and then the dare was probably only to go out without her finery on, not starkers. And the bit about Peeping Tom, the one pleb who looked and got blinded for his trouble, that was a misreading of a Renaissance painting of the scene – the bloke peeping through the letterbox was supposed to be the husband himself. 'Now they have a tour guide who goes round on horseback every summer, wearing a body stocking. Talk about the tail wagging the dog.'

'How d'you know all this?'

'Local knowledge, isn't it.'

Clive felt happier than he had done in ages. He sat back and enjoyed his beer and watched the people around him. As he picked his way between the tents in search of the toilets he noticed some people had marked out their own little front gardens with planks of wood, and sat on lawn chairs. Flags flew from the tops of tents like heraldic colours so that friends could find each other. Every now and then there was someone making a spectacle of themselves: a beautiful girl dancing, a lone guitarist, a bearded loon Clive's age lying down stark naked, tanning his tadger.

He queued for ages on a marsh of urine for a porta-loo, and when he got back Rose had gone. He got another beer and wandered to the Eco field to see the inventions that would save the world – an electric skateboard thing, a solar oven, a thing for turning old newspapers into firewood. He talked with a bloke who was building an ark in anticipation of global warming. A few stalls down there was a guy fretting about groundwater drying up. Clive informed him that Scotland was exporting water again, but the man wasn't very grateful.

He looked in at the Comedy tent, he caught half a play, he even had
a sit down in the Christian tent for people who needed a bit of peace and
quiet. Back in the beer queue he ran into Danny and some more Kiwis,
and they watched a few acts together. They were all excited about seeing
some New Zealanders play, and while most of the English sat them out,
Jo danced on Danny's shoulders and was projected on to the big screen.
It didn't take much to make people happy or proud.

As the sun went down camp fires were lit. The valley was studded with
tongues of gold flame, and the country stars came out. Clive felt a slight
katabatic wind, a coolness descending from the hills. With beer in his
veins it felt lovely to be able to know the right name for things in nature,
he only wished Rose was there to be impressed. He was sad that she'd
vanished. Still, everyone else seemed to be having a good time – teenagers
snogging, going ape, or just face-down drunk, beer vendors doubling their
prices, drug peddlers moving out from under the cover of the trees . . .

Just when he thought he was in the middle of a great pagan celebration
of life, all the bars and fast-food places closed and Clive found himself
scrambling for a warm can of beer and some crisps from a one of the
Cockney lager spivs. The stage lights went out and he hurried up the hill
to the coach park.

Rose was sitting in the driver's seat with the radio on when he got back.
That song was on again, 'Head high, head held high . . .', altogether too
jolly for Clive. It turned out Barry had come by and got them in backstage
and they'd had a great old time eating for free and, in Barry's case, loading
up at the bar and sniffing around the groupies. Apparently the Kiwis were
staying to party with their band, but everybody else was waiting to go.

Clive put a brave face on it, but his mind was spinning with beer and
laments for himself. He was always getting cut out of the loop. It was like
the black-tie crowd at university. Suddenly and without any warning they'd
be swarming, off to some social-calendar event or ritual he had no idea
existed. He tried to remember the thing about no man being an island,
who had said it and what they meant. It was the sort of thing his mother
would have known, once.

5

Progress

Rose nudged him awake. Everyone was off the coach and gone into the night. Barry had left a pile of green armbands on the dashboard.

'Ugh. I feel a bit rough,' said Clive.

She smiled. 'Better get a cab to Streatham. We want you back here at nine tomorrow.'

That 'we' again. It was enough to carry him all the way home.

A nap and a shower later it was happening all over again: Barry as he scanned the queue of boarding passengers for nice girls; Rose's face as she glanced in her mirrors; the Westway as they shot towards the west country; the fields, the plastic containers of scrumpy, the Tor on the hill. Clive repeated his commentary, with interest.

'I suppose a lot of you have heard of ley lines and are hoping for a ley experience, so I'd just like to point out that they are, in fact, bollocks. All this *newage* (and I mean to pronounce it that way) about them being navigational aids for aliens or paths for ghosts or places of special earth energy ... please forget all that right now. The whole thing started innocently in 1921 when a Herefordshire businessman called Alfred Watkins was sitting in his car one summer afternoon during a visit to Blackwardine in Herefordshire. He consulted a local map and noticed that a number of prehistoric and other ancient sites like churches and burial mounds in the area were in a straight line. Watkins reckoned that these lines were the remains of Neolithic tracks linking holy places and stone monuments. As many pagan sites had been Christianised over the centuries, this explained why churches were also on the route. He published his findings in his main book in 1925, called *The Old Straight Track*. Most archaeologists thought he was cracked but a few fellows did set up the Straight Track Postal Portfolio club, where people sent their ley line photos and research to each other. Sort of like a tweedy people's internet. Anyway his big theory was that where these lines crossed there would be bigger sacred spaces, and also at these points, markets. So what he was really saying was places like Stonehenge were the mega-malls of their day. The word "Ley" comes from the Saxon word for cleared glade and is linked to "lea" meaning a "tract of open ground". But that'll just confuse you. Watkins reckoned the chalk figure known as "The Long Man of Wilmington" in Sussex was a drawing of a prehistoric land surveyor establishing some ley lines . . .'

'The chalk bloke with the y'know, the wotsit?' asked Barry.

'No,' said Clive. 'That's in Dorset. This one's in Sussex. He looks like he's got a thin spear or stick in each hand. In the 1770s he had a rake and a scythe, and in 1873 the Duke of Devonshire had him "restored" and outlined in yellow bricks. Some say he was drawn by Roman soldiers because he looks a bit like Denarius of Vetranius who's on a seventh-century Roman coin, some think he's a Saxon farmer, or a Saxon warrior . . . then of course there's the usual legend about two giants fighting and the one who got killed lying where he fell. Mr Wilmington, the big loser. Makes you wonder who makes this up doesn't it? Anyway, ley lines . . . the Ley Line Club, like a lot of things, ended when World War Two started, but in the Sixties the New Agers, hippies and flying-saucer enthusiasts got hold of the idea. It only takes a couple of dodgy books to kick off a whole movement.'

Clive licked the corners of his mouth. It was hard work keeping his mouth going.

'There was an ex-RAF pilot, called Tony Wedd, who got a whole book out of a spurious connection between ley lines and orthotenies, which are the lines between flying-saucer sightings in France. He in turn influenced two Englishmen, Philip Heselton and Jimmy Goddard, who revived the Straight Track Club in the form of the Ley Hunter's Club. All these bad ideas have come together under the heading "earth mysteries": whale channels, dowsing, UFOs, geomancy . . . all that bollocks.

'It wasn't helped by the fact that people rediscovered *The Goat-Foot God*, a 1934 novel by Dion Fortune, also known as Violet Mary Firth, in which she talked about lines of terrestrial energy linking ancient sites of cosmic power. Dion was the sort of Twenties occultist who reckoned Freud and Jung didn't know as much as her about the human mind. Her family motto was "Deo, non Fortuna", Latin for "By God, not by Chance", which is where she got her magic name Dion Fortune. Of course she had visions of Atlantis when she was four and later in life believed she'd been a temple priestess there. Temple priestess, note. Not a temple cleaner, or a mud-farmer. She was kicked out of the Order of the Golden Dawn and formed her own order known as the "Fraternity of the Inner Light", discovered Glastonbury in 1923 and retreated here to the Celtic Otherworld regularly, where she had conversations with the Greek philosopher Socrates, the nineteenth-century Chancellor of England Lord Erksine, and Merlin. History does not record what Socrates had to say to her.

'Nutters aside, you can see why otherwise sensible people get interested in this stuff. Pigeons, whales, honeybees and bacteria can all navigate using the Earth's magnetic field. The physiological feature which enables them to do this is a tissue containing a substance called magnetite. Magnetite enables them to sense magnetic changes and has been found in human tissue associated with the Ethmoid bone in front of the vertebrate skull. But as for a special "Earth energy", that's crap. They did a thing called the Dragon Project in the 1970s, at the Rollright stone circle in Oxfordshire, using science, photography, dowsing, psychics, the full Monty. After ten years they concluded there were no strange energies, but there were anomalous effects in known energies like background radiation and magnetic field. So next time some hippie comes up to you with a dowsing rod you can safely tell him where to stick it.'

He looked around the bus. Every eye was upon him.

'Nowadays people claim they have ley lines in Seattle and South America and all over the shop, but they're usually students who read Bruce Chatwin's book *Songlines* in their year-off and have too much time on their hands. The thing about straight lines is they were also believed to be the perfect roads for the souls of the dead. There were "fairy ways" in Ireland, the Vikings had special straight roads along which they carried their dead chieftains to burial, the medieval Dutch had doodwegen, or death roads, and the Germans geistewege or ghost roads. So when people see a TV documentary or coffee-table book about Nazca in Peru, where there are straight lines marked out for miles on the desert by ancient tribes, or the Bolivian altiplano, where they have the same thing, straight lines running across the mountains from shrine to shrine, or the ritual roads of Chaco Canyon, New Mexico, which are made by clearing stones by hand and don't lead any-where, they start thinking, "Yes, this is a global thing, there must be a global grid of power lines . . ." And then they usually try and sell you something.'

He paused to take a sip of water, and said off-mike, 'Hey Rose, this isn't the way we came yesterday . . .'

She tried to suppress a smile. 'You *have* to tell them about *this.*'

Below them in a valley was a wheat field, pale gold in the midday sun. A third of the way across was a fifty-foot crop circle, made of flattened wheat, with concentric circles inside. Overlaying it was a triangle, on each corner of which was another small pattern. One looked like the flywheel of a farm machine, a circle with swirling spokes. Another looked like a rigid spiral that stepped down every ninety degrees ending in a blob. Everyone on the coach cooed and took pictures. Rose pulled into a turning point and they all got off to look. There was a farmer and a young man sitting at a table at a break in the hedgerow charging admission. Several people were wandering around inside the circle, giggling and having their pictures taken, or being conspicuously sensitive.

'Four pound a head, getcha tickets ...' said the young man. Clive and Barry noted he spoke with a Thames Estuary accent.

'You might want to consider, before you go in,' said Clive loudly to his group, 'that crop circles only started in 1976 when two English chaps called Doug Bower and Dave Chorley decided to have a laugh and hoax a UFO landing. They made them in the night, flattening the cereal with a plank of wood, and their only problem was coming up with better designs as oral accounts of the mystery spread. It wasn't until 1980 when they did one below the Westbury White Horse in Wiltshire that Ufologists got excited. Two of these, Colin Andrews and Pat Delgado from Hampshire, wrote a book on it, *Circular Evidence*, and their theories in turn influenced the designs by Doug and Dave. That's what you call a positive feedback cycle. Also a meteorologist called Terence Meaden got in on the act, saying crop circles were caused by mini whirlwinds, but as the designs got more complicated he started working in theories of Neolithic religion and Earth goddess stuff. More and more hoaxers were producing their own circles, and it wasn't until the early 1990s that one of the papers – a middlebrow tabloid called *Today* – revealed the truth. As a result *The Cereologist* crop-circle magazine lost its editor and everyone was embarrassed for a year, but then everyone forgot about it and abnormal service was resumed. There are enough pranksters, theorists and tourists now to support this cottage industry. In fact, cottage industry pretty much sums up the English economy today. Just thought some of you young people might like to know the history of this little corner of our heritage industry.'

The farmer looked pissed off but his accomplice was grinning and telling everyone, 'Not true, 'snot true!'

'Is that right?' asked Rose.

Clive nodded.

The passengers were still leaning over the hedge, looking. It proved just too tantalising. A couple of Spanish girls broke away and paid the farmer, whose baggy face broke into a triumphant smile. Then a Canadian couple followed suit, then some Americans they had made friends with. Then the deluge.

Rose thought it was hilarious.

'Come on,' said Clive, shrugging. 'I'll buy you a ticket.'

When they got to the festival the three of them made a beeline for the bar then took their drinks back to the grassy slope. Danny turned up with a couple of guys all in black. They had pipecleaner legs, dyed hair and wrap-around shades, and stood around smoking and looking bored, which annoyed Clive. He didn't like people pulling rank. It was agreed that they would all meet up at the backstage gate at five. He wanted to break his day into varied chunks – some wandering, some Rose-snowing, some relaxing alone, and hopefully, some poking around backstage seeing how the celebrity class lived.

'So,' said Clive, when Barry had gone off with some women he pretended to know, 'what's it like driving a coach?'

''Salright,' she said. 'For now.'

'Do you have anything you'd really rather be doing?'

'Yeah, but I'm still saving up.' She paused, and he waited till she toppled over into confession-mode. 'One day I want to have my own bike garage – classics. Triumphs, Nortons, BSAs ... Fix 'em up, all original parts, rebuild them, trade them ... there's loads in Europe just sitting around in barns and things. The market's there, especially now people realise that all new bikes are full of computer chips. They want something oily and loud, something they can tinker with. Something to remind them of the good old days. Something analogue.'

'What do you ride?'

'Sixty-three Bonny,' she said, looking very serious. In an instant Clive saw back through the years to the proud girl she must have been, little Rose frowning as she boasted about a dolly or some school success. He thought of Tess. Quickly he banished the thought.

'What did you think of my talk about Jesus coming to England?' he said suddenly.

'Eh? Oh that. All right.' She hesitated. 'You're not a God squadder are you? I hope not.'

'No. I should have said though, Jesus was into British bikes.'

'And how's that?' she said, looking both sceptical and curious.

'Says so in the Bible. "And his Triumph was heard throughout the land ..."'

Her face broke into a smile and she chuckled, and picked at her shoe, and laughed a little more as she replayed it in her mind. She had tiny wrinkles around her eyes, the marks of travel through her thirties. Clive couldn't remember very well what his wife had looked like in her thirties. When it was happening it was hard to judge, life. But looking at others was easier. He wondered if Rose came with much baggage. That was the woman thing – all's fine until they move in and start unpacking their personal agony – what Mummy did, what Daddy wouldn't do ...

'What was that book you were reading, the first time you drove me to Stonehenge?'

'What, the day Ray died? Just puzzles. Why?'

Clive was relieved to hear it was neither highbrow nor lowbrow. 'Oh. Riddles and suchlike? Hey I know a riddle. OK, get this: A dead man is lying in a field with a ring around his finger. What happened?'

'Heh-heh, well, it can't be anything to do with marriage, that's too obvious. Let me see ...'

She sat up, staring off into the distance, giving him the chance to look at her changing eyes.

'I'll have to think about that one,' she said.

After his afternoon wander he was forty-five minutes late getting to the backstage gate, such were the crowds packing the festival's dusty avenues. The vibe was totally different from the day before. An air of domesticity had developed – nice domesticity. Familiarity. People knew where they were, they felt comfortable being themselves. Helped by the drugs, the beer and the sunshine, they let each other pass first, complimented strangers out loud, smiled unprompted. The dust and the queues were shared approximations of hardship.

The girl guarding the VIP-area entrance sat at a plastic garden table with a sheaf of papers on a clipboard.

'Sorry, you can't come in without the silver wristband or a pass.'

'I'm meeting my friends here ... can't I just go inside and find them?'

'Sorry.'

'Come on, I'm sure they're in there. Do you know Barry? Barry Bergman. Look him up.'

She sucked her teeth noisily and gave the list a quick scan.

'No, he's not down. You'll have to move, you can't stand here.'

Clive tried to peer into the VIP Valhalla, but the tent had a corridor that bent round to the right. Eventually he gave up and moved back out to the common ground, where young kids lurked hoping to spot a star, and where the privileged came when they got bored with their status. Clive watched for a while, sitting on the grass next to another discarded wreck. He imagined Barry and Rose backstage, deep in discussion with one of the stars, like ... he looked at the programme. 'Van Morrison?' he muttered in disbelief. The man next to him gave a sympathetic nod.

'That old bastard, he's been around longer than me. And what's he ever done, really?' Clive moaned. 'Bloody "Brown-Eyed Girl". Supermarket music.'

'Ha!' said the other. 'Made some records. Well, one good record.' He was gangly, his face was a pasty white and his teeth were jumbled and tar-stained. He looked genuinely ill, but there was life in his eyes. When he smoked he tugged the heat through the cigarette and smacked his lips like every drag was the last. He wore a black shirt and grey pegs, and his leather Oxfords were dusty. Clive cursed himself for ending up with his own sort again.

But he quickly found out this bloke was not normal. He spoke in a hard northern accent, part mithering, part scathing, and he spoke at length, roping Clive in by asking questions, taking his mind off his worries.

'Trouble with this place is it's full of people who think Van Morrison is their dad. It's the first time we've had a generation that's exactly the same as their parents – smoke dope, listen to the Rolling Stones, wear the same sort of clothes. There's no gap, that's why they're not very creative. No friction. What do you do mate?'

'I'm a tour guide.'

'Ha! You should come round our way, Salford, there's plenty to fooking see up there. Take your tourists to see me Mam, when she goes out she gets done up and has a good time.'

Clive watched him swigging at his can of Falcon Superstrength.

'Seriously though, you been doing that all your life, riding round on coaches? Don't look it.'

Clive was sick of this, so he anticipated the question. 'No. I used to be a teacher but I got sacked for having an affair. With a pupil.'

'Ah! How old was she then? Fourteen? Fifteen?'

'Yeah.' Clive stared him down, until he went on.

'Must say, it's hard to talk to people my own age or just younger, they have no sense of history. I feel like skipping a generation. I can't imagine what this country will be like in thirty years. We were on tour in Wales and it was like the fucking *Wicker Man* – end of the night, they're all pissed, singing Welsh songs, running around outside. The bouncer's going "You're English, you'd better stay in the van"; and they've all got Welsh flags and stuff. We go back to the van and there's like 3,000 Welshmen with fucking torches going "Adoobedoobedoo". Imagine if that was fucking Germans or something!'

'You're right, we've got a blind spot for ourselves, the English.' Clive paused. Perhaps he wasn't so bad. 'This is a very bourgeois question, but what do you do?'

'I sing in a band.'

'Oh. I'm trying to meet some people backstage but I've lost them.'

'You don't wanna go in there anyway, it's horrible.'

Another door closed to him. Clive excused himself, and spent his second day out of the loop wandering the fields again, visiting the same haunts until limitations of the festival irritated him. He started seeing the same people over and over, like being in a small town. He went high up the hill and lay down with a four pack. He saw his singer come on, wearing the same grey pegs and muttering something like 'British people in hot weather', but it was hard to make out. When the evening cooled Clive went back to the entertainment tents. At the comedy stage someone with big sideburns and a purple lounge singer shirt was just finishing his set. Clive only heard the punchline: 'Kiss my goitre!' and the crowd laughed the laughters of recognition, satisfaction and relief all at once, and clapped him off. They turned from the stage with bright eyes, yapping about how great he was, pushing past him into the fresh air.

Clive didn't feel much like talking on the way home. At Victoria he felt a pang of the old misery at the prospect of going back to his horrible flat. He promised himself he'd visit his mother as soon as possible. Blood suddenly seemed a lot thicker than water.

The third day Clive woke up with a cold, a hangover, and a mind-numbing sleep debt. He lay in bed in his stripped apartment and let the final trip to Glastonbury proceed without him. He dozed until evening, then plugged in his little radio. He knew the sound of that crowd cheering. Two DJs, one an improbably chirpy girl, the other with a fake London accent as slippery as a jellied eel, introduced a live broadcast from the festival. He imagined himself there, having a rotten time. The horrible thought came to him that maybe his country didn't need him after all. Clive was back, and the world said 'No thanks.'

6

The Trouble with Tina

'The trouble with Clive was, he had no ambition. He gave up too easily.'

Christina was talking to her psychotherapist. A long silence.

'There's something I've got to tell you. It's complicated.' She took a deep breath. 'I've met a man.'

'Go on.'

'You know how Jeffrey turned out to be a big phoney and he never actually listened to any of his opera CDs or read any of those books on his shelves? Well this guy is a lot less pretentious, yet he has a solid background. He was a client ... I know, you're not supposed to mix with them ...'

'I don't see why not. In your line of work ...'

'But he was such a charmer. I did a placement for him in the West End. He was relocating from Richmond for business purposes and wanted a small office/home office. He said he'd be working from home with a computer and a cellphone, it was the wave of the future, and he had just broken out of corporate tourism and was going private. He said it was very lucrative. Anyway we went on two dates, the first time to a movie and then after that to dinner, a lovely Thai place, and that's when I said "Oh I know someone who's a tour guide," and he said "Really, who? I know a lot of people in the industry," and I said "No, you won't know him he's nobody, just starting out," and he said "No go on I might," and when I said "Clive Pointing" he laughed and said not only had he hired him at Wonga, he'd just hired him again at his new company! And then we put two and two together and it turned out he'd been right there the night me and Jeffrey had run into him in Soho, when they had the row in the street. The same night me and Jeffrey broke up. His name's Alex and he seems *really* nice. He's divorced but it sounds like a similar situation to me, he just married the wrong one.'

She paused and thought.

'It's a bit of a dilemma really, because it means I might see Clive again and I don't want to. But I do like this fellow. He's quite young. Only thirty-two. He looks older though, in a dignified sort of way. The problem is, if I trust his judgement, doesn't that mean I'm wrong about Clive being a big loser? Or has he suddenly come up with some reserve of ambition that I never saw in all the years we were together?'

'How does that make you feel?' asked the therapist.

'Well, it makes me feel as though my judgement isn't very good. And perhaps that applies to Alex too? And . . . to you?'

'Have you considered forgiving your ex-husband?'

'Absofuckinglutely *not!*' she exclaimed to the ceiling.

There was silence for a couple of minutes. The clock ticked loudly.

'We have to end now, I'm sorry.'

Tina craned her neck and looked around. 'Is it time already?'

'I'm sorry, yes it is,' said the therapist gently. 'We can talk about this next session.'

Tina got up from the couch. She looked up at the therapist with a puzzled expression and left, forgetting to pay.

7

Happy Hour Again

As Clive walked up the path to his brother Gordon's maisonette, he noticed rather a lot more dog faeces than normal. High-bandwidth coils of it were parked exactly where the feet might tread, some yellow, some tan, shining under the sodium street lights. As he approached the front door an object slammed itself against the glass panel from the inside, scaring him, barking furiously.

'Easy Naz, easy!' he heard his brother saying roughly. They wrestled for a moment longer until Gordon got his face through the crack.

'Oh, 'syou. Where the fuck have you been?'

'Nice to see you too,' said Clive. 'Can I come in?'

'Spose so,' said his brother gloomily.

Clive had a sudden panic that his mother might not be well. Might even be dead. He hurried in. She was in bed, with the TV perched precariously on the end where her feet would once have reached, before her skeleton had started shrinking.

'Mother?' he said.

'Ah yes Clive, I'd like to have a word with you.'

He turned to his brother. 'How's she been?'

'What do you fucking care?'

'I *fucking* care. Now tell me how she's been!'

Gordon looked shocked. He didn't know how to handle him, or the tan boxer dog that was trying to rape his leg.

'Worse, then. Worse than ever. I've 'ad the nurse in. 'Ome 'elp.'

Clive sat down at the bedside and held her hand.

'Mother, it's Clive.'

She looked surprised and pulled her hand away, then appealed to Gordon with her eyes, seeking protection or explanation.

He spoke quietly, struggling to form the words. 'I'm sorry I went away, Mum, I'm so sorry. I just couldn't take it any more.' His feelings overcame him and despite his brother looking on, Clive started to sob, pressing his face on to the old counterpane. Crying hadn't changed since he was a boy. The facial meltdown, the pressure in the brain, the voiceless gasping. The defeat of the self. The bedspread smelt the same as it had done for as long as he could remember, musty and flowery. He hoped to feel her touch on his head, that was all that could console him, but she remained aloof. He looked up and she was looking back at him in horror like a duchess being slobbered over by a wino, and the sight made him feel even more desperate. The dog was grunting, its claws catching noisily on the carpet. Clive's heaving sobs were shaking him, and the bed, and the TV on it (his mother was watching *This Is Your Life*), when he felt a hand on his shoulder.

'Easy,' said his brother.

It was enough. Gordon may even have been talking to his dog too but that didn't matter, it was just the feel of a sympathetic hand that drew Clive back to the land of the living. He regretted all the times he had called Gordon a moron, to his face and behind his back, and wanted nothing more than to stay there in his little flat. He looked around when his tears were gone and his brother even smiled at him as he wrestled with the rampant dog. 'Down Naz, down or I'll put you out again,' he said fiercely. 'He's a little bugger. I haven't been walking him much lately, except when the nurse is here. What have you been up to anyway?'

Clive felt full of love for his brother. 'Listen, have you eaten?'

He shrugged.

'OK, good.' Clive ran down the road. There was a mean row of shops, including an Indian restaurant which hadn't been decorated since the Sixties, and a supermarket that stayed open late selling cigarettes and beer to underagers. He ordered three chicken tikka masalas – he had read somewhere that they were now the country's most popular 'eating out' dish, if you didn't count chips – then ran next door and picked up eight cans of lager from the padlocked fridge.

'She likes curry,' said Gordon approvingly. 'Did you get any for the dog?'

'Er, no . . .' They each threw a hot chunk to the dog who hoovered it off the carpet, licking the thin nylon dry. Mother ate hers in bed, noticing nothing but the TV, while the boys sat in the main room. The food tasted good. Clive remembered the strong tastes and smells of his first meal after the river. After eating they each started a new can.

He felt warm inside and grateful, thanks to the big cry. He explained about Albion, and how busy he'd been. He saw his brother's sceptical look lock on to him like a missile and then confessed the rest.

'I know it was daft but ... I tried to do myself in. It just got too much. I thought I had nothing to live for. But I changed my mind.'

'What happened?' Gordon looked very interested. Suicide, torture, executions ... they were all subjects that featured prominently in his book collection.

'Well, I floated like a cork. That's all I can say. I floated, and then I swam to the side and got out.'

'So it was like a sign that you shouldn't do it? That it wasn't your time?'

'Erm ... Yes ...' said Clive hesitantly. 'I suppose that's how I took it.'

Gordon looked well impressed. He paddled the dog hard with his slippered feet to express his satisfaction, and the dog looked up with mad eyes and a mouth full of rubber.

As Clive drank and talked to his brother (the dog cost a grand from a bloke in the pub) he realised how bad things had been just moments before. Everything had failed him – death, work, love ... yet he felt he could make a life for himself, somewhere in this triangle of failure. At least he had one point of reference on the horizon, his brother.

'Thanks for ... you know ... that,' said Clive.

Gordon ignored him, paddling the dog even harder.

'Can she string her thoughts together?' asked Clive.

'Not really. She has her moments. Mostly though she's doing, y'know, old poems.'

He leaned over and picked up a thick book of English poetry. 'I've started reading her these when she's bad. Keeps her brain in gear. She might remember you, if you stick around,' he said with a trace of bitterness.

'I know ... I'll be here more often now. I'll come every other day.'

Gordon shrugged. Having an aggressive dog seemed to have calmed him down. He clamped the dog's head between his knees and poured some beer down its throat. 'Heh heh heh, he loves his lager.'

Clive flicked through the book, then went over and sat by his mother. *This Is Your Life* was just finishing. The person whose *Life* it was stood

surrounded by friends and family, all smiles. Clive remembered watching
the show once when it was some old footballer ... Danny Blanchflower,
that was it, who didn't want a *Life*. When the presenter popped out to
surprise him with the big red book he told him to 'piss off'. It was quite
a scandal in those days, and confirmed his parents' opinion that no good
could come from watching ITV. He imagined himself and Gordon sitting
in jackets and ties in the front row at their mother's *Life*. What if all those
people they'd known in all the different towns they'd lived in came back
and said 'Hello, Mrs Pointing, we remember you when you gave that cheese
and wine party ...' Sad memories which added up to little, and too easily
evaporated.

'Mother do you know this one? "On This Island", by W. H. Auden.'
He read:

> '"Look, stranger, at this island now
> The leaping light for your delight discovers,
> Stand stable here
> And silent be,
> That through the channels of the ear
> May wander like a river
> The swaying sound of the sea.

> '"Here at the small field's ending pause
> Where the chalk wall falls to the foam and its tall ledges
> Oppose the pluck
> And knock of the tide,
> And the shingle scrambles after the
> sucking surf,
> And the gull lodges
> A moment on its sheer side."'

She tilted her head back and joined in.

> '"Far off like floating seeds the ships
> Diverge on urgent voluntary errands,
> And the full view
> Indeed may enter
> And move in memory as now these clouds do,
> That pass the harbour mirror
> And all the summer through the water saunter."'

'Auden. I never know what he's on about,' muttered Clive.

'He was woofta wasn't he?' said Gordon.

'He's saying go to the seaside and be thankful. Dover.'

'Really, Mum?' Clive read it again to himself and it was none the clearer, but he spent a pleasant hour reading more until she fell asleep. Then he sat with Gordon, finishing the beer.

'We should do a trip to the seaside, Brighton or somewhere. There's a lot of Regency stuff down there. The foreign tourists lap it up.'

'How's that going anyway, the old guiding?'

'Uh ... it's OK. I shouldn't grumble. There's a nice girl driving the coach but I don't think she'll stick around.'

'Well if you go to the coast tell me and I'll come along. I might bring Sand ...' He stopped himself, embarrassed.

'*Sandra?* Who's Sandra? Eh?'

'She's this bird ... this woman I met. Just down the pub like.'

'Oh, I see. You're a dark horse.' He found it fun to tease his younger brother again.

As he rattled home on the Tube he made a new list:

1) See Mum every other.
2) Plan funeral.
3) More Albion.
4) Move flat.
5) Sort out Tess.

8

Into the Mediasphere

Barry, his dad, Alex and Rose.

That was the delegation that arrived at Clive's door. They'd come down in the pink taxi after recovering from the festival.

'Clive open up! We know you're in there!'

He opened his door to see them all looking very concerned.

'Where've you been? We thought you'd fucking topped yourself. You were such a miserable cunt when you left ... what happened?'

'Yeah Clive,' said Rose, 'what happened? I thought you'd never made it home. We tried calling Danny on his mobile but he was still at Glastonbury.'

'I ... I had a bad cold that's all. Sorry, I should get my phone re-connected.'

'Well, come on we've got a shitload of bookings. The Princess Di Connection is about to leave,' said Barry.

'The *what?*'

'We're fully booked, we need you,' said Rose. 'We're doing half days to Althorp House and we need your help.' She pronounced it correctly, 'All-thrup'. She meant business.

'But I ...' Clive was going to say he didn't know anything about the royal family, apart from that they were a bunch of inbred Germans and feckless Sloanes, and that no one better exemplified the recent entrance of talentless bluebloods into self-regarding celebrity culture than Diana, Ex-Princess of Wales, when he looked at their faces and saw how serious they were.

'Let me change my boxers and I'll be right out.'

They waited for him in front of the house. Clive hurried out pulling on his jacket against the cool morning. He took a deep breath of the sweet air. It had that dewy smell that promised another hot day. Even Streatham got some summer. In the cab Alex made a formal announcement for his benefit.

'Er, henceforth from now on Rose is a partner in Albion Tours. We feel she brings to the table excellent experience in the field of, er, navigational skills ... and, er ...'

'I got the coach dirt cheap. I know a bloke. I must admit I felt a bit sorry for you lot at first, but then I realised I could quite enjoy this lark. So long as we change the scenery often enough. There's nothing more boring than doing the same run twice a day all summer.'

Clive looked at Barry.

'Well it's the twenty-first century innit? Birds are doing all sorts of jobs. Only the other day my eldest girl Shell says to me she wants to be a ... wossat thing with the wig?'

''Airdressa?'

'Pop star?'

'Judge?'

'Barrister?'

''Assit, barrister. Hundred sheets an hour, they make.'

'Just what we need, more lawyers,' muttered Clive.

Alex raised his voice. 'Anyway, the bottom line is, basically, more money for all of us. Rose and I have been advertising with absolute *laser* precision in all the right places, we're fully booked for the *west* of the week.' With the whiff of success in the air, they talked excitedly as the car cut through the streets of Camberwell and Vauxhall up to Victoria.

The coach had ALBION TOURS painted in silver on green down the side. About thirty women holding flyers showing Diana's face rushed forward as it became clear they were about to be let on.

'Hold it ladies, hold it! One at a time!' shouted Barry. More flyer people turned up – European ladies dressed in smart casual wear with their reluctant handbag-toting husbands, some confused German campers, the inevitable pairs of Japanese girls, and a handful of black Americans. Diana seemed to cross international barriers.

Alex looked on with pride. 'Our decision to advertise on the web seems to have paid off.'

'Are you coming with us?' Clive asked him.

'Yes. I'm very interested to see how the Princess's brother has handled the operation. I've long been an admirer of Charles. He's a canny businessman. And apparently he's a *fucking* good bloke.'

Once on the MI Barry got on the microphone. He gave them the whole Diana story, from the childminder with the hatchback and the see-through dress to the theme-park mum assassinated by Mossad and the British Government. Clive raised his eyebrows at this point and cast a glance at Rose, but she just smiled back.

'It was up this very motorway that the body of Her Royal Highness was transported by the Royal hearses. Tearful well-wishers were lined up along the entire route, fifty miles, throwing flowers off bridges at the vehicle. The motorway was closed by the Government, and truly you could say the entire country came to a standstill that day. I myself was transfixed in front of the television.'

Clive suspected that the Bergmans were just the sort of family who would have taken a day off to mourn, especially as there hadn't been a proper gangland funeral out there for a long time. 'MUM' flowers at fifty quid a letter, that's what it was all about. Clive himself had gone to the shops as usual on the morning of her funeral, and had noticed plenty of people about. As he walked past the bookmaker's the door opened revealing the usual packed and smoky house glued to the racing on telly and the form on the walls. The supermarket seemed pretty full as well. Not deserted anyway, the way the media told it. He fell into a fantasy about what Rose had done that day. He imagined her in the front garden working on her motorcycle, polishing the chrome. In just a vest. And shorts. It was a nice day after all. Maybe with the radio on in the background. And changing stations to avoid all the Diana crap.

'My colleague Clive will now fill you in on some of the background to the Royal family tree.'

Clive looked surprised. So this was why Barry was so keen to have him aboard. He took the mike.

'Well ladies and gentlemen. The Spencer family is an old English family. The house at Althorp dates from 1508, but they've been knocking around a lot longer than that. As you'll see in the church in the village of Great Brington, they have their own private chapel in which twenty generations of Spencers have been buried. This sort of thing is very important to us English. You might remember her brother, the Earl ... er, what's his name?'

'Charles!' snapped Alex and Barry together.

'Yes, Charles, Champagne Charlie ... at the funeral he called her "The unique, the complex, the extraordinary, and irreplaceable Diana," and said she didn't need her royal title to *be* someone ... He was saying *we* the Spencers have been around a lot longer than that lot in Buckingham Palace, and if anyone's an English aristocrat around here it's us ... Well, that just about sums the English up – looking down on the Queen and her brood because they've only been here for a couple of centuries, that's the kind of highly evolved snobbery this country specialises in. And you'll find it at all levels – the nurse who looks down on the dinner lady, the black cab that cuts up the mini cab, it's all part of what makes our little world go around. Actually if you want a real souvenir of today, make sure you pick up a tub of Diana margarine or the Diana colonic irrigation kit, they say more about this country than all the postcards of designer frocks. Can you imagine any other country falling into such a squabble about how to market her? No one had a clue what to do, the families were arguing, the money men and the marketers were unsure what level of bad taste they could get away with, and on top of it all everyone had an opinion, including people like me who thought they didn't give a flying ... hey!'

Alex tried to wrestle the microphone off him but Clive pushed him down, saying, 'OK OK, I'm nearly finished. I'm just setting the context!' He looked out at the bemused punters. 'Anyway, it's probably obvious to all of you, you're not going to the English Graceland or anything. Don't confuse her with someone who actually created anything. She's got no product to sell, that's why she'll fizzle out. Diana didn't really do anything, apart from play her Wham! records and go to the gym. So in a few years nobody will remember what she was remembered for. Already there are little kids who know nothing about her other than what their mums have told them. I know because my little girl has got the whole story garbled more than once. God knows what her mother's telling her now.'

He clicked off the microphone. There was silence.

'Er, how about a bit of a singsong?' shouted Barry.

It was quiet for a few seconds until one of the black women put up her hand.

'I read somewhere Lady Di's favourite hymn was "How Great Thou Art"? Is that true?'

Barry didn't have a clue. 'Yeah, that's right. Does anyone know the tune? Or the words? Come on ...'

The lady started to sing, with a deep, deep voice.

'Then sings my soul ...'

Her friends shut their eyes and jumped in. Soon six gospel voices filled the coach, piercing the drone of the engine. The women's voices sashayed around each other, curling syllables with extra notes until the sense of the words was lost, but the passion was evident. Everyone else on the bus looked on with a mixture of awe and embarrassment.

Barry cut them off as soon as he thought he had heard the last note. This wasn't his idea of a singsong. He was pissed off at Clive, but knew it would be unprofessional to cause any more of a scene.

When they got off the coach he went up to him. 'Keep your fucking opinions to yourself in future, OK? They haven't paid seventy quid a head to listen to your *Guardian*-reader crap.'

'I don't read a newspaper, for your information.'

'Yeah well, just shut it.'

'Look, if you want to explain the history of the monarchy, be my guest.'

Barry scowled and walked off.

'Hey Barry! You never told them about the Diana's Death Panties.'

Barry soon had worse things to worry about. The Althorp tickets that Stu got him were fakes. The forger had spent so long on the hologram and the watermark that he'd forgotten the basics – the date.

'Bollocks! Bollocks!' Barry cursed through his teeth until the veins stood up on his forehead. The old bloke on the door said there was no way they could pay their way in, the rule was 2,500 tickets a day and this being the first week of July they were sold out. He looked back at his brood, took a deep breath and went for it.

'Ladies and gentlemen, there seems to be a misunderstanding with the, er, capacity of Althorp. We won't be allowed in for another hour.' Everyone groaned and looked at each other. 'However, I guarantee we'll get you in.' He ordered everyone back on the coach, telling Clive to take them round the village and meet him at the top end of the estate in an hour. Barry then had a word with Rose and fetched something wrapped in sacking from the boot.

Clive didn't know much about Great Brington, so he told them about the misplaced tourists instead. 'I don't suppose any of you would ever mistake Stratford in East London for Shakespeare's birthplace but it sometimes happens. The same thing's been happening for the last few years at Althorpe-with-an-e in northern Lincolnshire. Lincolnshire is the flat, dismal county between Yorkshire and East Anglia that gave us Alfred Lord Tennyson and Margaret Thatcher. Anyway the Althorpe up there is spelt with an -e on the end, but that hasn't stopped hundreds of people (including a team of French journalists) turning up there thinking it was Di's last resting place. Only 120 miles wrong. People are always arriving at the local pubs and hotel looking for Diana's grave. They've had cycling honeymooners from Holland, Australians, Germans, the lot. The landlord of the Dolphin Inn said he was thinking of digging a pond at the back of the pub and charging £1-a-visit. It wouldn't surprise me if he did. There's a great entrepreneurial spirit at loose in the land, after all.'

Great Brington wasn't so great. It was a village of two hundred people with a post office and a reading room and that's about it. They wandered around declaring everything 'cute' and annoying the locals by saving their money for the gift shop at Althorp. Clive hadn't been there before, but he gathered from the curtain twitching and the swaggering Range Rovers that it was one of those insular English dormitory villages where everyone acts like they're in London or the *Archers*.

'Bit of a cock-up on the ticket front, eh?' He said to Rose. Alex was off sniffing around, talking to shopkeepers to see if they knew Diana or her *fucking* good bloke of a brother.

'You don't seem that bothered,' she said, looking him in the eye.

'I'm not. I trust Barry to sort it out. I've been a worrier all my life. A few weeks ago my life changed completely, and one of the things I promised myself was I'd stop being a worrier. It doesn't get you anywhere, does it? It's a hard habit to break but I'm getting there. Thanks for coming round this morning, by the way. I've been having a hard time, personally.'

'Just protecting my investment,' Rose said, rather more coldly than she intended.

Barry met them on the grass by the wall that ran around the Spencer estate, standing on a clump of poppies. The red brick was only waist height but had a tall chainlink fence on top of it. The view of the grounds was blocked by bushes. Everyone trooped off the coach. There were ravens in the trees above his head, and circling over the nearby fields were birds of prey, once-endangered sparrow hawks dark against the blue sky. The tourists were delighted to be out in the fresh air, deep in the English landscape they had read about all their lives. To them the fresh poppies against the ancient mossy wall made a telling contrast, which they photographed and videotaped, but they also had the scent of royalty in their nostrils and wanted inside. Barry looked nervous.

'OK ladies and gentlemen ... we're going in.' He made no attempt to explain, but helped each person one at a time up on to the low wall and through the oval hole he had cut in the wire.

'Here we go then,' said Clive to Rose.

'I'm staying with the coach. Don't want to get towed. Take some snaps for me.' She winked at him.

In the grounds Barry led his group as tactfully as he could around the perimeter of the estate, following the crude map on the back of the ticket. They were heading to the house when they emerged from a clump of azaleas bang in front of the lake where the princess was buried.

Pleasantly surprised, he launched into his commentary. 'This small island was chosen for its privacy and was blessed by the Archbishop of Canterbury. However, the bridge we're standing on was specially built for access. Before that you had to come across in a boat ... like King Arthur to the Isle of Avalon.' The crowd clicked off hundreds of shots. The air was filled with the whirring of mini camera motors.

They proceeded on to the grave itself, which was marked with a stone, and Barry explained that she was buried facing the sun. They stood for a minute's silence and more photo opps. Clive borrowed a Polaroid and got a shot of Barry standing on the grave with two of the gospel singers grinning madly and Barry doing his serious face. After a few minutes though the people got restless and moved on. It was just a tiny patch of ground with nothing else to see.

Barry was very happy with this unexpected result. 'Here, Clive, who's that geezer buried in Paris ... ?'

'Er ... Jim Morrison?'

'Yeah, the Doors singer. We should do a trip there. People love to pay their *rispecks*.'

'Yes, Barry.'

Barry's excuse, when the beadle confronted him as all fifty of them came around the corner of the stables, was that they had been looking for the toilet. The group spent a pleasant half hour in the Princess's museum, which was full of the dresses she hadn't had time to flog off, plus some schoolgirl mementoes cobbled together by the family. Everyone seemed to be having a great time, but Barry called it a day when he saw a TV news crew interviewing two of his women. He steered them away and out the gates as swiftly as he could.

Rose was waiting to load up and soon they were on their way, racing across the countryside to the MI.

'Jesus!' said Barry. 'That was a result.' He was all smiles again. The bolt cutters sat on the empty seat next to him.

Something seemed missing.

'Alex!' shouted Clive. 'We left him behind.' Barry cringed and got out his phone.

Alex, it turned out, had just introduced himself as the CEO of Albion Tours to one of the locals when the word went out about a breach of security at the Estate. Burly men in Barbours pulled up and immobilised him while they talked frantically on their own phones and summoned the police. Alex's rang until it went to voice mail, since his hands at the time were wrenched behind his back.

By the time they got back to north London the *Evening Standard* lunchtime edition had SECURITY BREACH AT DI'S GRAVE on the front page. By teatime Barry's phone batteries were nearly dead from giving interviews. By eight o'clock Alex was out on bail and bookings for Albion were going through the roof.

He eventually pulled up outside the Shakespeare in a taxi looking very angry, but the others just laughed at him.

'Cheer up, Alex,' said Rose. 'Just think of the bottom line. We no longer have to pay for brand-building.'

'I could get a fucking criminal record out of this. All because of you three idiots!' he said, his voice going high with anxiety.

'Shut up,' said Barry. 'Criminal record? You don't know the meaning of criminal record. Wait till you've been inside, then you'll know about criminal records.'

They all looked at him nervously. 'Nah, not me you plonkers. Me brother. Trev.'

'What did he do?' asked Rose, her eyes wide. Clive had never seen her like this: he hoped she wasn't one of those women who loved nutcases, or wrote to murderers, any of that.

'It was a travesty of justice. He got in a ruck down the boozer. With a copper. He'll be out soon.'

'Big party?' asked Clive. He and Rose had been in the Shakespeare most of the afternoon. He was feeling very contented, several pints worth. The calls kept coming in on Barry's mobile. So many people were trying to book the Princess Diana Connection that Rose set up the website to take credit-card payments. The local news came on and they cheered the two gospel women's soundbite about visiting the island, and they cheered even louder when Alex's petrified face was shown, hands cuffed behind him like a common criminal.

Barry's dad came into the pub, his shellsuit legs aswish with urgency, he'd heard all about it on LBC. Then Stu turned up – he'd sorted out

Althorp tickets for the rest of the week, this time legit. Even the forger was dining out (on lager) on his brush with fame, somewhere in East London. Barry was in forgiving mood.

By chucking-out time a couple of the national papers were on to the story, Barry was photographed relaxing in the Shakespeare, and everyone was having a laugh. Even Alex managed a smile. When Clive said that on telly he looked like Charles the First being led to the scaffold, he took him seriously and sat up straight. He told everyone how he sensed he might actually be related to the Spencers (Clive's bit about them looking down on the Queen had triggered it), and Barry's dad said he could see the resemblance – 'No 'air and no facking chin!' – which made everyone laugh again, and Alex pointed a finger at him like he was dead serious, then smiled and said 'Kiss my goitre!' and they laughed more, and the bar staff came round shouting '*Finishyerdrinks please! Thankyouverymuch!*' so they went and stood outside in the warm night air still talking and hogging the pavement, and as they broke to go their separate ways Rose said she was walking back to her flat in Vauxhall and Clive said he'd walk with her, and the next thing she was inviting him in.

9

Sod off, Ma'am

'I don't mean to be patronising, but I think I can help you. It's your kings and queens isn't it?'

'There's just so many of the bleeders I get 'em all mixed up.'

'How many do you know?'

It was Clive and Barry's lunch break, a week later. They were on Shakespeare time. Albion was going great guns, the Di Connection was bringing in daft amounts of money. What they really needed was to split up and take a coach each, but Barry had been resisting it. He was like a yokel in a West End play trying to hide his functional illiteracy. Clive guessed though. 'How many kings and queens do you know right off the bat?'

'Er, well, the Queen. Obviously.'

'Elizabeth the Second, obviously.'

'And 'Lizabeth the First.'

'Obviously. What do you know about her?'

'Er, big collars, white face . . . wasn't she the one who was tight? Wasn't she a virgin? Or was that Victoria?'

'No, Victoria was pretty tight but she had lots of kids. Victoria was in Victorian times — you know, top hats, the Crystal Palace, India.'

'Yeah, course. She had a face like an old boot.'

'Victoria's the one who didn't believe in lesbianism. And she had all the table legs covered up. When her husband Albert died she had the Albert Memorial built for him. He had his cock pierced.'

'Straight up?'

'That's what a Prince Albert is. Stops it flapping around in those riding breeches. So Elizabeth the First ...'

'Who was she again?'

'For Christ's sake ...' Clive stopped himself. For a moment Barry looked meek, like a boy. 'She was the Virgin Queen.'

'Oh yeah. Wasn't she something to do with Shakespeare and all that lot?'

'Yes. Same era. She went to plays, she was no bimbo. She read Latin and Greek, spoke French, Spanish and Italian, and read history for three hours a day. Which we all could do with.'

'Yeah but there was less of it in them days.'

'True.'

'Prick teaser wasn't she?'

'That was her foreign policy. Keep 'em keen.'

'OK, Elizabeth the First, Good Queen Bess, I remember now. And her sister was Mary ... a real dog. Cafflick bird?'

'Had a lot of people burnt. If you want to read about 'em have a look at John Foxe's *Book of Martyrs*. Protestants used to be burned at the stake. Sometimes their friends would give them a bag of gunpowder to speed it up. Pregnant women used to explode.'

'That's disgusting. What's it called again?'

'The *Book of Martyrs*. By Foxe. He believed the English had been chosen by God to fight the Anti-Christ Pope, the usual thing. But it's 2,200 pages long. Forget it Barry. Just think Bloody Mary, hair of the dog. Do you know any more? Any Edwards? There were a lot of them.'

Barry looked blank. 'What about Edward and Mrs Simpson?'

'Good. That's one. He was Edward the Eighth. You don't hear much about him because he packed it all in to marry a Yank. He was quite a cool dude – he was in World War One, the people loved him, he cared about the poor unlike some of them ... Anyway, because she was already divorced twice the Archbishop of Canterbury and the PM said no way, so he jacked it in. Abdicated. You won't see many monuments to him around. She lived till 1986. They buggered off to Paris, which is where the Royals always go when they've had enough.'

He tried to take it all in. 'Didn't someone else go to Paris? During the, uh, what was it, the Reformation? Oliver Cromwell and all that? Now there's a dodgy geezer ...'

'You mean the Restoration? OK – you have to know your Charlies. Charles the First had his head cut off. He had long hair and made a big production of smoothing it out on the chopping block. He also wore two shirts to his execution so he wouldn't shiver. It was January.'

'Didn't the cunt have a coat?'

'History doesn't record why he didn't wear a coat. I suspect it was because he was a vain bastard and liked pirate shirts. Anyway he was King at the time of the Civil War, which lasted from 1642 to 1649. It was the Roundheads versus the Royalists, or the Puritans versus the Cavaliers, or the Republicans versus ...'

'So who was Oliver Cromwell again?'

'He was a Lincolnshire farmer, Puritan and MP who rejigged the Parliamentarians' army after their early defeats, called them the New Model Army, and ended up being head of the country when Charlie lost his. He had pages from the Bible pasted round the cannon mouths when he put down a rebellion in Ireland. You know that song, "Oliver's army is here to sta-ay ..." He had a warty face. Some MP said at the time, "His linen was plain and not very clean, and his voice was sharp and untunable." Anyway he made a bollocks of it in the end, made himself Lord Protector of England. He also put down the Levellers for being too radical. You know how we're famous for our free speech?'

'Er ...'

'Well, the Puritans were into free speech. Up to a point. Milton, Cromwell, all that lot. After he died his son Richard took over and he was crap. Pretty soon Charles's son came back from France and was restored, King Charles the Second. He was the one who was dogging Nell Gwynn on the side – in fact, out in the open. She was like the Barbara Windsor of her day. He brought in French architecture and dished out a lot of pardons. The theatres reopened and there were lots of whores everywhere, but the main thing is, since that time the monarch has never been much more than a pet. Sometimes they get ideas into their heads, like George the Third or Victoria, but generally they know their place.'

'Fuck.'

'Fuck is right. There's a lot of them. Look, we have to get back to the coach.'

Barry furrowed his brow. 'Hang on, I need to know this stuff. What about ... who was the first King? Of us. Of the English.'

'Ah well then, that's not so easy. There were plenty of kings during Celtic and Roman and Anglo-Saxon times. You know, King of a little patch of land, until he gets his head cut off. They reckon the first real King of England was Egbert, from 829.'

'BC or AD?'

Clive sighed. 'ADD,' he muttered. 'He was King of the West Saxons and you can sort of trace his descent. For a bit. We really should go.' He drained his pint and stood up. The sun cut through the pub smoke and lit up the bubbles as they slid down the inside of his glass. It was bliss to be alive. The pavements were packed with tourists who were delighted at the weakness of the pound, and with locals who didn't even notice.

'So who was William the Conqueror?'

'He was a French Duke who fancied himself as King here. Actually he had red hair and was descended from Vikings so it wasn't a big deal for him to pop across the channel and take over. You see, for a while there, the Danes sort of ran England ...'

'The Danes?'

'Yes, they weren't so bad once they settled in. Anyway after Ethelred the Unready we had Edward the Confessor, who was basically a wimp more interested in building Westminster Abbey than running the shop, and once he was dying everyone fancied their chances – his wife's two sons, one of whom was called Harold, plus the King of Norway, and William over in France ... anyway Harold had himself crowned King but it didn't last very long. He beat the Scanders up north at Stamford Bridge – no, not that one – then had to race back down south and got an arrow in the eye off William, which made him William the Conqueror, and that was the end of him. From then on we were French.'

'*French?*' asked Barry, stunned.

'Yeah. The rich spoke French, the rest spoke a kind of garbled English, you know, Anglo Saxon. Beowulf?' Barry looked hurt and confused.

They reached a stand selling tourist crap – plastic police helmets, black cabs, beefeater dolls, bum-and-tit postcards, rulers.

'Here, let me make it easier for you.' Clive pointed at a tea towel that showed the faces of all the monarchs from William the Conqueror onwards.

'William the Second. Inherited England off his father, sort of a second choice really, his elder brother got Normandy. His nickname was Rufus cos of his red face. He was gay, very gay – and mocked the churchmen around him. His big thing was blinding and castrating people, especially poachers who went into the Royal Forests, which his dad had massively expanded.'

'What a cunt.'

'He was killed by a crossbow hunting. Some say it was an inside job.'
'Hah.'
'His brother Henry took over, and died of overeating. He had over twenty bastards but his only legitimate son was drowned at sea. After that he never smiled again. So they say. Then there were a few more losers ... Why don't you point to a king and I'll tell you about him ... Right, Richard the First – the Lionheart. Liked to crusade.'
'Was 'e gay an' all?'
'No, crusade. Go to the Holy Land and kill the Muslims.'
Rose honked the horn.
'Hang on a sec, what about this pasty geezer?'
'Henry the Fourth. You know, Shakespeare? Part One? Bit of a rebel, always broke – Henry Bolingbroke. An OK bloke. Fought the Welsh. Died of leprosy.'
'This one looks like a cunt,' said Barry pointing a fat finger.
'Richard the Third. He was. Ruthless hunchback. A horse, a horse, my kingdom for a horse.'
'James the First?'
'Gay. Slobbering gay. Liked the theatre and witchcraft.'
'Anne?'
'Like John, Anne the One and only. Seventeen kids but none survived her.'
'George the One.'
'German.'
'Looks a cunt.'
'He was.'
'George the Two?'
'Hated his dad, hated his son. Last British king to lead the army into battle. Very German though.'
'George the Three.'
'Lost America. Quite popular here. Mad as a hatter in later life. Fifteen kids. George the Fourth, before you ask, slept around, was drunk at his own wedding, and was the Prince Regent – Regent Street, Regent's Park, Brighton Pavilion. Fashion victim.'
'Edward the Seventh?'
'Had it away with an actress, for which his mother Queen Victoria never forgave him. Gave him no power so he spent all his time opening new buildings, a bit like our Charlie. Smoked too much, shagged around, gambled. Visited America.'
Rose bibbed again.

'Henry the Eighth?'

'Cunt.'

'Edward the Two?'

'Wimp. And very gay. Not that there's anything wrong with that.'

'Stephen?'

'A mess.' Clive looked around. Rose was frowning at him. 'Come on let's go.'

Barry produced his wallet and bought two tea towels. They rushed on to the coach.

'Why'd you get two?' asked Clive.

'In case my missus dries the dishes with one I'll have a spare.' He stared at the imagery for half an hour until Clive roused him and made him get up and do his Diana.

10

What Would Barry Do?

The money came rolling in. Just as the early wave of Diana interest waned –
by the third week of July numbers were right down, because hardly anyone
was interested in trekking to Northants for a non-look at her grave –
new people started showing up asking for Albion. The first round of
recommendations had just hit. Alex was anxious, Clive didn't worry about
it, and Barry didn't think about it, but Rose was absolutely right. She said
there'd a be a three-week lag before new people started turning up, sent
by their friends.

A German girl would go back to Frankfurt and tell her friend in the
volleyball team that she *has* to go on an Albion tour on her upcoming
visit. The guides are a lot of fun because they speak plain English and
don't appear to get on very well with each other. Their phone line is
always busy and they don't seem to have a fixed schedule or itinerary.
She thought she was going to Oxford but spent most of the day driving
around the Cotswolds stopping at pubs and little churches. At Inglesham
they saw a Saxon church, warped and worn, then followed the Windrush
River to a medieval chapel built in the middle of a field at Widbrook. She
learned about the merchants of the wool trade making a killing between
the fourteenth and sixteenth centuries. Now she understood why sheepdog
trials are shown on television, and why the English have a treasured fantasy
of lovers lying in the grass, shepherd to shepherdess. Then she gives her
friend her spare stamps, old phonecard and loose change and tells her to
watch out for the guide in the jeans and trainers, he's a bit free with his
hands and tongue.

Rose turned out to be right about a lot of things. Right about where to advertise, right about saving money by not renting an office, right about Clive not being ready to get involved with her.

On that drunken night, after the initial Diana excitement, Clive chivalrously walked her back to her flat in Vauxhall. She didn't ask him to, but she didn't tell him not to either. The night air was muggy. He lingered at the door to the terraced house in Bonnington Square, asking her questions about real estate, fascinated by everything. He couldn't quite gauge her reactions because of the drink, but had lived long enough to know it was probably the same for her. Besides, his attention span was shot so he couldn't worry about anything for very long.

He lingered, asking about the renovation of the square (it had been successfully gentrified ten years before; he was trying to work out whether she was BC or AD) and she invited him in for coffee.

'My boyfriend's away,' she said, hanging up her bag in the hall. He didn't know whether this was said to contain him or free him up, but again, whatever he decided was irrelevant, because the lager was within him and he was going to act whichever way was most natural. There was a jumble of crash helmets, leathers and Belstaff on the floor. Her flat was on the ground floor and was well appointed. In the living room there was a white sofa and red and white Turkish rug, lit by a side lamp. There was one bookcase filled with CDs and the stereo, and another with books. The coffee table was tidy, with nothing on it except fat scented candles and two remote controls. There was something under it though, wrapped in newspaper.

She made him some instant coffee while he stood around in the fluorescent light of the kitchen, which made her hair parting look severe and her scalp pink. He wondered how awful he must look – how jowly, how porous, eroded by time – and was glad to get into back into the lounge.

She was wearing bike boots with her jeans, and put her foot out on the coffee table. They sat at either end of the sofa, at an awkward angle for talking. She put a copy of *The Puzzler* magazine under her heel to protect the surface.

'Oh yeah, I forgot to tell you, I figured out your riddle. A man is lying dead in a field with a ring on his finger. What happened?' She paused.

'Go on then.'

She smiled. 'His parachute failed to open.'

Clive was relieved. She wasn't a thicko. 'Very good. How long did it take you? Not that it matters ...'

'I dunno. Ten minutes.'

They talked shop. They laughed about Alex being arrested, then Clive tried to say something good about him but couldn't think of anything.

'We need him for the office,' said Rose.

'I know. There used to be a girl who did all that office stuff though, Maxine. I wish we could get her back. I don't know what Alex did. Played cricket.'

'We'll always need people like that,' she said cryptically.

'People like what?'

'You know, posh boys with no real talent, just the talent for being upper class.'

'It must be hard work talking in that deep voice all day.'

'Did you hear him when he got riled?' She did his voice. 'He got all whiny and afraid like this and was going to have a tantrum ...'

Clive laughed, pleased to have a scapegoat, but a bit worried about Rose being too cruel, too boyish. He got up and went for a piss, taking a peek at the bedroom as he went. The door was open. The king-size bed was neatly made. It looked very clean, like something in a catalogue. The shelves either side of the bed had more candles, and there were dried flowers and coffee-table books. The bedside lamp on one side was on and gave a soft glow. The other one was off, and had a crimson scarf draped over it. Everything else was put away in drawers and wardrobes.

The bathroom was similar – a toilet so clean you could have eaten sushi out of it, glass shelves for everything, fluffy towels to excess. But there was a terrible smell of solvent. He pulled back the shower curtain while pissing and was shocked to see the bath full of black liquid. It had chunks of metal in it. What looked like parts of an engine.

'What's that in the bath?' he asked her as he sat down, this time next to her.

'Oh that's a crank casing, big end, stuff like that.'

'Hmm.' Clive felt sorry for her, living with such a slob boyfriend.

'Where's your ... the guy you live with?'

'He's gone up north to a conference ... Oh, you know this Grand Up North Tour, we should do it with an overnight stay. There are places in Manchester where we can stick 'em, cheap. They can go out and have some nightlife, back on the coach in the morning and do the rest, then back to London.'

'I don't want to be worrying about a lot of luggage ...' said Clive, then realised what a moaner he sounded. 'Actually, that's probably a good idea.' He was still worrying about the boyfriend, trying to work out whether he was on the way out or not. He decided he must be, otherwise she wouldn't have invited him in. Unless things had changed since his day. He'd been out of the game a long time, after all. Things had been easy with that American girl with the purple bra. Forgot her name, but that wasn't the point. Nothing important had remained unspoken, or undone. He knew where he stood. Purple-bra girl had just heaved her sweater over her head and there they were.

But now he was back to the way he remembered it – he was afraid to ask, lest the moment be ruined, and she wasn't about to tell.

'Rose. That's a nice name, Rose,' he said wistfully.

'My mother was a gardener. She's dead now though. There's just me and me dad.'

'Oh, I'm sorry.' Clive quickly followed on with some stuff about his own mother and her lost mind, which Rose seemed interested in. He made out he visited her more than he did – as much as he intended to, in fact, so it was not really a lie. Then they reached the subject of his daughter.

She looked thoughtfully at the snapshot of Tess, neither cooing nor handing it back too soon.

'Do you see her much?'

He sighed. 'No. There's a lot of trouble with access and all that. I have a hearing next month, but my lawyers are terrible. Sometimes I think I should represent myself.'

'Ooh don't do that,' she said quickly. 'You might mess it up and then where would you be?'

'Well you know, I also have this other feeling sometimes. I know this is going to sound strange but ... my daughter Tess, she doesn't really like me. She doesn't even know me very well any more. I mean, I've been off the scene now for a third of her life. Or over half of her conscious life, the bits she'll remember when she's older. I'll just be this bloke who's in the videos of her fifth and sixth birthday parties, who left a few clothes in the wardrobe and who took her to the zoo at the weekends. I'm thinking it might be a good idea to make a clean break. Not see her again. Good for her, to not have me confusing her. Good for me too. Finding someone new is hard enough without having a child on board.'

Rose gave him back the picture and said nothing. They were silent for a whole minute.

'Look at these dampers,' she said, leaning forward suddenly and unwrapping the newspaper package from under the table. 'Off a Bantam. I just had them re-finished. Anodised and chromed by this little old man in Brum.' She showed him two shiny springs, about a foot long each and very heavy, part of the suspension from underneath an old motorcycle's seat. They looked like new, shining silver in the weak light. 'He's called Len and he worked for BSA for thirty years. He talks loike this, know wurroi mean?'

Clive handled them and tried to admire them, but ultimately couldn't think of anything to say. Maybe Barry was right. Maybe she was a lesbian. Motorbike boots? He was kidding himself.

He leaned across, very slowly, to kiss her, but she evaded him, very slowly, drawing back.

The ensuing embarrassment – good grief, look at the time, I'll show you out, yes of course – felt bad. But not as bad as he expected. Something in him was numb to humiliation. A bit of him had died over the summer. As he walked across the square he tried to imagine what Barry would have done. Barry, he thought, would pick himself up and move on.

11

Big Heart Bypass

The bus went rolling on and the money came rolling in. Clive and Rose had an unspoken agreement not to speak about his lunge and her refusal. In any case, there wasn't time. There was work to be done. Clive had to worry about Barry, to try and teach him some usable history so they could double their capacity. They had done the Cotswolds and Althorp, now they had to get the North going. They talked about doing day trips at first, just to get the feel of the place, as their northern knowledge wasn't great. At a meeting in the Shakespeare it turned out Clive knew the most. At least he had lived there for a bit growing up, so he didn't have Barry's instinctive distrust of everything past Wembley. (Barry liked Northern birds though, he freely admitted that. He'd met thousands during his Club 18 to 30 days. Shagged a lot of them too. They were easy, they were a good laugh, and they believed pretty much everything he said.) Rose said she only knew the major roads, but was happy to explore. She also had a friend from home who had moved to Merseyside, a woman copper. Barry and Clive looked at each other.

The big surprise was Alex revealing that he was a northerner himself. *Chester.*

'My father's side of the family were in Chester for generations. Centuries. It was only when my grandfather moved down south after he came out of the army that we moved to London. North country boy, I am,' he said, jabbing a thumb at his chest.

'Well, we're not going near Chester,' said Clive. 'It's too ... *nice*. It's a horrible place. It's like Surrey, with accents. All cheese shops, crypts and women's wear.'

'Where do you want to go then?' asked Rose, being all professional.

'Let them see some industrial heritage. I'm not against heritage per se. Rossendale in Lancashire – show them the cradle of the industrial revolution. Quarry Bank Mill in Styal, that's good – the cotton industry. Let's take them to the Ribble Valley, to the seaside at Blackpool, the Lakes, maybe across the Yorkshire Moors, Castle Howard . . .'

'They can't see all that in one day. Or two.'

'We'll just have to choose as we go. Whatever looks good at the time.'

Barry looked uncomfortable. 'Sounds like a lot of work.'

'Yes,' said Rose. She turned to Alex. 'What were the numbers like on the Midlands tour? The page views. On the website.'

Alex blushed – he'd forgotten all about that, the research he was supposed to be doing. The truth was he hadn't had much time for work lately. Most of his day was occupied with thinking about Clive's ex-wife Christina, in her lingerie.

'I had some calls . . .'

Rose commandeered the computer and looked it up herself. She graphed the number of hits and requests for further information for each destination, the Midlands and the North. The Midlands was winning by three-to-one. She shut the lid on the machine loudly. Annoyed at being left out of the loop, she went to get a round in.

'Oh well that's it then, the Midlands,' said Barry. 'I can be home for last shout.'

'No, I think the North is better. Come on', Clive said 'we can't change now. Alex? Alex.'

Alex hesitated, then sided with Barry.

'What about her? Rose? Does she get a vote? Hey Rose – Midlands or Norf, you decide.'

'Heart of England.'

Barry had a versatile mouth – he could laugh at Clive and finish a drink at the same time. 'So what's happening between you two anyway?'

Thoroughly tired of his insinuations, Clive said to him very quietly, before hiding his mouth in his drink, 'Shagged her.'

Barry's eyes nearly popped out of his head, and he swivelled in his chair to watch Rose returning. She was now *one of us*, and worthy of some *rispeck*.

12

Middle Class, Middle Aged, Middle England

Rose was right. The Heart of England worked out well for them. It seemed the Germans, Dutch, Belgians, Scanders, French, Swiss, Spanish, Czechs, Poles, Russians and Americans had an appetite for the gentle lands that stretched from Cheltenham in the south to Chester in the north, and from Coventry in the east to the Marches in the west. Especially the Americans. They came in droves. Where the natives saw only conurbations and unpopular accents, they saw river valleys and extra history. The home crowd saw a lattice of motorways and industrial estates. The visitors saw refurbished canals and factories drenched with meaning. If they were in the country for more than a few days, once they got over the Crown Jewels and Buckingham Palace, Oxford and Anne Hathaway's Cottage, Albion Tours was waiting (with its hazards going, illegally parked) to show them the rest.

And Clive was determined they should see it all. He got a manic look in his eye when it came to making decisions. Sometimes it seemed the only thing holding him back was his fellow countrymen.

'Ladies and gentlemen, today we will be making a loop of the Heart of England, taking in many historical and modern sights. As soon as we get off the M40 we'll be heading for a small town called Worcester on the River Severn, followed by Ludlow, which many people say is the most beautiful town in England. Then if you're *good* we might stop in at Berrington Hall, or Chester if you really want to, then we'll crack on to the Potteries, the West Midlands and back to London.'

He stood in the aisle holding the microphone like a talk show host, looking better than he had for months. Thanks to a diet of mainly Guinness and chewing gum the weight was falling off him. Plus he'd got some sun. The influx of money had meant he could shed his grey clothes, his high-street bargains and the plastic shoes that made his feet stink. Relegated too was the dark suit with the whiff of the dead man. Now he looked like a modern geographer: Gore-Tex jackets, microfibres, wicking shirts, high-end fleece that didn't bobble. He could have tap danced through the rain in his new semi-breathable superlightweight walking shoes, which also made him look five years younger. Not that it had rained in June or July. The country's weather was peaking, 25 degrees C guaranteed every day, continual news stories about ice cream and garden hoses and pretty girls sunbathing and global warming. The entire population was coming together on the same wavelength, under one blue sky.

Clive talked and talked and talked. He talked until white stuff gathered in the corners of his mouth and Rose would have to pass him her Diet Coke. He talked until he got used to the sound of his voice, until it felt like a part of him. It was like playing an instrument, a sensuous woodwind. He wondered if he learned circular breathing could he could talk all day without stopping?

Barry had to fight to get a word in edgeways. It was partly his own fault, because he still wasn't very good with his kings and queens (calling Charles the Second a 'shitout' because as a young prince he ran away from the Battle of Worcester did not go down very well, although Clive certainly knew what he meant), and he wasn't very quick to learn new areas either. This wasn't like London, whose infrastructure he'd known all his life, where he could just slot into place the social and historical stuff. Jack the Ripper was starting to look attractive again. Barry spent a lot of his time up the front listening. He limited the ladies and the newspaper to the journey home. Sometimes he'd try and chat up Rose, who made it clear that she'd rather be talking to Clive, who was now playing hard to get.

'One side of the country has the River Trent, this side has the Severn, the heart's main artery. If the country was a biscuit, or a cookie, it would snap in half somewhere around here, that's how close these two rivers come. The Severn has been an essential provider of food and communications for thousands of years. There are still Celtic coracles being used on it ... In fact until a few years ago there was an old chap who paddled across the river in a coracle every time they kicked the ball out of the stadium at Shrewsbury Town football ground. And though they no longer worship the river god around here, the local news crews still turn out every spring to film the Severn bore, a three-foot tidal wave that comes inland at the speed of a moped, punctual to the half hour.'

As they entered Worcester he pointed out the CrownGate shopping centre situated right in the middle of the small town.

'This is just the sort of thing that gets the armchair architects cross. Anything with "gate" in the name smacks of phoney medievalism, you know — *how could this concrete monstrosity have anything to do with walled medieval towns?* Like the Westgate Centre in Oxford. There's a certain class of English person who likes to get offended by modern buildings that are placed too near to old ones. Which is a shame really, as they seem to forget that when a lot of these places were built in the 1960s the economy was switching from manufacturing to services. People were getting interested in shopping. Now of course it's the number one source of entertainment, so they'll be pulled down soon to make way for buildings that are a bit more entertaining. So I wouldn't worry about it, just enjoy the view. If you could be here at dawn you'd get the view of the sun on the river, the bridge with the little lamps reflected in the water, the square tower of the cathedral in the background . . . that's enough to feed anyone's hunger for a romantic landscape. This whole place has a small-town attitude: when the river floods, the County cricket pitch ends up under water. And these are professionals. That's the equivalent of an American major-league baseball franchise being put out of action by traffic jams. But this is the sort of crapness we English love, proof that nothing is that serious.'

He led them round Worcester Cathedral. It was a mess of styles. 'You needn't feel bad about the shopping centre when you remember that this crypt was built in Norman times, chiselled out from beneath the Saxon monastery founded in 983. They didn't care about heritage, just getting the job done.' Upstairs he showed them the quire and the tombs of King John and Prince Arthur, and the lumps knocked out of them by Cromwell's men. Then he showed them the Prince Arthur Chantry. 'This place was built by Henry the Seventh when his son, Arthur, drowned on honeymoon with Catherine of Aragon. A chantry is a place where you pay other people to pray for your soul, or someone else's soul, so it can get into heaven all the quicker. The wealthy relied on it heavily, the way they rely on PR firms today to do their bidding. Nothing changes.'

Barry had to get his oar in. 'And Catherine of Aragon later went on to marry Arthur's brother, Henry the Eighth. And we all know what happened to her, eh?'

He took over, telling them the full gruesome story of the axe-happy

King, while Clive stood around waiting. He looked at the sad old flags hanging from angled poles in the servicemen's corner – rotting Union Jacks with gold fringes and military crests, faded by the sun, their creases permanent. He wondered what was stopping such a place from modernising. Two old dears in floral prints were selling postcards and paperweights, huffing and puffing over the change and the paper bags. Surely it couldn't be much longer before they'd be replaced by a teenager with a scanner, and the flags by projections. The churches used to be painted bright colours inside and filled with friezes and plaster saints before the Reformation, so that the illiterates could follow along. It wouldn't be so big a jump to go back to that.

It all made him worry about the future. In England the pace was usually set by those who were best at being shocked and outraged. Clive knew he'd done nothing to change things – a bit of dinner-party politicking, a petition hastily signed outside the supermarket ... For fuck's sake he'd never even chained himself to a tree. History might just push on without him, as it always had. But all the old certainties had fallen away just in his lifetime. What remained was a free-for-all. There was Barry, there was Alex, and there was him. Who knew who was right any more? Maybe he could call everyone's bluff by acting like he knew what he was doing and taking over history? And maybe that's how it had always been done?

'F'fuck's sake Clive, no more fucking cathedrals today, all right?' said Barry when they were back outside.

'Of course,' said Clive. He chose the phrase that would annoy his colleague most. Barry didn't scare him any more. Clive now was sure he could tailor any trip to keep the tourists happy. As the money began to flow in July he'd been excited at first, but once he'd got the new clothes and placated Mr Ahmet with some back rent, he found he wasn't that excited about money. Only two things fired him up: finding his way around the country, and making friends with Rose. And he'd largely put that on hold. He didn't feel like grovelling around a woman, and he didn't know how else to approach her. So she stayed on the bus reading her book, or eating her sandwich. He had a country to see, and information to pass on.

They did a drive-by on Leominster, a town of just 10,000. 'Seven hundred years this place has been a wool-manufacturing centre. Now it's a farm-implement centre. You know, there's a town down the road, Hay on Wye, which just sells books. That's it! Twenty used bookshops and a thousand tweedy people milling around, playing pocket billiards and looking for an illustrated Pepys. Anyway, the idea is it's a new economic model for saving country villages from depopulation. It's certainly worked in Hay, though it has limited application – we can't all corner a market can we? I can see it happening elsewhere though, a town giving itself over to music and records, say, and being inundated by people in Doc Marten shoes fretting about vinyl and complaining about digitisation ... Maybe some of you here have some capital and would like to invest? This is Europe after all, you're welcome to take a stake.

'I digress, as they say. Back to Leominster, spelt L-E-O Minster, which typically some middle-ager claimed was derived from the Latin *monasterium leonis*, the monastery of the lions, when in fact *leonis* comes from medieval not classical Latin and means "of the marshes". It makes you wonder who's in charge of making things up, doesn't it? Who do I speak to at the Ministry of Getting It Wrong?'

He stopped for a swig of water. He spoke swiftly, rolling his sentences into each other, then putting pressure on the odd word, emphasising it in slow motion.

'The church here has a Green Man fertility spirit carved by the west door. You see a lot of these around the country, though the local vicars used to be really embarrassed about them. Usually a bloke's face with trees growing out of his mouth, usual stuff, fertility symbols, rebirth, all that. For a far more embarrassing pagan symbol ask if there's a Sheela-na-gig, a carving of a Celtic goddess with her fanny wide open. There's one not far from here at St Mary and St David's church in Kilpeck but we're not going there. She's got both hands in it, looks like she's turning herself inside out. The idea is she's a Celtic goddess who appears as a lecherous hag to any future king and tries to seduce him. If she succeeds she turns into a beautiful woman and blesses his reign. See, the pagans just wouldn't let it lie, even when they were supposed to become Christian, they'd sneak their stuff into a little corner. The one I'm thinking of looks like it's been carved by Joey the Retard too. And can somebody here explain to me why they couldn't draw properly in those days? Talking of backward things, there's also a ducking stool here at the Grange Court, which was used for punishing dishonest tradesmen, scolds and wayward wives. The ducking stool was a doddle compared to trials by ordeal, which weren't abolished until 1219. Here's what you did. The accused had his arm bandaged up, then had to grab a stone from the bottom of a pan of boiling water. After three days the bandages were removed. If he'd been scalded, he was guilty. I mean really, ladies and gentlemen, and please excuse my French, but what the *fuck* was all that about? You won't be surprised to hear that

priests were excused trial by ordeal, and instead had to eat a piece of
bread *and cheese* before an altar. A prayer was made to God to send down
the archangel Gabriel to block the throat of the priest if he was guilty. If
he got the bread and cheese down, he was in the clear. Pretty tough, eh?
Oooh, I wonder who thought of that? Also, clergy could only be punished
in ecclesiastical courts, where the worst you'd get was a few thousand Hail
Maries, or maybe defrocking. This was called the Benefit of the Clergy, and
it also got you off capital punishment, which soon came to mean *anyone* who
could prove he was educated – that is, pay someone to help him memorise
a few lines of Latin at the eleventh hour in his cell – couldn't be executed.
Anyway King Henry the Second was against all this bollocks. The hard bit
for him was taking on the clergy, and stopping them appealing to Rome
all the time, which led to his quarrel with Thomas à Becket, the Archbishop
of Canterbury whose brains he had Security spread out on the cathedral
floor. They used to be great mates too. The people, being a soppy bunch,
thought this was terrible and started making pilgrimages to Canterbury to
his tomb, especially once he was canonised in 1173. And that, ladies and
gentlemen, was the true beginning of English tourism. Even Henry paid a
visit in the end, to make it look like he was sorry for slotting his friend.
I'm sure it's the same in your country – things have changed, things stay
the same. He cocked it all up in the end, Henry. He was married but he
fell in love with a girl from round here, Rosamond, daughter of Walter
de Clifford, who owned extensive estates along the Welsh Marches. She
was said to be a "masterpiece of nature" ...'

Clive paused for several seconds to make everyone imagine her.

'Anyway she was kept locked up in a tower in a maze, and his wife was
so pissed off she had her poisoned and turned her sons against him. In the
end he lost loads of land to the French – the real French – and just chucked
it in. They say he turned his face to the wall and said "Enough! Now let
things go as they may. I care no more for myself or the world."'

He paused again, then smiled.

'That's no way to run a country is it? You can't go round with a long
face all day.'

He went off deep into thought, staring out of the window at the
passing green.

At Ludlow, he became animated.

'We're now in Shropshire. This is Ludlow. Look at it. A castle, a square
church tower, a cluster of half-timbered buildings, the winding River Teme,
green fields just a stone's throw from the centre, ribbon development along

the A-road: surely this is one of the most beautiful sights in all England? This is what a lot of English people daydream about when they think of moving, but they never get round to it. Partly because they don't want to go from being a doctor or a mechanic to working in a cake shop selling flans and iced buns. Because there's not much here in the way of work. And of course we can't visit Shropshire without mentioning the celebrated English poet A. E. Housman. After a little setback — i.e. ten years as a civil servant — he swapped the marshes for the fens, and became a donnish poet who spent most of his life in Cambridge dreaming of the swains and hillsides back home. He wanted to be mistaken for a bit of a lad, a Shropshire lad, which I suppose is understandable when you're cooped up in an ivory tower all day. He wrote a lot about the landscape around here. He's quite a marketable chap. Up-marketable, in fact. You couldn't get a chip shop out of him, but a tea shop would be a worthwhile punt. Listen to this and see what you think. He's twenty and he's already complaining about feeling old:

> '"Loveliest of trees, the cherry now
> Is hung with bloom along the bough,
> And stands about the woodland ride
> Wearing white for Eastertide.
>
> Now, of my threescore years and ten,
> Twenty will not come again,
> And take from seventy springs a score,
> It only leaves me fifty more.
>
> And since to look at things in bloom
> Fifty springs are little room,
> About the woodlands I will go
> To see the cherry hung with snow."'

Clive looked around to see whether anyone understood it. Two Japanese girls smiled back at him.

'He was actually born in Worcestershire, you know, not Shropshire. He was ahead of his time, because he claimed to be a pagan. Now everyone's at it. Anyway, we're going to stop here for a pint — a pricey one too — at the Feathers, which got its name from the arrow-making industry. Arrows used to mean a lot round here. The longbow was an effective weapon used by the Welsh against the English (then later the English against the Scots

— we learned our lesson), sort of the Kalashnikov of its day. We'll skip the castle, you can see it from the ground. Besides, it's full of Elizabethan stuff. They all are, really.' He clicked off the mike and disembarked.

And so it went. Each day they came back to the area, and each day Clive went through his spiel, changing it, refining it, adding bits. He had no taste for saying the same thing twice, even to fresh ears, but he knew he had to. He looked back in amazement at his time teaching Geography. Every year he'd turn to the same page in the text book at the same week in the year. Dictate a few paragraphs about, say, the nationalised rail network and the Beeching Plan, then get the kids to do some colouring in. When things changed it worried him. When train routes started being privatised he wasn't sure whether to teach it in case it didn't feature in the national exams. He and everyone he knew were suspicious of change. What if things changed back? Or never changed in the first place? Who knew if those artist's impressions in the newspaper of the new city centre would really come true?

Now here he was unable to say the same thing twice.

'Are you all right?' asked Rose, near the end of their first Midlands week. He was still being cool to her, most of the time lost in his thoughts. She liked Clive's free-range talk. This streak of nonconformity had come from nowhere, and was spreading. Even the way he carried himself had changed — he walked tall, met people's gaze, seemed to have lost his fear. Unfortunately, he didn't seem interested in her. She had even ended up having her lunches with Barry in the pub.

'Yes,' he said.

'Worrying about the court thing with your daughter ...?' It was a hopeful statement rather than a question.

'It's coming up. But I told you already, it's probably best if I lose. I might just concede.'

She couldn't get any more out of him.

The next day he read a different Housman poem.

'This one's about a plough boy wondering what's going on in the world after he's dead. It's a dialogue with his best mate.

""Is my team ploughing,
    That I was used to drive
And hear the harness jingle
    When I was man alive?"'

'"Ay, the horses trample,
   The harness jingles now;
No change though you lie under
   The land you used to plough.

'""Is football playing
   Along the river shore,
With lads to chase the leather,
   Now I stand up no more?'"

'"Ay the ball is flying,
   The lads play heart and soul;
The goal stands up, a keeper
   Stands up to keep the goal.

'""Is my girl happy,
   That I thought hard to leave,
And has she tired of weeping
   As she lies down at eve?'"

'"Ay, she lies down lightly,
   She lies not down to weep;
Your girl is well contented.
   Be still, my lad, and sleep.

'""Is my friend hearty,
   Now I am thin and pine;
And has he found to sleep in
   A better bed than mine?'"

'""Yes, lad, I lie easy,
   I lie as lads would choose;
I cheer a dead man's sweetheart.
   Never ask me whose."

'You'd think a poem about sex, death and football would be more popular these days, but I'd never heard of it until today.'

In Stoke he spoke of the Potteries, and how the people didn't know if they were from the North or the Midlands and had the accent to prove it. Bookish people including his mother, he told them, call this area the Five Towns, though every inhabitant or travelling salesman knows there are six. Rose pointed out that the train station is in Stoke but the bus station is in Hanley, a fact he thanked her for and deployed whenever he could. As they stepped down from the coach into yet another street of Marks and Spencer's and WH Smith's, Clive told them about the City Museum. 'They have a memorial to a boy who died scavenging for coal. Nothing strange about that, until you realise that it happened in 1985, not 1885.' The crowd usually headed for Marks and Spencer's. He also thought of George, who used to spend Christmas at his sister's house in Stoke. He kept meaning to give him a call.

Some days he knocked Chester on the head, unable to stomach the manicured tweeness. Sometimes he ordered Rose to head straight for Walsall so they could see the leather museum, or Willenhall for the locksmiths. He loved the idea that half an industry had been wiped out by little magnets. Rose liked it because she met an old man there with an interest in data cryptography. She was very impressed that he had switched track from clunky iron locks to the abstractions of computer programming, all to stay ahead of the game. Clive tried to listen in but it was all gobbledegook. It was when driving through the Black Country that he discovered Merry Hill, the giant shopping centre, and wasted two hours of everyone's time there until one of the Americans complained that if she wanted to slop around a mall with spotty teenagers and buy shoddy goods she could have stayed at home, and take them to a castle *now*. She spoke too soon because he took them to Dudley Castle, a Norman ruin with a wretched zoo.

'You know you could have gone to Alton Towers,' he told her. 'It's the sixth-biggest tourist attraction in the country. And you *are* tourists.'

Barry stepped in, getting Clive to hold his tongue and go away. She was a big bruiser from Maine who worked in a call centre all day, so she was used to taking lip. Barry calmed her down with some lies about Clive being under a lot of pressure because of his mother and the Alzheimer's, scoring an accidental bullseye because she herself had cared for an elderly relative and knew exactly what he must be going through.

'What's number one?' asked Rose. 'British Museum?'

'No. Blackpool Pleasure Beach, eight million visitors, British Museum, six million, National Gallery where nobody *I* know has ever been, five, Brighton Pier, three and a half, Madame Tussaud's, three, Alton Towers, three. That's more than the *Toweralandan*. Hey Barry . . .' he shouted.

'Sshh. Leave him alone,' said Rose. 'Listen, we should do Blackpool. Tourists would love that, I bet none of them even know about it.'

Clive knew about Blackpool. His family had unwittingly gone there once for the day, with predictable consequences. Gordon had got lost in a penny arcade and Clive had to sit with his parents for three hours in the police station until he was found.

Some of Clive's pupils had been too, over the years. One of them, a real clever clogs, told him it was an 'ironic destination', a category which excited Clive momentarily by its novelty.

'What, do you think genu-ine American tourists and suchlike want to spend their euros in pubs, clubs and chip shops crowded with thieving Scousers, pissed Jocks and mad Geordies, slipping in sick on the boardwalk, stumbling into transvestite revue bars, or being pestered to buy bad Ecstasy by bullet-headed fourteen-year-olds?' He chuckled. 'Heh heh, that's a good idea. Meta-tourism. Come and see the natives touring. You're absolutely right, Rose.'

13

Growing the Company

Alexander White and Barry Bergman were having a pint together. They
were forced to talk to each other, since the other two hadn't arrived yet
for the strategy meeting. Alex recommended the Hen's Tooth draught ale
which he'd had once at Lord's.

'So Barry. What's your exit strategy?' he said condescendingly. Barry
looked up from the trivia machine when he had slapped his selection, D.
*How many goals to the nearest hundred did Pele score? A) 700 B) 900 C) 1,100
D) 1,300. Correct.*

'What are you talking about? I don't run from no one.' Then he
remembered that girl whose husband came home in the middle of the
day. In the back of his mind he'd expected a skinny white kid not the
seven-foot Rasta who was loping down the path to the maisonette. He
didn't wait around to see who would get the beating, he was out the back
door and over the fence in a shot.

'Business, Baz, I'm talking about business. How do you see your exit
from Albion?'

'I'm not going anywhere, *Al*. If anyone should get the boot it's you, yer
lazy sod.'

With exaggerated patience, Alex explained the world of business to him.
The idea wasn't to create a company and hang *on* to it, doing the actual *work*.
The idea was to grow the company and then sell it to a big corporation. Or
take it public. The first way they stood to make a tidy profit. The second
way they stood to become quite rich, but it was more of a risk. Having
'.com' after their name helped. Alex was obliged to explain all this because,
on Rose's insistence, the four of them had an equal share in the company.

In an ideal world he would just get rid of Barry and Rose, and keep Clive on at a salary. But this was not an ideal world.

'What do you mean, "rich"?' asked Barry warily. 'Kinell, General Knowledge.'

'Well ... a million each,' he said, trying to sound blasé.

Barry looked at him, then tutted. 'Bollocks.' He went back to his game. He read out the question. 'How old was Joan of Arc when she first heard voices? Fuck. A) 12 B) 16 C) 13 D) 14.'

'D, it's D, it's D! D, D, D, D, D, D, D!'

'Is it?' He slapped D. *Wrong*. 'It's *C* you silly cunt. Firteen. Still, I don't even know who Joan of Arc was.'

'She was a ... French saint. You know.'

'Yeah. I wish fucking Clive would hurry up and get here.'

'That's what I wanted to talk to you about. Remember Sir Clive Tiddell who used to run Wonga?'

'Oh yeah,' Barry smirked. '*Scum of the Earth*. Great series. Blowing his top like that at the camera, rule number one, never shove a cameraman ...'

'Well I hear he's very interested in getting back in the game. We could have a potential suitor on our hands.'

'Eh?'

'He wants to buy Albion.'

'Bit soon isn't it? Paint's barely fucking dry on the coach.'

'Oh the name would remain. This is a very, *very* strong brand. We grow the company, then we sell it. A million between us.'

'After three months?'

'This is a seasonal business, as you know. In this game one summer is like a year.'

The prospect of quarter of a mil had Barry excited, although he knew from experience that the bigger the figures, the bigger the bullshit. Which was why he had spent his life making the little runs, shuttling back and forth, whether it was Kos or lately, Coventry. His dad said the same, you make the money by taking lots of little fares, not by hanging around at 'Eafrow.

'So what's *your* exit strategy then? Bollocks, look at this: What fell on the Sahara on February 18th, 1979? How the fuck am I sposed to know that? A) A satellite. B) Snow. C) Two 747s. D) Six inches of rain.'

'It's got to be A, hasn't it?' said Alex cautiously.

'I think B. Snow. Innit? It never snows in the fucking Sahara. I know, I've been there mate. On the backova camel. Well, Morocco anyway. Hey!'

Alex had already slid his hand in and pressed A. *Wrong*. The correct answer flashed. *B.*

'You useless cunt! It *was* snow!'

'Oh.' Alexander White shrugged, but didn't apologise. There was no time for that now. 'Basically, if we can get rid of Clive and that girl we can make a more streamlined deal with Wonga. And I know for a fact that Sir Clive is likely to be more sympathetic to us, as Britannia alumni, than he is to those two – a banned teacher and a lesbian mechanic. He's a friend of the family, after all.'

'You're fucking Clive's ex-wife aren't you?' said Barry suddenly with a smirk. 'What's she like?'

Alex spluttered, 'I am not! I am not! Where on earth did you hear that? This is an outrageous lie!'

'I have my sources,' he yucked. 'A certain little lady who has access to your e-mail or whatever the fuck you call it.'

'That bitch! The little ... Don't you *dare* tell Clive ...'

'Nothing to do with me mate.'

'Well that's it then, she's going.'

'Quiet! What country contains the highest point in South America. Oh? 'kin Jesus. Where's Pointing when you need the fucker? A) Venezuela. B) Brazil. C) Argentina. D) Chile.'

'Gotta be the Argies, the one you least expect ... Get your fucking hands off ...'

'I think it's Chile.' Alex pronounced it Chill-ay, because he knew about wine. 'I'm telling you.'

'Argentina.' But Barry wasn't sure.

A hand poked in between them and hit the B button. Brazil. They both spun round. It was Clive, with Rose in tow. Alex glowered at her.

'All right Clive. How's it going?'

'Brazil,' said Clive.

They looked at the screen. *Wrong*. The correct answer was Argentina.

'Fackinell I knew it! I knew it! You dozy gits. You just cost me twenty quid! You fucking ...'

'Sorry, I used to know that,' said Clive, still smiling. Rose laughed loud and long. Alex glared at everyone and supped his Hen's Tooth.

Clive got a round in, they moved to a table, and Rose brought the meeting to order. 'Revenues for the last week are up 12 per cent. We are now sold out for the Midlands for the next month. The question is, do we want to keep doing that or do we try something different? I say we hit the North, like we discussed. Blackpool, The Lakes, Manchester, Bradford …'

'Yeah why not,' said Barry with a shrug. 'I'm sick of the *fooking Brummies.*'

'Now hang on a minute,' cut in Alex. 'Let's not kill the goose!'

'What fucking goose?'

'It could be perilous to suffer any fluctuation in revenues at this point,' said Alex.

'Perilous to what?' asked Rose. 'We work for ourselves, remember? We're free to do whatever we want. We could drive round in an empty coach if we wanted at the moment. Who's gonna fire us?'

'I agree,' said Clive. 'The North. Come on, vote and let's get the fuck out of here.'

They all stared at him.

'Er, Clive, that's the other thing,' said Alex, trying to sound concerned. 'We've been wondering if you're all right?'

'Yeah. All this effing and blinding's not like you, you're not the quiet geezer I first met just a few months back. In this very boozer'

'I'm OK,' he said defensively.

'You're drinking, I never see you eat, you still don't have a telephone …' said Rose gently.

'Yes, this is all rather odd behaviour. I wasn't aware of it until the complaints started coming in,' said Alex. He was about to play his ace sooner than he thought.

'What complaints?'

Rose had a couple of sheets of paper printed out. She slid them across the table to him but they stuck in some beer. Clive leaned over and read them aloud without touching them.

'"Dear Mr Albion, I wish to complain about the behaviour of your guide Mr Pointing. I and my mother took your Heart of England tour recently and were disgusted by his repeated use of cuss words and blasphemy …"'

'Daft Yank,' said Barry.

'"To Whom It May Concern, I had the misfortune of using Albion Tours on the occasion of our thirtieth anniversary to transport my wife and I to the majestic confines of Warwick Castle …"'

'It's my wife and *me*, fuckface …' said Clive. He read on. '"Blah blah blah, twenty minutes … blah blah blah … Cromwell's helmet … blah blah blah … irrational discourse … Where do we get these people? Rose, put a note on the next ad – No Nutters.'

'This is bollocks,' said Barry. 'So long as they don't try and get their money back who cares? Free market, innit? Free speech. Isn't that right, Alex? Clive's done nothing wrong.' He winked at him.

'Well, I think so too,' said Rose. 'But Alex asked me to bring it up, so I did. Didn't you have something you wanted to say to me?' she asked the young man.

Alex blushed deeply. 'Er, er ... no.'

'So!' said Clive, with finality. 'Next week, up North. And Alex you sort out the hotels. Is that it, can we go now? This is my night-off from looking after my mum and I feel like getting absolutely wankered. And don't worry, I can hold my drink as well as any of you.'

'Where are you going?' Rose said hurriedly.

'Out local with Danny the Kiwi. And Jo, I think. What about you lot?'

Rose shrugged her shoulders.

'My brother Trevor's homecoming party tonight at the Swan. The old man's picking me up ...'

The old man Ron walked right in the door on cue clutching his keys.

'Come on!' he said, his eyes popping out of his Cockney head.

As Barry got up to go, he casually invited Rose to go with them.

'Er, I don't know. Er, Clive, you should come with us.'

'Hurry up!' said the key jangler.

Clive liked the sound of that. 'What about you, what are you doing tonight?' Clive asked Alex, whose blush had just faded but now returned.

'Nothing, nothing ...'

'Well come with us then,' said Barry with a devious grin. He knew he had him. Alex swallowed and pretended all was cool. All five got in the taxi. Ron was doing his special West End driving, swinging into side streets that none of them knew existed. His philosophy was 'Always avoid the river'.

'What about your mate the New Zealander?' Barry asked Clive, who was perched opposite him on the jumper seat, hanging on to the hand strap.

'Fuck him. He'll be all right. You know I really don't like Streatham. I really want to move. It depresses me going back there at night.'

'That's true, it's a shithole.'

'Where are you these days, Alex?' asked Clive. 'Somewhere in the West End I hear?'

'He's just round here, off of Portland Place,' said Barry loud enough for his dad to hear. Alex was praying they wouldn't go anywhere near his flat. He imagined Tina sitting outside waiting for him in her car, with the little girl. And calling him. *Right now.* He slipped his hand inside his pocket and turned off his phone.

14

Ordeal by Lager

The Swan was so packed and hot that dozens of people were standing outside in T-shirts pouring chilled lager down their throats from straight glasses. Everyone greeted Barry as he pushed his way through the crowd, and he put on his serious face. His Adam's apple bulged and he had no time to look after the new friends he had brought with him, so Rose decided to take control of their little group. She steered them to the bar, got the drinks in and tried to keep Alex quiet. She already felt out of place without hearty boy opening his gob and making everyone stare even more.

'That must be Trevor, the tall one in the corner,' she said. It was standing room only, loud with chatter and juke-box pop. There was a low stage with silver tinsel behind it, and above it a twelve-foot banner that read 'WELCOME HOME TREV' with the logo of the sponsor, Lord Archer lager. Trevor was a taller, thinner version of Barry, and he sat surrounded by men and women who laughed a lot and talked loudly. They watched Barry and Ron pick their way through the crowd and greet him with handshakes then hugs, shoulder slapping and hair tousling, like footballers congratulating each other. Father and brother squeezed themselves in and were swept up in the conversation. Stuttering Stuart was there, with his arm around his girlfriend. Next to her was a small blonde in a tight green dress. Practically busting out through the lycra, her stomach was swollen like a beach ball. She was talking to another Bergman son in a black polo neck. Barry's three little blonde children chased each other around the table, squealing and occasionally supping from Cokes. A very old man at the end of the table stared and smiled, making minimal movements. He wore a jacket and tie and a flat cap, looked about ninety.

'That's Barry's granddad,' said Rose.

Clive was impressed that she could work all this out.

'What was this *Trev* in prison for again?' asked Alex, looking around the room, fascinated.

'GBH,' said Clive.

'No it weren't. Resisting arrest and assault,' said a thin black youth who overheard them. Clive guessed it was Errol the lookout for Barry's street-seller brother Craig. 'He got in a ruck with a copper and bit his ear off.'

'What did he get?' asked Rose. She felt a bit tatty asking, like a prison girlfriend, but she was determined not to be squeezed out of the conversation by the men.

'He did sixteen months of an eighteen-month sentence. Scrubs.'

'Gore blimey guvnor, it's like the bleedin' East End, innit?' said Alex in his below-stairs accent.

They both shushed him and Errol turned away.

'Oh, kiss my facking goitre!' he said with a drunken swagger, and laughed at his wit.

'I wish you'd stop saying that,' said Clive with a frown. 'Hey, Rose, I've been meaning to tell you, I've got a riddle for you.'

She smiled, glad he was taking an interest.

'I should warn you that they tested this riddle, and seventy-seven per cent of junior-school children got it, but only twenty-two per cent of university students. OK. What is greater than God, more evil than the devil, the poor have it, the rich want it, and if you eat it you die.'

'Huh.' She furrowed her brow. '*Huh.*'

'Money,' said Alex confidently.

'The poor have it? *Money?*'

'Oh.'

Rose muttered for a minute but got nowhere, then declared she needed some time. Alex started blathering on about his university, how great it was, how the cricket team was the best in Scotland, how he had opened for them for two seasons, and how well England were doing against the Aussies. The series was now two-nil to England with one drawn. 'I reckon I could have played at county level if I'd put my mind to it.'

'And what county would that be? Cheshire?' said Clive.

'Middlesex,' he replied, thrusting his webbed chin forward.

'I thought you lived in Richmond? That's in Surrey.'

'Yes, Mama and Papa live there, but we take all our cricket at Lord's.'

Out of nowhere a girl standing next to them butted in, giggling. 'Oh, *Mama and Papa! Mama and Papa! So* nice to meet you. And does one get out to the country much?' Her mates, two tanned girls in tight tops, cracked up and they all began doing the voice, 'Hell*ooo*! *Jolly* good show! *Mama and Papa!*

Alex grinned stupidly. Three girls, good. Piss-taking, bad. Rose looked askance at them. They had piled-up cleavage and piled-up hair. She herself was looking tomboyish, sweatshirt and jeans. She thought about what she had on underneath – a white T-shirt, another Triumph. If it got any hotter she'd be forced to reveal it, and that wouldn't be very good with all the totty about.

She and Clive watched as Alex tried to communicate with the poodle-haired girls. It was embarrassing, but he was up for it. So was Poodle Number One. Her name was Joanne and she was fascinated with the fact that he ran a travel company. She was soon shouting over the noise that she loved 'olidays, and that the *freeovem* had all just been to Kos, and a few months before that, shopping in New York. Clive expected to be drawn into the conversation at some point, to balance out the numbers, but he and Rose were completely ignored. So he turned to her. She felt like an old friend.

'Rose, what do you think will happen at the end of the season? I fancy taking off somewhere for the winter. Bali. Or Western Australia. Somewhere where civilisation doesn't really reach. I've always wanted to go somewhere warm and quiet. You know, I was a Geography teacher, and yet I've never been to the Southern Hemisphere? Or any of Asia? All I've done is Europe and some North America. Hiking in Canada – it doesn't exactly broaden the mind.'

'Well, I've got the coach payments to make, I suppose I'll keep on working.'

'What, you bought the coach? I thought it was leased?'

'No, I told you, I invested. Bought it for fifty grand. Ten down, the rest over five years.'

'Blimey. Or should I say, gore blimey. So you're really making a go of it.' He looked at her, impressed, allowing some of his warmth to show. They were speaking just at a level where Alex couldn't hear over the din. An old Soft Cell record was on the juke box. *Baby, baby, where did our love go?* 'I assumed you'd have the winter off too.'

'If I did I'd stay in England anyway. Spend it in the country. See my Dad.'

'Oh yeah. Meriden. And the motorcycles. Of course. I forgot.'

'You should do other guiding.'

'I suppose. I'm not sure I have patience for it.'

They both stood there thinking about the winter. Neither felt they knew each other well enough to affect the course of history, but they liked each other enough not to settle for Fate.

A big cheer went up and everyone turned to look at the corner. Barry was on stage trying to shush the crowd so he could address them.

'Speak *ap!* Speak *ap!*' people shouted.

Someone passed him the microphone. 'Trevor asked me to say something tonight, because as you know he's a man of few words. None of which can be repeated in front of a family audience.' Everyone laughed. 'Anyway, we're here tonight to welcome Trev back into the community after his time inspecting HM's West London Hotel.'

Barry was smooth. He only hesitated to let the laughter die down, catching each wave on the backwash.

'Anyway, while you were away Trev, some of the lads here at the Swan . . .'

'And ladies!'

'. . . Right you are, some of us here had a whip round and we came up with this, get you on your feet again.' He handed over an envelope of cash. 'That's nine hundred quid. Don't spend it all at once. And don't spend it at the bar tonight!' Laughter. 'Oh and there is one other thing.' Barry produced something from a plastic carrier bag. It looked like an award. Everyone was straining to see.

'What is that?' asked Clive. 'Looks like a . . . Something white. What is it?'

Someone had bought a pig's head from the butcher and cut off one of the ears. They had then taken an old football trophy, sanded the player down to a stump and in its place mounted the pink, rubbery triangle of porcine cartilage.

'That's for making a pig's ear of the last fight you were in,' said Barry, and handed it over to his brother, to much talk-show hooting.

Rose and Clive looked at each other and rolled their eyes. Trevor clasped his envelope with one hand and raised his trophy with the other. He had the look of prison about him – short hair, and wearing the clothes he went in in. An out-of-date England football shirt, baggy jeans, trainers that made people think 'poor fucker'. Everyone was laughing and applauding though.

'Must be tough being banged up for so long,' said Rose, a little wistfully. 'Why d'you think he's so popular?' Errol heard her and took his fingers out of his mouth and stopped whistling to say, 'Diamond geezer, Trevor. He runs the Legal Aid Centre on the estate.'

'What, he's a *lawyer*?' said Clive. Now his eyes were popping.

'Yeah, went to University and everyfing. Cambridge wannit? Summit like that. Stu!' he shouted to the brother who was on his way to the bar. 'Where did your Trev go to university? Cambridge wannit?'

Stu leaned forward and tried to reply.

'C-c-c-c-c-c-c-c ...' He stopped and tried again.

'C-c-c-c-c-c-c-c ...' He still couldn't get it out. Clive was now very keen to know. A life was hanging on the next vowel. Stu paused. He had a rule whereby after two failures he waited a few seconds to compose himself. It was supposed to take the pressure off, and also reassure the listener that he was aware how difficult it was for them to listen to a stammerer. He tried again.

'C————' This time he could only get the initial C out, followed by airless straining. He gave it another shot.

'C-c-c-c-c-c-c ...'

'Was it Cambridge?' Clive asked. 'Cardiff? Canterbury? Kent, yes, Kent, Kent? Hmm. C, c, c, c, c ...' He wracked his brains. Rose couldn't come up with anything either.

'C-c-c-c-c-c-c-c ...'

They were in agony waiting.

'C-c-c-c-c-c-c ...'

Stuart gave it one last try.

'C-c-c-c-c-c-c ... Olchester!'

'Ah Colchester!' All three of them echoed him in relief.

'Fuckinell,' said Errol. 'Colchester, Cambridge, same fing, I knew it began wiv a C.'

'Essex. That's it. University of Essex at Colchester. A fine town, a fine town, Roman in origin. Whew!' said Clive. He was ready for another pint of Lord Archer's.

The music had been cranked a couple of notches. Trevor worked the room like a brideless groom (Barry was on that case), saying thank you to everyone. He arrived at the huddle of bourgeois strangers. Clive expected him to pass right by, but no. Trevor introduced himself, and even thanked them for coming. What's more, his accent had none of the gear-shredding glottal stoppery of his brothers. He was relatively well spoken. Seeing him empty-handed Rose offered to buy him a drink.

'Archer's please,' he said grinning. 'What do you think of my banner? Five quid a letter. Barry got it done. I owed him a tenner. I bet him they'd make me do the full stretch.'

Rose found this very amusing, which annoyed Clive slightly. Her Puzzler mind got it before he did. Still, she was off to fetch more drinks, and that couldn't be bad.

'You looked a bit surprised when you heard me speak,' said Trev.

'Oh, well, er, no . . .' said Clive, completely taken by surprise. He had no idea he was so transparent. Then he realised he should be honest. 'You're right. A skinhead in an England shirt, just out of prison, I was expecting a right-wing, neo-fascist yobbo, but you're obviously not one of them.'

Trev smiled, which gave Clive a sinking feeling, like he was about to say, 'Well, actually . . .'

'Well, actually, if you want to meet a genuine right-wing, neo-fascist yobbo, talk to my brother. Ossie, the one over there in the black polo neck. He runs the *Pit Bull*. Renamed himself Oswald after *Sir Oswald Ernald Mosley, 1896 to 1980.*' He spoke quickly, in a mock-academic tone. 'That was about five years ago. His real name's Darren.'

Clive stared across at this Darren. He had never actually been in the same room as a real live fascist before. This was certainly more exciting than Islington.

The karaoke began on the little stage with the silver streamers. First up was another girl with the poodle haircut who sang like a cat on heat. She sang 'I Will Always Love You' introducing it as the theme from *The Bodyguard.* She stood stiffly, passively waiting for each lyric to scroll along, and then kicked lumps out of the melody. It was torture on a sliding scale, and the big note, the song's payoff, was the death blow. Even the old people abandoned good manners and made faces at each other. After a few more songs there weren't any girls left so some oldsters got up. The first was a fat geezer in a turquoise shell suit who sang the Beatles's 'Hard Day's Night'. Then his wife put her cigarette down and sang one, shaking her fat arse around: 'Doing the garden, digging the weeds,/Who could ask for more?/ Will you still need me, will you still feed me,/When I'm sixty-four?'

Clive watched in fascinated horror. This was worse than the school pantomime, when the teachers who were into pop culture and political correction would rewrite *Dick Whittington* or *Mother Goose.* Dick complaining about Hackney housing policy. Widow Twanky defending the rights of cross-dressers from the Pacific Rim. Clive would volunteer for door duty so as not to have to hear the terribly sung rewrites of pop songs.

Clive bought a round, then someone else included him in a round, and time began to accelerate. One of Barry's tow-headed girls, the middle one, was chasing her sister round the pub, and crashed into his thigh as she passed. Automatically he put his hand down to steady her, for a second thinking she was his own girl. Like a lover who takes the hand of a stranger in the supermarket by mistake, then turns and lets it go in embarrassment, he realised what he had done and excused himself. The girl ran off, oblivious, but he couldn't shake her warmth from his palm, and again realised how much he missed his own little girl.

High table had been reconfigured. Rose was talking to Trev. A couple of seats along, even Alex was gassing away to the girls, chucking back Hen's Tooth and showing his class. In a flurry of hair and stilettos, the three poodles got up and screeched 'New York, New York'. Next up a drunken man crooned Bob Dylan's song of sodomy: 'Lay lady lay, Lay across my big brass bed ...' Clive saw an opening and squeezed himself in where he could talk to Rose. He studied the trophy, the pig's ear was duct taped on to the eroded footballer, and it had thick blonde hairs growing out of it. He'd only been there a minute when Ossie from the *Pit Bull* came back from the Gents and sat opposite him.

'So you're the head of Albion then,' said Ossie.

'Not the head exactly. The four of us are equal partners.'

'Well I think it's a great thing that you're doing. Very patriotic.'

'What, fleecing the foreigners? I don't think we've contributed much to the Treasury yet, tax-wise ...'

Rose glared at him.

'No, I mean celebrating England.'

'Oh that. Well, it is a beautiful place ...'

'Beautiful, and proud.'

'And proud, you're right about that ...' He said it neutrally, but Rose thought otherwise. She kicked him under the table. He glared back, as if to say *What?*

'So anyway, this *Pit Bull*, I haven't seen it in WH Smith's ...'

'Oh I can get you a subscription if you want, just fill this in ...' He pulled a postcard out of his pocket. It was a slick photo of an all-white puppy, except for the red cross of St George PhotoShopped on to its spine.

'Oh,' said Clive nonchalantly. 'I usually do all that kind of thing on the internet. Less paperwork ...'

'We're not on the web yet.'

'Really? Well I'm sure *Rose* here could get you up, she's a dab . . . ooh.' He rubbed his shin with his other foot. ''Scuse me. Foot's gone to sleep. Anyway, so what's your target demographic?'

'Patriotic Englishmen aged eighteen to thirty-five. We cover all the subjects that interest this sector – sport, clubbing, fashion, dogs, music, *vijoe* games, celebrities, pinups.'

'So if Errol over there was to pick it up and start reading, how far would he get?'

'That's a trick question,' said Ossie, unsmiling but unruffled. 'I can see what sort of a teacher you used to be . . .'

'What sort is that then?'

'A lefty.'

'I don't see how you can deduce that.' Clive kept his calm. 'Anyway, so if Errol was to read about video games in your magazine, would he find anything to offend him? I mean, do you only review *Stormtooper 3*, or are you a bit more *open minded?* Do you seek out the patriotic angle in everything?'

'I don't think the likes of Errol would be buying our magazine,' he said, and sniffed.

Clive looked into his blue eyes. He was like Barry at his nastiest, but there was no chance of the Bergman smile creeping in. Ossie was several years younger than Barry, and not nearly so heavy-set. He didn't appear to be into fashion, but he looked quite smart. Like he worked in an office, maybe went to meetings.

'So tell me something, something I've never understood about the Right. Britain's finest hour was what, according to most people? The Battle of Britain. Sending the Nazis packing. But your lot run around with Hitler posters and SS daggers. What's the thinking there?'

'We admire some of the achievements of the National Socialist Government and Third Reich . . .'

'Oh yeah, the Thousand-Year Reich that only fell short by 988 years,' interrupted Rose, getting a bit testy.

Clive continued, 'That doesn't change the fact that if you were born at the same time as your granddad you would have had to fight them. Would you be happier if they'd invaded and won?'

'Well, Hitler had a plan for us. He was going to save the Anglo Saxon for breeding purposes. He saw that we were an integral part of the master race. England conquered the world after all.' He spoke in a plain Estuary accent, in a matter-of-fact way designed to seem unflustered at all times.

Clive shrugged as if to give up on the crackpot Nazi.

'So are you breeding for England now?' asked Rose with a smirk. 'Are *you* the future of the master race?'

'Well actually no, not me personally. But I'm doing my bit with *Pit Bull.*'

'Do you run horoscopes?' asked Clive cutting back in. 'I never know how magazines do them. Do you ever go back and see if they came true then fire the writer if they got them all wrong?'

'Our horoscopes are syndicated,' he said flatly.

'OK, so you have this style magazine for young Englishmen. What I don't get is how you can tell how English they are? Do you have colour charts like in a wallpaper shop – match your skin against this pink? Do you go by genealogy? How many years back do you have to go to find a bit of Irish or Jew or Latin before someone stops being an Anglo Saxon? Three? Four?'

'Five actually,' said Ossie.

'Oh good, answers at last.' Clive was getting mean. 'So tell me this: Who are the English? People descended from just Angles or Saxons? What about the Jutes? The Danes? Half the towns in Yorkshire, Humberside and the east coast have Scandinavian place names, and the people are the kids of Vikings. And what about all the French and Flemish influences here over the years? And what about the original Celts?'

'We believe in the repatriation of the Irish back to Southern Ireland. Our priority is jobs for the English, which means sending back anyone who has arrived here in the last ...' He hesitated for a second. '... Fifty years.'

'Ah, it's *fifty* years, is it? And what about someone of mixed race. You know, half Angle, half Rastaman?'

'He would have the option of repatriation to the country of his gene pool, or Class 2 Citizenship. Living in a restricted community.'

'Kind of hard to get through parliament, that,' said Rose with a laugh.

'We believe that there are methods of effecting political change. Including force.'

'So you think this country could see fighting again? Civil war?'

'It's possible. Some would say inevitable.'

'What about this ethnic cleansing then? Would there be any of that? I see you already have the black polo-neck.' Clive was enjoying himself. 'Would you, Ossie Bergman, pull on the old ski mask of the ethnic cleanser?'

Ossie hesitated, as though he hadn't admitted this before. 'If necessary.'

Clive sighed. 'Well I just can't imagine English people rolling out of bed, collecting their arms and going round the estates herding people into lorries and trains for the Chunnel. Or Holyhead. Is this going to happen all over?'

'We have supporters in all the major cities.'

'And it'll be what, city versus country? North versus South? To be frank, I can't imagine a load of Brummies or Geordies taking orders from you.'

'White versus non-white. Like I said.'

'And what about the Scots and the Welsh? They're pretty white,' said Rose, trying to get her oar in.

'They'll be encouraged to live in their own countries.'

'Hmm. Well that's depressing,' said Clive.

'I don't think so. I foresee a happy nation, with jobs for all and a strong, independent identity.'

'No, I mean it's depressing that you waste your time on this garbage. Still, I don't think enough people will give a fuck enough to join your crusade.' Clive smiled and took a slurp of his Archer's.

'We will stir the people up. Make them realise what a great nation this is and how it's being dragged down by the enemy within.'

'Oh cobblers!' said Clive. 'You're living in the past. If this still is or ever was a great nation it's no thanks to you and your magazine.'

Oswald remained calm and stared back in an 'I'll-remember-you' way. 'I'm sorry you feel that way,' he said. He produced the latest issue from his bag. 'Give it a read anyway, you may change your mind.' On the cover was a pop group from Essex. One of the singers had accidentally wrapped himself in the flag at a football match and been dining out on it ever since. Among the cover lines was KISS MY GUIT-ARS! A WHITE HISTORY OF ROCK AND ROLL.

'Thanks. I'll be sure and tell all my friends,' said Clive.

Another line read: BABY NAMES: GEORGE IS BACK!

'You know,' Clive said, unable to resist, 'Saint George wasn't always the patron Saint of England. For years it was Edward the Confessor, a mild-mannered religious man. It was Edward the Third who bumped him for George to placate the Genoese bankers he was in debt to.'

'That sounds like Zionist propaganda to me,' said Ossie, rearranging his buttocks in the chair.

Clive got to his feet and offered to buy him a drink but it was

declined. Rose came up to the bar with him, keen to get away from
the table.

'Creepy bloke, eh?' she said.

'Yeah,' slurred Clive. He stared, distracted by a momentary lust for her.
He wanted to take her apart, then her reassemble her exactly as she was.

'People like that, they just want a fight,' she said. 'Maybe he just needs
a good shag. He sounds frustrated.'

Clive didn't know what to say to that. Though he laughed in his face, the
neo-fascist disturbed him. He tried to imagine what he would do when they
came for him, some day in the future. He saw himself in bed when they came
knocking. Could it be like that? Bodies in shell suits being exhumed from
mass graves in the English soil for United Nations cameramen? The bloke
in the pub you never got on with suddenly escalating things, torching your
flat in the middle of the night? Rule by yobbo, rule by toff. The drunken
ticker tape of horror raced through his mind. Check points. Foreign media.
Fourteen-year-olds in basic training, the little brothers of the kids he used to
teach. They'd have to interrupt the football season. Clive and Rose huddled
together under the M&S duvet. Stormtooper bullies half his age kicking
the door in. Herding him down the stairs in his boxers. Making him kneel
while they decided whether to shoot him. Putting a cheap Chinese rifle to
his head. Rose screaming.

'Yeah. Really creepy.'

Barry came across. There was now room to walk about in the pub.
'I see Alex scored,' he said. 'He's outside having a knee trembler with
that Joanne.'

'You're kidding,' said Clive, sobering up at the injustice of it all.

'Well, she's sucking his face off anyway. So what you think of my
brother Ossie? Bit serious, inne.'

'Seriously fucked up,' said Rose, defiantly.

'Yeah, he can't help it.' Barry was still being extravagantly nice. Rose
went to the Ladies, and Barry sent Clive over to meet his granddad, while
he got up and scrolled through the karaoke machine. More Beatles. He
picked 'Revolution I', which he sang in a shouty, yobby sort of voice
which worked quite well. It made Clive think of John Lennon's reedy
Scouse and all its reverb: 'You say you'll change the constitution Well
you know, We all want to change your head . . .'
You tell me it's the institution
Well you know,
You better free your mind instead

But if you go carrying pictures of Chairman Mao
You ain't going to make it with anyone anyhow
Don't you know it's gonna be alright
Alright, Alright . . .'

'He's a great lad isn't he?' said Clive, looking at Barry as he settled in next to the old man.

Granddad smiled and nodded.

'Life and soul of the party. I work with him. Clive Pointing. And you are?'

The old man picked up what looked like a lighter off the table and pressed it to the underside of his chin. His voice came out with robotic electronic buzz, the sound made by a vibrating electrolarynx.

That's my grand-son.'

Naturally, Clive pretended not to notice, staring at the man's flappy old skin, which was penetrated by thousands of white stubble hairs. Barry's granddad carried on, gesturing to Barry's wife Christine. She was sitting back, her hard round belly the centre of attention. *'Three beaut-i-ful daugh-ters he has. And an-o-ther nipp-er on the way.'*

In between takes he breathed hoarsely.

'Oh yes, I hear it's a boy,' said Clive.

'Errp?' honked the robot voice. The old man looked shocked.

'Barry's, er . . .' Clive knew he'd put his foot in it.

'A boy? I did-n't want to know!' he HAL-ed. *'You stup-id bag-ger what you go and tell me that for? You sill-y cant . . .'*

'Oh, I'm terribly sorry,' said Clive, 'I thought . . . I thought everyone knew.' He looked around for an escape. 'Sorry. Can I buy you a drink? Come on, what is it, Archer's?'

The old man threw his head back and slapped his electrolarynx down on the table. One of the little girls who had been watching them lunged forward and grabbed it, then disappeared into the crowd with her sisters.

He tried to protest but empty air gasped from his throat.

'I'll get it!' shouted Clive. 'Just stay there!' He was feeling very drunk and bumped his way through the crowd, making a full circle of the room. He cornered the girl by the cigarette machine. She squirmed and giggled and finally he pried it from her hot little hand. He waved it at the old man, who tossed his head back again, still looking annoyed. While Clive waited at the bar he studied it. *VoiceMaster*, it said down the side. He gave it a sniff – it seemed clean. Then he turned it on. It hummed, making his hand itch. Slowly, he put it to his throat.

'Yes, *wotyouavaingmate?*' said the bar man.

'*Four pints of Arch-ers. And three Peps-is. And three pack-ets of crisps.*' Now his voice was robotic, totally transformed from the regular Clive. It had just one pitch, but it was resonant enough to cut through the glass and metal bar noises.

The bloke behind the bar thought it was funny, and Clive laughed back. '*And one for your-self,*' he chanted. He loved his new voice. '*I'd have a cig-ar too, but they don't fit in my trach-e-ot-o-my hole. I need an ad-a-pter.*'

People either side of him were smiling too, everyone loved a wag, and for one minute Clive loved being it. Back at the table he handed over the machine to the grumpy granddad. The girls took their crisps and Pepsi and said thank you, even little baby Di.

Barry came and sat down next to them. He tried to persuade his grandfather not to sing.

'*I al-ways sing,*' said the old man. His electronic voice had a lilt to it, a slight reverb. '*Berg-mans al-ways sing.*'

'But I just did.' Barry turned to Clive, grinning. 'You can't keep the old family down.'

'Why so many Beatles songs tonight?' asked Clive.

'Oh it was our Craig who got hold of the karaoke cartridges, kinda limited selection where he goes. What about you anyway? You sing?'

'Never tried it, but ...' said Clive. He was feeling very bold. He had just remembered a Paul and Linda joke. Barry's song had brought it all back from nowhere. It was old, but he'd been meaning to tell Barry a joke ever since the TWA one. He put his arm round his shoulder and pulled him closer.

'Listen. The McCartney kids are at the family ranch, anxiously waiting for news of their mother. Paul comes out from his wife's bedroom and says, "Kids, there's good news and bad news. The bad news is your mother's strength and will to live has been sucked away by her awful disease, and she died a few moments ago. The good news is ... it's steak and chips for dinner!"'

'Naaaar-har-har, naar-har-har!' Barry was pretty pissed too. 'Never heard that one before ..., naaaar-har-har, naar-har-har!' He *facking* loved it.

'It's a bit old but ... uh,' Clive was feeling very drunk. He couldn't finish his sentence. His body was full to the brim with beer.

Granddad saw his opening, and no one could stop him. He got to his feet, to massive cheering, and sang 'Run Rabbit Run' all the way through. At the end, everyone who could stand up to applaud, did.

15

Blue Sky Work

It took Clive a couple of days to piece together what happened at the Swan and after, and after all that there were still bits missing.

The first day he had the mother of all hangovers. He'd drunk two Guinnesses in the Shakespeare, seven pints of Archer's in the Swan, and bought two bottles of Grolsch to go which he drank on the train. All he could do was lie in bed and groan. At six in the evening he thought he had the all clear to get up and eat for the first time in twenty-four hours, but was only half way through his steak and kidney pie and chips when he rushed to the window and spewed spectacularly. Then he went back to bed. He couldn't listen to his little radio because his ears were so sensitive, so he abandoned himself to his mental news ticker instead.

He remembered Rose was nowhere to be found as he was leaving. Nor was Alex. It was a lock-in and he'd bailed some time around half past midnight. He remembered stumbling out into the street. Ron's taxi was still there. He remembered being in the West End all of a sudden, schlepping through Covent Garden to Leicester Square. He remembered Clapham Common, walking across it, worrying about the gays and the police. And then somehow he got home, undressed and fell into bed.

On the second day things were a little clearer. He remembered getting up onstage and doing karaoke. He groaned as he remembered whipping out Barry's granddad's electric voice box and singing an old ELO song, 'Mr Blue Sky'. Clive had no idea what the reaction was. No one stopped him anyway. He was in a world of his own. That was the best way to perform onstage anyway. And he remembered talking to Barry's wife Christine. She was the opposite of what he expected. She was sweet and gentle, for a start. And really beautiful, in a way Barry didn't deserve. She perched her youngest, Diana, on her lap while she talked, trying to fit her in around her swollen tummy. Words came back to him. He remembered her saying she didn't want her to be called Diana after the princess, in fact, Christine didn't 'give a stuff about the Royals. What have they ever done for us?'

The North was due to start the next day, so he had to check in with the others. First he tried Alex. He got him on his mobile. He heard a woman's voice in the background so he apologised and made it quick.

'Er, yes, it's all on for tomorrow. Meet at the usual place. We've almost got a full coach. Er, bring your overnight bag.' Alex was crapping himself. He had an unsuspecting Clive on the phone, Clive's unsuspecting ex-wife in the room with him having tea (she'd just 'popped in') and an unsuspecting East End slapper somewhere out there who had his business card, waiting for him to call. He bluffed. 'Of course I'll be coming along myself. First *twip* on a new *woute* and everything, I have to suss it out, have some face-to-face with our clients.'

'What clients?' asked Clive puzzled.

'The er, guest-house owner for starters.'

'It'll probably be some old couple who couldn't get in on the ground floor of the nursing home business so this is the next best thing . . . Well, whatever. It's up to you. Hey, did you see Rose the other night?'

'Yes. She went off with one of the Bergmans.'

'Oh.' Clive was crushed. 'Thanks.'

'Ciao.'

Rose didn't have a mobile. 'Hello, this is Rose, leave a message for me after the beep. If you want to talk to Nick, try him at his mother's on 0207 321 6110.' Clive hung up rapidly, shocked, running through best-case scenarios for what might have happened to the live-in-boyfriend. *Nick.* Nick sounded steady.

Barry was having a pint in the Shakespeare with his dad when Clive got hold of him. Yes, everything was on for the next day.

'Nice party the other night,' said Clive, hopefully.

'Well, you're a dark horse, you enjoyed yourself that's for sure, Naaaar-har-har, naar-har-har!'

After the nausea and the bad memories and the insecurity it was nice to trek up to Dollis Hill to see Gordon and his mum. He brought her dog roses, picked from the railway embankment, like the ones she always planted wherever they lived. So many times she'd had to abandon them, but she never gave in, she always planted some more. They smelt sweet and the pink petals had white bases, and shaggy yellow stamens.

He met Sandra, Gordon's new girl. She was all woman. Dyed, teased hair, beauty spot, green eye shadow, eye liner, mascara, face powder, touch of blush, red lipstick, earrings, necklace, bangles, hefty bosom, red and black top, black bra strap showing, cinched waist, large bottom, matching red skirt and jacket, long shanks, ankle bracelet, butterfly tattoo, high heels, painted toes. It was odd seeing his little brother with a grown woman. It had been such a long time. She smelt of bootlegged perfume, and had a nervous laugh. She was very nice to Gordon and his mother. She had just cooked dinner and insisted on feeding Clive too. She worked in 'a office'.

Clive was glad to shut them in the living room and sit with his mother. She was bad. She didn't look at him, and only seemed to listen when he read from the book of poems.

He found a load by Percy Bysshe Shelley. He asked her about him but she said nothing. She didn't look like she understood. Maybe she was just tired.

He read out one of the short ones anyway. '"England in 1819. By Percy Bysshe Shelley. Composed in 1819, First Published in 1839." Huh. Wonder what kept him?

> '"An old, mad, blind, despised, and dying king,
> Princes, the dregs of their dull race, who flow
> Through public scorn – mud from a muddy spring,
> Rulers who neither see, nor feel, nor know,
> But leech-like to their fainting country cling,
> Till they drop, blind in blood, without a blow,
> A people starved and stabbed in the untilled field,
> An army, which liberticide and prey
> Makes as a two-edged sword to all who wield,
> Golden and sanguine laws which tempt and slay,
> Religion Christless, Godless – a book sealed,
> A Senate – Time's worst statute unrepealed,
> Are graves, from which a glorious Phantom may
> Burst, to illumine our tempestuous day."

'Hmm. What do you think, Mother? Bit of a ranter.'

She said nothing.

He read a few more, but it made no difference, so he sat in silence with her. Sometimes he'd listen for her breathing, just to make sure, like he used to with the baby.

16

Hit the North

'You need a phone,' said Rose. They were churning their way through West Hampstead to the MI, the bit where coach drivers usually concentrate and huff and curse, but which Rose could have driven one handed if she wanted to. She concentrated on Clive.

They had forty-four passengers, most of whom seemed respectable – Koreans, Americans, Scanders, Germans, even a few Eastern Europeans. Best of all was the French showing – eight of them with their coloured pullovers and faded jeans. The French usually skipped *L'Albion perfide* and headed straight for Scotland, but something about the North must have appealed to their contrarian instincts. Forty-four was a disappointment though. There were several no-shows, which she put down to advertising on the internet, the medium of the flaky. Alex blamed the shortfall on the weather, his theory being it was so nice people wanted to stay in London. She concluded he was an arse. Alex was sitting directly behind her, giving her funny looks from the start. She could tell there was something cooking in that devious Sloane brain. He looked like a plonker in his three-piece suit with his moulded MH briefcase on his lap. He'd muttered something about corresponding with a genealogist up North and how he'd been invited to visit an archive at Dunham Massey, a Georgian mansion just outside Manchester. *Tosser*, she thought.

'I don't like mobiles,' said Clive. He sat across from Alex in the other front seat, with a splendid view of Rose's left cheek. She had the kind of clear, pale beauty that grew on him. Some women he thought of as attractive, but on later viewings he realised he'd imagined most of their charm. Rose was the opposite. There was nothing plain about her at all.

The more he looked at her the more beautiful she became. Her features seemed to reconfigure over time, like a photo developing before his eyes, like the face of Ophelia floating to the surface.

'They give you brain tumours.'

'They do *not*,' she said, smiling at his naivety. 'I admit, you don't need a land line, but you need something. I couldn't get hold of you yesterday.'

'Why did you want to? I got all the details off Alex.'

She said nothing. Shagging a Bergman had put her in a tricky position. If she wasn't so proud she would have regretted it.

Barry was sitting in the seat behind Alex, chatting up a pair of Barcelona birds. They were small and brown and fashionable, and totally out of their depth in England. They had no idea what to avoid over here. In Spain it was easy – they only mixed with nocturnal people, and their grandparents. In England they had to get up at ugly hours like 8 a.m., and turn in at the time they would normally be going out for squid and bull's testicles and Cava and E. '*Crazee Eenglish,*' they told their friends on Barry's phone. He was feeling sorry for them and let them have five minutes long distance each. Barry understood the European mentality.

'Well if we're making good time, I'll sort you out at Luton,' said Rose.

Clive said nothing. He didn't always get Rose. Nothing about her seemed to fit any pattern, he had no idea how to handle her. His ex-wife Tina, now there was someone he pretty much understood. Her aspirations could be plotted in a straight line. She wanted two kids, nicely spaced. Enough money for private-school education, two decent holidays a year and house redecoration every three. There was a pony in there somewhere but the pony could be bumped depending on how other things went. The Sunday supplements were her Bible and the property sections were her bread and butter, it was that simple. Until Clive went off and did it with a schoolgirl.

In no time they were in Luton. Clive stood up and told the people about Dunstable, just for something to say. He and his brother had been there years ago for someone's birthday party in a night club. In the mean little town centre they'd got dark looks from the locals, and the whole affair ended in a brawl at midnight when gatecrashers decided they had had enough. Clive and Gordon escaped into the street and got a mini cab all the way back to Milton Keynes. They found out later that the birthday boy ended up in hospital, losing an eye.

The punters shivered when they heard the story, and looked fearfully out of the window as though a mob would emerge any minute from between the office blocks and storm the coach.

'What did you have to tell them that for?' hissed Alex from behind his *Telegraph*.

Clive shrugged. 'It's real. Better than telling them about the land use or the Civil War connections. There are a lot of Italians connected to the brick industry in Bedford, should I tell them that?'

Alex huffed, and wondered about ditching all three of them. That was the trouble with doing business in this country, you just couldn't get the talent.

'Come on you,' said Rose. She stopped the coach round the back of the main terminal at Luton Airport. Together she and Clive jogged through crowds of holidaymakers until they reached a check-in desk.

'Hallo Rose! Come to see the boys?' said an old fellow loading luggage on to the conveyor.

'Yeah. Is it all right if I bring him in with me?' she asked, cocking her head at Clive.

'Gooarn then, I won't tell.'

They went through into a corridor behind the check-in. Clive could see people loading bags on to trailers, kids standing around smoking and laughing. They went though a door, down another corridor and came to a small office.

'Yo Rose, wassup?' said a small black kid with acne and a Greater London accent.

'Binny, this is Clive, he needs a phone.'

He led them over to a desk, where a bony white guy was sitting reading his tabloid. He seemed pleased to see her too, putting his cigarette down to shake her hand. Everyone was really nice to her. He opened his desk drawer revealing a mountain of mobile phones.

'Where do these come from?' asked Clive, his eyes wide open.

'Oh, daft gits who leave 'em on the planes. This is *naffink*. We get all sorts. Pagers, laptops, jewellery ... They'd lose their 'kin heads if they weren't screwed on.'

'Drugs,' said Rose.

'Yep. Balloons full of whatever. People panic and dump them under the seats and in the toilets. The dog coppers get them though.'

'So you're the guys who clean the planes?' he asked.

They both looked offended.

'*Fack* off, we're not cleaners. We're supervisors, Lost Property. *Cleaners!*'

'Sorry,' said Clive. Rose frowned at him.

'Anyway,' she said. 'Have you got anything nice?'

He warmed to her. 'As a matter of fact I have.' He pulled out a brand-new Nokia, and rattled off its features. 'You'll have to re-programme it . . .' he said.

'No worries, I'll do it myself tonight. Gotta run. Thanks.'

She pecked him on the cheek, then gave the black kid a quick hug.

'Thanks,' said Clive, backing out after her. They smiled at him. The double doors swung shut behind them.

'Rose's in love then,' said the white bloke.

'Yeah,' said Binny. 'Poor bastard. Someone should tell him. He doesn't know what time it is.'

They had lunch at the Little Chef. Sunbaked sausages, dry pies, chalky chips, oily eggs, sour coffee, wet pastries, and bad attitude from the Fag Ash Lil on the till. Everyone left feeling a bit sick and doing currency conversions. The mood onboard was still good, until they approached Manchester.

Clive was all set to take them round Quarry Bank Mill and Styal Country Park. This was a cotton mill built in 1784 that had been preserved and tricked out with post-industrial proles pretending to be the industrial proles. But Alex protested, saying there was no time and they had to get on to Dunham Massey. They had a row about which they should do. It was the first Clive had heard of any fucking genealogy, he said, but Alex claimed that since they'd stopped at Luton, they should stop for him too. Rose protested but he told her she couldn't vote, she had to concentrate on her driving. She fumed silently, not exactly able to come over and argue her point. Alex then tried to sell it as an opportunity for the passengers to learn something about the workings of the English aristocracy, and Clive appealed to Barry, who wasn't listening and abstained ('Leave me out of it.'). Clive capitulated. 'OK, OK, fine. I'll just tell them about it instead.' So he spent the next ten minutes on the microphone describing the glories of the coming of industrialism.

'You think Silicon Valley is impressive, well, this area is the Silicon Valley of its day, although cotton was the great raw material. Egyptian and American cotton were brought in and turned into calico cloth by machines for the first time. The mill is built on the River Bollin and at first used a fifty-ton waterwheel to power everything, but switched to steam and a beam engine in the 1840s. The owners, the Gregs, were still around in the 1950s when it went bust. Cotton work, like chip manufacturing, can be done a lot cheaper in the Developing World. It's five storeys high and looks like a factory should – dark brickwork up against a grey river, high windows . . . there's even an Apprentice House where fifty workhouse orphans would crash in their little wooden boxes after a twelve-hour day. What makes this place historic is the fact that the owners were early liberals, reformers – do-gooders. They wanted their workers to have more than a robotic existence so they built a worker village at Styal, with relatively spacious rooms, toilets and vegetable gardens. However, history does not record whether any of these people went on to become petty thieves and Victorian scallies, or pamphleteers and pioneers of social reform. At least the Gregs let them have a pub, that's all I can say.' He went on in this vein for a while, ending, 'Of course you won't be seeing any of this because Mr White has different plans. Today he's going to take us to a house called Dunham Massey where he's going to establish his family *credentials*.' They really were starting to hate each other.

At Dunham they strolled through the deer park and the orangery, then took a tour of the sumptuous Edwardian interior. Clive protested that he couldn't exactly ad-lib on a place he'd never heard of until a few minutes ago, and suggested Alex say a few words, but he bottled it and let the old girl from the National Trust do the work. He looked at the Huguenot silver and the walnut furniture with a proprietary air.

After the tour Alex took the lady aside and explained who he was.

'Oh! Goodness!' said the guide. 'I have your papers already. I'm afraid the Master of the house had to go into town on business, but he left the results of his search for you here.'

'Hmm.' He'd been expecting the full Monty – the firm handshake and the welcome-to-the-club smile. Barry was outside having a smoke with the Spaniards. Clive and Rose ambled up to see what was going on. Alex opened the folder. Inside were ten sheets of printout detailing his family history as far back as records went, back to the 1400s. After he turned the first page he went white. Then a muscle in his lower eyelid started to twitch. Then he chewed on his lip. A few of the passengers were hanging around too, as they'd been promised a show. The aristocracy in action.

'What's it say? Read it out then,' said Clive.

'Are you sure this is right?' Alex asked the old lady. 'I think there's been a mistake.'

'Oh, I don't think so. The master has been working on it for days. Oh, before I forget, I have to give you this.' She passed him an envelope.

'What's this?' he asked, horrified.

'Well it's his bill. He said there was no hurry. Any time this week.'

'I'm sorry, I'm afraid ...'

'Come on, what does it say?' asked Clive. The group around him murmured too.

Alex suddenly turned on his heels and stormed out of the building. He walked quickly, his buttocks clenched, down the path and back on to the coach. He was still there fifteen minutes later, staring at the back of Rose's seat, when everyone was rounded up. Motionless. Deaf to the world. Clive couldn't get any sense out of him. He gripped the folder between his legs and stared.

Barry was the last one on. He had a big grin on his face. He had just found out the Barcelona girls were very up for going out clubbing in Blackpool. Tired and emotional foreign girls at 2 a.m. were his speciality.

Manchester got knocked off the itinerary. Clive insisted on going to Rossendale, a small valley around Bacup and Todmorden that he fervently believed was the 'cradle of the Industrial Revolution'. Rose was past caring. So long as they reached their hotel in Blackpool that night before the traffic got bad, fine. She was still smarting at being disqualified from voting. If she had to park in a field and everyone had to yomp through sheepshit for a mile to the top of a grassy hill at four in the afternoon, that was fine by her.

Clive stood on the slope near an abandoned mill, a tiny structure from the very first days of industry. 'We've had a Glorious Revolution in this country which wasn't that glorious, and we've sat and watched while the Americans and French had their revolutions ...'

'Interfered!' shouted a bearded American man. He wore sneakers with his belted raincoat, and seemed like a bit of an intellectual. His wife kept giving Clive the eye.

'... But one thing we can call our own is the Industrial Revolution. It was faster and more spectacular than the Agricultural Revolution, which is exactly what you need to capture the imagination. When you see a painting like Turner's *Rain, Steam and Speed* you can see what it was all about: change accelerating, almost beyond control. I know you people get all excited about your cable TV and your internet, but all that's modelled on what happened here. A few imaginative people saw the power of a flowing stream and soft water for making good cloth cheaply, and let it spread.'

Clive was quite worked up. He put his head back and looked up at the sky.

'Can we go back now?' asked a German woman. 'What about Blackpool?'

'Yes, we can go back now. Blackpool will still be there.' Barry led everyone on the trudge back to the coach, where Alex still sulked.

Rose and Clive were the last ones. 'Clive.' She rarely used his name. He looked down at her serious face. 'I need you to do me a favour.'

'Huh. What?'

'Help me get rid of Alex. I can't stand him.'

'What do you mean, get rid of him?' He looked a little worried.

'Kick him out of the company. Fire him. Vote him out. We're the board. If you can get Barry on our side, he's gone. Will you talk to Barry about it? Please?' She had such a sweet face when she begged. For a Tomboy, she had surprising reserves of personality.

'OK. But why don't you talk to him?'

'I ... I can't. Me and Barry ... I have issues with Barry.'

'Sounds interesting,' said Clive, enjoying her discomfort.

'I'll tell you all about it one day.'

They started walking down the hill together.

'So when do I get to meet the boyfriend? Is he still up North?'

She looked surprised. 'No. Nick's not living with me any more.'

'Oh!' His heart gave a little surge of joy. 'Watch your step.' She nearly trod in some sheep pellets.

'I loved what you said about the revolution. It makes me feel better about this country, knowing we had ours already.'

'I love being up North in the summer. What do you think of Blackpool?'

'Never been.'

'Really? Gosh. I think you'll love it.'

The first thing they saw as they pulled out of the backstreets of Blackpool and on to the Front was a large, red-armed woman thrashing her toddler. The coach passengers were alarmed. One of the Americans videoed the incident and swore she'd report it to the police. The next sight was an unconscious bloke propped up against the prom wall, his shirt over his head and a stream of piss threading its way from his heel to the gutter. It was 6 p.m.

The Tower loomed over their guest house like a Soviet radio mast. The conditions in the hotel were fairly Eastern Bloc too. The MacDougalls, the savage Scottish couple who ran the place, did not believe in wasting money on redecoration. The guests gasped as they hauled their wheelie bags and holdalls up the narrow carpeted stairs and pushed open the lightweight doors, revealing knife-edge beds and sinks the size of junior urinals. Hot water was bought *'fefty pee'* at a time, and room keys were attached to large wooden blocks to prevent people walking off with them. The fifteen guests dumped in the prefab annexe out the back were even more shell-shocked.

Clive stood over Rose as she hooked his new Nokia phone up to her laptop and re-programmed it.

'You're pretty good at all this computer stuff, aren't you?' It was the first time he had expressed any admiration for her, and she blushed slightly, and worked on, serious and silent.

'Done. Get someone to phone you and you're set.'

Alex walked in, still unsmiling. 'I'm not very impressed with the owners,' he said. 'Bloody riffraff. They told me we had to be out by ten tomorrow or pay for two nights. Huh, you have the exact same phone I have. What are we all doing tonight? I must say I've never been anywhere quite so tacky before.'

Clive and Rose both sighed. Clive spoke. 'I think we should take them out for dinner, the menu here looks intolerable. There's only so much Method-tourism you can take. Let's walk along the Golden Mile and see what happens.'

Barry came in and said he thought of leading a group up to Robert's Oyster Bar, so after losing ten stragglers to culture shock, thirty of them set out walking along the prom. Everywhere there were people yanking their kids along, shrieking with laughter, kissing in doorways, staring each other down, stuffing cod into their faces, drinking from cans, struggling with shopping bags, checking their reflections in shop windows and stepping into traffic. Barry knew the feeling well – a whole town electrified, up for it, *largeing* it, having a good time. The Albion customers peered into shop windows at the crammed-in novelties – glass animals, willy warmers, imitations stools, Dad's Matches holders, gorilla masks, porno videos, football crap, bongs ... most of it was stuff designed for sitting around at home having a laugh, stuff to do with getting pissed, getting laid, or just getting. Every few yards was a boozer, a fortune teller, candy floss stand, T-shirts, cheesy electrical-goods auction, amusement arcade. Clive loved the place for the sheer numbers – six million people visiting the funfair at the Pleasure Beach, sixteen million coming to the whole resort – and he felt the need to pontificate, educate and illustrate.

'As a resort, Blackpool used to be quite upmarket. At the end of the eighteenth century it took at least a day or two to get here by carriage from Lancashire or Yorkshire, so only a select crowd could afford to come. However, as soon as they opened the railway in 1846 the mill workers started coming by the millions in Wakes Week, when their factories closed for the annual holiday. Pretty soon the piers, promenades and music halls sprung up to cater for them – they used to advertise "Open air dancing for the working classes" on Central Pier – and a mass market was born. Despite the fact that you can get all the sun, sex and sangria you want on a cheap package to the Mediterranean, people still find reasons to come here. For pensioners it's a throwback to the days of their youth, for younger people it's a good place to compare Saturday night activities with people from around the country, for families it lets all generations be as infantile as each other, and for human geographers and intrepid foreigners like me and you, well, forgive me for saying it out loud, but it's a chance for a bit of meta-tourism, a chance for a bit of vicarious fun. I wish there was a nicer phrase, but slumming it will have to do.'

'You know slumming started in the East End?' said Barry suddenly.

'No, I didn't know that Barry. Why don't you tell us about it?'

Barry had worked his way through the *Ripper* book and discovered slumming. 'There were 900,000 slum-dwellers East of Aldgate Pump in the 1880s. Rich people would get all dressed up in their black clothes and take a Hackney carriage out to the East End to have a look at the wretched urchins, drunken whores, footpads, sailors and mothers of ten who peeped out from broken windows in the dead of winter. And they loved it! It gave them plenty to talk about at their dinner parties.'

'History doesn't record whether any of them became reformers. But I bet some of them did. The Victorians weren't all bad,' added Clive. 'The Salvation Army was on the front line, as usual.'

They lost a few more people on the way. Robert's Oyster Bar was magnificent though, 120 years old, heavy with the smell of Victoriana – cockles, whelks, and mussels, which the Americans denounced as a health hazard but the French all consumed gleefully. Guinness put them in a better mood and pretty soon they were relaxed. Alex was the only miserable one amongst them.

'Samatta, Alex? You look down in the mouth,' said Barry with a sly grin. 'Could it be anything to do with ... THIS?' He whipped out the manila folder from the genealogist.

'How the *hell* did you get that?' he said jumping up. 'You *barstard*. Give it back!' He lunged across the table but Barry easily avoided him and began reading the contents out loud.

'White, Cecil, Major General, died 1921, age sixty-two. Son of White, Cecil, Captain, died 1900, age seventy-one. Army family eh? But what's this ... White, George Gordon, Justice of the Peace, died 1856, age fifty-five.' He skimmed down a bit.

'Incomplete, incomplete, unknown, unknown, White, Jonas, Provost, died 1812, age fifty-seven. Let's see ... Whyte, Luke, died 1795, age twenty-five, Sydney Australia (Tr.) What does "Tr." mean?'

'Transported?' said Rose.

'Aha! Oh here it is. Sentenced at Chester Town assizes for *sheep* stealing! Naaaar-har-har, naar-har-har! Wait a minute!' Alex was trying to grab the paper but Barry easily handed him off and read from the other. 'Whyte, Arthur, died 1722, age forty-five, Liverpool. Hmm. There's a lot of Liverpools here. Oh here we go. Wyte, Jed, died 1645, Preston, age thirty-five, hanging (treason). Preston's not far from here ... Wyatt, Alfred, died 1590, age forty, poisoning. Farrier ... Wossat then?'

'Someone who shoes horses,' butted in the bearded American. He knew his stuff.

Alex's face was scarlet. He stood, but seemed powerless to stop it. His will was crumbling.

'Here's another horse-shoe geezer, and another, and another, and another ... Wyatt, Thomas ...'

'Ooh, does it say anything like courtier or poet?' asked Clive.

'... Died 1533, the Wirral, *poisoning*. What an unlucky bunch. Wyat, Henry, died 1485, HDQ ... HDQ anyone?'

'Hung, drawn and quartered!' said several people at once.

'HDQ for blasphemy. Wight, John, died 1450, nail maker, age thirty-three, drowning. Wyght, Jon, died 1422, age forty, hanging (sorcery and adultery) Wrexham. Oh dear.' He winked at Alex, who was so mortified he was now seated. 'Nearly it ... Wight, John, peasant, died Ruthin, Wales, 1399, hanging, murder. End of records.' At this point Barry could have played it two ways: said something to the blubbing wreck opposite him, or filled his lungs with air and let out the Bergman battle cry.

'*Naaaar-har-har, naar-har-har! Naaaar-har-har, naar-har-har, Har-har, naar-har-har! Naaaar-har-har, naar-har-har!* Peasant!' he gasped. 'Sheep stealers! *Taffs!*'

'Sorcerers too,' said Rose, trying to suppress a smile. The foreigners got
the hang of it and joined in the laughing translating to each other and
generally spreading the message: the Englishman does not have so much
to be pompous about any more.

'Never mind,' said Barry. 'You're one of us now. Naaaar-har-har,
naar-har-har! Your round I think.'

Clive tried to be nice, seeing him in such pain. 'Come on Alex, don't
worry — it's not where you're from, it's where you're at!'

'Horseshit,' said the American.

Alex grabbed the folder back and walked out, disappearing into the
prom crowd.

Clive had to admit it did put him in a good mood. He had another
drink and fell into conversation with Rose. He was pleased to see she was
the most merciful amongst them. When Barry's Catalans went to the toilet
together he poked Clive drunkenly and asked him to tell a joke. 'What
was that joke again? The one about the Royals?'

'Eh? I don't know any.'

'Yeah you do. The one you told my Chrissie the other night at the
Swan. When you were pissed up.'

'I told a joke? About the Royals? She's getting me mixed up with
someone else.'

'How can that be, she said you couldn't keep your eyes off her all
night . . .'

'I . . . I . . . well, that's . . . I was looking at her, you know, she's pregnant,
that's all . . .' He tried to steer things but Barry wasn't bothered. He'd
remembered the joke.

'OK peeps, here's a real English joke. Courtesy of Clive here, the dark
horse. The Queen and Princess Di are driving down the road in their Range
Rover when they're accosted by a modern highwayman. "Hand over all your
cash," he says to the Queen. "My dear man," sez Queenie, "I am the Queen
of all England, and therefore do not need to carry any money."

'"OK, OK,' he says, and turns to Princess Di. "In that case *you* can
hand over all of your jewels." And Di says, "I have no need of jewels, for
I am the most beautiful woman in England."

'By this time the highwayman's getting a bit pissed off, so he says, "Right
then, get out of the car and I'll take that instead." And he drives off into
the sunset, leaving Princess Di and the Queen sitting on the grass verge.
And Di turns to the Queen and asks, "Where on earth did you hide all
that money you were carrying?"

'"I stuffed it up my snatch," says the Queen with a laugh. "But what about you. Where did you manage to stash all your jewels?"

'"I stuffed them up my snatch as well," titters Di.

'And Queenie sighs and sez, 'It's a shame Fergie wasn't with us, we might have been able to save the car. Naaaar-har-har, naar-har-har! Har-har, naar-har-har!'

'That's a bit sexist,' said Clive, which made Barry laugh even more.

'That's funny, cos that's exactly what Chrissie said when you told it to her. Har-har, naar-har-har! Urrrrrp! Scuse me. Oh here we go ladies. Right, who's coming on the pub crawl?'

'Count me out,' said Clive. 'I'll catch up with you later.'

'Same here. I need some air,' said Rose.

They left together, stumbling out into the high latitude light. It was August, and though the evenings were drawing in, they weren't drawing in very fast. Nothing could dampen the summer-holiday spirit. They made their way on to the sand where the last donkeys were still waiting, motionless. The beach smelt of sewage and salt water, the fine old seaside smell. It felt beautiful to walk along the wide-open sand, away from the screaming voices and the electronic swoops and bloops of the machinery of entertainment.

'Do you want a ride?' said Rose.

'Sure,' he said. At this point, Clive would have done anything she suggested. The news that the boyfriend was off the scene had given him new hope, and she seemed to be more open to him. Her donkey was almost blond and walked with a steady gait. Clive's was like a four-legged bale of pubic hair, and about as lively. Rose romped home, laughing at him as she lapped him coming back. 'You've been out of the saddle too long!' she shouted into the breeze.

It was the first time they'd had real fun together, and Clive liked the feeling. He dragged her off to the Pleasure Beach where they got passes and rode the old wooden roller coasters, working their way up to The Big One. As he read the specs Clive secretly thought he was going to puke – a vertical drop of 235 feet sounded like hell. He bluffed it though, and when it came to it – with Rose next to him hooting and waving her arms in ecstasy – he not only survived, he enjoyed it. They checked the monitor and bought an instant digital photo of themselves at the peak of the ride, at the point where the ground had just fallen away beneath them. Clive was staring ahead in terror, his face slack and his white knuckles gripping like an Action Man. Rose, meanwhile, looked serene, eyes half shut, half a smile on her face.

It was open until eleven but the guard was changing. Queues were forming outside the night-clubs, lines of twitchy teenagers and well-dressed workers. They ran into Barry. He'd traded his two Iberians in. Now he was with the back end of a fifteen-strong gaggle of hen-night girls from Barnsley, all bare-legged and all bare-armed. The odds were just too good. The American in the trench coat, Ed, was with him, looking the worse for five ciders, and a beady-eyed little Frenchman. He practically begged Clive and Rose to come along. Clive spent an hour in the shadows of an ear-splitting rave club, feeling old. Rose tried to get him to dance but it wasn't his scene. Some of these kids were young enough to be Amanda. He was happy to get out while he was ahead, leaving them to it. He was old. Strolling along the front while a harvest moon lurked over the radioactive septic tank of the Irish Sea was enough for him, for now.

17

The Spontaneous Overflow of Powerful Lager

'Good job you came along for that face-to-face,' said Barry, greeting Alex at breakfast. Mr Bergman was just tucking into his second round of sausage, fried egg, black pudding, bacon, beans, mushrooms and weeping tomatoes. He was freshly shaved and had on a clean shirt and striped tie. Alexander White, on the other hand, had spent most of the night on the pier with a bottle of gin, rethinking his life. At one point he had even considered casting himself into the all-consuming sea, but the tide was going out so he dithered, imagining what it would be like to land in two feet of turdy brine. The moon set and the only other people around were two teens fucking standing up behind the ghost train, and even they didn't take long. He walked the Front again, looking at the revellers, trying to imagine being related to any of them. Some girls laughed in his face. A tram crept up on him making him jump. He threw his empty Gordons bottle on to the sand and a copper made him go and pick it up. Alex crept home at dawn and lay on his bed, dressed, thinking.

'Go to hell, Bergman.'

His hangover only hit him when he smelt the fat and saw the grey bacon going round in Barry's mouth like boxer shorts in a dryer, and he suppressed a heave. He refused all food except for tea, so offending his hostess Mrs MacDougall, and sat there, trembling, his nightmare coming true again every thirty seconds. He put his phone on the table.

Clive walked in looking a little delicate too. He lay his identical phone out proudly, and sat down opposite Barry. It was second nature now –

expecting to be entertained. The other guests were drifting in, including the Spanish girls.

'So how's the nutty raver . . . here, what happened to you last night?' Barry asked him.

'What happened to you's more interesting,' said Clive.

He lowered his voice. 'Result. Model. From *Barnsley*. Can you imagine?'

'Ugh. I'd rather not. What, a hands-and-feet model for the *Argos* catalogue?'

'Now, now, don't get jealous. Just because you're getting nowhere with . . . Speak of the Devil.'

'Morning all,' said Rose cheerfully. 'God, you two look rough.'

'They are, darling. I was just about to tell them this joke . . .'

'Don't!' said Clive and Alex together.

'Pub landlord is shutting up for the night when there's a knock at the door. He opens it and there's a tramp who asks him for a toothpick. He gives him the toothpick and the tramp goes off. A few minutes later there's another knock. When he answers, there's another tramp who also asks for a toothpick. He gets his toothpick and off he goes. There is a third knock at the door, and a third tramp. So the landlord says, "Don't tell me, you want a toothpick too?"

'"No, a straw," says the tramp.

'So the landlord gives him a straw, but he's puzzled, so he asks the tramp why he wants a straw and not a toothpick.

'And the tramp says, "Simple, Gov. Some bloke just threw up outside but all the good stuff's gone already."'

'Oh, please! Come on!' said Clive.

Alex stood up and walked rapidly but unsteadily to the front door. Seconds later came the hurling and the plish-plash of stomach contents on crazy paving.

'Oh shite,' said Rose. 'That's the end of us.'

Mr MacDougall heard his wife shouting and came out of the kitchen in his apron to investigate. There were accusations and recriminations in two different accents, and a flurry of rumours in broken English around the breakfast room.

Mr MacDougall marched in. 'That's it. Out, the lottayee. English pigs. Animals.'

There was no point in arguing. Albion Tours staff helped their customers from the building as graciously as fire marshals. A few of them looked a little startled and fluffy haired, but they made it to the coach.

They were heading for the Lake District but since they had a bit of extra time, Clive got his wish and took them via the Ribble Valley. From Preston ('sheepshagger land' Barry told Alex delightedly, who was ashen faced and looking at his shoes) they went to Clitheroe and the Forest of Bowland, which was actually a treeless moor called a 'forest' on account of it being a Royal hunting ground. They poked around the Norman castle then went up Pendle Hill, where Clive told them about the Pendle Witches.

'Obviously there's not a lot going on round here, so you can imagine how quiet it was in 1612. That's when ten women were accused of being involved in satanic rituals, most of the evidence coming from one small child. They came from two feuding peasant families who were so broke they used to roam the countryside begging, cursing anyone who refused. It's hard to say how justified they were. In those days it was quite normal for churches and good citizens to take in and feed beggars, unlike today. Anyway, a few of them confessed and it ended with them all being hanged. They're a good marketing opportunity, especially around Halloween, and I personally like the story because it's an early example of, well, a successful witch hunt initiated by children. You know, all that *Oprah* stuff, "I'm suing my parents because I'm not an astronaut ..."'

'What's wrong with Oprah?' asked the wife of the raincoated American. They weren't speaking to each other. 'I was *on Oprah*.'

'What, in the audience?'

'No, I was on the show.'

'What were you?'

'She was a modern-day scourge,' said her husband.

'And I was *acquidded*, so fuck you!'

An embarrassed silence descended on everyone.

'So!' said Clive, being jolly. 'Onwards and upwards, eh? To the Lakes!'

Nothing Clive could say prepared the passengers for the majesty of the Lake District. He did start to explain about how it was an area of volcanic uplift that had been eroded by glaciation, which left a series of triangular peaks, U-shaped valleys and finger-like lakes radiating from a central point somewhere around Scafell, but he quickly gave up. He let the scenery just come upon them. As the peaks grew higher and the valleys steeper, he could not compete with the sight of scree-covered slopes and dark-green valleys patchworked over by dry-stone walls, so he left them to it.

Rose was taking them the weird way round. She thought she'd worked out a way to avoid the tourists by cutting along the south side, but there were tourists everywhere. There were so many tourists ('eighteen million a year,' according to Clive) that Albion's tourists took pictures of them. They sat on stone bridges in twee towns writing their postcards, they held up traffic dragging their feet on lanes without pavements, and they spent their leisure euros in vast quantities on duck-handled umbrellas, mint cake, pasties and phone cards. Rose got so pissed off she led them further into obscurity, until they found themselves in a valley called Wasdale Head. Clive suddenly remembered where they were from an old field trip and hustled everyone off the coach, making them climb several hundred feet up the bare hills until they could look directly down on to the flat fields. The stone walls made up a crazy pattern, a bizarre clutter of irregular fields, not just L-shapes but battered oblongs with corners missing, twisted trapeziums and scrawny strips. Clive felt a surge of pride.

'This gives you an idea of what life used to be like in this country. Farmers have been elbowing each other on this land for centuries. In the 1600s there would have been fifteen, twenty little farms strung out along the track in this valley, and now there are only two. It's as if they signed the ground before they left it, so that sedentary folk like us would have an idea of what hard work really is. There's another more practical reason why these walls are so wide – some of them are ten feet across, you could drive a coach along them. It's because the peasants here have spent hundred of years pulling the stones out of the soil so they can plant crops, and they had to put them somewhere. I suppose the modern farmers keep it this way for the tourists, or maybe they just can't afford to shift all that rock, they and the animals just work around it.' Clive stared at the scene again. The ground looked like a paint-by-numbers picture that had been filled in with all different greens. 'This,' he said, as though to a minibus full of impressionable adolescents, 'this is splendid. This is *splendid.*'

Barry hadn't bothered getting out of the coach. Nor had Alex, who had nodded off. Nor had a good third of the passengers. They watched Clive waving his arms around half way up the hill, pointing with his furled umbrella, and hoped he would hurry down soon.

A pub lunch soon sorted them out, during which Clive lectured them on the Lake poets.

He took a vote on where they should go next: Beatrix Potter's Hill Top Farm, or William Wordsworth's old house, Dove Cottage at Grasmere. It took a lot of negative campaigning about the old bag Potter but finally he got the votes to see the Wordsworths's museum-home. He was one of the serious poets that reminded him of his mother and her hobby. Better than going to see a load of crap about some kid's book, as he told Barry.

'God, I read enough of those to my Tess to know what a rip-off kids' books are. Ten quid for two hundred words and some crappy drawings. You know that Postman Pat's from round here?'

'Stands to reason dunnit? Postman Pat and his black and white cat. Twat,' said Barry. 'And them thick cardboard pages. They love to chew 'em. That's why I only get 'em *vijoes* now. You can't chew a video, can you? Besides, you can slap it in any old time. Not like reading a book.'

'Oh, Barry. You're such a ... fucking ... *yob*,' said Clive, not without affection. Barry took it well.

'Just be careful who you say that in front of, that's all,' said Barry, not without menace.

Dove Cottage turned out to be a poky little hole. Nasty cold flagstones. Hard furniture. A mean little fire. Black wood everywhere so it seems too dark to read by candlelight. It was made of stone and had a slate roof, and the windows were tiny. Everyone shambled through after the guide like people in the property market. The guide pointed out that it used to be a pub called the Dove and Olive. Barry looked around with sudden interest.

'That's my dream, that is.'

'What, to live in a pub?'

'Above one. Own it. Come down, pour a pint anytime I want. Play some pool. Have me mates round. Course I'll never have the money if I keep doing this.' He looked troubled for a moment. 'I need a big score. I need the really big score if I'm ever going to do it.'

'Like this lot. Always broke, till it was too late,' said Clive, referring to the Wordsworths.

They saw the floor spaces where Coleridge and De Quincey used to crash, and all the other loafers who couldn't pay their rent more than two months in a row. Wordsworth's babies slept in baskets in the kitchen, and he did his writing sitting in a weird angular chair with everyone tramping through. His sister Dorothy did most of the housework, and had her own little cube where she wrote her arselicking journal. After a bit, William married some local bird called Mary.

'So, he'd go off walking with his sister and write her love letters and all that. D'you fink there was anything, you know, going on there?'

The guide was speechless and turned bright red.

'No, definitely not,' said Clive loudly, taking over. He'd read a bit about them in his anthology. 'They were soul mates. Dorothy helped him with his poems, made fair copies, talked about them. The thing with his poems, and Coleridge's, they were meant to be simple, almost innocent. Simple language, everyday subjects, but with a lot of emotion. No one was doing stuff about farm girls and cuckoos then, not really. He even sent a copy of his *Lyrical Ballads* to a politician with a note saying see, "Men who do not wear fine clothes can feel deeply." He had a motto – "Plain living and high thinking".'

Rose tugged at Clive's sleeve to shut him up. It was an etiquette thing, stealing another guide's thunder.

'I'm just *saying*,' he protested. The guide hustled everyone to have a look in the next room. It was where the kids slept when there were too many people staying. It was the size of a closet, had three external walls and even in August it felt like a fridge. The walls had recently been papered with yellowed copies of *The Times* from Wordsworth's day, a heritage touch. Barry read out the numbers for the National Lottery of 1800.

They skipped the museum and shop and stood outside while Barry smoked.

'Plain living and high thinking. That's a nice idea,' said Rose.

'It's the opposite of Barry. Hey Barry, how does it feel to have met your antithesis? Your complete opposite'

'I'd never dog my sister like him, if that's what you mean. Sister-in-law, maybe,' he said with a grin, and flicked his cigarette butt at Clive, making him leap out of the way. 'Where are we staying tonight anyway?'

When they found Alex, they discovered he had cocked it up again. He had booked a hotel in Kendal but forgotten to confirm, so they'd been bumped and had to spend the night in a businessmen's hotel off the motorway. Clive spent the evening in the bar talking to the passengers, trying to keep them entertained, listening to their tales of their homelands and looking at their family snapshots. Alex was still sulking and looking ill. Barry disappeared to his room with one of the Spaniards. And Rose spent her evening playing with the computer. Clive was knackered when he got to bed.

The last day of the North was worse. They had great intentions, but traffic and time were against them. The highlight was a visit to Salt's Mill near Bradford. Even though it was one of his favourite destinations, and said so much about the country, Clive was tired before he was half way round it. It was a big old mill that had been tuned into an art gallery.

As the tapered chimney stack appeared on the horizon, he spoke up. 'As you'll see, it's just a big mill with a load of modern art inside. And shops. Book shops, fashion boutiques, expensive Northern health food cafés ... On the one hand it's a fantastic building, huge, *huge*, nestled in the hills, on a river of course, like a cartoon of a mill. The bloke who owned it, Titus Salt, bearded Victorian, had five "worsted stuff" factories in the Bradford area doing spinning and power-loom weaving, plus thousands of people working from home combing wool and weaving – a bit like today's telemarketers and envelope-stuffers. Only he tried to be a bit nicer to his workers, which is why he built Saltaire, the model worker-town attached to the mill after 1850. He made sure there was a chapel, a library, a gym, decent workers' cottages for five thousand people, rent-free almshouses for pensioners, a hospital, a concert hall, a school, and a park (no smoking, no swearing, no gambling). The idea of this paternalism was to establish a relationship between master and man devoid of class antagonism. He wasn't the first, by any means. You've seen Styal, there was also Thomas Ashton's village at Hyde, Richard Arkwright's at Cromford, there was a firm called Price's Patent Candle Company that moved from Vauxhall in London to Bromborough Pool on the Wirral, with lots of open spaces, a forerunner of the garden cities of this century. There was another one near Newry, Northern Ireland, called Bessbrook, built by a flax-spinner Quaker called John Grubb Richardson. Like Saltaire, it was built without a pub or a pawnshop, to save people from themselves. All of these people were active in the reform movement, and they needed it round here. Bradford had 100,000 people by 1850, up tenfold in fifty years. They were all huddled in without a thought for their welfare, and the pollution was unbearable. Listen to what George Weerth, a German poet living there, wrote in the 1840s.' Clive read from *Saltaire, An Introduction*, a dog-eared pamphlet he had brought with him,

' "Every other factory town in England is a paradise in comparison to this hole. In Manchester the air lies like lead upon you; in Birmingham it is just as if you were sitting with your nose in a stove pipe; in Leeds you have to cough with the dust and the stink as if you had swallowed a pound of Cayenne pepper at one go – but you can still put up with all that. In Bradford, however, you think you have been lodged with the devil incarnate ... if anyone wants to feel how a poor sinner is tormented in Purgatory, let him travel to Bradford." '

The passengers were happy to get off the coach and mingle with the rest of the tourists. Clive was surprised that there weren't just the faintly bookish, Ramblers Society liberals his mother would have nodded at, but plenty of jeans-and-trainers families with their pushchairs, sulky adolescents and diminishing attention spans. Clive wondered if they had run out of theme parks to patronise, or maybe they had got the art bug?

He walked round with Rose. There was a load of art on display by David Hockney, the artist associated with Mr Silver, the man who bought the mill and turned it into a palace of Sunday afternoon leisure. Hockney was the quintessential English artist – he moved to California for the tube socks for thirty years, but lately he had come home to die. Or at least to play the elder statesman.

Clive and Rose inspected the huge canvases with their sweeps of acrylic paint. All around them people were perfecting their ten-yard stare, trying to look interested in the blobs and daubs.

'This is a self-portrait, isn't it?' said Rose.

'It says here that's Peter Grimes, from the opera.'

'Well why's he in his Y-fronts?'

'I don't get it.'

'This one's a load of fields in the Dales. It says here he scanned the original and e-mailed it to his gallery, but they couldn't open the attachment, so he had to do it again from memory on the day of the opening. It says the paint was still drying as the champagne corks were popping, and the critics declared it a great success.'

'I hate it. I wouldn't hang it in my home'

'Your home isn't exactly a 4,000 square foot penthouse or the lobby of a bank, is it?'

'You know Rose, I'm sick of my flat. I decided last night, I'm moving out.'

'Where to?'

'A hotel. That's what I want. I'll use the money I've saved over the summer to pay for a hotel until I find somewhere else.'

''S a bit risky, isn't it? What do you think of this one?'

'Looks like two Spaniels that have just gone through six months of harrowing quarantine at Heathrow. Well that's my motto, isn't it? "Who dares wins."'

She giggled, fonder of him when he laughed at himself.

As they were standing in the sun for the last passengers to board, he said to her, 'I'm tired Rose. I'm just tired. This country takes it out of me.'

'It's been a bit of a hack, hasn't it?'

'This country has too many pieces.' His Nokia rang. 'Wa-hay! My first call! I bet it's Barry. In flagrante with some gift shop teenager ... Hello?'

'Clive? Is that you?' said the woman's voice he knew best.

'Tina? Is that you?'

'What on *earth* are you doing answering Alex's ...' The penny dropped. She'd blown it.

'You must have picked up Alex's Nokia by mistake. Uh-oh,' said Rose with a smirk. She was glad it was all going down. She was glad Alex was about to be exposed, and that the harridan Tina was about to be demoted even further in Clive's mind.

'Why are you calling Alex? What could you *possibly* want with him anyhow?' said Clive, getting angry. 'For Christ's sake ...'

'OK, well you might as well hear it from me. I'm seeing Alex. It's that simple. He loves me.'

The wispy-domed Sloane got up from his sulking spot on the coach and came out to find out why they were using his name.

'It's for fuckin' *you!*' said Clive, pushing the phone into his chest. 'Damn,' he shouted, and kicked the side of the coach. 'Damn! I'm such an idiot!'

'Hey watch my livery!' shouted Rose. 'Kick the tyres if you have to.'

Even in his anger he was touched by Rose's thoughtfulness. He was falling in love by increments, like the freeze-frame on one of Danny's videos. This, he knew, was an increment.

He kept on kicking though. He kicked his way round four tyres, then walked up to Alex while he tried to finish the call.

'Are you fucking my wife? Are you fucking my wife?' He switched his intonation to be like Travis in *Taxi Driver*, then started shoving Alex's shoulder. 'You screwed my wife, and then you cheated on her with that East End slapper?' The American guy in the raincoat came over to see if he could mediate, and Rose stepped up too.

'Fuck off! Leave me alone you psycho!' Alex kept shouting, in between trying to talk to Tina on the phone. He wanted to break up with her anyway. He just wanted to get away from everyone who ever knew him and start again. But he couldn't think straight with that oaf Clive pushing him. 'Stop it or I will not wesponsible for my actions,' he boomed.

Barry came jogging across to enjoy the action. His first task was to intervene with the interveners so the fight could take its natural course. He yanked the Yank back by the belt and pushed him into Rose's path. Meanwhile, Alex had had enough. He pressed the 'END' button to finish the call, then banged the phone down on the bridge of Clive's nose.

'Oooh!' Barry was impressed. But not so impressed with the ensuing brawl, where both men grappled with each other, staggering about, Clive with one leg hooked round his adversary. They toppled backwards against the coach and fell on the ground in a heap.

'Oh dear. This is em*barr*assing,' Barry said to Rose, and left her to help pull them apart.

'Gwarn, you cool off,' he said frog marching Alex a few feet to the bushes. He quite liked saying it. He imagined one day saying it to his son, catching the feisty seven-year-old giving some bigger kid a pasting.

'You're fired!' shouted the young CEO at Clive, who had his head tilted back, trying to stop his nosebleed. 'You're all fired!'

It was left to Barry and Rose to get the show on the road again. Clive took a seat at the rear, Alex bristled up front. As Barry suspected, they paid the price when it came to handing the beer mug round. After three days of Albion's undivided attention, the assorted respectable Koreans, Americans, Scanders, Germans, Eastern Europeans and French raised a miserable one pound forty-three between them, plus two dimes and a Canadian quarter.

The passengers had all vanished into the evening at Victoria. The hazards were going and the four of them stood together on the pavement.

'So shall we do this here, or in the pub?' asked Barry, feeling like the default leader.

'Here,' said Clive.

'Here,' said Alex.

Rose shrugged. 'I say we should take a few days to think about it and then decide what to do.'

'How can we?' asked Clive sarcastically. 'We've all been fired.'

'Shut your face, cradle snatcher,' growled Alex.

'Now, now, ladies, we don't want any more trouble,' said Barry with a wicked grin. 'OK, I propose we split everything four ways and fuck off into the sunset. Agreed?'

'Agreed,' said Clive.

'Absofuckinglutely,' said Alex.

'So long as you don't think you're getting any part of the coach. I own that coach . . .' said Rose.

'Don't worry, darling your coach is safe,' said Barry. 'Right then. See you when I see you.' And with that Barry turned and walked away, heading out east. He didn't even duck into the Shakespeare.

'Well what about the money then?' said Alex, chewing his fleshy bottom lip. He hadn't had the chance to do any embezzlement yet and was terrified somebody else had beaten him to it.

Clive shrugged. 'You and Rose sort it out. If there is anything, split it four ways.' He turned to Rose. 'That's it then.' He paused. 'It's been nice knowing you. Bye.' Inside he was a boiling mess of emotions, all of them unspeakable.

She frowned then looked down at her motorbike boots. 'Seeya.'

Clive strode off to Victoria station. He considered having one in the rail bar, then thought better of it. He was a little bit sick and a little bit tired, and walked towards the river instead.

And then there were two.

'So you never told Clive about me and his ex-wife?' asked Alex. He was curious as to why anyone would want to do him a favour without his ordering it.

'Nope. There's a lot I don't let on about. Call me and let me know what Sir Clive Tiddel says.'

Alex was gobsmacked. She walked away.

18

Summer of Love

Clive's real summer of love got going the very same evening, when Rose pulled up next to him as he stood staring off Lambeth Bridge.

'Hurry up, there's people behind me. Get in.'

He obeyed. 'I wasn't going to chuck myself in,' he said. 'Just in case you thought.'

'I didn't.'

'I was actually just thinking, which newspaper or magazine would be the best place to look for a flat share.'

'They're all the same. All a load of psychos. I can see why people get married.'

'Yeah, you're right there.'

He accepted her offer of a cup of coffee and watched amused as she squeezed the fifty-three-seater into tiny Bonnington Square. Inside the clutter of helmets was reduced. A lot of the nice coffee-table books were gone. He made an early trip to the toilet while she was in the kitchen, and saw the dried flowers and the candles were gone, but the motorcycle parts were still in the bath.

Maybe she is a lesbian? he thought, remembering Barry was right about some things. He noticed some spines on her shelf – the *Radio Spares* catalogue. This was a technical catalogue of every nut, bolt, grommet, piece of electronic equipment or street furniture that had been invented. All the stuff the tourists photographed but the natives ignored, like switch boxes and hydrant markers, traffic-light controllers and red emergency buttons . . .

'You like *Radio Spares*? I love this!' He exclaimed. 'We had it at university in the lab.'

'Like it? I've *been* there. I've been to the warehouse in Corby for parts.'

They were both impressed. Clive explained how he loved all the things people filtered out, things that were just too common to care about, or too confusing to worry about. 'It's like the unspoken language of the landscape.' He felt he had gone a bit too far, so he added: 'Some of the names in there – we used to think they were so funny. Things like vice-jaw tools, banana plugs, caged nut-insertion tools, deep-throated g-cramps . . .'

'I know! L-shaped ball-driver sets, clinchnut riveters, oblique-tip cutting nippers, fire-resistant sheaths . . .'

She seemed game, so he opened a volume and looked for some of his favourites. 'Look at this: gland adapters, vacuum pick-ups, suction lifters . . .'

She was giggling a lot now, and took over,

'Stiff nuts, cheese head screws – Ugh! Deary me! – *crab* clamps . . .'

'Look, look! – for kinky people, p-clips, precision liquid dispensers . . . and for the man in one's life – semi-delay fuses, tip cleaners . . .'

'And for the busy woman – bush kits, parts washers, hand probes . . .'

Rose was nearly crying with laughter. She had to stop and catch her breath. 'Look, here's Alex's section: handsavers, gripping gloves, manual motor starters, wrist-support gloves and two-hand relay units!'

Clive was laughing hard too now. 'This is perfect: stroke counter, butt splices . . . male stud coupling . . . Ha ha ha . . . male-to-male adapters . . . stainless-steel butt hinges . . . gender changers. And for all the lesbians out there, knock-on ball knobs, tool positioners, flexible probes, industrial joysticks, two-piece inserts and insert extractor tools . . . and look at this . . . Wiggler sets, mounted sweet spot devices, right-angle connectors, and ring and bush mounts . . .'

He started to close the book . . . '7-in-1 strippers, precision linear shafting, heavy-duty twins, ball attachment . . . Oh and something for Barry's wife: *locknuts.*' And snapped it shut. 'Can you imagine the nerds putting this together?'

'God that makes me laugh,' Rose said when she collected herself. 'How come I've never met anyone else before who thinks that's funny?'

He shrugged, leaving things to calm down, going into the kitchen to make more tea. He felt like he'd been drinking, he hadn't had such a laugh for so long.

'I solved that riddle at last,' she said presently over the tea. 'What's greater than God, more evil than the devil, the poor have it, the rich want it, and if you eat it you die? *Nothing.*'

'Well done. I should add, I didn't get it. My little girl did.'

'Which one?'

'What do you mean, which one? Oh.' His face fell. 'So you know about Amanda?'

'Barry told me. Big mouth,' she said. She wasn't the least bit apologetic, but neither was she outraged about him screwing a fifteen-year-old.

'We only, you know, a few times. If that's any consol ... mitigation.'

'I suppose the judge thought so.'

'There was no judge, no trial. Just a, er, meeting with the headmaster. That reminds me, I've got to find out what my barrister has got planned. That hearing about my daughter. The one who solved the puzzle.' He paused. 'You know, I assumed all those candles and flowers and coffee-table books were yours, and the bike parts were the bloke's.'

'Nick. Yeah. You need to work on your thinking. I'll lend you my motto: "Assume nothing." He moved out, to his mum's.'

'Oh. I'm sorry.'

'Why?'

'Actually I'm not. I'm glad.'

Another increment, this time in plain English. The room rang with the sound of what he'd just said.

She put on an LP, squatting to pick out a track. The first second gave it away.

'Oh no, not more Beatles!' said Clive.

> *He's a real nowhere Man,*
> *Sitting in his Nowhere Land,*
> *Making all his nowhere plans*
> *for nobody.*

'What's wrong? I'm putting this on for you.'

'Why *me?*'

'You sang it at Barry's brother's do. Don't you remember, or were you more blotto than I thought?'

'Oh no. Not this as well.' He held his head in his hands as the words came over him:

Doesn't have a point of view,
Knows not where he's going to,
Isn't he a bit like you and me?

She got used to his modest theatrics pretty quickly and laughed at him, singing along partly in imitation of him, partly to winkle out the meaning.

Nowhere Man, please listen,
You don't know what you're missing,
Nowhere Man, the world is at your command.

He's as blind as he can be,
Just sees what he wants to see,
Nowhere Man can you see me at all?
Doesn't have a point of view,
Knows not where he's going to,
Isn't he a bit like you and me?

Nowhere Man, don't worry,
Take your time, don't hurry,
Leave it all till somebody else
lends you a hand.

He's a real Nowhere Man,
Sitting in his Nowhere Land,
Making all his nowhere plans
for nobody.

'Oh God. What else did I do? I really should lay off the beer.'
They talked all night. They talked about Barry and Alex. The hours were counted out in pots of tea. They talked about their ex-es, parents and his daughter. They talked about Amanda, and what he'd been thinking, and he told her what a mistake it was, but added that no one had asked for his version of things, and how it was all complicated but hopefully behind him. 'Even in the midst of a family, it can be very lonely,' he said. 'I felt like no one was watching. What can I say? "The awful daring of a moment's surrender".' The light gradually came up, electric blue at first, then silver. They talked about themselves. It was like being young again.

They got a charge just being together, with the world all before them. Clive didn't go for the lunge this time, but they did agree that it would be nice to see each other sometime soon. A day out.

He walked back to Streatham, floating all the way. As he passed the Oval he thought of the cricket ball, and George, and how he should give him a call. He lined up all his people in his mind. He could use his new Nokia.

George didn't answer. Nor did Danny. And Tina had her machine on.

In Streatham the Sue Ryder shop was just opening so he wandered in. He chatted with the women for a while, thanking them for the suit. Poking around among the ugly vases and abandoned fitness equipment he found a megaphone. StreetThunder, it said on the side. All it needed was batteries. He tried it out in the street, with a squeak of feedback his muttering came through loud and clear, making the shoppers turn and stare: 'Testing, testing, hello hello, oops sorry.'

Bad news greeted him back at the flat. Jo heard him coming in and came running down to give it to him, then partly blame him: Danny was in hospital. Some blokes had come round and battered him two days ago. Danny had gone through Clive's window to sit in the garden when they burst in, three men in sports-casual wear, with baseball bats. They trapped him up against the substation fence, grunting while they laid into him. He had a broken collar bone, a broken eye socket, a chipped ankle, and lots of bruising.

'Who were they?' she sobbed. 'They must have been after *you*. They were your gangsters, weren't they?'

Clive couldn't exactly say. They could have been dead Dave's gangsters too, the voices in his head, but he didn't dare argue the toss with her. He confessed he had no idea, and once she had calmed down, found out that Danny was relatively OK and taking visitors in hospital.

The backlog of his mail had been cleared. Rubber banded together were months of credit-card bills, legal bills, lawyers' threats, and a brick of junk mail. The only things of pressing concern were a message from Tina's lawyers saying the date of their hearing had been moved to next week, and to expect the legalese equivalent of a good arse-kicking. And something marked 'HM Prison Brixton'. Curious, he sliced it open.

It was from George.

Dear Clive,

Maybe by now you have heard about my plight. All I can say is be wary of what people say until you hear all the facts from me. I am currently on remand in this beastly prison for a crime I did not commit. When you get this please visit. It is very difficult for me in here.

Yours Sincerely,

George.

On the phone, all they would tell him was George was 'Section 43'. For his own safety. And that visiting was restricted.

He decided it was a good time to move. It didn't take long. He called a mini cab and sat on the end of the bed with his one bag packed, waiting for the honk outside. He noticed in the mirror that his love handles had nearly gone. The ceiling pipe was still partially bent. Packing up always made him feel melancholy, but leaving this place was exciting. Looking out at the substation one last time he promised himself he'd never sink so low again.

He asked the cab driver if he could recommend any hotels in the West End, but she didn't have a clue. He hopped out to enquire about rates at a few places – South Molton Street seemed like a good place. Mainly because it said in his book that William Blake lived there, bollock-naked with his teenage wife Kate and his acid-engraving gear. But they were asking mad prices only a tourist would pay, hundreds a night. He ended up at the Waddington near Paddington, not a million miles from the scene of his tryst with American Amy and the purple bra.

The room was comfy – TeasMaid, cable television, clean shower. On the scale of things, it was nice enough to let a woman see. Every morning he had his breakfast in the dining room with the credit-card backpackers and the European second honeymooners. He spent a lazy week strolling round town, pottering in markets, climbing towers, reading the papers while drinking espresso at pavement cafés, and sprawling on the grass by bandstands. He lay on his back looking at the clouds and called Rose a couple of times, leaving messages. All talk of Nick was already gone from her machine. He got rather fond of the television too, and found himself heading home in the evening for a sitcom or the news. When he went round to see his brother Gordon and Sandra he had more to talk about. His mother was mute now.

It was while he was chuckling away at *Howzat!* the hilarious cricketing quiz show one evening that Rose rang back.

'Hiya Clive. I've got some good news about Albion and the money.'

'Rose. At last. How lovely to hear from you. Actually I've got some bad news about Danny the Kiwi. And my mate George. And my court hearing too.'

'Well, we should get together.'

'Absolutely. I really want to go for a drive in the country. That's what I want. You know, me and you. St Albans, Suffolk, East Anglia, Meriden . . .'

'Sounds cool. We can go on my bike.'

'Er, I've never been pillion before. In fact I've never been on a motorcycle before.'

'Hmm. Maybe you're right. It'll be freezing anyway. And I only have one lid now. Never mind. I'll come up with something. How does tomorrow sound?'

'Tomorrow sounds beautiful.'

Tomorrow was beautiful. They had the fifty-three-seater to themselves. She pulled up outside his hotel, smiling her multiple smile – self-satisfied, excited, benign. She had her fair hair in two plaits, and wore a summer dress and cardigan. As he stepped on board he was hit again by the smell of commercial-grade Draylon and sunlight on plastic, bringing back memories that were only a few weeks old: Barry on the mike, Alex hugging his briefcase, tourists bleating about toilets. None of that mattered, since he had the whole day ahead of him with Rose. Maybe two – he'd brought his overnight bag. He knew they couldn't fit everything into one day.

He explained that he wanted to visit Danny the Kiwi in Tooting Bec Hospital first, then George in Brixton. She was cool with that. She liked Danny the Kiwi.

'Switch your mobile phone off,' she warned as they walked through the electric doors. 'They interfere with the internal network. Set the alarms off.'

He obeyed. It was nice knowing someone who knew such marginal things, knowledge that slipped through the cracks.

Danny the Kiwi was a pushover. He wasn't blaming Clive at all, and was seriously on the mend, bones knitting, bruises yellowing . . . he was even making bedpan jokes. More important, he had something to write home about, and tons of ideas for a movie script about gangsters. He thought he remembered them saying something about Dave, the former occupant, as they pummelled him, but as he had concussion he couldn't be sure if he imagined it. His doctor said he might remember in time, but it was best to try and forget it and get on with his life. He was sorry to hear about Clive moving out, but Rose jumped in and invited him to a barbecue later in the month.

'What barbecue's that then?' said Clive as they hurried back to the coach which was parked in a handicapped zone.

'Oh I just made it up. Give him something to look forward to. And you know what those people are like for their barbies.'

Clive let it go. New Zealand was not really barbie country, the climate was too mild and ... well, fuck it. He silenced his inner pedant.

Seeing the stubbly Head of Geography blubbing on the other side of the glass was a lot harder for them both. He asked the guard to give George the cricket ball from the Test Match. The guard inspected the three gilded lions, bright on the glossy red leather, and put it in a zip-loc bag. Rose went to look for a coffee machine to give them time to chat. George's story was that he'd acquired a computer over the summer and was experimenting on the internet – latest scores, fantasy cricket, geology newsgroups – when he had stumbled into a chat room and struck up a relationship with a girl who said she was sixteen. He enjoyed chatting to sWEEtI6 in a chaste and responsible manner, just as the young teachers did at school, face to face with their pupils. Chatting. Answering questions. Giving advice. Unfortunately, when he agreed to her requests to meet him at Manchester Airport, he made a big mistake. As he came beanpoling through the gate looking for the McDonald's he was approached by a Granada news crew and three detectives from the CID and led away to an interrogation room. Twenty-four hours later he was on remand in HMP Brixton, handing over his shoelaces, making up his bed and slopping out from the last guy. Who had hanged himself with his own Y-fronts. It was a very bad situation.

Clive felt himself being drawn into something he was keen to avoid, yet trying to offer solace out of the goodness of his heart. He especially wanted to get the conversation over before Rose came back.

'What you want is one of those, er, civil rights lawyers. You know, someone who champions free speech and all that.'

'I have retained a lawyer but he's useless. He doesn't seem to care. Chap who did my conveyancing in the Eighties.'

'Oh dear,' said Clive. 'Look, I'll look around for someone on the outside. A Family Law specialist, or one of those Legal Aid people. Don't worry. Gosh look at the time, Rose and I have to be going. OK George, pecker up. I'll come and see you, er, soon.'

He told Rose the whole story as they drove north across London. He felt a bit sick. London was all muggy and congested, he just wanted to get out and see the wide open green.

'Sounds like he did nothing wrong, technically,' she said. 'But ... you blokes. You should just learn to keep your hands to yourselves, and your eyes on the road. That's all I can say.' She frowned.

Clive had nothing to say to that. She was right.

The difficult mood lasted until they crossed the M25, then it lifted like a summer fog. Neither of them had ever been to St Albans, but they'd heard good things about it. It had a lot of history. When the country was one great potential tourist trap, St Albans looked attractive.

'So, I'll tell you what I know about St Albans,' she said as they approached. 'It's sposed to have a bit of everything. Important Roman town once; the British tribal Queen Boadicea kicked the Romans' arses there ...'

'Mrs Thatch used to like being compared to Boadicea — strong woman, rebelling against European rule, scorched-earther ...'

Rose frowned at the interruption.

'Of course, she didn't have much to choose from. In terms of female role models. History being written by men and all that,' he added hastily.

A little smile curled around her lips. She liked him being outspoken, but she also liked a bit of obedience. That worked for her in the past. That's why Nick got the boot, ultimately. Old Nick got his poles reversed, he didn't know when to grovel and when to shine.

He watched the curling corners of those lips. He had never seen them do that before. He wanted to kiss them.

She continued. 'They have a medieval clock tower, a sixteenth-century water mill, Ye Olde Fighting Cocks which is another one of those "oldest pubs in the country' where Oliver Cromwell slept but probably didn't get a round in. And a big fuck-off Norman cathedral.'

They walked across the park to the ruins of Verulamium, the Roman town. Low walls, outlines of nothing.

'I know one thing,' said Clive. 'This is Blue Badge country. Oh God, I know *her*. Quick, this way.'

The guide he'd spotted had studied on his course. She always did her homework and led the hunt for future failures. Like Clive.

'I've listened to those people and most of 'em could be replaced by a Walkman. There's not many that say anything memorable.' She paused. 'Like you.'

He felt a flush of pride, and love.

They paid into the museum, which was good for a few murals and amphorae. Clive got an overwhelming sense of layers upon layers of dead people, former inhabitants. 'You know I can never shake the feeling that they were all very unlucky to have missed on refrigeration and wide roads and comfy automobiles and anaesthesia and satellites.'

'I agree,' she said. 'Things just keep getting better and better. Material things, anyway.'

'I bet the Romans felt like that. Course, being stuck out in Britain must have been crap if you were used to lolling about by the pool in Pompeii. Then again, it must been fun in England when they left. I always wonder what it would be like to live in the Dark Ages. Pulling down Roman temples to make an outhouse. Using statues for catapult target practice. I wonder what I would have been? Probably something boring like a schoolteacher. A private tutor.'

'I'd love to have been a pagan priestess. Celebrating nature and stuff. Doing rituals.'

'Like in the *Wicker Man*?'

'Yeeeah!'

Another increment. This time towards lust. They were coming faster and faster.

'If I was in the *Wicker Man* I'd be the poor sod who gets the run around and ends up roasting with all the lambs.'

She laughed. 'You have a very strange view of yourself.'

'Sometimes I think I'm the last man on earth who thinks like me. I think I'm an island. And then I look around and I see I'm on an island with millions of other people who think they're an island.'

'People think I'm an island, but I'm not. I'm very ... what's that Latin word for "touching"?'

'Contiguous?' he said.

'Exactly. That's me.'

They walked up the lane, resisting the pull of Cromwell's boozer, to the cathedral. Its nave was indeed built in the Fuck-Off Norman style. Clive told her that St Alban was the first English martyr, a Roman soldier who was decapitated in AD 204 for sheltering a priest. His fourteenth-century shrine got a good hammering during the Dissolution of the monasteries, but the Victorians, as usual, restored it.

'These empty old churches,' she said. 'They're just big museums. Badly run museums. They should turn them over to the homeless.'

'Can you imagine a load of winos and roughnecks in here? It'd be as bad as Brixton, or Rampton. Besides, the Anglican Church owns too much land. If they started giving it away there'd be a big property plunge.' He looked at her apologetically. 'Sorry. My wife was an estate agent. You get like that.'

The town centre seemed cosy. The clothes shops were terribly nice and the pubs had CAMRA stickers and bearded, Clive-type jazz.

'I could live here,' he said. 'Maybe. Or maybe not. Didn't I read somewhere that St Albans is the most violent town in England? I think at night when the "colourful" street market closes this cashpoint is surrounded by junior thugees and a thousand young men spill out of those pubs and kick each other's heads in . . .'

'Visiting's OK, but I couldn't live in a tourist town.'

'Do you fancy seeing the Gardens of the Rose at Chiswell Green? You know – Rose, roses,' he said grinning.

'Nah. No time. Anyway my mum named me after the herb, not the flower. Rosemary.'

'Rosemary, you're lucky. My parents plucked my name out of the air. Left the rest to Fate.'

They were happy to have ticked off another sight, but wanted to get out into the country. Rose cut east across the land, against the grain of the transport system.

'I love this,' she shouted to him. Clive was wandering around the coach, enjoying the space, looking out from all angles. 'Going crosswise. Taking the B-roads. It's like stroking a cat the wrong way. I mean who are these people that live round here? Why do we never hear from them? It does my head in thinking about it.'

They stopped in Saffron Walden. The heat hit them when they got off, it was 30 degrees. People were sitting out on every available piece of grass. They went into the BP shop and bought egg sandwiches and a big bottle of fizzy water, and shared without wiping. Clive bought a book, *Have with you to Saffron-Walden*, by Thomas Nashe, because it said on the back he wrote it out of gratitude to the town. He hid there when he was on the run from the militia for being a Catholic in Shakespeare's time. He read her a bit as they walked. 'This Nashe bloke was a total piss-taker. He sounds like Barry. Crikey, look up there!' he shouted, putting his hand on her shoulder and pointing her towards the horizon. High in the bright blue sky a shining silver object floated. It looked like a tiny moon, bright and round as a ping-pong ball, but it was far too small even for a day time moon. Clive began talking very quickly.

'You know what they do, don't you?' Clive never stopped to wonder whether she might, he was just dying to tell her. 'It's a weather balloon! How marvellous. I haven't seen one for years. Years!' He looked at her with such a light in his eyes that she let him continue.

'The weather stations, a thousand of them all over the world, they send them up every day, noon and midnight, Universal Coordinated Time, carrying these things called radiosondes, which are basically mini weather stations, they have all the stuff on them to measure temperature, humidity and atmospheric pressure, and they just rise up and up, thousands of feet, transmitting the data back to the ground. It's not just the, you know, state-run weather labs, the military have their own, and then there are the hobbyists and amateurs ... they reckon about a million of these things go up every year, and they all burst and come crashing down to earth, but you never see them, that's the weird thing. When me and my brother Gordon were little, one passed over where we lived, I'll always remember, it was in Milton Keynes, it was just sailing overhead, and all the neighbours came out to watch, it was quite spooky, someone said it might be a UFO or a Russian A-bomb, but then it was on the radio later that it was just a weather balloon that got off track ...' He caught her smiling at him, and shrugged. 'It was a big deal. That's the only time I've ever seen one before now, in real life. We were only little kids. I think they're so beautiful. They start off about eight foot across and expand as they rise because of the decrease in atmospheric pressure, until they end up about twenty foot across and then they pop. And that's the end of them.'

'Where do the bits go?' asked Rose.

'Oh, they just land somewhere. I mean, it's the equivalent of a lot of stuff every year, I think I read somewhere it's like forty lorry-containers' worth of matter, but it's mostly polystyrene and little batteries and wires, no one ever seems to get hit by it, like they do with frozen lumps of blue toilet water from planes ... but you're right, it's pollution ... but on the other hand, it's a trade off for the data. We need the data.'

Clive didn't have a problem with data, he was trying to digest all the feelings that had just been thrown up, thinking of when he and his brother were little boys, how bright and shiny the world had seemed to them, and letting Rose in on his world without expecting it.

He took a chance, and went on. 'They're like butterflies, or fruit flies, they just live for a short while, do their business and that's it. Just up and up and burst and that's it.' He felt a bit queasy, having stumbled across a metaphor for his life. Something that summed up his dutiful insignificance. Rose let it sink in for a minute while they walked.

'Don't you want to know the news about Albion?'

'Oh yes. I totally forgot.' He'd been so high on her presence all day, and now this, he didn't give a flyer about Albion Tours.

'Alex has found us a buyer. Sir Clive Tiddel.'

'The man who ruined Wonga?'

'The very same. Anyway, at first Alex was chucking round six- and seven-digit figures, but he had lunch with him yesterday and got something a bit more realistic. Sixteen grand for the name, split four ways. I did some checking and he's not holding out on us. The moron. Four thousand pounds each and the name Albion belongs to Tiddel. I'm up for it. I haven't asked Barry yet, but I'm sure he will be. Alex is too – he says his rent's due, and his cricket team's going on tour to India.'

'Four thousand's fine by me. I'm well rid of it.' It amused him, Sir Clive throwing money at a name. 'Couldn't the stupid git just think of one himself?'

'That's not how it works, according to Alex.'

'He's a slippery eel that Alex. You know what he said to me when we were doing the Midlands? He said if I'd help him get rid of you and Barry it'd be very worth my while.'

'He did? The *wanker.*'

Clive ran his hand through his hair. 'I think he felt threatened by the two of you. Which annoyed me – why wasn't he threatened by me too? What made me such a pushover? Anyway I told him to get knotted. In no uncertain terms.'

They went quiet.

At four in the afternoon they were on a lane driving through a sea of wheat, white-gold against the blue sky. England never looked so good. In each field there was an oak tree, twisted and broad, clear in every detail like a bonsai. Gentle green slopes rose in the background, barely a hundred feet high.

'This is so beautiful,' said Clive, breaking the silence. 'This is my favourite thing. This is England to me. Let's pull over.'

She drove a little further then found a spot, pulling the empty coach off the B-road and up a tractor path. They walked around. They held hands.

His heart was knocking, but his voice was firm.

'Do you want to … walk out there?' he asked her, looking down and catching her eye for a second. She looked more beautiful than the first time he had properly looked at her, way back at Glastonbury festival.

She nodded.

19

Coming Home

After that, Clive knew he was ready to die. Not that he wanted to. But at least he wouldn't go out complaining. He'd plumbed the depths of his good fortune, and now knew where he stood in life. He was a lucky man. A beautiful woman had given herself to him, and he had acquitted himself well. They lay on their backs half-covered by the cast-off clothes looking at a patch of sky. It was dark blue, August evening sky. The soil beneath them was black clay, text-book friable from the long summer. He could see where the machines had planted in straight rows, nothing growing between.

'Do you want to hear a poem? I've got my book in my bag.'

'OK,' she said. 'Keep quiet though. I'm worried a farmer will came along and blast us with a shotgun. I've read about that happening.'

'Put your head here where you can hear then.' He had a poem earmarked. 'This is by another bloke who claimed he was mates with Shakespeare. He died in Deptford in a pub fight. Stabbed in the eye. Anyway. It's called "The Passionate Shepherd to His Love", by Christopher Marlowe.

'Come live with me, and be my love ...'

'Oh I know this one, it was on telly.'

'On telly?'

'Yep.'

> '"And we will all the pleasures prove,
> That hills and valleys, dales and fields,
> And all the craggy mountains yield.

'"There we will sit upon the rocks,
And see the shepherds feed their flocks,
By shallow rivers, to whose falls,
Melodious birds sing madrigals.

'"And I will make thee beds of roses,
And a thousand fragrant posies,
A cap of flowers, and a kirtle,
Embroidered all with leaves of myrtle;

'"A gown made of the finest wool,
Which from our pretty lambs we pull,
Fair lined slippers for the cold,
With buckles of the purest gold;

'"A belt of straw and ivy buds,
With coral clasps and amber studs:
And if these pleasures may thee move,
Come live with me and be my love.

'"The shepherd swains shall dance and sing,
For thy delight each May-morning;
If these delights thy mind may move,
Then live with me and be my love."

'It's got it all hasn't it? Roses, wool, swains, varied topography.'

He read her a few more until she felt cold, and then they dressed, a little shyly as it was all new to them, and neither felt that pretty. They walked back in single file through the track of broken wheat, and picked straw off each other by the coach.

They drove through the twilight until they found a Red Lion Inn, where there had been rooms for hire for five hundred years. Clive was surprised – there was very little awkwardness. When they had nothing to say, they said it. They ate in their room and watched television sitting up in bed.

For the next forty-eight hours they wandered wherever they wanted, against the grain and ignoring the clock. They went to Boston, Lincolnshire, a small port on a river that leads to the Wash, which had been pumped up by EU money. They had Radio One on, and the overly-familiar DJs made everything feel compressed, as if the whole country was in the same room. They passed through many little villages, peering out at the descendants of the eel-eating fen slodgers. They saw lots of satellite dishes on thatched roofs and menfolk wandering around shirtless in football shorts, and everyone looked very happy. Then they cut south and west down to Nottingham, where Rose revealed she had been to University (Electrical Engineering). He hadn't even thought to ask, but was secretly pleased. She took him to a tourist pub, the Trip To Jerusalem, built in a sandstone cavern beneath the castle and supposedly the oldest pub in England. The name came from the fact that Crusaders used to meet there for a bevvy before going off to fight the heathen, and you couldn't get a beer in the Holy Land.

'The more I travel around this country, the more I realise how little I know,' he said.

'Just keep going then,' she said, her 'life-should-be-a-laugh' laugh bubbling up again.

They played trivia and won together, then they played pool and she beat him three − nil. He'd only ever played one person before, George, who was even worse than him.

He asked to see Meriden so they continued south.

In the middle of nowhere they spotted a field of long green grass and made love again. They could hear the traffic just a few hundred yards away. Afterwards he was high as a kite.

As they walked under a pylon she suddenly shushed him, like she'd seen a bird or a rabbit. 'Look!'

He looked up at the electricity wire. 'What the hell is that?'

A small orange machine was inching its way along the live cable. Behind it, it paid out a second, curly cable, also orange, that looped round the first one like ivy.

'Oh my God! That's Energis!' She whispered. 'That's it! I never thought I'd see one!' Her mouth was wide open.

'What is it?' She seemed so excited he had to know more.

'It's the telephone company, they're laying more cable. That thing's a robot, it comes out here on its own laying fibre optic cable. Instead of digging up the ground, they use the surplus capacity of the pylons.'

'That's a good idea. Leveraging the old infrastructure?'

'Exactly! Wow!' They stared for five whole minutes until the thing was half way along the wire. 'Wow!' she said again, her eyes shining.

A few minutes later, as they walked on, she turned to him.

'I have a question for you,' she said. Normally this would have been ominous, but with her he was happy to answer.

'You know you said yesterday "This is my favourite thing, this is *my* England"? Well, what else? What else?'

'God, there's such a lot. Lots of things, mad things, beautiful things . . . What is England to me? Roundabouts. Three-inch breakers.' He thought for a moment. 'Unsolved cattle maimings. A ten-yard queue at a free phone box. Catfights at the Harrods sale. Celebrities mentioning their bowel movements in interviews. Stopped clocks. Car manufacturers' recalls . . .'

She smiled.

'I'll tell you what it is, Rose.' From his backpack he produced the megaphone. 'Hello everybody, hello! Can you hear me? Oyez, oyez . . . that's French by the way . . .' There was a whistle of feedback, and his voice had a rough electronic tang to it, and cut across the landscape.

'Army surplus stores. Fans who turn up to boo at Luton Airport. Hanging baskets that drip. Tweedy men who work for 1950s wages. Hand-inked bus passes and home-made tax discs. Judges dressed as babies. Supermarket closings. Wreathes on a grass verge. An ex-con's paper bag. A twenty-one-year-old junior school teacher coming third in Miss Great Britain. Grandparents handing their grandkids back. Old sweets made for the nostalgia market. A new Blue Peter presenter. Chilled lagers. Old maids cycling to therapy. Engraved shotguns. A steaming filly. Petrol-station glasses. Riverside pubs. Obsessional litigants. Unwitting homosexuals. Vote-counters. Foster parents. Wheelchair heptathletes. Pensioners who shout "Stringemup" at Black Marias. Empty mental homes. Cream eggs. Pubs at 11 a.m. Grocers apostrophes. Rebel commuters on the tracks. Rejected astronauts. Nobel Prize winners who still go in to work the next day. Giant graffiti on motorway bridges. Isle of Man masochists. Soup after school. *Double entendres.* Picnics in lay-byes. That Peel bloke when you least expect him. Wind in the willows. Outrage at the Olivier. New pop stars. Farm boys on dirt bikes. Indignation. The longest day. The hottest day. Silent libraries. Cable burning. Have you had enough?' he asked her, and the world in general.

'No!' she shouted from fifteen yards away. 'Tell me more.'

'Riots. Sue Ryder shops. Agents for this and that. Moaning. Tower-block demolition. Executives with carrier bags. Criminals in their court suits. Scallies blocking the handicapped ramp. The dead old lady and the hundred cats. Pubs at 11 p.m. African night-shift cleaners. Bonfire night. Fat. Light-aircraft tragedies. Green-flash pumps. Smoking footballers. Sponge swirl ceilings. Shakespeare outdoors. Vomit in corners. Three squaddies looking for a country pub. Midges. Temporary frost. Visiting dignitaries. Swords reversed. Car-boot sales. Vacuum-tube valves. Paddle boats. Roman numerals. Monogrammed hankies. Cones. Knot gardens. Troublemakers. Quink. Asian Babes. Victorian swimming baths. Tartan shopping trolleys. Scabs. Tank crossings. Frog crossings. Pelican crossings. Pigeon fanciers. Genetic engineers. Poets. The detention centre at Heathrow. The Burger King at Heathrow. Social climbers. Rock climbers. Windmills. Toast. Dole offices. Postmen hiding letters in a hedge. Film critics. Slot machines. Redesigns. Anthrax. Cheese rolling. Twats in Union Jack suits. Waistcoats. Sellotape culture. Need I go on? I could go on.'

Rose was smiling throughout. 'Save it! Save it for next time I'm sad.'

On the way to Meriden she decided to stop in Hinckley, Leicestershire, because she wanted to see the new Triumph factory. Down a bare road on an industrial estate they found the modern unit, and were just in time to slip into the boardroom where a roomful of men in Hein Gericke gear were being briefed for the afternoon tour. They donned their earplugs and were shown around the plant, where workers assembled the snazzy sports motorcycles. They even made some of the parts there, or at least, finished them off. The last third of the trip was the actual assembly line, where youths in coloured polo shirts added parts to the hanging bikes as they passed slowly by, like beef carcasses in a slaughterhouse.

'These kids look like they could be working in McDonald's,' she sniffed, but she was impressed that it only took forty minutes to put a whole bike together. She looked enviously in to the testing room where every few minutes a lad in overalls rode a fresh bike on rollers, at ninety miles an hour, helmetless. Clive hadn't noticed, but she had a pierced clitoral hood and was curious to know if they shook like the Triumphs of old.

As they drove away, she seemed a little conflicted, explaining that the new factory owner, John Bloor, was just a builder who had bought the Triumph *marque*, or name, as an investment. On the other hand, she was wide-eyed at the thought of riding one of his sport triples.

'Do you want to see my dad's estate?' she asked further down the road. 'He might even be around. He's retired but he still goes in a lot. One of those blokes, you know.'

'*This* is his estate?' asked Clive in amazement as they pulled up at Charlecote, a Tudor manor set in huge grounds.

'There's a deer park where Shakespeare is sposed to have poached,' she said happily. 'And a river runs through it. Two in fact – the Avon and the Dene ... what? Wha-at? Why are you staring?'

'This is your dad's estate?'

'He doesn't *own* it. He manages the land.' She laughed at him. 'What, did you think you'd scored with an aristo there for a second? Oh Clive, your imagination.'

They met the old fellow walking along with a dog and a shooting stick. He did look a bit like an aristocrat – red faced, gruff with strangers, dressed like a bum – but he was very pleased to see his Rosemary and gave her a proper hug. They didn't stay long, Rose had ants in her pants. She decided they were going up north to see her friend the woman police officer. It was twilight as they crept up the M6, passing the glass tetrahedron of the RAC centre in Walsall.

'That's where I used to work,' she said, with some pride.

'Do you want to go in?'

'You know, I wouldn't normally, but I think I will, just for a sec. Give me your phone.'

She talked to someone as she pulled off the motorway. In a few minutes Clive was being led through the slick reception to a room where RAC guys sat around like firemen, playing cards and taking the piss out of each other. They were all pleased to see Rose though. She had a private word with one of them, a nice-looking chap, and they headed for the door. 'He's just gonna show me his new ride,' she reassured Clive. Twenty minutes later they were back, cold from the night air.

They got going again. He liked the motorway at night. Half an hour up the road, in the middle of nowhere, she suddenly got excited.

'Look here Clive, look up ahead. Look!'

'Where? What?'

'At the signs. Look!'

'I can't see ...' Then his mouth dropped open. 'Well I never,' he gasped.

Strange words were scrolling across one of the electronic road-works signs in the hard shoulder.

CLIVE ... POINTING ...

She slowed down but they were still doing fifty.

'What does it say? Go back!' he was getting all excited.

'There's another one up ahead.'

And there was: CLIVE ... POINTING ... I LOVE ... CLIVE ... POINTING ...

He was blown away, she was grinning madly.

'Did you do this? How did you do it? Oh Rose. Oh Rose.'

'What do you think eh? I hacked it. Using a telly remote control. That's how they programme them. They're all field-programmable, microprocessor controlled. I've done it on the London Underground too, me and a mate, you know those red ones? Some are done from central command, some by radio-telemetry. Once you know the commands, you just go out there and point and shoot, like you're watching telly ...'

'O Rose. I tell you what I think. Rose, I love. Rose I love. Too. That's ... that's the most romantic thing anyone's ever done for me. And I don't normally give a stuff about romantic.'

She was very pleased with herself. They stayed the night at the WPC's Barratt home in Warrington, on the fault line between Liverpool and Manchester. Sally the WPC had the next day off and was going to ride her horse. She wanted to be a horse copper but had failed the exam, so she was stuck in a patrol car. Like Rose, she didn't own a car. She didn't like tin boxes. She hadn't given up hope though, she was going to take the test again.

As Clive and Rose lay in the dark together in the single bed, she asked him another question.

'Clive? You know you read all those other people's poems, which are very nice and all, don't get me wrong ... but do you have a poem of your own?'

'What, do I have a poem in me?'

'Yeah.'

'I don't know.' He thought about it for a minute. 'Er, sort of. I've never really thought of it before. Doing my own poem. It's not really a poem, because I'm just making it up. It won't be around in the future. It's not very good, but it says how I feel. And it's in English.' He cleared his throat.

'When life is hard,
I want to cling to this soft rock
My island home,
But better still
Put out my arm and hold my Love.

'That's it. That's pretty much how I feel. Sorry it doesn't rhyme.'

'That's really nice,' she said. They were silent together for a moment. 'Say it again.'

When they wandered outside after breakfast into the close, Rose cursed. One of her tyres had been slashed. Clive thought it might be due to her aggressive parking – she was blocking someone's drive by a few feet, and he'd seen people have words over less – but Sally explained it in one word.

'Kids.'

They got the bus to where the horse was kept, a beautiful black stallion she called Stalker. The Mersey was small and sluggish where they were, sunk in its grassy banks, unlike at the great port twenty miles away. There was a huge electricity generating station across on the edge of the flood plain, with rows of different types of pylons marching off to the different cities, and thousands of transformers bristling behind fences.

'I bought him at a police auction,' said Sally proudly. Clive stood around while the girls groomed the animal and Sally happily shovelled shit. As she rode him around, Rose asked to borrow the megaphone.

'Watch this. He's a real police horse.' She put it to her lips and spoke in a voice that echoed off the fences, 'Mr Clive Pointing! Mr Clive Pointing! Come in, your time is up!' The horse barely dipped his head, continuing in a straight line.

'The police are all right, aren't they?' he said to Rose. 'I get on with the police. It's lawyers I can't stand. My lawyers, they're idiots. I've given up on them. In fact . . .' He looked at his watch. 'They'll be in court cocking up my custody hearing in a few hours.'

'What? *Today?*' Rose was mortified.

'Yes.'

'*Today's* your court date and you're not even going? You didn't even tell me?'

'Now hold on . . .' She looked furious.

'So today you're just giving up on your daughter, just like that. What's her name, Tess. Well poor fucking Tess, that's all I can say, having a father like you. God, you make me so . . . Ugh! I can't even speak. You *arsehole*.' She threw the megaphone down in the mud and stomped off.

Clive sensed he had done something wrong. He looked at his watch again. Even if he got a taxi he'd never get to London in three hours. Even on the fastest motorcycle he wouldn't make it. And she wouldn't have him on the back anyway, she was so angry. He went over to her where she was telling Sally all about it.

Sally, however, was hit with a wave of sympathy. Not just for the little girl, but for her friend, who had only the night before been telling her how deeply she had fallen for this oddball older guy who seemed so calm, and so rooted in the here-and-now. She even had a teaspoon of sympathy for *him*.

'What about your mates at the airport?' Sally said.

'The freight lads? Even if they did have a plane going in the next hour, we'd never get to Speke. Cabs won't come out here.'

'You could take Stalker.'

'Are you kidding?'

'Why not. He could do with a good run.'

Clive had already made up his mind to do a U-turn. If it made Rose feel better, he'd do anything to get to court. He'd still lose his daughter but he'd hang on to Rose.

'Can that thing carry both of us?'

'Course he can.'

'Can you ride, Rose?' he asked.

'*Course* I can,' she said, still cross, but half her mind racing ahead.

'Well. Let's do it. As they say on the telly.'

He got some black looks for his humour, but on the whole he was a good passenger. They trotted along, cars giving way when they saw the green police jacket Rose had borrowed. At one point she even had the horse pick his way down a grass embankment, across a dual carriageway and back up the other side.

'Isn't this illegal?' shouted Clive, but she didn't answer. Then the tiny airfield and the Ford factory became visible. Squeezed in between the two was Speke Hall, a Tudor mansion.

She avoided the terminal and headed straight for the back of one of the hangars, where she tied up the horse after Clive had dismounted. With a thump. A young lad in a boiler suit shouted across at her, smiling. He seemed pleased to see her, wiping the oil off his hands as he spoke, but not offering his hand to Clive.

'Terry I need something going to London. *Anything.* Now.'

'Ooh, I dunno,' he said. 'The Heathrow goes at five.'

'That's too late,' said Clive. She glared at him.

'We've got the parcel plane going to the City Airport, but it's already taxiing.'

'That's it, that's perfect. We're practically going to the City anyway. Can you get us on? Please Terry? *Please?*'

Her begging worked. He led them to an unmarked transit van and they headed out to the plane waiting on the asphalt.

'Why do you have no number plate?' asked Clive, unable to contain his curiosity.

The lad Terry launched into a delighted description of the scam they ran. The airport vans didn't have to be licensed since they never went on the public highway, and even after several years, with low mileage they could be sold off to unsuspecting punters as nearly new.

He jumped out and talked to a fat kid on the plane who shrugged, allowing them on board. Inside the cramped front section of the tiny plane Clive and Rose were given the fold-down jumper seats, like the kind in Ron Bergman's taxi. The piggy lad who let them on sat cross-legged on the floor rolling a joint and chatting to Rose as the shuddering plane took off. As it soared high above the gaping Mersey, Clive commented, 'You know Speke Hall was the home of one family, the Watts, for centuries. In 1921 the estate was almost the same as it was in the eighteenth century – little plots and cottages. Course the National Trust got it and sold off chunks to the local authority ...'

Silence. Rose looked embarrassed, and rolled her eyes at the lad apologetically. He lad looked up at them, amusement in his piggy eyes.

'So, I wonder if Alex is related to these Watts?' he said to Rose.

'Shut up, I'm still cross with you.'

He kept quiet and looked out of the window instead. The view was majestic. It was a hot, clear day and he could see every road, every house, every above-ground-swimming pool, every hilltop cairn, lorry, river, haystack and bus shelter. The plane didn't cruise very high but he could see the curve of the Earth and the blue haze of its edges. He saw deep into Wales to the Irish Sea, and on the other side way across the East Midlands, where he had been the day before.

All the while the fat Scouser chatted about his perks. How him and his mates, being privileged airport workers, could go anywhere they wanted for free. Sometimes they'd just go to a club, in London or Newcastle, wherever was happening and handy. Best was he could just ask his girlfriend where she wanted to go on holiday and she'd say Costa this or Florida that and they'd be off the next day, connecting flights and long haul, all free. Sometimes they took a jumper seat on a freight plane, sometimes they kicked back with the paying punters in coach. They had mates in immigration everywhere who would just wave them through, usually though a side door or back office, sometimes through fire doors and across grass. It didn't matter, there was a community of airport workers around the world who recognised each other's laminates.

As he listened, and wondered again about Rose, at how different she seemed, and how special, he recognised roads, the M5, the M6, the M1 ... there was the geomantic shopping mall of Milton Keynes, his spiritual home, and suddenly, London. They landed amongst the private jets and European workhorses of the City Airport. Rose did all the thanking, and the fat Scouser said any time and good luck. She warmed to Clive slightly in the taxi, and within minutes were spilling out of a cab at the courts. Marion, his terrible barrister, was just going up the steps.

'Bang on time!' said Clive grinning.

'Get in there,' said Rose. Then she added, 'You lucky sod, Clive Pointing. Just remember how lucky you are.'

Epilogue

'Naaaar-har-har, naar-har-har! Naaaar-har-har, naar-har-har!' Barry was on the roof garden telling jokes. 'Here's another one. Michael Jackson and his wife are in the recovery room with their new baby son. The doctor walks in and Michael asks, "Doctor, how long before we can have sex?" And the doctor goes, "I'd wait until he's at least fourteen." The midwife told me that one, straight up! Naaaar-har-har, naar-har-har!' People who didn't know Barry tittered, unsure of themselves, but he hardly noticed. Someone refilled his drink. The sun made his blue eyes bright and his face slightly creased as he squinted. He was on good form.

'Here's another. This one's for you, Dad. Old geezer gets put into a nursing home by his son. He doesn't know if he's going to like it at first, but he decides to give it a go for his son's sake. First morning in the nursing home he wakes up with a hard-on. Out of nowhere, a beautiful nurse walks in, kneels down, and gives him a blowjob without saying a word. Geezer gets on the phone to his son and says, "Son! I love this place! Thank you so much for putting me in this nursing home!"

'And the son says, "Wow, Dad, you sound really happy. What happened?"

'The old man says, "You won't believe it. I woke up this morning with a hard-on, and the most beautiful nurse I've ever seen in my life came into my room and gobbled me senseless. Didn't say a word."

'"Well, that sounds great, Dad. Congratulations".'

'"Thanks, Son," he says and hangs up the phone.

'Then later that day, the old man is walking down the hall in his zimmer frame. He slips and falls and can't get up. A big ...' Barry glanced about him and whispered the next word, '... *black* male nurse comes up to him, rips his pyjama legs down, shags him up the arse, and leaves him lying there in a heap. The old man crawls to a phone and calls his son. "You have to get me out of here, Son, this place is mad!"

'So the son says, "What happened, Dad? You sound terrible!"

'"Well, I was walking with my zimmer and fell over and couldn't get up. Then this big black male nurse came up, ripped my pyjamas down, and shagged me up the arse!"

'"Well, you know, Dad," said the son. "You got a blowjob this morning. You have to take the rough with the smooth."

'"No, you don't understand, Son!" wails the old man. "I only get a hard-on once a month. I fall down three or four times a day!" Naaaar-har-har, naar-har-har! Naaaar-har-har, naar-har-har!'

He got better laughs this time. Barry was useful at a party, and Alex was glad he invited him.

It was August Bank Holiday Monday and they were all in the roof garden of Alex's friend Sophie's huge white house in Notting Hill. The carnival was thumping away down below, the streets a boiling mass of people, inching forward like lava. Every so often a new sound system would come round the corner into the leafy square, followed by a hundred youths dancing and pumping their fists in the air, or a float would go by trailing skanking parents and school children. The voices of MCs on microphones echoed off the buildings and overlapped, as did the sounds of soca, reggae, hip hop and house music. The owner of the house, Sophie, went amongst her guests with a jug of margaritas, welcoming everyone. She had the poshest, fruitiest voice Clive, or Barry, or Rose had ever heard, but there was a warmth to her smile, and a cheek to the way she engaged with people that put them at their ease. She even seemed to like Alex, and spoke to him in his own language.

Alex White had come through – big time. The amount he got from Sir Clive Tiddel for Albion Tours was higher than anyone expected. They each netted out with eleven grand. This was perfect for Barry – it meant drinks all round at the Swan, new trainers and dresses for the girls, and spending money for a late-season break in Ibiza (someone at the old travel agent's in Mile End sorted him out). Not enough left to put down on a house, but they were happy where they were for the time being. Besides, they had the new baby, it was not a good time to move.

For Alex it was good because it gave him some breathing room while he looked for a new job. He was thinking of going back into the English

Language teaching game – he'd had some offers. Sir Clive was keen for him to carry on his superb stewardship of Albion, but Alex wasn't too sure. He didn't want to push his luck and be found out as an oik *and* an ignoramus. He knew Clive wasn't interested, and Rose was just a coach driver, they were ten a penny. He had invited them all to the carnival to give them their cheques, in the hope that if they were sufficiently disoriented and drunk they wouldn't ask to see all the paperwork and the bank wire, which was not that different from what he was giving them, he was just shaving a little off for himself, a service fee. He calculated correctly. In the event no one cared enough to ask.

'So, Rose,' said Barry, 'what are you up to these days?' She and Clive had just arrived, and after negotiating the protocol with the hostess and getting Bloody Marys from the catering staff, steered their way directly to the people they knew.

'What do *you* think?' she said, raising Clive's hand up in hers and winking.

'Oh I see, bit of this, bit of that . . .'

'B-b-b-b-b-b-bit of the other . . .' chipped in Stu. Stu's girlfriend cuffed him round the head and told him not to be so effing *shtupid*.

'Didn't think I'd see you here, Stu,' Rose said.

'I got S-s-s-s-s-s-sophie some P-p-p-p-p-pavorotti tickets once,' he said with mild indignation. 'It was m-m-m-m-m-m-me what introduced her to that Alex.'

'Strue,' said Ron, scratching his gut.

'Where's your other brothers?'

Father and sons glanced at each other, hesitating, until Barry said, 'Ossie was fitted up on a charge, and me other brother Trev . . .'

'The one with the ear?'

'Yeah . . . he's gone down the station to get him out. This afternoon.'

'Oh dear,' said Clive, quite pleased. '*Pit Bull*-related activities?'

'Nah, that folded. He was selling perfume outside Harrods with Craig when he got nicked.'

Barry's dad joined in. 'Daft fucking copper didn't know the score. Rookie. I told him they put the young ones on duty on Bank 'Olidays. Anyway. He'll be all right. We couldn't miss this party. See that posh bird over there?' – pointing at a pretty girl in a black dress. He called her over, with much oi-ing and whistling, then introduced her as the girl who was going to make a documentary about him and his cab. Ron got the nod on the condition that he get his cab painted black again. No newspaper ads, no tampon ads, just straight Hackney Carriage black like in the postcards. He gave her a squeeze and a wet kiss on the cheek, which she greeted with an ironic roll of the eyes.

Clive handed over the sixty quid he owed in bets. They all chatted some more, having to speak louder to be heard over the braying of a clutch of hooray Henries near by high on cocaine and frozen vodka. Danny and Jo were there too, Danny on his crutches showing people how to shotgun Rasta Lager from the bottom of the can. Grudgeful neighbours complained of the smell of marijuana so the police arrived – one black WPC. Barry thought she was a stripagram for a minute and made as if to grind with her, which she didn't like, but she ended up staying for a glass of sasparilla and dancing with him anyway when her favourite song came on, 'Heads High', the reggae tune that had haunted the summer and was now popping like a thousand balloons.

Clive had invited his brother and Sandra. Their mother was rapidly going downhill. The doctors had opened her up and found a gordian knot of things wrong with her, about which she had been unable to communicate. After two long nights of discussions and sadness, and some sensible counsel from Sandra, they decided it was best to let her just go. He wanted to tell Gordon in person about the Albion windfall, and about his plans to put most of it towards hospice care for their mother. And he wanted Gordon to meet some nice people for a change. In fact Clive had invited everyone he knew, keen that they should meet Rose.

The drink and the heat started going to Clive's and Rose's heads. They'd been off alcohol for a fortnight. Alex came sidling over giving Clive the look like he wanted everything to be water under the bridge.

'So where's your little girl then?'

Clive checked the corner of Alex's lips for sarcasm before he was sure he should answer earnestly.

'Tina's come around. She says I can have her, weekends. It was that therapist. He persuaded her. Or whatever it is they do. I'm happy.'

Everything had resolved itself that day in court. Tina had fallen for her psychotherapist, without realising it, and he had been pretty generous to her, seeing her for an extra week during August when he was supposed to be not working. He explained that a protracted custody battle wouldn't be very good for the little girl in the long run, and that it might be best to make peace with Clive. Consequently, Tina dropped her claims and Clive Pointing agreed to pay a fixed amount of support in return for more relaxed access. The psychotherapist was a great believer in people.

He knew Clive would be a good father. The lawyers had nothing to do and went home.

Barry's little girls were running about, drinking people's drinks and climbing up the flower trellis. The eldest stopped and looked at Clive shyly, recognising him from the boozer. He waved at her and she ran off smiling.

'So where's the wife?' Clive asked Barry.

He called Christine over. She was looking radiant and slim again, and all the hoorays were leering at her. In her arms she had a new baby.

'Oh God, I forgot about your baby! What's he called?'

'*She*,' said Christine, before Barry could say anything.

'Hmm, that's an interesting name. Is it ... is that a pop star or something?'

'No you plonker, she meant *she*, her. It's a girl! This is me little girl. We haven't named her yet.'

Barry cradled her, curling up with pride. 'Beautiful, isn't she? Just like her mum eh? Eh? Eh?'

Clive was amazed at his turnaround and exchanged a smile with Rose. Barry jabbed his thumb at them, saying, 'You two wanna get started soon, before it's too late ...'

'Er ... change the subject Barry.'

Clive got to talking with Barry's wife again. He wanted to apologise for the Fergie joke he had told when he was drunk.

'Oh, don't worry about that,' Christine said. 'I told you I don't have no time for the Royals. Although actually I do like Fergie, she's all right. Well she's almost one of us, isn't she? Besides, it's a fairy-tale ending innit? An amicable divorce. Lovely kids.'

Clive agreed. An amicable divorce was a fairy-tale ending. Things had turned around for him since that May night when he'd thrown himself in the Thames. Being cut adrift seemed to be working for him, for now. He knew he didn't fit in to the world, but neither, it seemed, did many others. The old certainties were gone, but he was coping. Rose was still a mystery to him, but he realised how lucky he was to have her at all. He and Rose freshened their drinks and stood looking over the crowd in the square below, speculating out loud about where the people all came from, and how they would all get home – what Tube stations were closed, what buses were running. Then she turned and nodded toward those around them on the roof.

'What do you think of all *these* people Clive?' said Rose.

Clive was in love. He knew, absolutely, for sure and for certain, when he'd gone round to Rose's flat and seen the photo of them on the roller-coaster wedged in a frame on her bookshelf, even though it was still on the outside of the glass. That was enough.

'I think I'll probably never see any of them again,' he said. 'But I'm sure there's plenty more where they came from.'

ACKNOWLEDGMENTS

Words by John Lennon and Paul McCartney taken from the song
'Lovely Rita'
Words by John Lennon and Paul McCartney taken from the song
'When I'm Sixty Four'
Words by John Lennon and Paul McCartney taken from the song
'Revolution I'
Words by John Lennon and Paul McCartney taken from the song
'Nowhere Man'
All by kind permission Sony/ATV Music Publishing

"Don't Stand So Close To Me" Words and music by Sting
© 1980, Reproduced by permission EMI Music Publishing
Ltd/Magnetic
Publishing Ltd, London WC2H 0EA.

WH Auden "On This Island"
Phillip Larkin "The Mower"
Reproduced by permission of *Faber & Faber* Ltd

AE Housman "Loveliest of Trees" and "Is My Team Ploughing?"
Reproduced by permission of The Society of Authors

George Weerth, translation by Alan Farmer and Janet Reynolds in
"Saltaire: an introduction to the village of Sir Titus Salt" by Jack
Reynolds (Bradford Art Galleries and Museums, 1985)